Sorrowheart

Dreamland
Deception Island
Ropedancer's Fall
Sweet Narcissus

Sorrowheart

M. K. Lorens

A Perfect Crime Book

DOUBLEDAY

New York   London

Toronto   Sydney   Auckland

m
Lor

A Perfect Crime Book
PUBLISHED BY DOUBLEDAY
a division of Bantam Doubleday Dell Publishing Group, Inc.
1540 Broadway, New York, New York 10036

DOUBLEDAY is a trademark of Doubleday,
a division of Bantam Doubleday Dell
Publishing Group, Inc.

Book Design by Claire Vaccaro

Grateful acknowledgment is made for permission to reprint from the following:

Die Sonette an Orpheus and "Herbsttag" in *Das Buch der Bilder* by Rainer Maria Rilke. Reprinted with permission of Insel Verlag from *Sämtliche Werke* by Rainer Maria Rilke.

"Sailing to Byzantium" by William Butler Yeats. Reprinted with permission of Macmillan Publishing Company from *The Poems of W. B. Yeats: A New Edition*, edited by Richard J. Finneran. Copyright 1928 by Macmillan Publishing Company, renewed 1956 by Georgie Yeats.

Excerpts from "East Coker" and "Little Giddings" in *Four Quartets*, copyright 1943 by T. S. Eliot and renewed 1971 by Esme Valerie Eliot, reprinted by permission of Harcourt Brace Jovanovich, Inc.

Library of Congress Cataloging-in-Publication Data

Lorens, M.K.
    Sorrowheart : a Winston Marlowe Sherman
mystery / M.K. Lorens. —1st ed.
        p.   cm.
    "A Perfect crime book."
    I. Title.
    PS3562.07525S67   1993
    813'.54—dc20   92-36467
                                            CIP

ISBN 0-385-46781-8
Copyright © 1993 by M. K. Lorens
All Rights Reserved
Printed in the United States of America
May 1993

1   3   5   7   9   10   8   6   4   2

First Edition

To Kathryn, who knows the heart of sorrow

and

To Gordon, whose eyes see more than is good for them

Was ist deine leidendste Erfahrung?
Ist dir Trinken bitter, werde Wein.

—*Rainer Maria Rilke*
Die Sonette an Orpheus (The Sonnets
to Orpheus), II, 29

What is the worst of your sorrows?
If the drink tastes bitter, turn yourself
to wine.

Sorrowheart

I.

Hard-Luck
Stories

One

She might have been dead, to look at her.

He stood naked beside her bed, seeing her as if he had just killed her, judging her and himself with the passionless detachment of a practiced murderer.

It was the same, this moment of displacement, whenever he risked staying the night with her, waking, perhaps, once or twice to wander the house, prowl the dark garden, or roam the sleeping campus whose barren steel and glass towers loomed like patient predators above her wild, mad kingdom of woods, orchards, small meadows, and herb patches. He was accustomed to take long night walks, and he would rise from her often, when sleep deserted him; she never seemed to notice, and sometimes he stayed away a day or two, a week, to punish her, mocking himself for a fool. Tonight, though, he had come back, undressed, and slipped into the bed again beside her to lie sleepless, fingertips barely touching her, adrenaline pumping, too alive with her to rest.

The sky over the Hudson grew cold with buried light as he crept from her side this last time to stand watching. He knew he would not see her again. She had pushed off the bedclothes in her sleep— grappling with the mortal enemy, as she did every night—and the pale shape of her shone like glass, as if he might reach out his hand and thrust it through the aging richness of her flesh and find the web of nerves and the stubborn bone beneath, beyond them the sheets she lay on, the lumpy old mattress, the rusty, protesting bedspring.

All other lovers, wives, friends, had been childhood stumblings. In her, he had at last, almost too late, grown up. Grown suddenly, fatally, old. If he had ever had some other country, he had it no more. She had swept him clean.

He owed her everything. Now he must pay his debt.

I'll kill him for you, he thought, looking down at her. *If he beats you down, I'll kill the bloody ravaging bugger.*

He closed his eyes for a minute, did not like what he saw there, and opened them again, perversely fixing them on her to heal himself.

It was early November; even the bushes of herbs in her rambling gardens had surrendered to the cold, crouching weak-sapped in a wild profusion only she could unravel. There was frost on what remained of their silvery leaves, frost on the cloudy glass of the two ramshackle greenhouses at the far end of the path of broken, heaved-up bricks that wound past the house; frost crept up the diamond panes of the long bay window beyond her bed, but every night, to save money, she shut off the heat in the large faded bedroom. The cold grew deep by morning, when the two drew apart; the nipples of her breasts were hard with it now, but though her body registered the cold involuntarily, Elsa did not seem to notice it, did not reach in her sleep for blankets. Her senses, exquisitely alive when she woke, deserted her entirely. In sleep, she was a perfect, absent warrior.

Jaffer smiled, looking down at her. "Balm of hurt minds," that was what Shakespeare called sleep, the silly old berk. Nice turn of phrase, that, though; he probably bled fifty bob out of some noble get for it, paid off the bar bill. So much for the classics. Poor old fart, knew bugger-all about it. Should've asked her. Should've asked Elsa the Great.

"Sleep is the price you pay for waking up, my dear," she'd told him, pushing her dime-store glasses up on her long, beaked, blue-

4

blood nose and turning sideways, elbow on the table, a thumb and forefinger tilting her chin back to give him the view. The profile that should've been on all the coins. Elsa. Lady Elsa.

High-boned, the eyebrows dark and unplucked, eyes wide but far from innocent, a veil of suspicion that never left them, not for all the kindness, the open honor of her. The hair long and graying goldish brown and so kinked with natural curls she wept and yelled and cursed him when he combed it for her. The skin so tanned by her garden work it blended with her hair and made her all one piece, the color of a lion on the sand. That was how he would remember her.

If I buried you now, he thought, *in the heaps of orchard leaves, no one would even see you there till spring. You would belong only to me.*

Her fingernails were always short, under their tips perpetual black crescent moons of loam she never bothered to dig out. The belly full, but flat, the hips narrow, thighs long and supple, legs brushed with curling brown-gold hairs. "Shaving the legs?" she told him when he made some clever crack. "A thing for kitchen maids, my dear. A vulgarity. Pfu!" Elsa sectioned the world in half—things to be bothered with, and things to be left to the servants or the gods.

Except that for her there were no servants anymore, had not been since the war, when she was a girl. No servants, nor gods neither—not that it made the slightest change in her philosophy.

How in the spinning world had she selected *him,* old Jaffer Swan, to bother with? After more than a year in her kingdom, he still avoided the incredible reply.

I'm afraid you almost love me, he thought. *You don't love Graham. You never did, not that way. But you could almost love me.* It came to him like a dull unlocalized ache that suddenly sharpens into pain, bright and specific. He had not dared confront the qualification before; now, he could not avoid it. *Almost.* It would make it easier for her, at least, to lose him. He bent and brushed his lips delicately across her breast. As usual, she did not seem to notice him at all.

Jaffer shivered to his soul and looked round for something to wrap up in. Though he disliked the sight of his own body, which at forty-eight was thinning into absolutes, it was the hour as much as

5

his nakedness that made him shiver. He mistrusted beginnings, containing, as they did, an infinite number of probable failures.

"What do you do?" she'd asked him when they first met, when he'd strayed in to look for work at her almost-solvent garden center. "How do you account for yourself?"

He had stared at her across the geranium bench where she was potting up seedlings, while the warm, jungle air of the greenhouse shimmered with the cobweb beauty of Mozart playing on a small tape recorder clipped to the waistband of her trailing skirt. With her high-necked blouse and her wild hair pinned up and her Berlin accent tinged with London and her way of asking hard questions softly, she had seemed adrift from some old planet—a little superior, a little terrified. In her presence, he felt like Alice before the Red Queen.

The house, too, had daunted him at first. It was crammed with china, fine etched glass, leather-bound books strewn around like old newspapers. An honest-to-God harpsichord perched in one corner of the study, heaped high with yellowed music scores. It was a small house by the scale of its time—just before the First World War, before the Somme, the Marne, the Ardennes. Long before Dachau, Buchenwald, Stalingrad, Dresden. It might have been, he often thought, the vanished house of Elsa's vanished mother, the three narrow stories on the Essener Strasse that would have been Elsa's inheritance, shrunken from its childhood glamour into the reality of sagging boards and flapping shingles.

There were only four real bedrooms and just the one old bath with its grumbling plumbing, and not even a fireplace. Instead, there was a gleaming white tile stove her papa had sent for from Vienna when they settled here. Using the money his new American wife didn't know what to do with, Professor Bergner filled her house with small beauties—tiny, glass-doored cupboards tucked into corners or hidden under stairs and holding bits of cobalt or of ruby glass, pressed flowers from his careful garden, miniatures painted on bone and hung on black velvet ribbons. Just when you began to take the place for granted, carved panels turned suddenly into doors and opened into marvelous rooms with no other purpose than one's being there, being alone and wholly oneself in them. A wall that looked ordinary one day would suddenly blossom the next with a Manet lithograph or a drawing that must've been a Hals. Wherever you didn't expect it, a dusty treasure materialized.

About these wonders, Jaffer kept mum. For all Elsa knew, he thought Franz Hals was a used-car salesman. For all *she* knew, he was just like bloody old Graham and only looked at pictures on the wall in the doctor's office. Not that *he* ever went to doctors, frigging bloody Graham Worthing. Healthy bastard, barrel chest and ruddy cheeks, every spare minute out in the barn whacking at his punching bag till it hollered uncle. Not even high blood pressure or a nasty cholesterol level, goddamn him to hell. He would probably live forever. Goddamn him anyway.

But it wasn't just the pictures and books that amazed Jaffer. He'd grown up with the precious and the fucking rare, hadn't he? And ditched the lot to balance on the grubby edge of the universal pissoir most people spent their lives in. He preferred it. Old iron, old bones, old rags. All Jaffer wanted now was to step softly through the lives of others, taking care to cause no more smashups as he went.

Beautiful things, therefore, did not dazzle him. It was her. Elsa. The way she was with them. When they lived with perfect things, most people got like his mum and granfer. Rembrandts were wallpaper, Bach was elevator music, Gerard Manley Hopkins wrote the verses for those greeting cards of theirs. Oh, that was a prize, that was. The God's Grandeur line, they'd called it. Sold a treat, too, got Granfer on the Honors List that Christmas before he cashed it in. For himself, the old bugger had preferred a nice whodunit, thank you very much.

They'd bloody merchandised the whole of Western culture and now they were bored with it, they were ready to go slumming with the amazingly third-rate, the current Blue Light specials in the center aisle of the junk-culture supermart.

This might be the way of her husband, Graham. Graham, who could sell anything to anybody, though his cash flow was always mysteriously down. But it was not the way of Elsa. She could not pass a picture without stopping to look, amazed, as though it had just been painted specially for her. My Last Duchess, her husband called her, in an uncharacteristic display of third-form literacy. But it was true. She cherished them equally—the books, the paintings, Jaffer himself, the harpsichord, the gaggle of chatty females in her gardening classes, her husband, her two Harvard sons, her old stepmother, and her improbable house.

Not equally, he thought. *Not that.* In the last account, the only thing she valued was the house.

As a girl, when she first came to live there, she had given it a name in the old European way. She called it Trauerherz. The heart of sorrow, peace without hope. Sorrowheart.

The name had long ago been forgotten. Even she had laughed at it when she told him the story. They had been through the war then, they were full of sore places, she and her papa. So, Sorrowheart. Now there were other wars.

At the college, they looked down from the sixth-floor office of the new chancellor and though she had no legal claim to it as yet— her stepmother, Maxima Bergner, still being very much alive—they simply called it Elsa's Place, and they were right. Her soul—the word sprang unwelcome into Jaffer's mind, and though he tried to drive it out, it clung, incontestable—her soul had a dwelling such as ancient spirits had. The place was hers, and no one else's.

It was set like a hermit's cell among pear trees and apricots. A tangle of briar roses bloomed pale blush in early summer; an orange trumpet vine overwhelmed the front porch and climbed the roof and grew its way through the cellar bricks. There was a hay meadow, too; she kept it for its fragrance in the hot nights, and to taunt ''the progress nazis,'' as she said. Beyond the small meadow, against the latest college parking lot, was a dense grove of Austrian pines, their scent as sweet, almost, as the hay, the ground underneath deep with brown needles, littered with sticky cones. And near the greenhouses, almost hidden by grass she only cut three or four times a summer, were the herb beds, her papa's pride and joy, once carefully plotted and groomed, now rank and lunatic and all her own, as the whole place was, holding out against all probabilities. Without her, it could not have existed; without it, Elsa, thought Jaffer, looking down at her, would have gone up in smoke.

"What do you do?" she had said to him insistently, that months-ago day across the geranium seedlings.

Jaffer's eyes were wide and dark blue and his thinning crown of fine sandy hair blew back carelessly in the draft from the greenhouse doorway. A darker brown moustache drooped gently at the corners of an even mouth that seldom smiled.

"I disappoint people," he told her, his voice soft, a deep tenor, set far in his throat, the words articulated with the mouth barely open. A lip-reader would have despaired of him, but Elsa didn't. She only watched him curiously, her eyes absorbing him, as he shifted the weight of the backpack of books he was never without. "It's my life's bloody work, see. I'm a professional disappointment."

With a phalanx of highly respectable aunts and prominent god-damn uncles, a mother who thought she was Empress of Birmingham, an ex-wife or so, and three assorted kiddies, all goosestepping around the planet giving evidence against him, not to speak of any number of former employers, disgruntled landlords, a bookie or two, and at least one bank with a rubber-check complex, he'd told her only a bit less than the truth. Born in London just too late to claim the good old Blitz as an excuse, he'd drifted—after a skirmish or two at Oxford—out to the States hoping to settle in like the homesteaders in the John Wayne movies.

Which were, of course, pure bloody cock. Marked men, those homesteaders, even when the cattlemen didn't hang them from the barbed wire. There were always the goddamn prairie fires, weren't there?

Always.

So, after the homestead went up in smoke on the Minnesota prairies, after the big range war was over and he'd finally pulled himself off the barbed wire, Jaffer set sail north, across the border, first to Winnipeg, then sweet Toronto, full just then of pregnant, lank-haired American darlings and their ponytailed boyfriends, sitting cross-legged in the Bloor Street doorways, banging "Blowin' in the Wind" on cardboard guitars. Jaffer would reach into his backpack crammed with books and pull out his clarinet and let the cold Canadian sun dance on it, and, leaning his broad, oarsman's shoulders on a doorway of his own, he would play.

> Redwing blackbird, flying low,
> Make my home in the rain and snow.
> Redwing blackbird, flying fine,
> Hard luck's just a state of mind.

The notes rose and drifted and overwhelmed politics, and sometimes an old sod with a bottle in a paper sack would shuffle by and stop to sing a line or two, or just listen, round-eyed, while the Dylan-clones and the Bay Street brokers and the blue-haired darlings with shopping bags from Eatons and the team preachers and the Buddhist monks with begging bowls all curved and buckled and broke with melody, forgave themselves and came back new.

But Jaffer did not forgive himself. Not even the Blackbird could make him do that. Not even Elsa.

She was a good ten years older than he, was Elsa. Hard to tell, the bitch lied about everything, made up her life as she went along. You never quite knew when you were being had. But the slight sag of the tight belly, the droop of the full breasts, the tension along the jawline and in the corners of the great browny-black eyes—he'd marked her down as coming up hard on sixty. With her memories, she had to be.

A boxcar full of deportees, so crammed together they could only stand up, hugging one another, all the long journey. Among them Elsa's mother, who was amazed to discover she was one-eighth Russian Jew, her huge dark eyes unblinking as she stood very straight between the other women, looking at nothing, no longer able to see her small daughter or her husband who watched her, their eyes burned dry with grief. The train, they were later told, arrived at a small, cinder-blacked station far to the east; more than half the women frozen to death.

The blood and hair on the rifle butts of the beautiful, blue-eyed boys who stopped under a lamppost to light their only cigarette and sing "Stille Nacht" in voices like choirboys.

The forbidden radio, played at a whisper, ears smashed against the speaker, to hear for a split second the voice of Winston Churchill, who no matter what the papers said had not been killed by heroic Nazi pilots, who was still free, still breathing English air.

The trees in the Tiergarten bowled down like ninepins, their great roots plowed naked by the Russian bombs, then the British, then the American.

The bombs. The firebombs.

She'd told him none of this, of course, when she was wide awake. In her sleep, though, jagged fragments were torn from her dormant consciousness, and Jaffer collected them, pieced them to make pictures, imagined what was left. They were the only truth he had of her. In her sleep, she never lied.

There was something more, though, something which even in the random fallout of her unconscious she kept buried away in the dark, silent stream that was her center. Something which, if he knew it, might explain her and the house and the feckless marriage and the two insufficient sons. Which might even explain this unexpected infidelity in a woman to whom truth was everything, in spite of her lies—perhaps because of them.

Might even explain Jaffer himself, what in him had wakened her at last and made her almost love him. Almost.

As he stood watching, Elsa shuddered slightly, a tremorlike groundswell that began with a tiny muscle beside her mouth and ran down her body to her toes, tensing her shoulders, drawing her fingers into a fist, pulling her knees up tight, then, finally, jerking her long, narrow feet as though she were being hanged. Her eyes were squeezed violently shut; she seemed to be in pain and he believed she was, although she had told him often enough that he was wrong.

He supposed it was the answer she always kept ready for Graham, in case he noticed. In front of her husband, she would never admit to pain. Not that she was too proud, or that she did not trust him. Graham Worthing was nothing if not dependable, and she loved him as she did all other steady, useful things. But it would have damaged Graham to know. He could not have managed it and would have held her to blame. Her infidelity he tolerated and ignored, was even, Jaffer thought, a little glad of. But Graham did not know what to do with pain.

Jaffer laid both his thin, cool hands across her eyes and felt her lashes brush his palms. Slowly her body seemed to relax and she curled onto her side, diving deeper into sleep again. He wrapped himself in the blanket she had thrown off and moved silently across the creaky floor to the heap of his clothes in the corner. Elsa made a faint sound in her sleep, a kind of rising whimper, faintly interrogative, and he turned from the growing daylight to look at her. He could not imagine her anywhere else, in any other room or any other bed. The calm that is the heart of pain. Trauerherz. The bastard wanted to take it away from her, knock it down and burn off the fruit trees and smash the greenhouses and plow up the beds of herbs.

If that were all. If that were bloody-all.

Kill him, thought Jaffer, lighting a cigarette and drawing deep on it. *Somebody has to go and kill the bugger dead.*

Two

The worst thing about being nearly eighty-four years old, thought Maxima Davenport Bergner, settling herself in the bentwood rocker near her bedroom window above the rose garden, was that you could never sleep late. Age woke you bitterly, burrowing into the marrow of your bones. She slept only intermittently during the dark hours, and by five A.M. the bed was mild torture; by six, she couldn't lie there another second.

She had been brought up to luxuriate in sleep, to rise slowly, eat sparingly, dress with the utmost care in immaculate style. Few costumes, but the most exquisite, chosen on the annual shopping trip to Paris with her mother. She conjured in memory the burgundy silk from Erté, the one they'd bought in 1929, before the Crash. Her father, formidable Aylwin Davenport, who never speculated with his inheritance, had lost nothing, and the Great Depression washed over them here in their small-town fastness like a fairy-tale ogre in *The Brothers Grimm.*

Where was she? Oh, yes, the burgundy silk. That and the cream satin she'd been married in. Unconventional for a wedding dress, that décolleté. But she had always had her own style. She could still wear the thing, she'd tried it on one night when she couldn't sleep.

Only a little pull across the shoulders. She supposed she slumped a bit.

What else? The sleeping late, of course. Her maid—shared with her sister Vivian, but loyal only to her as everyone was—her dear maid, Lily, would've wakened her at— Nine, had it been? No, surely not. Ten? Yes, ten. With a fresh orange in perfect sections, and dry toast and strong coffee. Never tea, which was—according to her father—an indulgence, and certainly not cocoa, which was practically dissolute and taken only by cads and literary Frenchmen. It was always coffee. Strong, bitter, hot, marvelous coffee.

How long since she'd dared a sip? Three years, was it, or—no, surely it was nearer five. Bad heart, the quack had said. Funny how young they were turning out quacks these days. No more solemn graybeards; all the medicos were slim and peach-fuzz faced and permanently adolescent. Very likely they'd invented a pill to guarantee youth, which they only passed out to each other. Or an operation. These teenage quacks were fond of knives.

So, no more coffee for old Max. No more cigarettes. No passions of any sort at all. A bad heart, indeed. Certainly she'd lived by it too long, and it was tired. But bad?

She reached into the Limoges box her husband had given her and took out a cigarette, the Black Russians he'd liked, wickedly strong and containing God-knows-what they said was tobacco. She lighted it, drew in the forbidden smoke, and leaned back, trying to think of nothing.

It wasn't possible. Her mind was fogged with hate. It never left her now, had not for years. Usually it remained unfocused, venting itself at random over minor episodes—those foul herbal brews silly Elsa gave her instead of coffee, or the smell of Graham's after-shave, so strong it made her head throb. Scarcely realizing she did so, she would contradict her stepdaughter's slightest remark, snapping like a kennel bitch, insisting on a superiority she had never needed, never wanted before.

But, then, she'd never been old before. It was always there, in the dark corners of their minds, even Elsa's, who loved her, whom she loved. *You are old,* they thought. *You are nothing.* If you did not hate, at Maxima's age, you were either a fool or a saint, and she was neither.

Most of the saints, of course, had died conveniently young.

Now, though, she had something definite to hate. For the last two months, since their battle over the house began, she had felt stronger, settled and calm, aimed like an arrow straight at *him.*

She conjured his face. Oval, but short-chinned, folds of empty flesh below. He had been fat, once, and despised himself for it, punished himself into thinness. An ugly, out-of-balance mouth, the lower lip pouting slightly, the upper almost invisible. No beard nor moustache, a face full of tiny scars, as though he nicked himself with the razor constantly. The nose, at least, was satisfactory, though the ears were so close to the skull they looked artificial, as if they'd been stuck on with tape. The complexion was muddy, flooded with dirty crimson when he was angry.

That was where they differed. Maxima hated, which was a function of the soul. James Temple Macauley, chancellor of DeWitt Clinton College—*Doctor* Macauley, as he insisted on being called—was merely angry.

Which was a function, thought the old lady, breathing deeply of the dark, vile cigarette smoke, of the lack of balls.

Cowardice simmered and festered and turned brutal; in time, it simply bludgeoned the soul to death, as it had with James Temple Macauley. She'd met such men before, in her father's time at Clinton College and again in her husband's. Academe seemed to breed them, disguising their brutalities in snide wit and petty gossip, smearing their venal power games with the gloss of an intellectual nobility they had long ago surrendered, if they'd ever had it at all. If they were small men, they did it merely to survive, to get tenure, to make their house payments, to send their children to upscale colleges, whether they had any business there or not.

But if they were ambitious, such things were not enough. Men like Macauley needed monuments, they needed to delude themselves with petty immortality. And most of all, they needed battles they were guaranteed to win. Impotent as fixed tomcats, they picked fights to prove themselves, and then made sure the fights were rigged. The one thing they could not stand was to come up the loser in full public view, and that was exactly what she had in mind for James Macauley. But though she might relish the triumph, Maxima feared the aftermath. If he lost to her this time, he would come for her again, and time was on his side. Such men had the patience of cats too, of single-minded hunters; you could always tell it, by the eyes.

She shuddered, thinking of them. Mad eyes, they were, staring out of an empty cave. Flat blue eyes that never saw you though they never looked away. Burnt eyes, too long in the desert of himself.

Though she had no real religion and no idea what God might be, Maxima Davenport Bergner had prayed fervently for the last two months that James Temple Macauley might die before she did. The universe deserved to be rid of him.

That, she thought with mild amusement, that and the house were the only things they had in common, she and Macauley. He wanted her death as much as she yearned for his.

Until he came blowing in like a cold west wind—they'd re- cruited him from some western university, she could never remem- ber which and it made no difference anyway—Clinton College had been content to leave things as they were. The two pastoral acres of her father's property were surrounded, now, by campus, with a dormitory on one side, the tomblike obelisk of the new administra- tion building on the other, each with its tarred expanse of parking lot. Maxima, though, had never—till now—felt threatened or en- trapped; daughter of a chancellor, wife of the late esteemed profes- sor of European history, she had been part of Clinton College from her girlhood, she breathed and ate and slept the place. As her father had in his day, she gathered the best of the old guard of faculty— preposterous, curmudgeonly Winston Sherman and bemused Edward Merriman of English, stiff-necked little Halverson of classics, and tall, elegant, sarcastic Piers Ambrose, the magician, novelist, medievalist—in her dim parlor for sherry and cakes on Sunday evenings. She even winked a sardonic eye when she tripped over the students fumbling their way to love under her apricot trees in their annual *sacre du printemps*. She loved Clinton and felt loved by it, as though they were partners in an enterprise that had somehow managed to entice time to a standstill. In her turn, she lent the place a virtue— the flavor of survival.

Until he came, Macauley. He and that two-bit Machiavelli he brought with him as administrative assistant, Norman Shumaker. The campus, they told the city council, simply had to grow. It needed *Lebensraum*—parking space, room for another dormitory. The college was a major source of income for the city of Ainsley—Macauley and Shumaker had all the figures, and figures, being neutral, can be made to say anything. They had never offered to buy her out, unless you counted a vague hint over dinner at some college function. They knew, Macauley and his bullyboy, that Maxima would never sell, no matter how much they offered, that the house, the two acres of garden were not replaceable, not exchangeable with any other, could not be hoisted onto a truck and set down anywhere else. She was an immovable object, she and her house. Abruptly and overnight, entirely without notice, they asked the city council to condemn.

"Rubbish!"

She had gone herself to the first reading of the motion. The moment played like film against the retina of her mind, over and over, herself at the podium, painfully forcing her shoulders straight, voice trembling with disgust. Why had she not mastered that quaver? They had thought she was about to bawl, the fools; the eight bland faces of the council members had looked embarrassed. She could read their thoughts. *Silly, sentimental old woman.* That there should be, somewhere in their dispensable universe, one irreplaceable thing— how could she explain it to such creatures?

"Clinton College is a private institution," she told them instead, as calmly as she could. "It has no legal right to demand condemnation."

17

The city attorney, leathery Henry Jurgens, shook his rusty white mane and glanced at Norman Shumaker where he slouched in the corner next to Macauley. Shumaker nodded and Jurgens shook his head again. You could almost see the wires being worked.

"Legally, Mrs. Bergner, the city can condemn any property that is required by the public interest, no matter who requests it. It's entirely up to the city to define. *Pro bono publico,* you see. That means—"

"Rubbish!" said Maxima. "And I speak perfectly good Latin, thank you very much, Henry, a damn sight better than yours. What you mean is, I ought to go home and fold my hands in my lap and wait for the verdict like an old cow for the butcher's van! *Pro bono publico?* Parking lots for the public good?"

"But economically speaking," insisted Councilwoman Lucy Maclaren of the Third Ward, "anything that's good for the college is good for Ainsley. In these economic times—"

"Rubbish!" she said again. "I believe I ought to know as much as you about the good of that college, Lucy. You only graduated from it, and by the seat of your pants at that, as I recall. I was born into it. I married it. I have lived in the crook of its elbow for eighty-four years, and my home was here before the first stone of the place was ever laid. The good of the college—I—I—"

Hate engulfed Maxima. She could feel herself slipping downward into uncontrol. She glanced at James Macauley's face, and his eyes blinded her. She brushed a hand over her cheek and felt someone touch her arm. Elsa was beside her. Dear Elsa.

"Mutti," she whispered, "sit, before you fall down."

Mutti. Mummy. Elsa had only twice before called her by that pet name, which belonged by rights to the vanished mother, the ghost Maxima had never quite been able to exorcise. Mostly it was Madam Max, or simply Max. But not this time.

Such bitter tenderness was the final blow. Maxima reeled in the ferocious brightness of the fluorescent lights; she felt fragile as rice paper, old as the oldest god. Suddenly, without intending to, she sat

18

down—*plonk*—in the chair Elsa had placed at her elbow. The audience tittered, the man from the local paper tried to wipe off a grin, and the girl from the radio station cleared her throat pointedly.

Ridiculous. A ridiculous old woman.

"I would like to speak."

Elsa had always been soft-voiced, and at first, in spite of the microphone, they barely heard her.

"Speak up, please!" honked Mayor Tebbs. He looked like one of the Cheeryble Brothers, but looks were deceiving. He had a name in town for hard dealing and for bargains struck in back rooms. "Speak into the microphone!"

"I would like—"

"State your name!" This from a thin councilman with a face like a rubber Halloween mask, a scowling presence in a flashy suit and too much hair dye. "State your name and address for the record!"

A shudder ran through Elsa and she grasped the podium with both hands, hard. As a girl, after Berlin had fallen, she had once been taken in for questioning by the Russians. Almost no one came back from such arrests. Sometimes they were heard from years afterward, somewhere in the east, in Russia or Poland. Sometimes they had a secret, or a skill, or they had angered someone in the Russian zone. Sometimes they were cases of mistaken identity, punished by accident for someone else's crime. Maxima's husband could hardly bring himself to speak of it, as though the knock might still come on his door in the night, the unmarked car pull up the drive and wait there, hungry for his daughter's life.

They kept her five days. She had been just fourteen.

"Name, please!" barked the councilman.

"Elsa Bergner Worthing," she said clearly, forcing the words out like bullets. "I live at—at Twenty-seven Garden Road, my stepmother's house. My—my gardens, my greenhouse. My business will be—"

Mayor Tebbs interrupted her impatiently. "Yes, thank you, Mrs. Worthing. But you understand, this is only a first reading. You'll have

1 9

four more weeks, two further readings to present your arguments and any petitions or legal objections you may wish to offer. Leave it to The System. We must have faith in The System." He tipped back in his chair and locked his fingers together over the expanse of what Maxima might kindly call his chest, looking like a self-satisfied cinnamon bear.

"I do understand," said Elsa softly, but so clearly that even the bored young girl from the radio station looked up from the tabloid she had hidden under her note pad. "But *you* must understand. The system, any system, is not a machine. It is a jackass, sir, and it works for the one who gives it the biggest carrot or beats it with the biggest stick. My mother and I have no carrots, my dear sirs, and the sticks we have are not very large." Pride in this alien stepchild swelled in the old woman. "But believe me," said Elsa, pleasantly, "we shall beat like hell. Oh, my word, yes."

That had been more than two months ago, the decision held off by one continuance after the other. Tonight it would end. Winston Sherman, ever the Nosy Parker, had searched the records and discovered that the action was entirely without precedent. No city council had ever condemned a private house at the request of a private institution before in the history of Ainsley, New York. The council, torn between an untenable legal position and an overwhelming desire to kowtow to James Macauley, would vote on the motion tonight.

Unless Macauley capitulated. Unless he gave way.

But even then, public humiliation would only strengthen his desire to be rid of her. Time, time was her enemy. In time, he would win, and the world—or all of it that mattered to her—would fall to him.

Unless the Devil takes him and he falls down dead, thought Maxima. She would have no peace till he was dead.

Downstairs the telephone rang and she heard Elsa's bare feet pad out of her room across the hall and thud down the stairs to answer it. It had rung before, during the night, and no one had gone down. Telephones were distasteful to the old woman—she refused to answer them herself—and finally it had stopped its ringing. Perhaps Elsa had gone down without her hearing last night. She could be silent when she chose.

There. Elsa had answered, the clear voice rang loud up the stairs. Soft-spoken everywhere else, the girl had always shouted into telephones.

"Graham? My darling, good morning," cried Elsa, delighted. "Where are you?"

Graham. The husband. The drone.

Maxima sighed and drowned out her cigarette in the cold remains of the cup of coltsfoot tea Elsa insisted would cure her cough, though nothing ever did. With a stubby hand she drew the thin curtain back to look at the morning, to feel, if she could, the astringent cold of the frost-brushed glass. Except for the pines, the garden trees were bare now, the twisted, spiked branches of the apricots and the gnarled old pear limbs naked and vulnerable.

There was a wind from the east, and if it had not been for the wind, she would not have seen the slender, lonely figure in the gray windbreaker. He wore it unzipped and it flapped when the gust struck him. Elsa's lover, Geoffrey Swan.

As Jaffer stopped to zip his jacket and turn up the collar against the cold, Maxima appraised him: the muscular back, the long, agile thighs, the delicacy of his steps through the deep orchard grass, the elegance—entirely unconscious—of his head.

A good choice, she had thought so from the beginning. The first sensible thing the girl had done in years, far more interesting than Graham. Maxima detested Elsa's husband, and the two sons they had produced, Paul and Jordan, were only slightly better—kind enough, and good-humored, but what did all that matter, when the essential piece was missing, the wordless thing that comprehended, discerned, forgave?

Graham and his sons had no such level. They would not have wanted it; it had no practical translation into dollars and cents, real property values, bearer bonds, or commodity prices, no mechanical parts, no defining subclauses. Intuition, imagination—to Graham, they might as well have been a vestigial tail or a web between his toes.

But not to that slight figure out there in the wind, making his way through the pear trees. He was no Graham Worthing, this lover of Elsa's. Maxima had known it the moment she saw him, bent over his work in the greenhouse. Geoffrey Swan, the displaced Englishman who tied up the herb bunches and potted the chrysanthemum slips and sprayed the fuchsias for white fly and read aloud to his lover when he came to her at night, in a deep, soft undertone—from Eliot, was it? No, it was Yeats, almost always.

> Consume my heart away; sick with desire
> And fastened to a dying animal
> It knows not what it is. . . .

Such was Jaffer's way of making love, to enter the mind before he attempted the body. Elsa's father, Alois Bergner, dear Alois, had been the same, becoming inevitable to Maxima, courting her with his tender, subterranean voice, reading from Rilke as they sat beside the fire in her dark living room.

> Wer jetzt kein Haus hat, baut sich keines mehr.
> Wer jetzt allein ist, wird es lange bleiben. . . .

Whoever has no house will never build another. Whoever is alone, will be long, long alone. Sometimes she thought Alois had married the house as much as her. Certainly he had loved it as though he had grown up in it just as she had. And Elsa, too. They came home gratefully to this gentle archaism of a patch of nineteenth-century ground.

Whoever has no house will never build another.

If they took the house from her, if Macauley defeated her with those fools on the council, it would be the end of her. As it was, she couldn't bear the thought of change around her. When chairs grew rickety and unsafe to sit upon, she would not let them be thrown out or even sent away and repaired. She defended them with her life, pushed them into forgotten corners and harbored them. When a tree died of cold in the orchard, she refused to hear old Axel Engstrom's saw whining. Axel, who had been her husband's friend, who knew more about trees and plants than even Elsa did, would scold and cluck at her like the old hen he was, but Maxima could not bear to be the vessel of change. She let the wind do such work, and the load of ice, until the barren branches fell of their own weight. Each loss diminished her; unless she fought, there would be nothing left, nothing to stay for. Graham stole her treasures and sold them, and she held her tongue, adding up her secret score against him. He might as well have cut off her arm. They were the geography of her existence.

Wer jetzt kein Haus hat, baut sich keines mehr. If there was no longer any place in the world that could be defended. . . .

I want to die, thought Maxima Bergner. *Christ, let me die.*

The slim figure of Jaffer Swan disappeared into the darkness of the pine grove and the old woman was alone. She loved him, she was certain, as much as Elsa did. She hated the weekends, when Graham came huffing and puffing home from Manhattan and Jaffer slept God-knew-where. There was danger in him, as there always is in poets, certainly. When such a man breaks, the fragments are dagger sharp.

Still she waited each night for his step on the stair, pausing at the door of her stepdaughter's room across the hall, always hesitant. Then, when he had gone inside, Maxima would get up and open her own door. She could not often make out the words once she had lain down on her white bed again, but the tone of voice drifted into the dark room, calming her. There was an odd strength in it. The man had been beaten and survived.

In the end, that was all there was in the world—those who held the stick and those who felt it.

"I want to die," said Maxima softly, through clenched teeth. "Sweet Christ, I want to die."

She had a gun ready, in the drawer of her dressing table, oiled and loaded. Alois had never got over his wartime nerves, and he had slept the better knowing it was there. His final solution, he'd called it. Now it would be hers.

I want to die, she thought again.

Her old eyes took in the garden, the bare trees, the tower—Macauley's tower—rising over them.

"But not before *he* does," she murmured. "Amen."

Three

"Such an early hour, I'm half asleep! Look, it's not yet eight! So, my dear, you are already at the office, or what?"

His wife's warm, dusky voice, as always, was soothing to Graham Worthing. He began to be less afraid.

"Yes," he lied, "I am. Naturally. At the office. Where else would I be?"

His office was a three-room suite in a building on Madison Avenue just off Fifty-Third, and it cost too much. He had had to give it up weeks ago, but he had not told Elsa. He worked now—when he worked at all—out of the condo he'd bought on West End Avenue when the ad business was booming, back in the purblind Eighties. That euphoria had given way to a low-grade fever of sorts, then to a gnawing angst. Now there was only a hollow cavern of dismay.

The slump wasn't Graham's fault, of course. Several of his best accounts had gone under. The Arabs were grabbing everything. Then came the Japanese. These successive invasions had washed over Graham Charles Worthing, eroding him a millimeter at a time. He became estranged, submerged, made few contacts, answered his telephone with trepidation.

Then, too, he'd been cautious, slow to get into video presentations, which he had always mistrusted. All these factors added up; one by one, he let his assistants go, then his secretary. He sat alone in the silent, expensive office, watching the Madison Avenue traffic roil and churn below him. In time, he might have worked his way out of it.

But there was no time. The long hours he spent alone high above the sidewalk crowds, surrounded by the exposed frauds of his professional life—the silent computer only the missing secretary knew how to use, the rows of files containing information coded and labeled and stored according to some mystical system he could not penetrate, the three telephones through which good news never arrived —all this made one thing plain to Graham Worthing. It, even more than the high rent and his lack of funds, had made him close his office and go to ground. Time had at last run out. Something in the fabric of things had given way.

"I—I thought I'd come in early this morning, get things cleared up," he lied.

He had gotten good at lying, even better than his wife. When his younger son, Jordan, came down from Harvard for a day in Manhattan, Graham booked a table at The Four Seasons, where Georges, the headwaiter, still remembered him though he had not set foot in the place for almost a year. "Gotta travel first class," he bluffed to the boy as they lounged possessively at the best table in the house. Graham pretended to read the menu, but his mind was scanning desperately over the credit limits of the plastic cards in his wallet, trying to decide which one he could present to Georges without embarrassing consequences when the bill at last arrived.

If he had been able to explain his real circumstances to anyone, it certainly would not have been to his sons. They were precious to him, more precious, even, than his wife; Elsa had not seemed to want children until she was nearly forty. First Paul, towheaded and blue-eyed, then silent, black-eyed Jordie, had come as complete surprises to their dazzled father, who had long since given up hope. He could deny the boys nothing, and the bills had begun to mount up, the college clothes and computers and tutors' fees. He paid them without a qualm. If Paul's blond perfection had grown lumpish, if Jordan's silent inwardness turned smug, Graham pretended not to notice. They were all that kept him afloat.

"Not to worry," he lied when Jordan made a grab for the bill. "Leave it to the old man."

And lying was not all. He stole, too. Twice, when payments from clients failed to arrive, he had abstracted small treasures from Elsa's curio shelves and china closets, sold them at good prices to antique dealers. A Steuben glass vase, tiny and rare and perfect, and a one-of-a-kind Wedgewood cream jug—or so the dealer told him. Graham would not have known, and Elsa did not seem to miss them. They were the old woman's, anyway—Maxima's—and she only came downstairs now to stomp through the house and out into the orchard, in all weathers and at all hours, barely noticing what was inside the place at all.

Graham cleared his throat. "I decided to come home tonight, Elsa. Not wait till the weekend. I thought I might—be some—use to you."

He stared out the motel room window at the cars rushing past on the Hudson River Parkway. He was not in Manhattan. Often at night he would take his car from the garage down the street and, turning it onto one of the fast highways, he would drive, hours long, the tape Elsa had given him playing over and over in the sleek deck of his unpaid-for BMW. The voice of some actor, faintly English but not quite—oh, yes, it was David Cromwell, old Sherman's foster son. A careful, probing speech, searching out unexpected meanings, a voice that darkened with private pain as he read. Graham had never been one for books, but he played over and over that sober voice, the words of Joseph Conrad.

We were wanderers on a prehistoric earth, on an
earth that wore the aspect of an unknown planet. . . .
we glided past like phantoms, wondering and secretly
appalled. . . .

27

The words wound through his consciousness as he drove, and finally, when it was almost morning, he had come home, at least as far as the motel. He'd chosen one of the new cut-rate places not far from the campus and his wife's house. Elsa wouldn't be likely to drive past in her rusting station wagon and spot his car outside the Cozy Inn. She wouldn't be driving anywhere. She'd be with him, with Jaffer Swan.

"I—I wanted to be with you tonight, my love," he said to her now. "The council meeting. I didn't want you to face it alone."

"Dearest Karl," she said softly. "How good, how good you are."

His middle name was Charles, and Elsa had made herself at home with it, using it only when she was fondest of him. She had never been quite comfortable with the artificial formality of Graham. At first she had teased him with it, but over the thirty-one years of their marriage, the distinction had deepened, become more subtle. Graham was the man of business who lived five days a week in an apartment in the city, dining with clients, managing their personalities like credits and debits; who slept now and then with some strange woman, perhaps beautiful, perhaps young; and who could not disguise it, not even over the phone, though he wanted to desperately, firmly believed he had. Graham was preoccupied, confident, immune to music, art, nature; aside from the materials he represented, Graham had scarcely read a book since he left school, had no time for the theater or even movies. Graham worked in incomprehensible, faintly distasteful ways at a job she disliked, a job she knew humiliated and cheapened the best that was in him.

The best was Charles—Karl, as she said. It was Charles she had married, a bluff, awkward, gentle lover, his passion wrapped in layer upon layer of endearing self-doubt. No strange woman had ever come near him; Charles was unswervingly faithful. It was Charles she would never leave, not even for Jaffer Swan.

Elsa's lover—the first she'd ever had since their marriage, Graham was certain of that—had not had the sort of effect upon her husband he had expected, even wanted infidelity to have. Instead of jealousy, shame, chagrin, he felt a secret joy. The nagging guilt of his own occasional adventures left him. The fear that even the Charles side of himself which she still loved could never give Elsa what she needed most, that he was, at bottom—had always been—insufficient for her, incapable—even this secret knowledge ceased to trouble Graham Worthing. He could simply love his wife, without being required to understand her. He could leave that to Swan, who seemed to know instinctively what Charles—certainly not Graham—had never quite taken in.

Jaffer Swan understood about the house.

"—so glad to have you with me at the meeting," Elsa was saying. "I think much better when you are there, my dear, you know, I keep my brain under control and don't go wheeling off the road. Like when you taught me to drive!" Her warm, breathless laughter spilled across the telephone lines. "Remember? Without you, I'd never have survived!"

"You know perfectly well you only pretended to let Graham teach you." It was Maxima speaking, that acidulous croak her voice acquired before she had eaten in the morning. "I taught you myself, and you were a dreadful pupil. But you certainly *did* know how. Only Graham would be fool enough not to know it. Where's my orange, Elsa, dear? My throat feels like alligator skin."

In his mind's eye, Graham saw old Madam Max, rose-colored quilted satin robe wrapped round her nearly twice, crepey skin of her throat visible where the top button was missing, bony arms protruding from the wide cuffed sleeves that hung loose on her, the thin hand with the absurdly careful manicure she made Elsa give her every Saturday, the long, crimson nails. Descending the stairs each morning like a nesting eagle, soaring and swooping for prey. He'd grown elephant hide for twenty years to bear her, put up with her till his boys were grown. Then he'd claimed the pressure of business, taken the apartment in Manhattan, asked Elsa to come with him, leave the house and the blessed orchards to Maxima.

29

Elsa had refused.

"Is that the fool you're talking to?" His mother-in-law made her voice louder than usual, knowing he would hear her. Graham glanced round him in the dingy motel room as though someone might have heard her, as though she had exposed him, even there. But he was alone, still alone. The realization came as a relief.

"Hush, Max!" commanded Elsa. "Karl, are you there, darling? When are you coming? I'll make the blue trout for dinner, a celebration. We're going to win, I know it now, now that you are coming to cheer for us. Macauley shan't have the house, and we shall have *blaue Forelle* for dinner, a regular party! I'll ask Winston and Sarah, don't you think, Karl, and that nice Mr. Zimmerman, the librarian? And Jonathan Lucas, such a clumsy boy, but sweet, and such a baby! He reminds me of our boys, dear, when they were first at college, all worldly looks and chewed fingernails and too many zippers. And little Krishnan, those perfect manners, we can't do without him! Did I tell you he's found a girlfriend now? Hallie, her name is. Harriet. Such a beauty, and a touch with flowers. She comes to my silly classes, but she's too good for them. Ach, that Mrs. Costello, and the Sheffield woman, no taste at all. Them, I won't invite! Oh, it's been so long since I could think about a party, I really must, before the meeting tonight."

The excited chatter suddenly stopped.

"To—to throw it in his face," she said. "Herr Professor Doktor James Temple Macauley. To live in spite of him. To celebrate."

The warm voice had grown deeper and stronger. It was blended of several pitches, and different emotions carried it higher, lower. Then suddenly it was dark and heavy and full of pain, like the voice on the tape. *Wondering and secretly appalled.*

The heart of darkness. Sorrowheart.

"I want to die here, Karlchen," said Elsa softly. "This place. The garden. The orchard. I cannot lose my life again. I shall ravel out, like old rags."

Graham was silent for a moment, staring out the motel room window. Outside, along the shoulder of the highway, a woman

30

struggled uphill on an old bicycle. It was hard work and she pumped away with determined legs, her shoulders straight, hands fisted on the handlebars, dark graying hair bound in one thick braid that hung down her back halfway to the saddle of the bike. As she did every Wednesday morning, Sarah Cromwell was going to Elsa's place to play the harpsichord.

"We will win, won't we, Karlchen?" asked Elsa, her voice almost a whisper.

"Of course," he said, too fast and without conviction. "Of course, my love."

Sarah Cromwell, the woman on the bike, the sister of the actor on the tape, would have made Elsa believe it. Even sour old Maxima could put courage back into her stepdaughter, and the silent resilience of Jaffer Swan, who seemed to let the world wash over him like a dirty tide over a rock, would make her want to endure. She had the three of them—her best friend, her stepmother, her lover. Why was she glad Graham himself had come? What could she possibly need from him any longer?

"You are kind," Elsa said, the darkness thinning in her voice. "You are kind to come and be with me, my dear."

You're lying again, thought Graham Worthing. *Did you get up from him and go to your window in the night and see me out there in the orchard, watching? Do you know how many nights I have come and watched? God, dear Jesus God how I hate you,* he thought. *How I hate Jaffer Swan.*

"About six," he said. "I'll be home about six tonight. Few things to clear up at the office. Good-bye. Good-bye, my love."

Graham hung up the telephone gently, as though it might break. Love for his wife flooded over him, and the wish to be free. Outside, the strict, stubborn figure of Sarah Cromwell on her aging lover's rickety bicycle caught Worthing's eye once more. Loathing for her seized him, for all of them—for Sarah, Maxima, Jaffer Swan, for Elsa herself, who valued him only for the side of himself that had made him a failure, ruined him. They owned a private universe that had no room for him.

31

It is impossible. The voice on the tape whispered in the ear of Graham's memory. *We live, as we dream—alone.* . . .

If they could only die, all of them, and the world could be clean and he could be truly alone, houseless, wifeless, childless.

If he could only kill them all.

Four

Today it was Scarlatti.

The perfect sonata form stated and restated itself, thesis, antithesis, synthesis, posing and resolving and posing once again at the root of Sarah's consciousness as she dismounted gratefully from the old brute of a bike and began to walk it up the graveled drive along the greenhouses, toward Elsa Worthing's squat, white house with its circular porch.

It was unthinkable to her that after tonight, if the chancellor had his way, the place could be gone within a month, the orchards leveled, perhaps, before the week was out. Once the city council okayed these blitzkrieg moves of his, Macauley lost no time. A street on the other side of the campus had been closed at his request six months ago, just after he arrived, and the air hammers had been at work the day after the motion was granted, tearing out paving.

Another parking lot, forsooth! The man was a dolt. Winston said so, and Win ought to know. He was certainly having enough of a fight with Macauley over the new "marketable" curriculum the Iron Chancellor—that was what Winnie called him—had demanded. The new administrative head of Clinton College was disliked by most of his faculty, especially the old hands like Winnie, Hugh Jonas, Piers

Ambrose from the history department and old Howard Halverson of classics. There were rumors everywhere—jobs would be cut, whole departments terminated, pensions sacrificed. Winston, who'd held out so long against forced retirement, was safer than most; he had his novels to write, the long career he'd forged over the years disguised as Henrietta Slocum, queen of the mystery novelists. But it didn't stop him from facing off against Macauley and everything he stood for. She was proud of that.

Only the computer experts and merchandising wonders of Business Administration and the ever-increasing tribe of coaches, male and female, seemed to like their new leader; their presence translated directly into dollars and cents. Sports meant big alumni bucks, and matching funds for athletic scholarships that more than matched their cost. Students could always be found to register for business courses, whose practical use was undeniable.

The rest, the old knowledge, was of marginal use, and those who treasured it, whose lives had been its priesthood, were the same. They were expendable, they were dead wood. And they were afraid.

Until she met him, Sarah had dismissed this muttered fear of Macauley as mere faculty-lounge paranoia. He was married, but his wife was seldom seen; they had no children, and they chose not to live in the rather grandiose residence on campus that went with the job. Instead, they moved into a development house as far from the college as possible, butted up against the grounds of Pineview Memorial Cemetery. Probably, Sarah had thought, the faculty wags were just pouting at this chilly distance. Maybe the man was only shy, or had too much good sense to waste his life in pointless mingling. She herself hated faculty parties, and so did Winston.

But then came the banquet when Macauley was installed as chancellor. At Winston's side, she'd moved along the receiving line to where he and his anorexic-looking wife, Helen, a faded blond with dark eyes like shoe buttons in a pale, oval face, were greeting the faithful. Helen took her hand mechanically, and Sarah looked up and smiled. The woman's face was blank as a sheep's, and when Sarah spoke, she seemed to shrink into herself, trying to disappear into the high-necked black dress she wore.

"If there's anything I can do to help you settle in," said Sarah warmly, "shops or tradesmen or anything, do let me know, won't you? I mean, if you need wiring or plumbing, some of these pirates will take your back teeth right out. God knows, with everything that's broken down in that old place of ours, I've got the local contractors pretty well weeded out, so—"

She could hear herself rattling on, as though she stood at a distance, listening, while the rest of her looked into the woman's face. Helen Macauley was frightened, white as a sheet except for two spots of brownish blusher on her cheekbones. What had she said to terrify the poor thing? Or was it merely the prospect of possible friendship that unnerved her?

No, thought Sarah. *It's him. The husband.*

Macauley was tallish, well-built, and his lean, punished body stood posed, mannequinlike, opposite the comfortable bulk of Winston. Win held out a big, square paw and the new chancellor seemed to consider for a moment, mildly surprised that congeniality should be demanded of him. Then he grasped the offered hand a bit too energetically.

But the oblique angle of his glance never completely left his wife. He watched her constantly, no matter who else stood before him.

"Are you going to be a thorn in my flesh, Dr. Sherman?" he said stiffly, with a flicker of perfunctory smile.

Winston snorted and let out a dragon-cloud of smoke from the Turkish cigarette he was never without. "That depends, kiddo." He peered at Macauley through the fog as a volcanic drift of ashes settled on the chancellor's impeccable dinner jacket. "Are you going to be a knife in my back?"

The evening had unsettled Sarah's nerves and kept her wide awake all night at Winston's side, thinking of the new chancellor. Being a musician, she was sensitive to sounds, to the subtle pitch of voices as they rose and fell. What had she heard in James Macauley's that denied her rest? What had she seen in the bleak blue eyes?

Le silence éternel de ces espaces infinis m'effraie.

The famous line of Pascal came suddenly into her mind as she lay awake, listening to the steady snoring of the man she had come to know, over the nearly forty years of their unconventional union, better than she knew herself. The one thing Winston Sherman could never be, not even by Pascal's eternal silence, was terrified. "Applesauce, kiddo," he'd say, and settle down to write the next chapter of whatever mystery his publisher was clamoring for now.

But the old Frenchman's despairing line might've been written expressly, she thought, for James Macauley. The silence of infinite spaces. That was what she had seen in the eyes, heard in the dull, unvarying voice. Not even his wooden-faced wife came near him. With his carefully shorn cap of snow-white hair and perfect posture, he might've been made of ice. At the center of an empty, whirling universe, Macauley was alone. His shadow was gigantic and it swallowed everything in its path.

And that, she thought with a shiver, made him dangerous. No wonder Helen Macauley was afraid.

But that dinner had been months ago, and the world hadn't ended yet. You could hardly hold one man to blame for the idiotic contrivances of a bankrupt culture.

Winter was coming, to Sarah's energetic soul the best season of the year. She shook off her forebodings, enjoying the early cold as she always did. Leaning the bike against the potting bench outside the greenhouse, she peered inside. Bunches of herbs hung on drying racks and a few of the wreaths Elsa and her gardening ladies made from dried flowers and fragrant sprigs of rosemary, lavender, and rue had been finished already and hopefully set out for the early Christmas shoppers up from Manhattan for the weekend. Old Maxima had money, but even if she'd offered it, Elsa would've refused. She worked hard to make the little garden center pay, but with two sons at Harvard, there was never enough money. Graham's business was crumbling, everybody knew it and nobody said it. But it was obvious. Elsa worked harder and harder, offered classes in the growing of houseplants and kitchen herbs, in flower arranging and design, deter-

36

mined to keep her share of the bargain with her stepmother. Maxima shared her house and the treasures with which her husband had filled it; Elsa and Graham were to pay the bills.

Sarah sighed, thinking of her own rambling white-elephant mansion. Bills, indeed. If she knew anything, the old woman had gotten the best of the deal.

Usually, people drifted in and out of the greenhouse at all hours, but it was early, and nobody was yet at work. Not even that strange fellow, Swan.

She had no idea why, but Sarah disapproved of Swan. Oh, not because he was sleeping with Elsa. That was hardly surprising, with Graham adrift and barely seeming to belong to the place at all anymore. Astounding, knowing Elsa's ideas about fidelity, but hardly surprising.

There was something about Geoffrey Swan, though. Something unpredictable and a little askew. Like a mistreated cat that might either purr or claw if you had the temerity to offer it love.

You liked him instinctively. He was quick and perceptive and often funny, slipping in and out of rooms as though he were on the lam. But being liked made him uncomfortable and, Sarah suspected, prone to do random damage.

Which didn't matter, of course, so long as he didn't damage Elsa.

If Sarah Cromwell had been able to choose a sister, that sister would've been Elsa Worthing. In fact, Sarah had a perfectly good sister, named Ellen. But they had been more apart than together; they understood nothing of one another, and even though they wrote and telephoned these days, the messages were conventional, polite, and tentative. With Elsa, she barely had to talk at all. Comprehension jumped between their two minds like a spark between hot wires.

Sarah had a house of her own, too, a rundown, once-pretentious mansion left her by her father, and she loved it because it contained her past, her life with Winston. But if she had been able to choose a house, it would have been this one. Sorrowheart.

The Scarlatti took possession of Sarah's mind again, carrying with it the remembered touch of the harpsichord keys, clean and precise as piano keys—for all their store of passion—could never be. Playing that rare marvel of an instrument of Elsa's restored Sarah's confidence in the essential order of things, their continuity, holed-up in secret places such as this. God knew where old Herr Professor Bergner had found the thing, but on its mysterious ebony keys the child Mozart might have practiced arpeggios, the portly Bach, beset by children, hacked out cantatas. However the harpsichord had got here, here it was, and for twenty years she had come to play on it. After tonight, she thought regretfully, all that might be swept away.

Order, even in the face of death. To assert it, she had refused to drive her car up to Elsa's place today. She had insisted on borrowing Winnie's bike instead, to venture out undefended in the presence of death. He and Eddie had tried to talk her out of it; somebody was killing lone women, there had been three deaths in the past four months, and age seemed to make no difference.

But in the end, Winston understood. He always did. Wholeness had to matter more than fear, or nothing would survive. Grumbling and complaining, he had lent her the wretched old bicycle and watched her from the window as she ground it down the drive.

She would phone him when she got to Elsa's, let him know she was safe. He would pretend he'd just gone back to steal another forty winks, and grouse a bit more, and she would feel his relief.

Three women dead—one old, one middle-aged, one hardly more than a child. Three women unmolested, almost untouched. Except for the track of a needle.

Overdose, they said. Improbable, but true.

Sarah closed her eyes for a moment, letting the sonata soothe her nerves, and it was only when she stumbled over something in the long grass that she became aware of another melody intruding upon the first. Like the Scarlatti, it was familiar, but her mind was too stunned to identify it just then.

She had wandered, preoccupied, into the orchard where the unmown grass of autumn was long and thick beneath the trees, clotted with fallen pears, wasp-stung and shriveled and rotting away.

It was under a big, cleft pear tree, a few stubborn fruit still hanging on its boughs, that the girl sat. It was upon her small feet, stretched out before her, that Sarah tripped and fell headlong into the littered grass.

The girl seemed asleep, but it was too cold for sleeping. She was slender, with heavy black hair that hung loose around her shoulders like a silky cape, and skin the color of dark honey. Her eyes were closed, the lashes long and black like the hair, the lips a perfect line. Her body was small and slender, dressed in blue jeans, a white silk shirt, and a scuffed brown leather jacket, the left cuff unbuttoned and the sleeve rolled up to bare the smooth forearm. Round her slim throat, where the shirt fell slightly open, hung a long necklace made of jagged branches of natural black coral, polished to a preternatural gleam. Her hand lay open in the grass as though it had held something precious. Now it was empty.

In the muscle of the left forearm, just above where the pulse should have been, was the telltale crimson track of a needle. She was dead.

Sarah knew it, but her mind refused the fact. The wind was up, and it was very cold. She reached for the girl's hand and held it, her fingers searching for a pulse. When her father, cynical old Erskine Cromwell, lay dying, he had kept her by him hour upon hour. "Take my pulse, girl," he would say, and wait, anxious, while she found it, wait for her to tell him he was still alive, to measure how much life was left him.

For this girl, nothing was left at all. There was no pulse. Sarah put two fingers delicately against the slender throat, although she had no hope. Nothing. No sign of brutality or of violence marred the exquisite figure propped calmly against the twisted tree trunk. Life seemed simply to have left her of its own accord, and death perfected her. It was unthinkable to move her, to look for wounds, to search for identification. It was unnecessary, anyway. Sarah knew who she was. She was the fourth victim, the girl who was to have been Krishnan Ghandour's wife, and her name—though now it scarcely mattered—was Harriet Glendon. Hallie.

39

The Scarlatti rose to a climax and ended, and that other melody, till now unrecognized, grew and took precedence, its unsung words carried to Sarah on the cold November wind.

Redwing blackbird, flying fine,
Hard luck's just a state of mind. . . .

She could just see him through the bare trees, a hunched, lone figure that might have been shadow, braced against the cold, and though he saw her, he made no motion.

Blackbird, blackbird,
Stumble and fall,
Blackbird got no home at all.

The bluesy notes of the clarinet drifted on the wind. Jaffer Swan was playing a requiem.

Five

Though I didn't hear it myself, that music of Jaffer's turned out to be the cue for my entrance—Yours Truly, Winston Marlowe Sherman, Ph.D., professor of English at Clinton College, known to mystery fans worldwide—well, in the state of New York, anyway—as Henrietta Slocum, dowager empress of the whodunit, and although I was fighting it like hell, I already knew I was about to become entangled as usual in another real-life crime.

And also as usual, Sarah was right. I hadn't gone back to bed once I'd seen her off on her defiant bicycle pilgrimage to Elsa's place. Oh, not that it wasn't tempting, mind you. The floors in this drafty old barn of ours felt like the polar ice cap at eight o'clock that bleak November morn. Outside, bare branches scraped a sky the color of used dishwater, and I could've sworn I heard a raven somewhere, croaking "Nevermore."

No kind of a day to defy augury, I thought as I stood in the front hall watching the love of my life pedal off down the drive. What had I let her get herself into? I yanked my seedy old tartan bathrobe closer around my Nero Wolfean midsection, and shivered mightily, from the cowlick in my shock of gray tweed chicken-feather hair to the ingrown toenail on my chilly big toe.

41

"Launch another one of those, Winnie, and an earthquake alert will go off up and down the eastern seaboard. Standing there shivering won't protect her. So put on your carpet slippers like a sensible hippopotamus, stop gazing after Sarah as if she were the lost Lenore, and do something about it!" Merriman shoved my long-distance specs into my paw. "Here. Look at her through these confounded things! You could lose her, you know. She's too damn brave for her own good!"

I rammed my glasses onto my beak and did as I was told, which, with my old pal Eddie Merriman—especially before he has his morning cuppa—is always a sound plan. And I had to admit he had a point. It was part of what had drawn me to Sarah Cromwell forty years ago, a rare practical intensity that applied itself to everything full tilt; it made her dauntless, but it also made her vulnerable as only the unconsciously brave can be. She worried about my forays out of the mystery fiction I'd written for so many years and into deadly reality, she was terrified when her brother David ventured into danger, but she hardly realized it when she put herself at risk.

Sarah had no choice, of course; she was unique. I'd known it the first moment I saw her, playing Chopin at one of her father's flashy parties. Awash in a life that seemed to be going nowhere, I took root in her and held fast. She offered me her house to live in, and I live there still. When her father was dead, her kid brother, David, became a little bit my brother and a little bit my son. Whatever I had of value after seventy years of living I owed to her. The possibility of losing her to sudden, swooping death was unthinkable.

But possibility it was.

The sight of Sarah perched elegantly on the lopsided saddle of my old bike, working the squeaky pedals with an iron will, sent a knife-blade of fear through me. Out there somewhere was a dark spirit that erased lives one after another, like so many smudges from a sheet of paper—a puzzle no amount of reasoning could solve, a silent malevolence no ordinary passion could excuse. Even the broad, all-fitting cloak of madness was too easy an answer for it.

A serial killer, that neutered term for a peculiarly modern horror. It was a hobgoblin that could turn up anywhere these days. Anywhere but here.

Ainsley, New York, isn't Manhattan, after all. It isn't even Buffalo, for pity's sake. It's a small, slightly batty haven with a population largely made up of commuters to city jobs who throng the aged depot each morning and each night return to tidy hives of development houses clustered on the wooded bluffs above the Hudson.

On one such bluff perches DeWitt Clinton College, an amalgam of feisty lads of the Old Brigade such as Merriman (now retired) and myself (still fighting it off); of barely literate undergraduates—I think especially of our football ace, Lance "The Bull" Carmichael who, in his seventh year at Clinton barely qualifies as a sophomore—and of half-educated Flower Power Ph.D.'s like our esteemed department chairman, Thomas Van Doren Sheffield, whose dissertation, titled "Reference Materials for the Study of Colly Cibber" consisted of a shoe box of colored file cards—quite a feat, to be fair, as nobody since Mrs. Cibber has ever, to my knowledge, had the slightest desire to study old Colly at all.

Add to these a few benignly dotty citizens-at-large like the Widow Megrim, Eddie's former landlady—Bony Blanche of the industrial strength Vienna Waltz perfume, the world-class collection of Perry Como's greatest hits, and the bold and roving eye, which roved in Merriman's direction once too often and drove him to sanctuary at our place years ago. Then, too, there's Elsa's stepmother, old Mrs. Bergner, a.k.a. The Claw, so called for the heart-stopping bloodred manicure she has affected since her flapper youth. And, last but not least, one Quincy Mapp, who holds the world's record as the oldest living man to steer a unicycle with his elbows. Quincy is now ninety-three, and can be seen every morning at eleven on Abbott Street, steering away like sixty.

A serial killer in such a place? It seemed impossible, but it wasn't. Whether the specter had descended on us like a plague from somewhere else during the past four months, or had risen slowly from some unsuspected darkness we had always, like a cancer, contained, it was out there somewhere. And so was Sarah.

"Why the hell didn't I ever marry her?" I muttered.

"Because I told you not to, Winnie," said Merriman's reedy tenor into my left ear. "You'd have lost her, you know. For some people, marriage is like asthma, it takes the breath away." He frowned and poured milk on his bowl of Oat Crunchies, thinking, I knew, of his late wife Gwendolyn, whose long-ago passing had made breathing a whole lot easier for him.

Thinking of Gwendolyn always means Eddie's about to give me a hard time. I decided to ignore him.

All I'd had for breakfast so far was my blood pressure pill, a fairly recent addition to my morning routine I could've done nicely without. The thing was as big as a Ping-Pong ball and tasted like musty suet, and every time I took it I could hear flights of angels singing, "Good night, sweet prince," in four-part harmony, with ad-lib riffs on the celestial harp. Right now, I needed something more sustaining.

I opened the fridge and began to browse among the leftovers, emerging with a slice of middle-aged pizza left from one of David's visits; his little girl, Gemma, like stout Cortez, has just discovered pizza, and leaves a trail of it wherever she goes. It suited my mood exactly—cold, heavy, and indigestible. I poured a cup of Mr. Coffee's finest to wash down the grease, and lowered my bulk into the chair opposite Eddie, braced for whatever was on his mind. He leveled his guns and fired.

"I don't know why you don't set to work properly on the business, Winnie," he snapped, "instead of fussing every time Sarah sets foot out the door. Surely there must be some connecting factor in these deaths. What does Lloyd Agate have to say?"

This was Lieutenant Agate, friend and former student and mainstay of the Detective Squad, Ainsley P.D.

"He had quite a bit to say, as a matter of fact," I replied with my mouth full of pepperoni. "Beginning with 'Keep your big nose out of this, Doc.' "

44

Eddie, as per usual, forged on. He seemed primed with information, as though he'd got the whole thing memorized. "Three women in four months. Mary Ann Godowski, the checker at Red Apple. Good-looking lady, as I recall. Not a beauty, but a certain quality of bone, and an intelligent eye. Mature, certainly. What was her age, would you say, Winnie? Thirty-five, forty?"

I swigged some coffee and scalded my throat. "I don't want to talk about it, Merriman," I croaked, and shoved in more pizza to cool my vocal cords.

"Old Mrs. Ten Eyck. Widowed, lived alone. Rented out a room to Lance Carmichael, didn't she? Could just as well have been Mrs. Megrim, you know, that's what I thought at the time—quirky old thing, on her own for years and years. Artistic, used to come to our sketching club till her asthma began to give her trouble. Still lifes, as I recall, and floral explosions in the Georgia O'Keefe mode." He took a swig of tea. "Then the third. If there are degrees of horror, her death is the most terrible." He glanced at me and went on, stern and inescapable, his blue eyes colder than I've ever seen them and staring straight at me. "Angela Cody," he said. "Only sixteen."

"Fourteen," I muttered.

"Ah, of course." He knew he had me. He relaxed into the nervous dither with which he always attacks a problem. "What's odd is, in such cases one always expects the sexual motive—assault, rape, tampering of some more arcane kind. Like that beastly film we stumbled into in Manhattan, fellows reshaping unclothed young ladies with hedge trimmers. Horror fiction as an art form."

"Except this isn't fiction," I muttered again. The chill began to thaw in Eddie's eyes, but he didn't let me up.

"The graphic horror being missing in all three ladies' deaths, it's next to impossible to recognize any motive, I mean no robbery or anything like that and no overt violence," he rattled on, "almost as though all three of them trusted the murderer, and then dying of poison—"

"Overdose," I said. "Well, more or less. And I won't do it."

"Of course. Overdose. Do what?"

45

"Stick my beak into it. Stir around in the grisly details."

It was a last-ditch resistance. Merriman studied my face, eyes narrowed. As I glanced over at him I suddenly realized he hadn't shaved. There was a definite shadow of gray stubble on his jaw, and it wasn't so much chill that lingered in the blue eyes as the milky film of weariness. The man must not have slept a wink.

"I see," he said quietly, and continued to stir his Oat Crunchies to mush with his spoon. "Have you talked it over with David at all?"

"No, of course not. He's taken this artist-in-residence stint up at the college for a rest from sudden death, and playing Othello for the campus players is as close as I want him to get to murder for a while." Believe it or not, I was playing Desdemona's daddy, and I'd been telling myself this venture into the limelight was all that had my nerves on edge. But Merriman and I both knew better. "It's—it's not the sort of thing I'd be any good at, Eddie," I said. "A nice ordinary murder with a clear motive, okay. But this—it's like a terrorist bomb, there's no predicting it, no preventing it. Besides, Lloyd Agate—"

"Dear Lloyd has told you to keep your hooter out of countless other messes, and you've never paid him the slightest heed before. What was it an overdose *of,* exactly, Winnie?"

"You know that as well as I do, confound you! Overdose of digitalis. Slows the pulse, too much blood gets pumped to the heart muscle, which is also slowed down and doesn't pump it out again. The heart simply explodes, more or less. Heart attack."

"No, I mean specifically, what *form* of the drug? Digitalin, digitoxin— There are a great many ways in which—"

"All right!" I said, staring at the last bit of pizza. "I'm *scared.* Is that what you want me to say?"

"It's a start," he replied, and got up to make himself another cup of tea. "It wasn't given in food," he went on calmly, "or anything of that sort, was it? I mean, the killer couldn't simply be raising a perennial border of handsome foxgloves, mashing them up, and inviting his victims in to tea?"

"All three women had been injected with the stuff. Different spots—upper arm, thigh, stomach. Always in the muscle, not the vein."

"Bespeaks an amateur who had plenty of time. Tricky to find a vein, unless you're trained for it, and absorption takes longer in the muscle." He frowned. "It's almost as if the murderer knew all three, as if they simply sat down and calmly allowed him to stick them with some unknown substance."

"Horseradish, Merriman," I growled. "You don't believe that any more than I do. None of those women consented to be injected to death. The killings may *seem* random, but somewhere there's a principle that connects them to somebody. I have to believe that. Somewhere there's a motive, and we'll find it."

"*We?*"

"All right, blast it! They. The police. Lloyd. It was a slip of the tongue."

"I see. Because you believe the killer may truly *be* choosing his victims at random, and the idea scares the pajama pants off you, you intend to simply sit on your hands and let Sarah and dear Alexandra and Elsa and silly old Mrs. Megrim remain at risk, when we might be able to help—"

"Oh, put a sock in it, Merriman!" I roared. "I can't stand you when you're right!"

He pursed his lips and sat primly dumping sugar into his tea. I scowled at the morning glories on the tablecloth.

"That's six spoons of sugar you've loaded into that cup," I told him. "I hope what's left of your teeth fall out. But you win. I surrender. Got a pencil on you?"

I might've known. Eddie dug in his sweater pocket and produced a stump of Number Two. Then he trotted into his sitting room—he rents the old servants' quarters off our kitchen—and returned with a legal pad.

"Okay," I said, "if we're going to do this, we might as well do it right. According to Lloyd's lab boys, the specific form of the drug

47

was called diginox. It's been on the market almost five years, prescribed for patients with a severe arrhythmia. Supposed to level off the heart rate as well as slow it.''

"Five years? Doesn't narrow the field much, does it?''

"It does not. Anybody with a prescription for the stuff is a candidate, along with doctors, nurses, pharmacists, anybody who handles the drug when it's produced and bottled—there are ways to get substandard pills on the black market, too, the way women used to have to buy contraceptives. Any family member of a patient with a prescription, a servant, a housekeeper—'' I forgot I wasn't wearing my slippers and kicked the table leg in disgust. "Hell! It's hopeless. And to top it off, I think I just broke my toe!'' I frowned and glanced at the clock above the back door. "Don't you think I ought to phone over there, be sure Sarah's made it safely to that confounded harpsichord? Damn thing's nothing but an attractive nuisance! Why couldn't she have stayed at home and practiced on that perfectly good Steinway in there?''

He just blinked and ignored me. "One puzzling thing," he said, "is that all the bodies were discovered out-of-doors. Fairly far apart, of course, but in quite public places. Nowhere that would cast suspicion on a particular house or neighborhood.''

"Which of course they wouldn't, if the murderer's got half a brain.'' I sighed and swallowed the last of my mug of coffee. "That's what bothers *me* about this whole thing, Merriman. The intelligence of the man, the control. As though he's been planning it for years and has it all worked out. The bodies always neatly positioned, left with dignity in some fairly handsome spot. Mrs. Ten Eyck was lying beside the chrysanthemum bed in Vandenberg Park. A hiker found Angela Cody under a pine tree in the Henrik Hudson Preserve by the river. How did they get there? Lloyd and his boys have run every test known to man, and there's no evidence those women were killed someplace else and then moved. They weren't drugged, aside from the fatal dose of digitalis. Not sedated so they could be injected, I mean.''

"The murderer must be mad, but the deed is not?"

"The victims have nothing in common except their sex. Different jobs, different parts of town, different interests, different ages. None of them seem to have had any enemies. No apparent motive, just what looks to me like a fairly intellectual desire to administer death. There's nothing rational about the choice of victims, and yet the death itself is—well, you said it before, confound you. It's gentle. Almost loving. It scares the hell out of me."

Eddie nodded. "I quite agree. As you know, I am never inclined to drop off to sleep in a hurry, but lately even a chapter of *Barchester Towers* fails to induce somnolence." I'd heard him in the wee hours, night after night, tootling away at that blessed old clarinet of his as he always does when insomnia strikes. He'd invented more versions of "Sophisticated Lady" in the past few weeks than Ellington. "The thing is," he said, "if I were to choose suicide, it's the sort of way, the sort of place, I'd do it in." Merriman sat staring at his thin, slightly arthritic hands, the skin mottled with his age, which was now past the midpoint of his seventies. "And if I chose to kill a fellow creature—even an animal—"

"Especially someone you were fond of," I said. "It's not likely the killer knew any of these women personally. As I say, there's no apparent element in common. And yet, there's a kind of empathy in the thing. Reminds me of that line Davy was reading at rehearsal last night. 'I will kill thee, and love thee after.' "

Merriman sat frowning at the sugar bowl. "Winnie?" he said softly.

"Right here, old sport."

"Go to the telephone. Call Elsa, and see that Sarah's safe. Do it right now."

I lumbered over to the phone on the kitchen wall and had my finger on the dial, when something seemed to explode out on the back stoop. There was a hammering on the poor old storm door that would've made Sherlock Holmes swallow his pipe.

"What the blue blazes!" I sputtered. I peered out at a tall, slope-shouldered silhouette under the overhang, and groaned. "Hit the deck, Merriman," I hissed. "It's our only hope. Don't make a sound."

"Now, Winnie," he told me in what I always call his nanny voice—like a spinster in starched knickers explaining to a four-year-old why poached eggs are good for him. "You know perfectly well that if you get down on the floor, I'll only have to let Thomas in anyway, to help me heave you up again."

"Winston," bleated a somewhat breathless tenor on the other side of the door. "I *know* you're in there, and we *have* to talk before the faculty meeting on Friday."

I gnashed my teeth and yanked the door open. "Sheffield," I said, "if you're going to start on me about voting for that new curriculum of the Iron Chancellor's again, don't. Just don't. For the first time in forty years of academic life, I'm actually chairman of a committee that doesn't stuff envelopes, bring cookies to the faculty tea, or sort the student evaluations, and I'm damn well not about to put my name to that piece of claptrap Macauley's suggesting! The curriculum committee will vote without undue influence from any quarter, thank you very much. Except mine."

"Are you going to let me in, or not, Winston? There's a north wind, and I'm cooling too fast."

I'd been standing in the doorway and Sheffield was still on the mat. Clad in a jogging costume of royal blue velour with natty white stripes down the legs, he was hopping up and down on the doorstep like an overdressed Easter bunny who can't get off the dime. He had a fleecy white bath towel pulled over his head like a monk's cowl, and that meant he'd come out without the famous hairpiece for which numberless Taiwanese goats gave their all. He never wears the thing when he's likely to work up a sweat on his jog. The glue melts.

I gave place and he jiggled in, only to begin a series of contortions designed to tune his overstimulated carburetor down a peg for contact with the sedentary classes.

"Do you want something, Thomas," I said, "or did you just stop by to scuff up my linoleum?"

He called a halt and began to tousle what remained of his boyish locks—a graying fringe of a sort of mousy beige, a color favored by his wife, the peerless Diana, known among us as Lady Di. Ever since the arrival of James Macauley, the Iron Chancellor, back in the spring, Tommy Sheffield had had a lean and hungry look. Diana's daddy, you see, has always been our Thomas's insurance policy. As a charter member of the college's board of governors, the old man made and unmade chancellors and chimney sweeps— not to speak of department chairmen like his son-in-law, who might've loved the chilly Lady Di, but whose heart and job security most assuredly belonged to Daddy.

But Daddy, alas, had handed in his dinner pail two summers past, a fairly showy exit made while waterskiing on a fjord somewhere in Norway. And Tommy had lost his leverage.

It was more than that, though. Sheffield knew something I didn't about the Iron Chancellor, and I was determined to pry it out of him before Friday's faculty meeting.

"Are you going to let me see that recruitment file on Old Ironpants, or aren't you?" I said, firing from the hip.

Sheffield had been on the committee that hired Macauley, after the retirement of old Chancellor Whitehead. I knew I could get my mitts on the file with or without Tommy; his secretary, Hannah, would sell her soul for a plate of my famous German chocolate brownies. But it would be a real moral victory for Thomas to give me the inside dope himself. For once in his life, I wanted him to stop flapping in the wind and take a side.

Mine.

"Grow a backbone, Sheffield," I urged him. "It was a mistake hiring the man, and you did what you always do. You nodded and smiled and signed on the dotted line, and now *all* our tails are in the Mixmaster. Do something about it! Confusion to the enemy! What do you know about Macauley that I can use to stop this pincers attack of his?"

He sighed and draped the towel around his neck like Rocky. "Coffee?" he whimpered, eyeing the half-empty pot. I poured him a

5 1

mugful and he sank into the chair next to Merriman. "You're the only one on the faculty it's really safe to talk to, Winston," he told me, dunking one of my chocolate raisin cookies in his cup. "Everybody knows you'll be the first one he throws out anyway. You've got nothing to lose."

"If James Macauley thinks he's going to get rid of me that easily," I growled, "he's got another think coming. I may not have your talent for political fiddling, Thomas, but I've still got tenure— sort of—and I'm no older than Piers Ambrose in the history department. If Macauley gives me the push, he'd better be prepared to give it to Piers, too, and we both know he won't do that, not if he doesn't want a front-page story in the *Times Book Review* the following Sunday."

Piers Ambrose—medievalist, prize-winning historian, amateur magician, and faculty rake of long-standing—had achieved in the past two years a sort of literary fame that I, who had fallen into the bin of mystery novelists thirty-five years ago and never clawed my way out, could only gnash my teeth over. His books were "literature" and his reviews the stuff that dreams are made on. "A new American voice for the Nineties," they burbled, "another Scott Fitzgerald, a second Hemingway."

They ignored, of course, the fact that my friend Piers was neither new nor American. He was three years older than my own three-score and ten; he was born, raised, and had grown to manhood in Montreal, dabbled in the theater with more talent than success, turned to scholarship, and had written eleven fine novels entirely ignored by the press and the world in general before, in his seventy-first year, a book called *The Sorcerer King* finally caught fire. Since then he'd become the local golden boy, trotted out to speak and sign his books at fund-raising lunches and formal dinners for doddering alumni.

I didn't envy him his status as the local literary lion, and to be honest, I didn't even envy him his newfound success. Piers was everything I wasn't—elegant, handsome, coolly cynical—but I'd always liked the man, and he deserved every ounce of his belated fame.

Though everybody'd groaned when Davy cast him as Iago to his Othello in our play, Piers Ambrose was proving the truth of his own magic; even in rehearsals, with no makeup at all, you'd have said Piers was just rounding into an energetic middle age—a man strong with the force of a secret life into which nobody, not James Macauley and certainly not Yours Truly, had ever been invited to pry.

"That's right," said Sheffield thoughtfully. "They really have no hold over Piers, have they? Macauley, I mean, and Shumaker. Piers could tell them where to get off. I mean, they wouldn't dare get rid of *him*. He's not the same as you. He's *important*." He sipped at his coffee. "You know him fairly well, don't you, Winston? If you asked his support at the faculty meeting, if you asked him to protest some of Chancellor Macauley's moves—"

"If Piers Ambrose sees a bit of mischief in the offing, he'll be Johnny-on-the-spot," I said.

"Oh, yes," chimed in Merriman. "Dear old Piers can't abide the smug and the stuffy, and the Iron Chancellor is both of those with bells on. Our friend will be delighted for a chance to put the wind up him. Shouldn't be surprised if he made Macauley's trousers disappear in a puff of smoke or levitated the podium during the opening speech."

"So if he found that someone—someone who'd given a great deal to the good of the college—devoted the best part of his life to education—was about to be—to be—due to the chancellor's new program, was in danger of being—"

I toddled over to the cupboard, snaffled the bottle of fruitcake brandy, and poured a healthy dollop into Sheffield's mug. He smiled up at me wanly and took a swig from the bottle instead.

"Are you trying to tell us Macauley's giving you the chop, Thomas?" I said.

"It's not me," he wheezed. "It's not even *you*. It's Krish. Krishnan Ghandour."

I sat down with a thud.

"Applesauce! The man practically lives in his office, he spends hours in those student conferences of his, he does more preparation in a week than most of us do in a month. He's—well, blast it, he's a damn fine teacher! If Macauley wants to give somebody the ax, why doesn't he take a look at Skip Winthrop, the sci-fi guru? *He* only meets his classes when the moon is right and he's been assigning the same three Bradbury novels in rotation ever since he came here ten years ago. If you need job cuts, you prune out the dead wood first, and Skip Winthrop has more deceased cells between his elfin ears than anybody I know. So why Krish?"

"Because, Winnie," Merriman reminded me. "Skip Winthrop is *Doctor* Skip, and our Krish is still laboring on that endless dissertation of his. He hasn't achieved tenure. And in the hiring and firing wars, very little else matters."

"But comparing a piece of cooked-up drivel about some ninety-five-page science fiction epic and a technical study in a field like linguistics is mixing coconuts with cabbages! Linguistics degrees always take eons, any fool knows that, and Krish's is coming along nicely. I'd rather have a first-rate mind in a plain wrapper any day than a third-rate intelligence with vellum and gold leaf. Besides, Krish has only just asked Hallie Glendon to marry him!" I shouted at the walls. It would do as much good, I knew from experience, as trying to reason with Macauley and his hit man, Stormin' Norman Shumaker. "They're trying to get a loan, shopping for houses, for pity's sake. Even if there were some sort of economic justification for it, there's no human excuse for firing a man just when his life is about to start! Confound Macauley, he's got a piece missing."

"It's the student evaluations, Winston," said Sheffield soberly, his eyes fixed on his blue velour knees. "He claims to take them as gospel. When he was chancellor of Belmont College—"

He hesitated, and I had to egg him on. "What did he do at Belmont? Come on, Sheffield, give."

"I'd—rather not."

"But you will. Diana's daddy can't help you now, Thomas."

"All right," he said, "all right! Macauley has a record of damaging careers when people cross him. Sometimes he uses the student evaluations to do it."

"But Krish has never crossed anybody in his life. I don't get it."

Sheffield shrugged. "I only know that three of the students in Krishnan's linguistics section gave him very negative marks in last spring's evaluations. Macauley feels—"

"No, he doesn't, he doesn't feel a thing. Student evaluations? My hat, everybody knows they're nothing but a sop somebody threw to student power back in the Sixties! Most of these kids are barely literate, and they're certainly not competent to evaluate the skills of a technician like Krish. Linguistics is a bear under any professor. Almost bombed out of it myself back at Iowa State."

"What was the complaint of these three dogs-in-the-manger, Thomas?" inquired Merriman. "Did they have a vested interest in damaging Krish, by any chance?"

"Well," replied Tommy, hitting the brandy bottle again, "as a matter of fact, I asked Hannah to pull their files, and all three were habitual class-cutters. Barely passing marks in most of their other courses. Krish was the only one who actually failed them, instead of giving incompletes. But don't you see? That won't matter to Macauley. It's there, in black and white. 'This teacher's grasp of the English language is weak and his communication skills are poor.' "

"You mean *theirs* are! My sainted aunt, Krish speaks better English than you do, Sheffield. Better than I do! And a damn sight better than that merchandising bilge Macauley spews out like Lavoris. 'Cost-effective.' 'Feasibility study.' I'll give him feasibility!"

"You say Macauley has a record of damaging the careers of people he takes a dislike to." Merriman sat fiddling with his pencil. "Blacklists, do you mean?"

Sheffield looked round as if he thought the place was bugged. "Sixteen years ago at Belmont, there was actually a death."

"A what?"

"A suicide. I don't remember all the details. But apparently a woman in the music department wrote to the board of trustees complaining about a slackening in the grading standards since Macauley's arrival. Nearly a third of the student body with straight A averages. Absolute permissiveness."

5 5

I couldn't help raising an eyebrow as I remembered Sheffield's own speech to us when he arrived to take over the Division of Arts and Letters about that same year, back in the misty Seventies. "It is the responsibility of every teacher to create a positive self-image in his students," he had purred. "The days of punitive, elitist grading are behind us. Even a regular attendance in class deserves grades above the average."

Translation: The mind is out of fashion and the benevolent tyranny of the feel-good fascists is riding high. Academic jobs are scarce, and bad grades, even when richly deserved, will drive away the customers. And we, with doctoral degrees stowed neatly in our back pockets, know damn well which side our bread is buttered on.

But a decade and a half had passed since then. The Sheffield gospel of benign self-interest, deluded by its own professions of nobility, enshrined in the sacred books of educationists and social theorists, had become a nightmare. It had been, I thought, a con game from the first, begun by a bunch of kids with flowers in their hair. Tommy had been one of them—a Yalie version, of course, and never entirely comfortable in anything but tweeds. But innocent of guile. The only person Sheffield had ever entirely deceived was himself.

In the last few years, though, things had changed. Power wore no flowers now. It flexed its muscles, eyeing the main chance. The pros moved in and took us over, and the game turned dirty. Political correctness surfaced on the campus like a twenty-year-old boil just coming to a head. The time was ripe for James Macauley.

"So this woman wrote to the Belmont trustees to complain," I said, "and Macauley trumped up a bad evaluation or two and got her fired?"

"It was worse than that. He dangled her on a string for two years, kept her on a conditional contract. If there was one bad evaluation, he called her into the office and raked her over the coals. The woman taught music theory, Winston. I haven't had it myself, but it's fairly technical, I understand."

"Technical? It's worse than trigonometry," I said. "Just ask

56

Sarah to explain it to you some time, Sheffield. I've seen those textbooks of hers from Juilliard, and they might as well be Sanskrit!''

"So it wasn't hard to find a few students who chafed under the complexity of the material and blamed it on the professor, as with Krish,'' said Eddie.

"And after two years on Macauley's hook, the lady cracked.''

I poured a little brandy of my own. I'd been dangling, of course, on Sheffield's very own hook ever since I reached retirement age, hanging on by the skin of my teeth to whatever bones he saw fit to toss me instead of my beloved Shakespeare classes. But with me it was a matter of stubborn pride, not personal survival. I had my mystery novels, and with or without Sheffield, I'd make a living. We both knew it, and it had become a battle of wits between us.

Well, my wits, anyway.

"She committed suicide,'' said Sheffield. "And now he's after Krishnan.'' He sighed. "You *could* speak to Macauley, Winston, but I don't think he'd listen. He doesn't listen to anyone except Norman Shumaker.'' He shuddered and sweetened his coffee. "But maybe if Piers were to have a word?''

I studied his face—not a thing I've often had occasion to do, since most of the time Tommy's features express nothing but the desire to make as few waves as possible. This morning, though, beneath the bland civility he has cultivated since he got out of diapers, there was a sense of determination and something I might— if I hadn't known him better—have mistaken for character.

"You really do care what happens to Krish, don't you, Thomas?'' I said gently. I was downright proud of him.

"Of course I care,'' he groaned. "It's the thin end of the wedge, Winston, don't you see that? If Krish goes . . .''

I sighed. This was the Tommy I knew and loved.

Eddie had been contemplating the brandy bottle and now he poured the last whisper of the stuff into his third cup of tea. "Of course Macauley doesn't take those evaluations seriously,'' he said. "He's found a lever, that's all, and he intends to rule the world with it. What we need is a lever of our own.''

57

Sheffield sluiced the dregs round the bottom of his cup. "He's bound to win, I suppose. There's something about the man, you know? He's a— He's a—"

"The word you're fumbling for, Thomas, is 'juggernaut,'" I said. "He's rolled in here like the Wehrmacht into Poland and attacked us on half a dozen fronts at once—undermining the curriculum, cutting staff, deflating the grading standards. But have you looked at the list of new administration jobs he's created in the five and a half months since he arrived? All the old boys like Fishy Finsbury in the registrar's office are out, replaced with twenty-three-year-olds who owe their careers to Macauley. He's created new jobs right and left up in that tower of his. 'Director of Planned Giving?' What the hell is that?"

"I believe," explained Merriman, "it's a sort of economic funeral director who goes round the deathbeds of promising alumni making certain the will's in order."

"He's tearing down every old building left on campus," I went on, "every ounce of tradition we had left. Now he's going after Maxima Bergner's place, and that's been a fixture here since Noah's feet got dry. The man's got to be stopped. But we need ammunition. Any more dope on that poor soul he pushed over the edge at Belmont College? Is that where he picked up Stormin' Norman? Where the hell *is* Belmont College, anyway, Thomas?"

"Wisconsin, I think," he said, "or maybe Michigan. It's in the file."

"Speaking of that file, you'll be delivering it to my office this afternoon, won't you?" I made for the telephone. "Meanwhile, just let me give the Sorcerer King a jingle. Old Piers has mingled with Macauley and that bovine wife of his more than the rest of us, maybe he's got something by telepathy. And I'll call Hilda Costello, the Queen of the Jungle Telegraph. If we can muster something juicy before the faculty meeting on Friday, and apply a little gentle blackmail—"

I reached for the dial at the exact moment the thing began to ring. When my feet touched terra firma again, I picked it up.

"For pity's sake," I gasped, "you made me bite my tongue! I mean, Winston Sherman here. What can I do you for?"

"Doc," said a woman's voice, "this is Dottie, the dispatcher at the Cop Shop?"

"Oh, hi, Dot," I said. My pulse was still thundering. "What've you got? Lloyd need that book on bloodstains I borrowed, does he? Because I can——"

"He wants you to meet him," Dottie said. "Another woman's been murdered. Our pal the Heart Specialist." It was something of a police tradition to give pet names to serial killers. "Lloyd got the call about fifteen minutes ago. He thought you'd better be in on it this time."

I was surprised. Agate had been so anxious to keep me out till now. "Where shall I meet him, Dot?" A twinge of fear shot through me. I'd got tangled up with Sheffield and his news and almost forgotten that Sarah had never phoned. My heart was doing calisthenics and my chest felt like lead. "Who's the victim?" I asked her, my breath heavy and short. "Where was she found?"

"Lloyd didn't say who it was," Dot answered. "But the body's out in Mrs. Bergner's orchard. Elsa's place. It was——"

I didn't hear any more. My breath wouldn't come and something heavy and black seemed to be pulled over my head and the light from the kitchen door broke and splintered and the room turned upside down. Something was falling on me and it was the sky, in pieces sharp as shattered glass.

She's dead.

I heard the words in my own voice, echoing at me from the bottom of a cavern as I fell and crashed onto the floor. I must've spoken them aloud as I collapsed, because Merriman was there, and Sheffield, and their faces, too, broke and shattered.

Sarah has been murdered, I could hear myself say. *She's dead.*

II.

The Invisible Lady and the Sorcerer King

Six

When I woke, her head was on my chest and her hand gripped mine.
I could feel her breath, warm and steady. I was grateful for it. I felt
very cold.

"Alive, are you?" I heard myself say. I didn't seem able to talk
clearly, and a sound like the persistent drip of water from a leaky
faucet kept drowning me out. "Or am I dead, too? What the hell's
been going on?"

Sarah raised her head and blinked and rubbed a hand across her
eyes. "Of course I'm not dead, you old ninny," she said, straighten-
ing herself with a squeak of the plastic chair beside what appeared to
be my hospital bed. "And neither are you. But you've had some kind
of attack, and you're in Ainsley Memorial and you've got an oxygen
tube up your big nose, damn you. How dare you, Win! How dare
you almost die without me?"

"Oatmeal and applesauce, kiddo," I muttered. "No question of
pegging out. Just slipped on a banana skin, that's all."

I pulled her close again, for the warmth of her. The hospital bed
was hard and small and mechanical, and I was a part of the machine
—cold as iron, and worked by wires and cogs. So long as I could
touch her, I was myself again.

"Can't somebody fix that faucet?" I grumbled.

"It's not a faucet, honey, it's a heart-lung machine," rasped a marginally female voice from the doorway.

I hadn't realized till then that the place had a door, nor windows either. An ample woman in a whistling white nylon uniform charged through the dim space beyond my bed, establishing the geography like a big white combat plane on a bomb run. She began to fiddle with the machine I was hooked up to.

"Doesn't make any sense at all." She sounded like a cross between George Raft and Marjorie Main. "Nothing abnormal here. Pulse is good, blood pressure perfectly fine. For somebody with as much gut as you're carrying around, that is." She aimed her bombsights at my central slopes. "Respiration seems good, too. Damnedest thing I ever saw!"

"Terrific," I said. "Then you can get this blasted radiator hose out of my nosehole and let me go home!"

"Not without doctor's orders, honey," she said, and dipping a nylon wing, she made for the door.

"Get old Pennington in here, then!" I demanded. "Where the hell is 'doctor?' "

"Aw," she told me over her shoulder. "He's gone for the day. He'll be in on rounds in the morning, bright and early."

"Morning? But it is morning! Isn't it?"

"Hell, it's almost two in the afternoon, kid. Be visiting hours in a minute. You want something, just ask for Hortense."

"*Dr.* Sherman, to you, you presumptuous old bag of—" I broke off. It had just registered. "Two in the afternoon? But it was—"

"They gave you sedatives, Winnie." Merriman came trotting in and perched himself on a chair in front of the picture window. With the light behind him, all I could see was his silhouette, and even that looked tired. "Green ones, I believe. And some sort of injection from a starchy little fellow with the rescue unit. Terribly efficient. Wouldn't let me come with you. 'Fraid I was too feeble, I expect. Took Thomas instead."

"Sheffield, ride in a rescue squad? Did they have to give him oxygen afterwards?" Feeling almost my usual self, I yanked at the ties of my hospital gown, which seemed to consist of two Kleenex with a noose around the neck.

"Tommy was here most of the morning, as a matter of fact," said Sarah. "He's been very kind and helpful and hardly like himself at all."

"Must be sickening for something," I growled.

"And David's outside with Alex," continued Merriman, "and Lloyd Agate's stopped by several times. You were deep in the arms of Morpheus, knitting away like the dickens at the raveled sleeve of care."

"Doped like a racehorse," I growled. "No wonder my head feels like cream of wheat. What happened to me, for pity's sake?"

Eddie shrugged. "You simply dropped the telephone and staggered a bit, and then you fell down. You couldn't seem to get your breath and your heart rate was doing flip-flops, bumping away like mad one minute and barely there the next. Thomas *said* he knew how to give the kiss of life, but he couldn't seem to pucker up when it came to it, so in the end we phoned nine-one-one. And here you are."

"When I spoke to Dr. Pennington"—Sarah pulled the extra blanket over my feet—"he seemed to think it might've been an allergic reaction of some kind. What did you have for breakfast?"

"The same pizza I had for dinner two nights ago, and I didn't fall over in fits then." I squeezed her hand as hard as I could; she didn't wince, just closed her eyes, a slight smile playing round her mouth. We both knew what I was allergic to, and it wasn't cold pepperoni pizza. Sarah wasn't lying anywhere dead, and I had had quite enough of hospitals. "There are more things in heaven and earth than are dreamt of in old Penny's philosophy," I told them. "Get me my pants, Merriman, and let's blow this joint."

"They're intending to keep you overnight for observation. And I wouldn't tangle with that head nurse if I were you, not in your condition."

The voice was soft but you could've heard the words across a stadium. It was David, tall and dark and hollow-eyed, walking around with the Moor of Venice like a shadow at his elbow, as he always did when he was in rehearsals. But the slight young woman who really came in with Davy, her mop of red curls pulled into a sort of exploding ponytail on the top of her head, certainly wasn't Othello; she was the English beauty Davy had married when he was in London with the Royal Shakespeare, the model Alexandra Hemmings as was, now mother of Gemma, friend and cohort of us all after a rocky beginning, and about to make her very own Shakespearean debut as Desdemona in our college play.

She bent to give me a sensible peck on the cheek, flinched slightly when her delicate freckled epidermis encountered the beard I hadn't had a chance to shave that morning, and gave my arm an energetic squeeze instead. "Don't be daft, Winston," she said. "They want to keep you till they're sure you can go straight back to being the same disgraceful old toot as always, and you'd better let them!"

"Naturally they *want* to keep me. Who wouldn't?" I said, yanking at my oxygen tube. "But I have no intention of being helpless in this excuse for a bed when that B-seventeen that calls itself Hortense comes swooping in again." I punched the buzzer on my pillow, then punched it again. "Besides, how can I help Lloyd with these murders if I'm—"

I stopped in my tracks. Until that moment, the reality of Sarah, alive and unharmed, had pushed everything else from my conscious mind, but somewhere at the back of my fogged memory Dot's phone call, Agate's request for help, the latest corpse found in Elsa's orchard, had all been silently waiting their turn.

"Sarah," I said. "The body? The woman they found this morning out at Elsa's—"

"*I* found her," she said quietly. David came to stand behind her, his fingers barely brushing his sister's shoulder, but Sarah's voice was perfectly steady though her eyes were very bright and her face, always pale, was nearly drained of color. "It was Hallie," she told me, letting go of my hand at last. "Harriet Glendon. Oh, Win, it was Krish's Hallie."

By the time I got myself out of the clutches of the fair Hortense, it was nearly three-thirty, the late autumn light already beginning to fail. David and Alex had taken Merriman home, kicking and grumbling and looking seedier than I felt. He seemed to have some personal stake in all this, and it was more than Sarah's right to go for a solitary ride on my bike. I would have to get him in a corner and find out what was up, but for now we had other business.

A cold mist hung over the Hudson as Sarah and I waited at the emergency entrance for Lloyd Agate's promised squad car. My favorite lieutenant hadn't kept Sarah for questioning once he heard about my flashy performance on the kitchen floor, but I'd phoned him from my bed of pain—along with every other citizen I thought might be able to spring me—and he wanted to talk to her now, while her memory of the morning was still clear. He'd be taking her back to Elsa's orchard, and I was determined to be there.

"I don't think you should, Win," Sarah told me as we shivered in the damp. "Lloyd won't keep me long. You go home like the others and get some rest and a decent meal. Not cold pizza!"

"I'm perfectly all right, I tell you. It was—an episode, that's all." I drew a deep breath of the cold, heavy air.

A mortal episode, I thought. *A dark wing laid for an instant across the vision of the still-to-live. A moment of free-fall that restores the balance, clears the sight, bestows that paragon of precious gifts: another chance.*

I exhaled and watched my breath smoke in the cold air. I felt omnipotent, as if I could do anything. *Alive.* The word rubbed itself against me, soft and grateful as a cat's fur. *Alive.*

I stuck my arm in Sarah's and yanked David's loaner stocking cap down over my shaggy locks. "Probably just gas. Can't get rid of me that easily, old kiddo. I'm in it for the count."

"Win, I've been thinking," she said. "About Krish. Nobody's

told him yet. Eddie phoned Blanche Megrim and she said he's in Manhattan at some convention or other, and she didn't know how to reach him.''

"Of course! The Atlantic Linguistics Conference, up at Columbia. Thank the Lord old Blanche didn't know how to phone him. When anybody cashes in, the woman turns into Paul Revere with a touch-tone phone.''

Some women take a peculiar kind of joy in publishing death notices, and Krish's landlady, though suffocatingly kind and well-meaning, was certainly one of them.

"That's just a one-day affair. Dinner to cap it off, then the nine o'clock train up here from Penn Station. We can expect him about ten-thirty, maybe eleven, if the commuter's late as usual. We'll meet him at the depot.''

All this, I thought angrily, when the man was about to lose his job to the Iron Chancellor's cost-effectiveness campaign. I've always held with the Bard that it is not in our stars but in ourselves that we are underlings, but my gentle Pakistani friend did seem ground beneath the heel of a fate he certainly didn't deserve.

"*I* want to tell him,'' Sarah announced, the words clipped off in that New England blue-blood accent of hers that deepens with her emotions. "I saw her lying there. How strange it was, and—and how beautiful—she was—'' She broke off and pursed her lips, fighting back memory. "I'll tell Krish. I must.''

I stood there in the cold, looking at her as though she were a stranger waiting for the same bus as mine, seeing her with the eyes of that second chance I mentioned. After forty years with the same person, married or not, it's easy to turn loving into a habit more comfortable to obey than to break. But Sarah was no habit. The strength of her drew me straight, as it had done from the first, the energy of her filled the parts of me the years of half-success had drained. Piers Ambrose could have his crown of laurels and his critical huzzahs, the magic tricks and the aura of mystery that had given him—even before his literary lionization—his pick of lovers all these

68

years. I didn't envy him, not a whit. Piers Ambrose was alone, and I had Sarah. I stood there in the cold, wanting her fiercely.

"I suppose you know I love you," I said. It came suddenly. I am not given to such declarations, and stood staring at my feet in David's borrowed tennis shoes, a half a size too small. "I suppose you know I'd marry you tomorrow, if you asked me to."

She shot me a look from under long dark lashes. "You see?" she said. "I *knew* you weren't feeling well!"

Lloyd was waiting for us in the orchard as the squad car pulled into the drive; I could see his broad back braced against one of the small, twisted apricot trees, his long, simian arms dangling at his sides. Agate is neither lightning-quick nor razor-sharp, but like the mills of the gods, his wits grind slowly and exceeding fine. Thought, with him, is an almost visceral process that involves his whole huge physiology, a sort of movement of the earth, and while he's on a case he might level the entire contents of the Metropolitan Museum with an accidental nudge and hardly notice. But I've never known him miss a bit of fiber, a stray hair, a footprint in the grass that might lead him to the truth, and he can sniff out a liar from a mile away.

Sarah and I got out of the car near the greenhouse where my bike was still leaning; we took the familiar path through the long grass, now sodden with the rising mist and beginning to freeze underfoot. Lloyd seemed to be alone, the shoulders of his blue nylon jacket beaded with the rain, his head bare under the dripping branches. He did not speak, and at first I failed to see the figure of Elsa Worthing crouched in the grass at the foot of a pear tree, her fingers raking the dead thatch of sodden brown, now and then unconsciously finding and discarding a shriveled, decaying bit of forgotten fruit. She wore an old raincoat of her husband Graham's and a scarf the same deep green as the grove of pines that rose beyond the orchard, her tangle of pale brown hair escaping round her face, clinging to her cheeks in the damp.

There was something of childhood about her, I thought as she looked up and saw Sarah coming toward her on the path. Elsa was that rare article, a woman of absolute innocence.

The kind, I thought ruefully, that does the deepest harm and walks away untouched and utterly unaware. I liked her very much indeed. And so, I could see at a glance, did Lloyd Agate. His eyes never left Elsa as she turned her attention to Sarah and to me.

"Ah," she said, "my dears. Such a tragedy."

She stood up and opened her arms, raising them slightly toward the gray sky, then took a step and embraced Sarah, her face, flushed from the chill and mist, laid tenderly on Sarah's shoulder. They had seen each other that morning only in the few stricken moments after Hallie's body was found. It had been Elsa who phoned the cops, though Sarah's instinct had been to call me first. In the end it was Elsa, too, who called our house, while Sarah broke the news to Madam Max. Then had come the frantic trip to the hospital, the long day of droning machines, sphinxlike nurses, puzzled doctors, and Yours Truly in a delicate condition. Till now, the two women had had no time to confide, to comfort one another.

The great gift, I thought, watching them together, granted to women and denied to all but the rarest of men, this wordless probing after pain, this laying on of hands in silent mutual sustenance. There was a bond between these two that even they scarcely seemed to fathom, one I could not enter and did not wish to. They were, in things that mattered, very much alike. Did I envy Elsa the precious bit of Sarah to which she held the key that locked me out? I did.

But if Sarah had never been born, said a small voice at the back of my head, *you might still have found someone to love you. Elsa.*

I saw her shut her eyes, and her hands, still at her sides, closed into fists, then opened and hung limp again, helpless. She pulled away from her friend and smiled at me uncertainly. "So? How is it, Winston? I heard terrors, hospitals, oxygen masks. But here you are!"

"Here I am," I said simply. At my feet an outline had been

sprayed on the grass with orange fluorescent paint. "This is where you found her, then?" I asked Sarah.

She nodded. "Just under the lowest branch, with her back against the trunk, as though she'd gone to sleep there and—and— simply didn't want to wake up. It was like—like—something from a dream. A fairy tale."

Sarah dropped to her knees, ignoring the cold and the wet, and Agate glanced at me but said nothing. His eyes returned to the face of Elsa Worthing and did not look away.

Fitting herself into the outline sprayed on the grass, Sarah sat down at the root of an old, cleft pear tree, one of the grandsires of Maxima's orchard. She straightened her back against the trunk, feet outstretched, hands laid open in the grass. "Just like that. I actually tripped over her feet and fell."

"Was she wearing anything around her neck?" Agate asked her. "A locket or a chain? Anything like that?"

"Oh, yes! A necklace. It was black, like onyx or black jade, I thought at first. When I looked closer, though, I recognized it. Black coral. It's very expensive now. Endangered, I think. It was highly polished. It gleamed in the sun and caught my eye even before I stumbled over her. I was thinking, you know, about the council meeting tonight, the condemnation. And I was listening to the music."

"Music?" It was the first I'd heard of that.

"Jaffer Swan," she said. "He was playing that clarinet of his, the song he always plays. 'Redwing Blackbird'—it's an old blues from the forties. Remember Win, from that little bar on Third Avenue, the saxophone player they had? I haven't heard it for years, until this morning. Well, I expect Swan's told you, Lieutenant."

"He might have," said Agate, "if we could've found him." He frowned in Elsa's direction. "He seems to have taken off early this morning, right after you saw him out here with his horn. We've got APBs out on him, but so far, nothing. I've got a man on the bus depot and the train station, and cars watching all the roads. He doesn't seem to have left town."

Sarah bit her lower lip, thinking and remembering. "I was here," she said at last, "on all fours. Hallie's feet were right there." She made a hollow with her hands in the grass. "I think I'd been hearing that song all the while, even before I found her, you know? At the back of my mind. Only it didn't register until then."

Agate looked skeptical, and I tried to explain.

"When you hook up with a concert pianist, Lloyd," I told him, "you get used to the music of the spheres. Sarah's spent most of her adult life with music, and there's a kind of constant tape loop that plays along in her subconscious. Sometimes it rises to the surface and drowns out things she doesn't want to hear—supermarket music, the neighbor's dog. Sometimes she hums Rachmaninoff in her sleep."

"I do not! And you've got a tin ear anyway, you wouldn't know Rachmaninoff from Gershwin!" She got to her feet and I began to brush her off. She slapped me away and did it herself. "But don't you *see?* Swan must've been out here for a while before I arrived. He must've seen Hallie sitting here. He couldn't have missed her, and he must've known she was dead. When I saw him, he was right there, beyond that pear tree stump."

She led the way among the trees and we followed, mushing through the wet leaves and the grass.

"He was sort of leaning here," Sarah went on. "He had that backpack he always carries, and his jacket collar was turned up. He was here one minute, and I was on the ground beside Hallie, and I meant to go to him for help, get him to phone the police or fetch you, Elsa, or *something.* But when I'd got up and got my bearings again, he was simply gone. It sounds ridiculous. Where could he have disappeared to, out here in the open? But it's true."

"Geoffrey Swan could *not* have killed that woman, Winston, or anybody!" said Elsa. "I told your policeman so this morning, but he doesn't believe me."

"Mrs. Worthing," said Lloyd, a careful gentleness in his deep voice. When he spoke directly to Elsa, he ceased to look at her and his eyes sought the dark grove in the distance. "It isn't a matter of believing you. Swan was seen in this orchard not far from where the girl's body was found. He may have spotted the killer, he may have some evidence we need, some fact he doesn't even know he has. He *must* know we want to talk to him. As Miss Cromwell just said, he couldn't have been out in this orchard in the light of day—which we know he was—and not seen Hallie Glendon's body. I want to find him. I'm *going* to find him. Now, do you know where he's gone, or don't you?"

"I told you," she replied, kicking at a tree root with a booted foot. "I have no idea where he is. But he did *not* kill that young woman, or any of the other poor things you have found."

"There's probably some perfectly reasonable explanation. Maybe his neighbors have seen him," said Sarah. "Where does he live, Elsa?"

Mrs. Worthing only shrugged. "How do I know? He comes, he pots some plants, he helps Axel with the heavy work. He goes away. Next day he's back. These men, they drift away. One day, I figured, he would move on. A warmer climate, easier work. Another one drifts by and stays awhile."

"But he's been here longer than that, Elsa. Longer than any of the seasonal people who pick the apricots or the benchers who work with the bedding plants in the spring. Swan's been here a year, hasn't he?" Sarah studied the even features of her friend's face, puzzled. "And he's *more* than that. More than just a drifter looking for labor. He's— I don't know. Complicated. Isn't he?"

Again Elsa shrugged, her clear, dark eyes fixed on some invisible tableau in the middle distance, where the mist was thickening into fog. I heard a car pull into the drive beside the greenhouse and cut its engine—one of Lloyd's boys, I thought, still on the hunt for evidence. With the mist and the growing dark, the deep grass that swallowed every footstep, they'd have the devil's own job finding any trace of Jaffer Swan.

"He came June, I think," said Elsa Worthing at last. "A year ago. It was geraniums, then, and cleaning out the herb beds. Yes, a year ago in June."

"And it's November now," I said, "which means you've known

73

the man eighteen months, you've filled out Social Security forms for him, you've paid him regular wages, you've worked with him day after day for a year and a half. And you have no idea whether he has a roof over his head at night or rolls up in a sleeping bag in a park somewhere?" I didn't believe her, and neither did Lloyd.

"He sleeps sometimes in the loft, above the garage," she said. "But there's no heat up there, and it's now cold, winter almost. Where he is now, that's his business." The tiny lines of laughter around her mouth and eyes were pulled smooth with strain. "I told *him* that already." She gave a nod in Lloyd's direction. "I saw you up there, sniffing over everything." The wide eyes narrowed, the head cocked on one side, and Elsa Worthing laughed. It was a strong laugh, as everything about her was strong, an honest laugh that had a cutting edge. "Did you find Jaffer's diary, Mr. Police, in which he records all his murders? Did you find his bottle of poison and his knife and gun? Hah! Ridiculous! The man is kind. To the bottom of his shoes, kind. Even old Madam Max cannot get him angry with her sour tongue. He reads, he thinks, he keeps his mouth shut, he watches and decides and then is loyal to his choice. If that is a killer, you might as well accuse me!"

Lloyd frowned, his foot braced against the tree stump where Sarah had seen Jaffer Swan. Agate turned suddenly upon Elsa. "Where were you last night, Mrs. Worthing?"

"I?" The word was breathless, as though he had just struck her in the chest. She knew he was attracted to her, and she had not expected this. "Where was *I?*"

"We spoke to your stepmother. Mrs. Bergner says she was awake most of the night and that very early this morning the phone rang downstairs. Nobody answered. She says it rang a long time, that you always go down to answer it when there's a late-night call, because it might be one of your sons or your husband. But last night you didn't get up. The phone stopped ringing. Where were you, Mrs. Worthing?"

"My wife was with me last night."

Graham Worthing, burly and ruddy-cheeked, built like a wrestler, his fair hair grayed to the color of bleached wood, had come up the path from the greenhouse. I could just make out the gleam of his expensive car through the trees—the car I'd heard pulling up a moment before. He was expensively dressed, too, a fashionable loosely cut suit, perfectly tailored to his muscular build, not a pull across the shoulders or a centimeter too much cuff at the wrist. A man with power at his fingertips, in absolute control—that was the impression you got at first glance.

Why, then, did I wonder, looking at him, if the suit were borrowed, if he had only rented the fancy car?

A displaced person, I thought. *A refugee.*

"I decided to drive up from Manhattan last night," Graham said, joining us. "I thought Elsa and her mother—stepmother, that is— could use a little moral support at the council meeting tonight. I've asked my lawyer to try and make it if he can. If you want to question my wife any further, I suggest you wait until he's present, Sergeant."

"It's Lieutenant, as a matter of fact," I told him. I dug in my pocket for my favorite Turkish smokes, intending to offer Worthing one, but found nothing, naturally, but a little grit and a broken match. My day hadn't exactly begun with precise planning. "Lieutenant Lloyd Agate, Mr. Graham Worthing."

Lloyd gave Elsa's husband a curt nod and a careful once-over. "Was it you who phoned, then, sir? Early this morning? You weren't here when I questioned your wife and Mrs. Bergner before, and I understood you were still in Manhattan."

"Matter of fact, I heard the phone. So did my wife," replied Graham. "But it was—inconvenient to answer. Just at that moment." He smiled vaguely and put a hand through Elsa's arm, intimating connubial delights. She drew close to him, tacitly concurring.

Agate made a note. "What time did you get here from Manhattan, sir? Close as you can remember."

"Around—eleven forty-five, would you say, my love?" He stood poised, balanced against his wife.

"I guess," she said. Her voice had grown soft, and peculiarly tender.

"Madam Max was in bed," said Graham with a smile. "I keep telling my mother-in-law, if she'd stay up later, she wouldn't wake in the middle of the night and lie there till morning tossing and turning."

"Did you see Swan when you arrived?" asked Lloyd. "Was there a light in those rooms over the garage? Any sign of him at all?"

Worthing shook his head. "Usually isn't, you know. Takes off after dinner—my wife cooks for him as part of his wage—and isn't seen again till around eight, when the greenhouse opens. Work isn't heavy right now—is it, my love?—and he doesn't show up at all some days. Born drifter. Might try some of the joints on the river, Mr. Agate. Sort of places a man like that wanders into. Makes casual friends. Only thing he's up to, really. In and out. You try the bars, you'll find they know him. Probably picks up some change with that horn of his when he can."

"Mrs. Worthing, what time was it during the night that you heard the phone ring and didn't answer it?" Lloyd was staring at Elsa Worthing.

"Round two, I'd say." The question had been put to his wife, but it was Graham who answered. "Yes, two A.M. Don't you think, my love?"

"But—" Sarah looked worried. "Graham, I got here just after eight this morning and your car wasn't here then. I passed the garage and if it had been inside, I'd have noticed. You can't shut the big doors for all the junk in there. Your car wasn't—"

"After eight, you say? Why"—Graham Worthing spoke quickly and a bit too loud—"there you are, you see. I'd gone to the depot, had a package coming in on the early train—at least I thought I did. I'd asked my secretary to send a few things on, so I could work from here for a day or two, till this condemnation business is settled. As it turned out, I phoned her from the car, and she'd forgotten to set her alarm. Can you beat it? My fax machine is down just now, and

Madam Max won't have a computer in the house. So I decided to drive into the city myself and pick up the files. Just now got back, and when I stopped for gas I heard the news from Jimmy, at the Esso station. Terrible thing, that girl. Terrible. My wife had enough on her plate already, all this trouble with the college, the city council. Now this.''

"You won't have to worry about that for a while," said Lloyd. "This is a crime scene, Mr. Worthing. Until these murders have been cleared up and the case has gone to trial, nobody will be coming in here with any bulldozers. The coroner has already told the city attorney, and Mayor Tebbs is going to table the whole condemnation proposal till further notice. There are some unusual things about Miss Glendon's death, some indications on the body that—'' He hesitated, then switched gears. "I want my boys to go over every inch of this ground, and that will take time. We'll be in and out for a day or two, and we'll tape off the immediate area, the tree where Miss Cromwell found the victim. Appreciate your cooperation.''

"So," I murmured, "Macauley loses this round, at least.''

Elsa looked up at Lloyd. "How long?'' she said.

"Like I say," he told her. "After the trial. If there ever is one. If we catch the guy." He scowled at Graham Worthing.

"Surely that's not usual," Elsa said, searching his broad features. "So long a wait? The police finish, they go on their way to the next crime.''

He squirmed a bit, tugging at his jacket with an awkward hand. "It's—an unusual case," he said. "Being outdoors this way. I—um —made a special request.''

Elsa put a hand on his arm. "You like old places, Mr. Police. Old life. A generous thing, your special request.''

Lloyd stared at his feet. "I don't like throwing things away," he said.

Graham Worthing stepped between them. "Thank you, Lieutenant. If you're finished with us now, I'd really like to see Elsa get some rest.''

He took his wife's elbow and turned her toward the house, but they had only taken a few steps when she pulled away and walked quickly back to me. She stood very close, spoke very softly. Her eyes were bright with the cold, and with something I could not put a name to, neither fear nor sorrow for the dead nor love for anything.

"Winston," she said in a near-whisper. "If your policeman finds Jaffer—"

"Elsa!" Worthing was calling her.

"What shall I do?" I asked her. "What about Jaffer?"

"Make him forgive me," she said, and almost ran to where her husband waited.

Lloyd stood looking after them as they walked together, hand in hand, through the mist-scarfed orchard toward the squat old house, its lights already on as the winter evening drew down, the wood smoke from Professor Bergner's tile stove perfuming the heavy air with the smell of burning pine logs.

"I don't understand," I said, half to myself.

"Neither do I." Sarah hugged herself against the cold. "I don't know why, but Elsa's lying. I think she knows exactly where Jaffer Swan is."

"They're both lying," Agate said. "That phone call Mrs. Bergner heard? Worthing had the time down pat, but that was because he made the call himself. I'll check with the guy at the filling station. I don't know where Worthing was this morning, but he wasn't in that house or anywhere out here, not till he walked up behind us a minute ago. I'd bet my pension on it."

"You think they're protecting Swan?"

"Elsa is," said Sarah. "Well, of course she is. If you sleep with a man—"

My mouth fell open. "Elsa Worthing, sleeping with—"

"Win, honestly, don't be such a goop. Of course she is. And Graham knows it. Didn't you hear the way he dived in and gave her an alibi?"

"Well, naturally, he wouldn't want her reputation ruined. He—"

"Oh, phooey! Men! *Her* reputation? It's his own reputation he's worried about, if you ask me. Or doesn't want their boys to know. If Elsa had chosen a more up-market lover, he'd probably have invited the man down for the weekend. But Geoffrey Swan is a loser. At least that's how Graham evidently sees him. And that makes him an embarrassment."

"But if Jaffer really spent the night with Elsa, he's got an alibi. What was the time of death exactly, Lloyd?"

"Sometime between one-thirty and two this morning."

"There it is again," I said. "Two o'clock. Were the others nighttime killings?"

"The Cody kid was, yeah. The Godowski woman was about seven o'clock in the morning, and Mrs. Ten Eyck in the afternoon, around four. No pattern there," said Agate with a sigh and a shrug.

"The cause of Hallie's death," I asked him, "was it—"

He nodded, anticipating me. "Diginox. Digitalis poisoning, just like the others. It's weird, though. Digitalis was the only substance found that could've caused the deaths, but O'Fallon down at the lab says they never find enough to indicate a real overdose, not in any of them."

"What they've taken shouldn't have been enough to kill them, you mean?" Sarah frowned.

"Under ordinary conditions, no. It should've made them sick, that's all. Almost as soon as the needle went in, in fact. But the symptoms shouldn't have been strong enough to keep them from calling for help or going for it, and they shouldn't have killed them. Only there's no sign of anything else that *did* kill them, either." Lloyd kicked at a clump of grass. "How well do you guys know this Swan character? Ever talk to him?"

"He doesn't talk much to anybody," I said. "The few times I've seen him, he's been pleasant enough. Englishman. Odd accent. I can't place the social class, the part of the country, nothing. David could. Or Alex. But we'd have to find the man first."

"All these murders never happened," said Sarah, "until *he* came here."

"That's the oldest logical fallacy in the world, kiddo," I told her. *'Post hoc* doth not a Jack the Ripper make. Anyway, if you're right and he was with Elsa last night, they've both got an alibi."

She snorted. "So why did he run? And don't tell me it was to protect Elsa's reputation!"

"And, for that matter, how did he disappear from this orchard? He'd have had to go right past you to get to the greenhouse, or up to the house to wake Elsa, and you say he didn't." I gave her a quizzical look.

She whacked my arm and I winced. Hortense's hypos had left their calling card. "Of course he didn't walk right past me, you old ninny! I told you, he was there, and then he was suddenly gone."

An idea taking shape in my mind, I began to move through the grass toward where the grove of Austrian pines began, their straight trunks like iron sentinels in the cold.

"He must've gone this way," I called over my shoulder. "These needles are thick enough to muffle the sound of his feet, and it stays dark in among these trees long after it's light everywhere else. He's quick on his feet, and he might've—"

I saw something move between the perfect trunks of the big old trees, and there was a rustling like wind among branches, though the wind had dropped as the cold mist rose.

Lloyd heard it too, and glanced nervously around him. "Creepy place," he said. "Cold as hell in these trees."

But Sarah seemed relieved. "Of course, you're right, Win. He *must've* come this way, and just crossed over the fence the way the students do. It wasn't magic after all."

I blinked and rubbed my eyes. "I wouldn't be too sure, kiddo," I said. "Look there!"

A tall figure in a black greatcoat and a wide-brimmed black velvet hat stepped clear of the trees for an instant, then was gone again, and though I tried to spot him beyond the fence on the open stretch of parking lot beside the administration building, he simply wasn't there.

"I don't see a thing," said Sarah, sounding worried. "Win, I think we'd better get you home, and right now, too! You're seeing things!"

Lloyd studied me with narrowed eyes. "What was it, Doc?"

"The kind of day I've had," I said, "I can't be sure. A little sleight-of-hand, maybe."

And without arguing, I let them fuss and bother and shoo me back to the car and take me home. I didn't mention it again, but I was sure of what I'd seen. The man had been watching us, listening to every word we said.

And if anyone could make a lonely drifter disappear into air, into thin air, it was Iago himself, my friend Piers Ambrose, the Sorcerer King.

Seven

Her husband's arm around her was an unbearable weight. Elsa Bergner—she had never stopped thinking of it so, even after two sons and thirty years of married life—felt herself, as she had for more than a year past, slowly drowning in the hollow center of the man she had married.

She had tried at first to connect Graham to the world she valued, to deepen and strengthen his own virtues—generosity, decisiveness, a grasp of the practical. If to these she had been able to add her own awareness of the dark and silent wolves that prowl through ordinary lives, there might have been some hope.

As it turned out, there was none. She could only go through the usual motions, kindly and skillfully, some part of her own nature permanently walled away.

It had taken no more than a month of marriage to teach Elsa Worthing her husband's limits. She was coupled to a blind man, too afraid of getting lost in a moral jungle of his own to acknowledge that others stumbled there lifelong, building civilizations in the dark and losing them to men like Graham Charles Worthing, who could reap fortunes from their own deliberate impercipience. Graham seemed to know by instinct that the huge complexities he chose not to see might've queered the deal for him, caused him at some crucial moment to hold his hand, splitting moral hairs while the fat profits went astray. He stuck blindly to the bottom line.

When friends in Germany wrote asking for his wife's help in rebuilding the ancient Church of the Three Kings in West Berlin, badly damaged in the war, Elsa was eager to go. It might have healed the endless wound those days had left in her. She wanted terribly to make the trip. But Graham dragged his heels.

"You see, Karl," she explained to him with infinite patience, "it's taken all these years to raise the money, and now almost everyone who remembers how the murals looked, and the paintings on the beams—they're all gone. Papa would've known, and he took me there to church. In my mind, you see, perfect—I must go and help *them* see it that way. You understand?"

"Elsa, Elsa," Graham said, smiling indulgently. "How long do you suppose this noble project would take? Hmmmm?" He didn't bother to lower his evening *Times*.

"Six months. Perhaps eight." What was eight months in the long span of history so cruelly smashed, so tenuous of repair? "It wouldn't cost much, I could stay with Franz and Klara."

At last he lowered the *Times*. "Travel is too dangerous for a woman alone, and I can't possibly spare eight months from the agency. Besides, wouldn't it be hard on you, going back?" Graham lit a cigarette. "Bad memories, I mean? What's the sense in raking all that up again?"

Did he think you left such things behind, like cracked china discarded in an empty house? At night, when Elsa fell asleep, the dark under her eyelids flickered with the dancing light of burning cities, bombed away. The fires ate through empty buildings, their broken windows hollow-eyed, and at each window was her mother's face. Bad memories?

"I saw that church bombed, my dear," she said sharply, wanting to hurt him. "I watched the walls crumble and the rose window smash and fall like colored icicles. Such things you don't forget, not even here. Maybe to build it up again, to see it rise—"

Graham shifted nervously, uncomfortable with history. He raised the paper in front of his face again. "Better send a check instead, my love," he said.

From that day on his wife began to see in him a peculiar threat. He was the new world, rich and assured, and caving at the center. She was the old, wise with sorrow, tolerant and gently corrupt, but too weak with batterings to stand alone. They might have completed one another. But Graham could only give, a bitter and lopsided charity. What she could offer was invisible to him.

The vague fear she felt in his presence reached its climax one evening in high summer as they walked together through the little meadow deep with hay. The new college administration building, which now towered over them, had just been rising then, floor by floor, the summer mornings loud with the curses of workmen, the very ground shaken by grinding monsters that moved earth, swung girders, raised beams. In Madam Max's parlor, the Spode and Wedgewood and the Steuben glass shook in their cupboards, and tiny cracks appeared from nowhere, carrying a silent threat.

Elsa had slept badly for weeks; her youngest son, Jordan, had not come home from Harvard for the summer. He had gone to California with some girl or other, and Paul, too, had defected from her, taken a summer job at the Stock Exchange "to make contacts," as he said. Their eyes were on the future, big with dollar signs and sex and self-importance. She felt they had discarded the old house and the gardens and herself with them. They were becoming the worst of their father, and the future would be the worst of *them*. Had she been right, after all, to dread having sons? Her arm in Graham's, she walked through the hay-sweet July evening lost in regret.

"Elsa, my love," Graham said, after a long silence. She could feel him watching her sidelong, sizing her up like a sales prospect. It meant he had some plan or other she was sure to hate. "I'm a practical guy," he said. "You know that. And you know the agency takes a lot of my time. Advertising clients want more devotion than a goddamn mistress."

He had never had a mistress, thought Elsa. He had spared her the fact of fidelity to any other single woman—she was sure that was how he thought of his silly career as a philanderer. A kindness to his wife to browse among lovers like a customer in some sexual bookshop, reading a word here, a word there, but buying nothing.

Elsa wished fervently that he might take a mistress and she would die, that she might infect him with some long disease, not fatal but weighted with shame. She wished he might be broken, and healed into strength. Then she would be free to leave him.

"What with the train rides back and forth every day," he went on, rubbing the sweat from his forehead with a clean handkerchief, "I lose almost four hours to commuting. It's wearing me down, Elsa."

It was true. His deep voice was heavy with exhaustion. He carried home his portfolios of advertising nonsense from the office and worked far into the night, papers spread thick across Madam Max's walnut dining table. Elsa stroked his bare arm, fond and sorry. Graham was not often without a jacket, but it was a warm night. As always, she wore long sleeves with the cuffs buttoned, though sweat beaded her upper lip and soaked through the shoulders of the cream-colored silk across her back. You could hardly see the scars any longer, but she preferred to keep them covered.

"You are tired," she said sympathetically. "What a good Karl you are, to put up with so much for me. So I can keep my wonderful old house, my trees."

She felt full of love for him then, as she had in their courtship. It was such moments that kept her from leaving him.

"It was best for the boys, dear," he said. "Only practical thing, when they were little. Couldn't find a better place to raise two fine sons. Fresh air. Exercise. No problems with gangs or drugs."

She bit her lip and smiled. When Jordan was twelve, she had caught him smoking pot. At seventeen, crack. Now, at sophisticated Harvard, he was all grown up and on cocaine. The bills he sent were —many of them—forged. She had phoned around to check. His father was paying for the boy's drug habit; Elsa went up to Cambridge to see her son and threatened to get Graham to withdraw the checks that came like clockwork.

Jordan only nuzzled her and laughed. If she took away the money, he might have to steal, he told her. Did she want a thief and a jailbird for a son? Did she think the old man could take it? Did she think Graham would believe her if she told him everything?

Elsa knew the answer. She had learnt it painfully on the night of their first lovemaking, when Graham's clumsy innocence had made her feel old and had moved her to speak at last about herself before it was too late—about the war, her vanished mother. Somehow, foolishly, she had wanted him to love her other self, the child lost to bombs and jackboots. Her head against his barrel chest, his hand lost in the tangle of her hair, she had scarcely begun to speak when she felt him tense and draw away, to sit on the edge of the bed, smoking one cigarette after the other.

"That's all behind you, now, my love," he said at last, brusquely. "Helluva business, but it's nothing like that here. You're somebody else entirely. You're mine, and you'll never have to be afraid again. There'll be no waiting in lines for food here, I promise you."

He had not made love to her again till they were safely married.

"He'll smother you with money," Madam Max had warned, "until you die of thirst."

And money was the last thing Jordan needed; in the end, Elsa had told her husband nothing. Either the boy would learn to live, or not.

After the first night she had slept with Graham, Elsa Bergner had never risked a confidence again, not even to Sarah Cromwell, nor to Jaffer Swan. Her war had never ended. It raged on still, in the solitary confinement of her brain.

Better send them a check, my love.

"I'm taking an apartment in Manhattan, Elsa," Graham had told her that hot July night in the hay meadow. "This place of yours has served its purpose in our lives, don't you think? I want to be close to my work, and a life in the city would do you good. You're too alone here, nothing but the plants and Madam Max. You think too much, and brood.''

"Leave Trauerherz?" The old name she had teased her papa with sprang unwished-for to her lips. She had never used it with Graham before. He had no German, nor any other tongue.

"What?" He squeezed her hand and frowned. He did not like the few foreign words that slipped from her now and then. "What did you say, my love?" he asked her sharply.

Elsa chose her words with care. "It would be wonderful, a few months in the city, Karl. Of course I'd have to find someone to stay here with Madam Max, a housekeeper. And someone to help old Engstrom with the gardens. He could manage the greenhouse on his own, but Axel has no head for figures, and he simply can't keep the cashbox straight. It would be—delicate. For me to leave. But a nice vacation.''

"That wasn't what I had in mind, Elsa," he said. "I was speaking of a permanent residence. I've already put a downpayment on a lovely apartment on the Upper West Side. Cathedral ceilings, marble entry. A huge terrace. Wonderful view.''

So. He had it all arranged, and she was to have, once more, no voice.

The Invisible Lady.

It was one of the magic tricks Piers Ambrose knew. It was what he had called her since the only night he slept with her, before her sons were born, before Graham. Long, long before Jaffer Swan.

Her husband went on describing the wonders of the new apartment, and Elsa said nothing, drawing deep breaths of the hay-scented air. In the day, it was buried in the acrid stink of burnt gasoline from the big earth-moving machines. At night, the world restored itself and gathered strength. She felt anger rising in her with the sweetness; she had already made the only choice he left her, and she hardly heard Graham as he went on.

"Your stepmother would be better off up at Oakview, anyway," he said. This was the swanky retirement villa on the hill above Lake

Tamarack. It had just been built and was allotting rooms. They cost a fortune, the price of honorable death. "There would be others her own age. Probably a number of people there she knows. They'd have something in common. Interests. Memories."

"Most people the age of Madam Max," Elsa said, her voice edged with disgust, "have anymore no memories, Graham. Most have hardly at that age a mind. They have fear. They have pain. Such things, who wants to have in common?"

"Yes," he said. "Max is bright. She's kept her mind. She's very lucky."

"Ah," breathed his wife. "And do you know how fast her lucky mind would go in such a place, this gulag of yours?"

"Oh, Elsa, really," he said, pained and embarrassed. "It's nothing of the kind and you know it, it's—"

She had to soothe him. If she did not, he would feel entrapped and would act on his own, stupidly, and all of them would pay for it.

"Of course, Karl," she told him, her hand again on his arm. "But don't you see, I can't leave her alone here, and she wouldn't want to go? I know she's difficult, but when I came with Papa she was good to me. Like a kind, prickly auntie. How can I push her away?"

They walked again in silence, out of the meadow and into the pine grove, the rare old trees cool and rustling softly in the warm air of evening. Beyond was the mess of construction, the great hole gouged into the ground like a bomb crater. Elsa shuddered and looked away, turning her back on it.

"I'll never get you to myself," said her husband suddenly, "not so long as that goddamn house is standing. Will I?"

She did not answer.

The Invisible Lady.

She.

Elsa could not have said when she began to think of herself in the third person. It was the thing in her that survived, that detached her from pain and let her breathe.

I might have surrendered to Graham's angry cry.

But *she* would not, the Invisible Lady, the voice from the secret hiding place underneath the floor.

"You won't come then?" her husband said, his voice husky in the half-dark.

"No," she said firmly. "Go to New York and live there yourself, if you must. But this is my place. Here I stay. If you want me, come and find me here."

After he left, to come only on the weekends like a less-than-comfortable visitor to the old house, Madam Max reveled in their freedom, strolling bare-breasted through the living room, the queen of the Amazons. As for Elsa, she humored the old woman, brewed herbal teas for Axel Engstrom's arthritis, held a few small classes in flower arranging for the local ladies. Mostly, with deep and hypnotic relief, she dug in the rich river dirt planting henbane, lady's-mantle, burnet, heal-all.

But it was make-believe, an idyll from a Greek myth. The Invisible Lady remained in hiding.

Only for Jaffer Swan had she come out.

"Elsa!"

Graham's voice jarred her out of her reverie, and the weight of his arm around her waist grew painful. Behind them Winston, Sarah, the tall, clumsy policeman, were eyes in the shadows, watching as husband and wife walked through the orchard to the house, their breath steaming in the damp November cold.

"You'll have to speak to my lawyer." His voice hissed in her ear. He took her by the arms and turned her to face him and his fingers dug deep into the soft flesh of her forearm. "Do you hear me, for God's sake? I *saw* you."

"What?" She could think only of the pain in her arm where his fingers clamped her. Why was he hurting her?

"Where was Swan?" he said. "Was he upstairs? Are you sure you didn't wake him when you came down to the orchard?"

Elsa pulled away, tired of his persistence. "You don't make sense, Karl," she said.

"Don't call me that!" His voice was a hoarse cry, stifled by his awareness of that old busybody Sherman and his tame policeman. "Don't you understand? I phoned you at two! It was my call Max heard. When you didn't answer, I came out. I was here, at the edge of the orchard. I *saw* you." His hands, still reaching for her, dropped suddenly, limp at his sides. "Oh, my love," he whispered. "I didn't see her, but I saw you come out of the workshop. I *saw* you after you had killed that girl."

Elsa shook her head dazedly and the deep green scarf slipped from her tangled mass of brown-gold curls. Then suddenly she took Graham's hand and kissed it. "I think tonight the bronze chrysanthemums will freeze at last," she said, and slipped past him into Sorrowheart.

Eight

La Maison de Dieu.

It was a bitter card, and it had turned up three times straight on Piers Ambrose's office desk since he returned from his expedition to the orchard on that darkening late afternoon. He sat and glared at it, his heavy brows gathered in a stormy frown. He considered laying out the tarot one last time. Better not, though. It would be tempting the forces.

Piers believed in many forces stronger than himself, the great invisible threads, some dark, some light, that wove the world and tangled up to form the human skein. He had an odd humility in the face of such truths, an abnegation hidden underneath the coat of arrogance that kept him clean. He of all people ought to perfect humility, having been disregarded for the best part of his life.

But not, he thought, defeated. He stared down at the tarot card on his desk. Never defeated. No.

La Maison de Dieu. What did it mean, that lightning-struck tower on the card? Defeat was the usual interpretation. Calamity, deception unmasked, the unexpected, sudden ruin. They were all superficial answers. The tarot was a tool for disciplining the thoughts and feelings that churned and surged round the great mysteries of death, despair, struggle, and defeat. No unseen supernatural finger steered the hand that laid out the cards. It was all in the reading. Piers studied the picture, letting his mind play over the images.

The house of God struck by the hand of God. A stronghold with carved lintels, colored windows, old and tough and made of the mountains that were the earth itself. Stones raining from the walls as the great storm struck from a blue sky. A cataclysm, certainly. The fall of overweening pride. The crash of a weak and house-proud race from a single, unexpected blow, a force of nature?

There were two figures in the picture, both male. One lay at the foot of the tower, smashed by the crumbling walls. The other was frozen in perpetual fall, caught headfirst midway between the broken turret and the earth. He could neither fall and die, nor rise and live.

Something was familiar about the figures and Piers shuffled through the cards. He had bought them from an old magic collector in Paris, on the Rue Silène, an eighteenth-century tarot deck, hand-painted, said to have belonged to the great German magus Katterfelto. The paintings of the Major Arcana were pale and exquisite, the faces of the figures glowing with a secret life, their eyes large and luminous. He laid them out one by one, the most powerful cards of all.

Le Mat. The Fool. He'd be tempted to stick that one onto Winnie Sherman, but you didn't joke with such things, not if you were Piers. The Fool was thoughtlessness, undiscipline, and sometimes panic fear, and none of those was Winston. His card, thought Piers with a catch in his breath, was *La Justice.* Justice, with scales and naked sword.

He had always been fond of Sherman, a man like himself of hidden talents, a man of masks and dodges he had worn and used so long he hardly knew them as disguise. A man who cared, as he did, for the balance and the truth of things. Winston knew these killings had to end, and he was stubborn as that implacable figure of Justice on the card. He had been out there in the orchard, nosing around where Hallie was found, talking to that policeman pal of his. Now that he'd begun, Winston would go tromping right through the business to the end, just as he always did. He saw things through. Another thing they had in common. Piers, too, would ride the mad trick to the end.

If only, he thought, Winnie did not stumble into his path before it was over. Once the next step was taken, there would be no stopping, no holding his hand, not now. It had gone too far.

Those four women.

Piers felt his heart jump, the uneven rhythm that warned him the pain was coming. He leaned back in the creaky office chair, braced for it. It began as a slow ache that struck his left shoulder first, then crept downward in great swelling waves along his arm until it reached his fingers. He pushed himself—he knew that—though his doctor issued glum prognostications. The business was nothing new to him; his heartbeat had been irregular at birth. To beat down death for over seventy years—it took a kind of madness, an overwhelming will that threw off every unnecessary fragment of connection. It was how he had let *her* slip away. Love had once, for one episode, invaded his desire, but even then his will had battled through and won. He almost learned to care for nothing.

But not quite. It was the one trick he had never managed to work.

Even now, at his age, he sometimes ached with it. He could feel it on the stage, with that exquisite wife of David Cromwell's. Love, the memory of love, staggered his heartbeat, brought the great, white pain in his shoulder and down his arm. The long damage of self-imposed loneliness throbbed through his fingers when he touched her, and he could see she was afraid.

Truth was, it was Piers himself who was afraid. He was, he knew, a man who had loved women far too well.

He had been married at nineteen to a woman of forty. Carlotta, that had been her name. Innocent fool that he was, she'd actually convinced him he had to marry her after one night of highly instructional fumbling. The Ambroses were a power in the lumber town of Deux Rivières, Quebec, pillars of the Anglican church, bankers, lawyers. There were a dozen stuffy uncles and a dozen frigid aunts to whom the florid, dowdy Carlotta was almost as much of a scandal as the one she could've made if he hadn't taken her down to Montreal and married her before a judge.

It was she who had taught him the tarot, though she used it cheaply and understood none of its truth. Piers did. He had an instinct for its magic from the first. One by one, he had played all the roles the cards offered, beginning with the first, the one in which Carlotta herself had cast him. For her he was *Le Mat,* the Fool.

After a week of marriage, he wished he could stop her gabbling mouth. After a month, he wished she would disappear. After three months, she obliged him. When the Goodbody Medicine Show and Travelling Circus pulled up its tents and left Deux Rivières, Carlotta went along. Piers found a note on his pillow in the bed still reeking of the honeysuckle toilet water she all but bathed in.

"It ain't your fault," said the note. Her handwriting was barely legible. *"You'll always be my Sugarplum. Only, hell, you know—I gotta get some air."*

Sitting on the honeysuckle bed, Piers began to laugh, slipped down onto the floor and lay there crowing like a madman, tears of delight rolling down his cheeks, his long legs kicking, and when the mirth—which was not hysterical relief but the first true moment of joy he had ever known—subsided, he sat up, clear-eyed and whole.

It was the first trick, and Carlotta was the greatest magician he would ever know. She had set him free.

Her Sugarplum had found it easy, afterward, to avoid entanglements, for he was married, wasn't he? He was susceptible and tender, kind, subtle, with a complicated center that drew women like a magnet. When he made love to them—and he did so even now, an old man's futureless love with the urgent edge of desperation—they seemed to understand instinctively that they merely formed one thread in the pattern of his complex life. He did not claim them, could not. He made that clear. And when one of them complained or argued—well, there was always Carlotta.

Surely she had been dead ten years or more by now. He tried to summon her face, to see it dead. He could not. The face he saw was the only one he had ever truly loved. A girl's face, very young, wide dark eyes watching as his magician's fingers stroked her, roused her carefully, quickening the dormant fire he sensed within her calm. He had been forty-something then. Almost the same age as Carlotta when she had seduced him. And the girl was barely of age, her twenty-first birthday just celebrated. He had lain with her—the biblical phrase was apt—in the long grass beside her father's herb garden, the sweet mingling of scents rising to them in the spring night. He had picked the leaves of lavender and crushed them in his palms and rubbed the oil against her pale skin, across the fading scars of wartime damage. They had been in sight of the house, of the old man's study window. There was a light inside, for Alois Bergner read far into the night. Eventually Piers had taken Elsa's hand and led her into the orchard where the pear trees were in bloom, and it was there, like some couple out of one of Carlotta's shabby novels, that they had crashed together finally, like two planets met by accident from orbits they had lost. The lithe passion of her had swallowed him whole and afterward he lay exhausted and old beside her, his ungovernable heart beating wildly, like death inside him. He dreamed the weight of her upon him even now.

Elsa.

She had been his second magician. She had taught him power and self-knowledge, from her stronger self. Only when he dared to write about her had his novels found truth and brought him fame.

She was the third card of the tarot deck. *Junon,* the Priestess. Wisdom, serenity, silence, mystery.

What a mystery she'd proven on that night, he thought ruefully. Perhaps it was just that after Carlotta and the others, in his middle age, he had craved newness. Elsa was a girl, she'd been protected closely since the war, Madam Max watching over her like a dragon and her father passing inspection on all her suitors in the classic German way. Until that night, when the light burned in the study window and Piers Ambrose led the girl into the pear trees. Could

9 5

the old man have orchestrated it, or Madam Max? Had he been meant to marry Elsa and make her a professor's suffocated wife? Oh, surely not.

The real mystery had been Elsa herself. Elsa, who was not innocent. If he'd anticipated terrified virginity, he had not found it. She was bold and direct with his body and her own. Almost deliberate, leading him and timing herself to find his rhythm. Her satisfaction, when it came, was deep, as though he had healed something in her, temporarily, at least. They lay until almost daylight, he watching as she dressed. She was complete without him. There had been no question of another chance. In all the years since then, she had never spoken of that night, nor even brushed against him as she passed the sherry at Madam Max's Sunday soirees. She seemed to have forgotten him completely.

He wondered if she'd read the books he made of her. He doubted it. Perhaps she was afraid he understood too much.

Piers Ambrose took a deep gasp of the stale office air as the pain in his arm and shoulder began to recede. He was old, old. In the Middle Ages he loved so well he would've been, with luck, a king's tame wizard, a Merlin on the wrist. Without the luck, an ancient mountebank, a juggler, dancer with bears, brewer of potions. He knew the herbs, of course, as most magicians did. Healing was woven in the mightiest of tricks, along with death. It fell to chance which would be used.

He sighed, relaxing from the pain. Old, old as Merlin tempted into endless sleep by a woman. As she tempted him. There was no escape from it, from her.

Four women. Their faces, pale among the trees. He closed his eyes to study them, but Elsa's features overwhelmed them all. He had seen Macauley watching her often through the orchard branches as she went about her work. Watching from the safe darkness of the pine grove, wolflike in the wind. Watching from his office window, high in the tower. Aiming his glasses, his infernal camera, at her strong, sweet body. . . .

Four women. Four. Falling. Falling from the Tower of God.

Piers opened his eyes again and turned another card.

Le Bateleur. The Magician. That, of course, was Ambrose himself, and—

Suddenly it dawned on him. The smashed figure at the foot of the stricken tower on *La Maison de Dieu* was painted exactly to match *Le Bateleur.* It was the magus who lay dead.

Piers Ambrose scattered the cards with a sudden spasm of his long, broad hands. But one stubborn card still lay faceup in front of him. He had the answer in a flash. He knew what he must do. The figure caught there in perpetual fall was exactly the same as that of *Le Pendu,* the Hanged Man.

It meant decisive action, that terrible figure, and he had seen it too often now to deceive himself. He would have to make the choice, there was no escaping it.

Piers could light fires from his fingertips, make flowers grow from lumps of coal, turn aside knives, and make bullets into silver coins. Death was an illusion he could manage, he was sure of that. As Iago had managed, tormented trickster that he was.

Piers Ambrose opened the drawer of his desk and took out the almost empty vial of diginox, laid the syringe beside it, and began to prepare himself.

How soon it would be, how much time was left, he did not know. He only knew it was not over yet. The four were not enough.

Someone else would have to die.

Nine

" 'Look where he comes.' "

Piers Ambrose paused as David made his entrance, a slender, blue-jeaned Othello sans makeup, striding preoccupied into the dim rehearsal lights on the littered stage of Gould Theatre. My own role, Brabantio, wasn't due for rehearsal till next Monday, and Sarah had been pretty emphatic about my getting some rest before we went to meet Krish's train from Manhattan, which would arrive at the Ainsley depot at ten-forty that night, more or less.

But I felt entirely myself again, and it was only Wednesday night. I would have no real rest till I confronted the Sorcerer King—or in his present guise, the honest Iago of Shakespeare's tragedy.

> Not poppy, nor mandragora,
> Nor all the drowsy syrups of the world
> Shall ever medicine thee to that sweet sleep
> Which thou owedst yesterday.

Piers Ambrose was a tender torturer. His Iago was a tough old captain, battered by long wars. Younger, slicker men who thought a battle was a game of wits had risen like skyrockets in a burst of false light, his corporals become his generals. Now he saw those years of loyal effort thrown away by credulous officials with more power than judgment. His wife had proved a fool, unworthy of him, and he did not trust her. No man had ever been more alone, and isolation made him as vulnerable as his victims. As he destroyed them, he destroyed himself, and knew it, watched it like the progress of a slow disease. Although his words were brutal, his deep voice was full of pain.

This Iago, I thought as I watched him, took life the way the Heart Specialist did, as deftly as a conjuror. Or a Sorcerer King.

I shuddered and shoved the ugly thought away.

Piers was a tall man, six feet three at least, and broad-shouldered, though his waist was well-defined, his hips narrow. He stood very straight, his long arms folded in front of him, shaman-fashion, his wiry thatch of unruly snow-white hair drawing the eye straight to him in the half-darkness of rehearsal lights. Despite his age, his broad face was almost free of lines, the skin clear and pale; in his youth, when I first met him, Piers Ambrose might have been David's elder brother, with the same black hair and deep-set dark blue eyes.

No schizophrenic slasher, though, had come for Piers, no plastic surgeon built back half his ruined face from photographs. About that damaged side of David's countenance there still remained a trace of disconnection. He had never entirely reconciled the two severed halves of himself, but he had learnt to balance on the scars, and dance.

" 'Othello's occupation's gone!' " Bless David, he didn't shout the famous line. He almost breathed it, straight into Iago's face.

Piers Ambrose stared, the deep eyes hooded and cool beneath startling still-black brows that slanted sharply upward from the nose. His lips were parted slightly and his breath was short. The tormentor was suffering his own tortures.

" 'Is't possible, my lord?' " he said softly, a hand on David's arm.

Suddenly Othello stood nose to nose with his torturer, his lips almost brushing Iago's. Davy grasped the lapels of Piers's black suede jacket and as he sank he pulled the older man down with him, his next speech passing like breath from his body into Iago's.

> Villain, be sure thou prove my love a whore!
> Be sure of it; give me the ocular proof;
> Or, by the worth of mine eternal soul,
> Thou hadst been better have been born a dog
> Than answer my waked wrath.

" 'My noble lord—' " breathed Piers, and took his victim in his great arms. In an instant, they had changed ages. David—Othello— was old, old as delusion, and Piers, though thirty years his senior, had the eternal youth of clear-eyed evil.

"God, what a pair," whispered Sarah. "Is there anything old Piers *can't* do? I had absolutely no idea what an actor he is! I actually tried to talk David out of casting him, told him Piers was too long in the tooth for such an active part."

"Makes you wonder, doesn't it?"

Merriman had insisted on coming along to rehearsal just as Sarah had, and here they were, stationed on either side of me in the dim auditorium. That way, if I decided to keel over again, there'd be one of them for me to land on whichever direction I toppled. Eddie looked and sounded tired, but excitement was carrying him along as it always does when we begin poking into trouble.

"An enigmatic fellow, our Piers, bless him," he murmured. "His various talents seem to have no limits. 'A sound magician is a mighty god,' and whatnot. Doth Faustus walk among us? Makes one wonder. My yes."

"It makes *me* wonder what the hell he's been doing *here* all these years, with a talent like that." I scrunched down in my seat. My own scenes with the old magus were brief, but I—who'd always prided myself on my grasp of Shakespeare and had often read lines with David over the years—felt totally eclipsed by Piers. The man had secret resources, daunting ones. And Merriman was right. I certainly did wonder.

" 'Now art thou my lieutenant,' " whispered David, still kneeling in Iago's strong embrace.

The wide gold band on Piers's finger gleamed in the artificial dusk as his long, heavy hands—an old man's hands, in spite of the illusion of youth—lifted slowly from Othello's shoulders and slipped along his throat, then wandered upward to caress the lean, shadowed cheeks and draw the ravaged face close, close, until at last his lips were upon David's. The kiss was long and deep, and at my side I felt Sarah tense. A few rows down from us, David's wife Alex, waiting her turn on stage, put down her magazine and leaned forward, her small hands braced on the seat-back ahead of her.

At last Piers drew away. The long kiss ended, but the final line was laden with lingering tenderness.

" 'I am your own forever.' "

There was a moment of stunned silence. It had been a master stroke.

"Well," said Merriman. "My word."

"Phooey," muttered Sarah. "That man is not gay in any sense of the word. I don't believe it for a minute. Not Piers."

"Maybe not," I said. "But certainly Iago. This one, anyway."

David rocked back onto his heels and I saw him take in breath. He, the director as well as the leading actor, had been as stunned by Piers's interpretation as everybody else.

"Act Two, Scene One, please," he shouted. "Montano, Cassio, Desdemona!"

He jumped lightly off the stage and into the orchestra pit, and I saw him hesitate for a minute down there in the dark, pulling himself together. Piers walked calmly off the stage to wait for his entrance in the new scene. Before David joined us, he paused briefly beside Alex, a hand on her red hair, as she and the others who'd been scattered round the auditorium waiting their turn lugged themselves up on stage. My colleague, Hilda Costello, doyenne of film studies, who was playing Iago's wife Emilia, shot me a look across the empty seats. This episode was sure to go down in her little black book of gossip classics.

"That was—interesting," Davy said with a soft laugh, as he draped his long legs over two of the seats in the row just ahead of us. "Had no idea our Piers fancied me."

"Maybe he doesn't," I said. "Maybe he's just a damn fine actor."

He gave me a look and grinned. "Maybe."

"But you think it's more than that?" This from Sarah, who looked mildly worried. Since the slashing, she's nervous of anybody who pays too much attention to her kid brother, even on the stage.

"Piers is—" He paused, as Hugh Jonas, who was playing Montano, and the two drama majors playing the Gentlemen loitered on the stage. "Okay," shouted David, "I'll cue the entrance."

He didn't even glance at the script rolled up in his sweater pocket. As an actor, he might've settled for the scenes he appeared in; as a director, he had the whole play by heart. It ran through his mind constantly, like that Scarlatti of his sister's.

" 'Hell and night,' " he roared, deadpan, " 'Must bring this monstrous birth to the world's light.' "

Montano and his companions made their entrance, and David turned back to us.

"Piers is an incredible instrument," he said in an undertone. "He has everything, you see. Most actors—me, for one—have the voice. Some even have the brains. A few have the nerve. But almost none of us has the words, too. Piers does. Oh, any decent actor can *speak* a line. But with him— It's as though he's writing it as he goes along. It's—new. You see? So these interpretations, stunning little touches like that kiss— They come from a part of him that isn't standard equipment. It's rare as dragon's teeth, that kind of insight. A writer or an actor who can feel and think in all genders, all ages, all races— Look," he said.

Iago was on stage again, flirting with Desdemona under his wife's very nose. Next to him, Alex was tiny and fragile—already at

102

his mercy as he took her hand and kissed it. I thought of Hallie
Glendon, and my ticker skipped a beat.

"Just be careful, kiddo," I said suddenly. "And keep an eye on
her."

O heavy ignorance; thou praisest the worst best. But
what praise couldst thou bestow on a deserving woman
indeed, one that in the authority of her merit, did justly
put on the vouch of very malice itself?

Alexandra, slight and pale under the heavy Aran sweater that
reached almost to the knees of her faded jeans, her wavy red hair
turned loose and framing the narrow oval of her face like gold fili-
gree, looked up at her Iago and smiled. In the dim light, the chill of
the empty theater, she seemed to carry warmth and brightness with
her. I had not expected her to be much good, a model trying to turn
actress and compete with her better-trained husband. But she had
surprised me. I thought, watching her, that at certain moments she
surprised herself.

Piers delivered his next speech walking round and round the
slender, bright figure, like a spider throwing invisible webs that caged
her.

She that was ever fair, and never proud,
Had tongue at will, and yet was never loud;
Never lacked gold, and yet went never gay,
She that could think, and ne'er disclose her mind,
See suitors following, and not look behind;
She was a wight, if ever such wight were—

He bent to speak into her ear, and with the last words his head
lay on her shoulder, one great hand below her breast.

" 'To do what?' " Alex whispered, and a nervous laugh, like a gasp, came from her without intention. Emilia—Hilda Costello—gulped and stared, and the kid who was playing Cassio looked at his shoes.

Piers straightened up suddenly and patted her on the bottom, the bold and impertinent soldier. " 'To suckle fools,' " he cried, " 'and chronicle small beer.' "

"Okay," called David suddenly. "Break, everybody! Back in fifteen." He got up and turned to me and there was anger in his face. "Eye on her? I'll buy a pair of bloody handcuffs." He loped at a half-run down the aisle toward his wife.

"Abracadabra, blast you!" I said, poking my head into the farthest cubicle of the men's dressing room backstage.

" 'Thou wretched, rash, intruding fool, farewell!' " cried Piers Ambrose.

"Wrong play," I said, lowering myself with a grunt onto a rickety old classroom chair. "Or had you planned to stab me behind the arras?"

"There isn't one," he replied, the deep voice muffled. "Macauley wouldn't foot the bill for a goddamn arras, even if he knew what one was. Aha! I come Greymalkin!" Piers had been fishing in a box in the corner ever since I entered, and now he emerged with a bottle and two slightly cloudy plastic glasses. "Haig and Haig?" he said, the Mephisto eyebrows raised.

"You're asking *me*? Just keep in mind who taught you to drink the stuff, and make it three fingers. Here, use my fingers, they're bigger than yours. It's been a tough day, even without you mixing metaphors. Greymalkin, indeed."

"I never mix metaphors or cocktails. Just plays."

He poured the booze and hopped up onto a bunged-in desk piled high with props from the last production our head of the drama department, Rex "Used-Car Harry" Osborne, had attempted before he went off on sabbatical. Used-car Harry is the character old Rex inflicts on the televiewing public every night during the ten

104

o'clock news, and his idea of a sabbatical was six months doing dinner theater on a cruise ship. If he'd been directing the Christmas Revels, this year's all-college production would've been *Auntie Mame,* and Hilda Costello might've come into her own, the quintessential aunt, a cross between Wallace Beery and Edgar Buchanan, with a dash of Margaret Hamilton thrown in. But the acting talents of Piers Ambrose would have remained in hiding, as they had done for all these years.

"Quite a performance," I said, sipping at the scotch. I'd stocked up on Turkish Delights, and offered him one. He took it, and produced a light from the tip of one index finger. "Was that supposed to dazzle me?" I asked him as he lit my smoke.

"Hell, Winnie," he said, folding himself into a modified lotus position, cross-legged on the desk top. "That old trick? I only pull it now and then to keep from getting rusty."

"I didn't mean the flaming pinky, kiddo. I meant the kiss. You're no more gay than I am, Ambrose."

He grinned, that wicked grin of his I can't resist. Each year at the campus Christmas Revels, when he favors us with sleight-of-hand and one special trick, one real classic illusion, Piers's broad, handsome kisser lights up brighter than the Christmas tree with that same delighted smile of self-congratulation at the moment when the grand illusion clicks.

"You don't say, Henrietta?" He inhaled the sweet smoke deeply, then breathed it out. "A man writing as a woman writing with the voice of a man? I've always had my doubts about that pen name of yours, you know. And your sleuth—is that what you call them, sleuths? Silly word. G. Winchester Hyde and that pal of his Sam Newlin—an odd couple if ever I saw them. We all have our dualities, Winnie. I chose to pull one of my own to the surface, that's all."

"And which one of your incarnations was it I saw in Elsa Worthing's orchard this afternoon?" I said. I polished off the Scotch and he refilled it. "Or was that just your astral body?"

He laughed. "No. Only my too, too solid flesh. I thought you'd seen me, but I didn't think it was the time. Saw your pal, the local Dogberry."

"His name's Agate," I said. "Did you hear everything he said all right, or would you like me to tape our next get-together?"

"She was a student of mine," he said, suddenly serious, the shoulders slumped. The lineless face seemed to collapse, and he was himself, a tired old man confronting unfathomable darkness. "Hallie was— She was one of my history majors, Winnie. She was very much alone here, until recently. She and your friend, young Ghandour—well, their paths didn't happen to cross till a few months ago, and Hallie thought of me . . . Her mother died before she could walk or talk, father was a scholar. Renaissance art history, I think. Irresponsible bastard, apparently—you know the kind. Sexual ethics of a badly bred stoat."

"Love them and leave them?" Piers's own reputation as a sexual adventurer was formidable, but I'd never heard a woman who had known him speak less than fondly of him. Perhaps, I thought, he did not leave them so much as set them free to leave him when they chose. It was the "loving" part I wasn't sure about. Oh, I could imagine him a gentle, tender, certainly a skillful lovemaker, his magician's deftness giving him timing and delicacy.

But loving? That was something from another sphere, one of patience and endurance, and a kind of breaching of the space between one life and another I wasn't certain Piers could manage, not in the long haul. He observed, he manipulated, he worked his tricks with empathy and a kind of subtle wisdom. His novels were the same. He could enter the minds of characters, slipping in and out at will. But only so long as he never committed himself totally to a single one.

Much as I liked him, Piers Ambrose was congenitally incapable of love. He had been drawn to Hallie Glendon's loneness, isolated as he was himself. "And Hallie thought of me . . ." he had said, leaving the sentence incomplete. It had implied that he'd been a father substitute, standing in for the Badly Bred Stoat. His age, her youth—

106

it was the conventional assumption. But nothing about Piers was conventional, and no relationship—including that with Hallie Glendon—was precisely what it seemed.

Whatever he'd felt for her, I wouldn't have said it could be love. Or was it only that it wasn't *my* sort of love? I sighed and ground my teeth as Piers went on.

"She graduated two years ago," he said, "but she stayed up here in Ainsley, wanted me to help her through her master's. She's been working at Columbia, under Raymond Parsloe. Twelfth-century economic development, Henry the Second. She might've been a brilliant scholar. Bleeding Jesus, Winnie. To take a life—"

I studied him. "I've watched you saw a girl in half, Piers. I've watched you shove swords through a man trapped inside a locked box. You swallow fire. You juggle with death every day."

"Magic isn't about death, you fool!" he cried. "It's about life! You saw the girl in two, and she survives! Life indestructible, beyond all illusions. Read Houdini, study Robert-Houdin!" He unfolded himself and slipped off the messy desk, to begin pacing the dressing room. "The others were bad enough. Mary Ann Godowski rented the basement flat in that duplex I own on Pine Street. I knew the old woman, of course, Mrs. Ten Eyck. Roomed with her years ago. And that child, Angela Cody? The daughter of Marian Cody, who types my manuscripts. Now Hallie. It's too close to me. Too damn close, Winnie. He's building an illusion, and I seem to be smack in the middle of it!"

"How did you find out about Hallie? It hadn't been on the radio or in the papers yet." Lloyd was very careful, as always, to keep things quiet.

"I was up in the chancellor's office, waiting to give Macauley a piece of my mind," said Piers, "and his secretary—the one with the remarkable bottom? As usual she was gaping out the window instead of dealing with the word processor, and she saw the squad cars down by Elsa's greenhouse. Well, I'm a sort of honorary member of the family, you know, and I thought old Madam Max had shuffled off the coil at last. So I phoned. It was Max who told me, as a matter of fact. I wandered in and out of there all day. Couldn't stay away.''

"What time was it that you phoned Madam Max?'' asked Merriman.

He and Sarah had agreed to let me have a few moments on my own with Piers, and Sarah had joined Alex and David for a cup of beastly backstage coffee. Eddie'd gone patrolling among the other actors, picking up gossip from the formidable Hilda; gloomy prognostications from Hugh "Tess of the D'Urbervilles" Jonas, our Thomas Hardy expert and Davy's Montano; and sounding out the conflicts among this cry of players with the accuracy of a born water witch. Unless I missed my guess, he'd been out there in the hallway for some time, listening to our conversation. Now he toddled in, scouted round for a receptacle, selected a moderately clean plastic coffee cup someone had discarded, and rinsed it with scotch. I winced as he poured the precious stuff onto a plastic prop palm tree in the corner; I could never abide the waste of decent scotch. Eddie refilled his cup and perched nervously on a folding chair.

"My point, Piers,'' he said, "is that, due to Winnie's delicate condition during the better part of the day, he didn't manage to visit the *locus in quo* till long after the troops of Midian had been prowling and prowling round that orchard. Policemen have generally oversize shoes, and they tend to obscure the view when performing their duties. If you were there early, before things began to get muddied up with official machinery, you may have seen something that was gone by the time Winnie got there.''

Piers Ambrose shook his head. "The police had already been there an hour by the time I phoned,'' he said. "I had one class, but I dismissed it, sent the young beasts to the library on a paper chase, and slipped across the parking lot to Elsa's.'' He gulped down what was left of his scotch and poured another, a hefty one. "They hadn't taken Hallie's body away yet. I saw her there.'' He downed the scotch all in one swallow and sat breathing heavily. "In the Middle Ages, they'd have taken the bastard and torn him apart and made

108

everybody watch it. Four horsemen, each carrying a rope attached to the murderer's arms and legs, would simply ride away toward the four winds and pull him into pieces. Fair exchange, I'd say. His screams for her long silence. A punishment to fit the crime and haunt the memory." He looked away. "He was there, you know. I saw him in the grove. I waited, hung back in the trees. Didn't want to get involved with the police, of course."

I raised an eyebrow. "Of course."

"I saw him, coming across the parking lot. He skirted the paths and moved through the trees till he wasn't more than ten yards from me. Odd thing was, he didn't seem to be paying much attention to what the police were up to, taking their photographs and measurements and what not. He was watching the house. And her. Elsa Worthing. She was there, standing in the doorway. He couldn't seem to take his eyes off her."

"You have to tell this to Lloyd Agate, Piers," I said, getting excited. "If you can help Lloyd get his hands on Swan—"

Piers smiled. "Careful, Winnie, your academic blinders are showing. Odd, isn't it, how even the best of us assume our brethren of the gown are immune to the common brutalities, let alone the uncommon? Look in your own backyard, Sherman. I wasn't talking about Geoffrey Swan. There's someone else whose presence among us coincides even more nearly than Swan's with the career of this peculiar murderer of ours. And *he* was the man I saw this morning, watching Elsa Worthing. I've seen him do it often, especially in the last few weeks."

My mind was racing. "If you mean who I think you mean—"

Piers stood up, the empty scotch bottle in his hand. The transformation took place before my eyes, a sort of magic I have seen Davy perform a hundred times and marveled at. In an instant, Piers Ambrose was once more Iago, the wide face set hard, the hooded depths of the blue eyes fixed, boring into the dirty floor at which he stared. He threw the empty bottle against the wall behind me and it shattered, spraying me with thick slivers of glass. When at last the words came, they were almost whispered.

"There are excellent arguments for public execution. He's one of them." He looked at Merriman and me as though we'd just materialized in front of him. "It was the King of Cups I saw, don't you understand? Of course it was. James Temple Macauley, our bastard chancellor!"

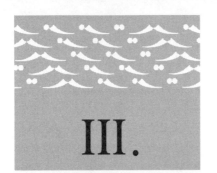

III.

The
Palace
of Pluto

Ten

He was the last to step off the train, hanging back to wait till all the other travelers had passed, a white wicker birdcage swinging lightly from his hand.

At the entrances to buildings I have often seen him stand and hold the door while a long stream of self-important boobies rushes past, taking his deference for the servility of a toady. When he gets aboard an elevator, he glances gently back along the hallway in case some hapless straggler is hurrying to catch the car. His landlady, fussy old Blanche Megrim, got a chauffeur, a part-time dishwasher, a resident Mr. Fix-it, and a balancer of checkbooks when Krishnan Ghandour moved into her upstairs front. Bringing his shark-finned Plymouth, the pride of his narrow, careful world, to a halt at four-way stop signs on our Ainsley hills, he will gently wave the other drivers one by one ahead before at last he pulls into the intersection himself, only to hit his brakes a hundred yards beyond to let a tardy squirrel cross the road.

Lacks assertiveness, scribbled the chairman of his doctoral committee at Columbia on the end-of-term evaluation.

The professor was especially annoyed that day, having just discovered in the wire basket on his office desk the last two chapters Krish had submitted for his dissertation, a complex linguistic study the professor only vaguely understood and so had put off reading for the past three months. No reason had been given him to bother in the meantime, after all. There had been no nagging phone calls, no bitchy letters of complaint from Krish. Nobody came to take the adviser out for beers at Mitch's Pub on Friday after class, creating a debt of fellowship he could not comfortably ignore. That was how the game was played, and only players could be winners.

But such games were a muddy channel where Krish would have drowned before he swam. Relying on the scholar's discipline, Krish waited in long silence, and was lost.

"These underachievers," said the adviser, sipping his beer while Mitch's jukebox played a rap record, "these goddamn all-but-dissertation bastards really piss me off."

"Fucking right," agreed Joe, the student who had brought him, sloshing a bit of beer on purpose over the unread pages. He had caught the note of anger in the professor's voice, the boredom, the sour taste of self-disgust. He gave it a focus. "Sonuvabitch part-timers, sitting on their asses in some knee-jerk upstate college, passing themselves off as the genuine article, for Chrissake. They're a goddamn waste of your time, man."

The professor nodded, his pulse thumping with the monotony of the rap record. Outside the uptown traffic roared, loud voices in soft island Spanish swore and flirted and made passes at the girls in tight T-shirts and big bright plastic earrings. It had been spring, then, almost time for another school year to end. It was a yearly ritual, the deep surge of private fear that rocked him when the weather warmed and the trees in Central Park leafed out again. He wallowed in despair, staring down at the puddle of beer on the pages of Krish's chapters.

Nagging phone calls fed his vanity, bitchy letters secured his sense of power, and these afternoons at Mitch's deadened his despair, made him feel young again and full of possibility. But the unread pages only stared up at him from the table, accusing him of sins he could not expiate—of self-indulgence, of puerile laziness, and

114

worst of all, of having given up years, oh, years ago, that final saving strength, the honor of the mind.

"Poor little bastard'll be stuck in that puddle-jump college where he works for the rest of his life," he said, "whether he finishes the doctorate or not. Never make it at a university like this one, you know. Get chewed up in a minute by the academic meat-grinder, an unaggressive wimp like that."

It was the only self-defense he needed. Released from his despair, he tipped back in the chair and launched into a delightfully irrelevant discussion of the Bergman retrospective being sponsored by the campus film society. Joe's questions were clever, his own elaborate replies especially cogent, his famous puns more deftly prurient than usual. The pounding rap rhythm brought his sex alive and he flirted boldly with Joe and his black-eyed Chinese girlfriend. When they all left Mitch's and went down to Harry's place on Second Avenue, the professor didn't notice that the pages he had not read, the hard-won pages that completed Krish's thesis, had been left behind among the dirty glasses and the empty Heineken bottles.

On Monday, when the professor made it to his office at last after a harrying subway journey from the Village, where he lived, he found a note from Joe paper-clipped to a chapter of his dissertation on Appalachian dialects. It was carelessly typed and badly spelled, the prose atrocious—as usual with Joe. The scholarship was all but non-existent and the subject had been dealt with nearly to exhaustion by far better minds. But the professor had enjoyed himself on Friday, and besides, his memory wasn't altogether clear on what had happened once they left Harry's. A simple gesture now would keep things on an even keel.

This is looking damn good, Joe, he scratched on the pages in bright blue marking pen. *A masterly critical job. Keep up the good work!*

It was only then that Krishnan's unread pages flickered for an instant through the professor's memory. He glanced into the wire basket on his desk, pawed through his briefcase, pulled open one desk drawer after the other. Of course, he knew, had always known. The pages were gone. Self-loathing seized him in the pit of the stomach, but he could handle that, turn it with the skill of a drum major twirling a baton, till it became a useful bludgeon.

"Fuck it," he muttered to himself. If, after all these years, he couldn't fake a few comments on a piece of graduate student crap, he wasn't the man he thought he was.

The last two chapters, he scribbled on a sheet of departmental letterhead, *will have to be rewritten. Scholarship is shaky. Recheck your sources. I'm not too sure your premise doesn't call the entire dissertation into question. And for God's sake, Ghandour,* he wrote, staring at the bleak expanse of his own insular and pointless past, his inescapable future, *be a little more aggressive, or you'll get lost in The System!*

To Krish, it meant another year of work, at least.

He had hoped the two chapters that finished his long, careful labor on the dissertation would be approved in time for him to graduate in the last spring of our old chancellor's term at Clinton College. Then would come the long-awaited tenure and a promotion, the beginning of a professional and personal life that had not yet materialized despite years of constant effort. He felt he had been alone too long; orphaned in infancy, raised by too many well-meaning relatives, shuttled from Lahore to London, then to Charleston and finally to New York, he longed now for permanence, for something and someone of his own, and Mrs. Megrim's rented room was not enough. Especially now that he had Hallie Glendon, the amazing silken-haired half-Pakistani beauty who had, to everyone's delight, selected our unprepossessing Krish to love.

But thanks to that afternoon at Mitch's Pub, his life was still on hold. Krish spent the summer and most of the autumn retracing with excruciating care every step of his research, examining his critical conclusions in long discussions with Merriman and me in the office after class, checking every period and comma of his footnote forms, reorganizing his bibliography. In the short autumn evenings he would drive out with Hallie beside him in the faithful Plymouth, past houses with For Sale signs in the lawns and down payments he knew he could not afford.

And Hallie would tease and laugh and ask if Mrs. Megrim didn't have another room to rent, and take his hand and kiss it, crashing down the walls of his reserve, amazing him with the simple, dazzling fact of being, beyond all expectation, loved. If hope forsook him, she found it lying discarded somewhere in the corners of his mind and put it, like a good housekeeper, back where it belonged. He could no longer remember what it had been like without her.

Lost.

The word roared in my ears as I watched our young friend coming toward us along the station platform, the wicker birdcage swinging from his hand, a smile of pleasure lighting his dark features as he spotted us.

Lost?

Too cheap a word, I thought. Too easy.

Not lost. Say, thrown away.

"A small remembrance," he said, grinning and holding up the birdcage for our inspection. "Hallie will like it, I think. I bought it in Chinatown. Having played, I confess, hookey from this conference during the afternoon. The papers, I am sorry to say, were remarkably undistinguished. Unoriginal in the extreme. Ambition, it is sad to say, frequently exceeding discipline. All in all, a crunching bore."

He began to walk and we kept pace with him, Sarah's arm through mine, her hand gripping my wrist for dear life. In a few steps we were in the station parking lot, the mist by then a thin rain freezing as it fell. Suddenly Krish stopped, his head on one side, and looked from one of us to the other.

"So kind of you to come," he said. "One appreciates to be met at the station. Deep obligation to you both, naturally. And forgive me. But why?"

Sarah's gloved fingers dug into my arm. "Krishnan," she began, "there's—" She broke off with a gulp and stood silent, and I felt a sort of jolt pass through her body, the unconscious electric charge brought by the vivid memory of what she had found in Elsa's orchard that morning.

I let her go and took Krish by the shoulder. "Come on, kiddo,"

I told him. "We've got the car over here. Let's get out of this muck."

He said nothing, just let me steer him to where the Olds we'd borrowed from David was parked. Krish got into the front seat and Sarah slid behind the wheel, started the engine, put the heater on. I wedged myself into the back, alone in the dark, and saw Sarah brace herself, gloved hands tight on the steering wheel.

She told him simply, as I'd known she would, refusing death the satisfaction of a cheap disguise.

"Krish," she said, "it's Hallie. She— She's dead, my dear."

I couldn't see his face. He sat hunched slightly forward in the car seat, both hands clutching the birdcage.

"Where is she?" he said.

At first I thought he hadn't grasped the truth. The voice was angry, but the edge was dulled.

"Where is she? She should not be alone!"

There was the dullness in his voice again, the weight it would carry, no doubt, for the rest of his life.

"I do not want her to be left alone!" he almost shouted.

"Krish," said Sarah. "It—it wasn't an ordinary death. She— I found her myself, and it was—she didn't seem to have been in pain, or—"

"Where have they taken her?" He was inexorable.

"The police, Krishnan," Sarah told him. "They— I don't think they're finished with their—with their work. She— Oh, my dear. She was murdered. In the night, in the very early morning, Krishnan. In Mrs. Worthing's orchard."

He said nothing, and his shoulders slumped back against the seat. There was a slight sound, like something cracking. His hands had crushed the fragile lattice of the cage.

"Where is she now?" he said quietly. His words seemed calm enough. "I want to see her."

I put a hand on his shoulder. "Not tonight, kiddo," I told him. "In the morning, I'll go with you and—"

"Pleeeeeeeeeaaaaaase . . ."

The sound was wild, half wail, half moan. He jerked free of me and burst out into the icy parking lot, a small dark figure in the eerie pink sodium lights, the crushed birdcage still dangling from his hand. He ran, slipped, fell, clawed himself up again to some precarious balance, and ran on, to disappear into the hopeless dark.

Lost. The word struck me, sharp as the icy rain. *Thrown away.*

I tried to follow but the going on that thin coat of ice was too much for me and I slid my way back to the car, to stand watching him, Sarah beside me.

"Dear Jesus Christ, Win," she whispered. "I didn't mean to hurt him so."

"Not you, old love," I said, holding her against me. "Not you."

And then I saw another figure come out of the shadow of the platform overhang, a tall slope-shouldered shape in the same blue jogging suit he'd worn that morning when he turned up at our back door.

Sheffield started after Krish across the parking lot, but his rubber-soled shoes slipped dangerously on the icy blacktop and he skidded past and would have fallen. I put out my arm and he caught hold and slid straight into me; for a moment we stood, the pair of us, in a kind of bear hug. Odd, when I thought of it. I couldn't remember ever having touched the man before.

"I ought to go after him," Tommy said shakily. His face under the unearthly pinkish lights was desolate.

Sheffield the politician, Sheffield the manipulator, Sheffield the bootlicker, Sheffield the henpecked husband, Sheffield the fair-weather friend—they had all stayed away tonight. There was only a rather silly man out here, frightened of emotion, not especially good at being human, awkward at loving and at being loved. But a man who was deeply sorry and badly needed to offer help.

This, I thought, was the Tommy who had induced me against my better judgment time and again to pull him out of the soup when he sank in over his eyebrows. In spite of everything, the chuckleheaded good intentions of the man were irresistible.

"Come on, you two," I said gruffly. "Get in the car. Krish

119

needs time to think, and Sarah ought to rest. We all need a good stiff belt. And I want to talk to you, Sheffield.''

He gulped and blinked. ''Me? You mean you're asking me to—''

''Tie one on,'' I said. ''That's the idea. Now, for pity's sake, get in the car, confound you! I think my ears are icing up!''

''How long do we have before another woman dies?''

Sarah sat cross-legged on the floor before our living room fire, sipping one of my hot scotch-and-lemon toddies, cradling it carefully between hands that still had not stopped shaking. She'd put into words the questions that were haunting all our minds: Who's next, and when?

Merriman, parked tentatively on the bench of Sarah's Steinway, took a sip of his brandy and soda and cleared his throat. He'd emerged from his private sitting room carrying a clasped manila envelope, and now he got up and marched over to the couch where I was sitting, Sheffield having usurped—blast him—my favorite sagging armchair. Eddie dumped the envelope into my lap.

''As you know, Winnie,'' he said, ''I'm in the habit, when something piques my interest, of taking cuttings from the *Guardian* and the other papers I read regularly. Squirrel instinct, I expect. Any rate, I've been saving all the bits and ends about our friend the Heart Specialist from the start.'' He shivered. ''Appalling nickname for the brute. But there you are.''

''Miss Godowski, July the eighth.'' I read the list of dates in Eddie's minute handwriting that was stapled to the flap of the file. ''Mrs. Ten Eyck, August seventeenth. Angela Cody, September twenty-sixth.'' I looked up. ''What's today?''

''November twelfth,'' said Sheffield. His long, lax frame was draped over my personal armchair and after having vacuumed up three of my toddies in quick succession, he was nicely sozzled—though still subdued—and slowed to a sip on number four.

''Which means that there have been—give or take a day or two—almost exactly six weeks between the killings,'' Merriman said. Obviously he'd been keeping track of the details for some time, that canny filing-cabinet brain sorting and analyzing everything.

"And six more weeks?" I tried a little calculation but my math rusted out somewhere after sophomore algebra. "That would be almost—"

"Christmas." Sarah poked the fire up and added another chunk of pine. "The week of Christmas. Dear Lord."

I shook my head. "The man's a brutal ironist. Death under the fruit trees. Murder at Christmas."

"Sexist." Sheffield mumbled the accusation into his half-empty glass.

"Beg pardon?" I said.

"Might have been a woman, not a man. Poison's a woman's weapon," he said.

"Who did you call a sexist?" I sputtered. " 'Woman's weapon'? I ask you!"

"Whom," he said. Those toddies seemed to have done something to the man. "And anyway, it doesn't seem very ironic to me. Romantic, I'd have said. Idyllic settings, death like a lover. All a little exquisite and Rossetti-ish. Straight out of the late Romantics. Sublimated suicide, all that."

I raised an eyebrow. "If we're up against a killer addicted to that Pre-Raphaelite piffle, I might as well resign here and now," I said. "But I don't buy it."

"Well, Winnie," Merriman chimed in, "there is another angle to the upcoming Christmas date. Might be a sort of schedule, as if our killer's planning some sort of climacteric for six weeks from now. Death of the earth in winter. The Yuletide idea, don't you know, burning off the corruptions of the past year and cleansing the world for renewal, druid-fashion, with the fires of Christmas. Something symbolic about these deaths, you know, I've thought so from the first. Means, location—everything. Ritualistic. Makes the whole thing seem unstoppable, like a natural force."

Sarah sniffed. "I absolutely refuse to consider druids! Besides,

I'm certain Hallie *knew* whoever killed her. If you'd seen her face, Win. Not the slightest flicker of fear. Quite—quite beautiful."

I hadn't seen Hallie, but I could imagine. It was what always set me nosing into real-life crimes, my writer's imagination diving into possibilities, exploring the world with a dozen pairs of suspect eyes until I knew their minds as well as I did my own, perhaps better. Oh, I made a joke of it, the long series of novels I'd written under that silly pseudonym, and my faintly effete detective, old Winchester Hyde. But the pseudonym was my freedom. It gave me the nerve to face death as an equal, to dive under the tidy surfaces of things I never could have stared at with my own two aging, myopic eyes. How could I explain, even to Sarah, that I truly *had* seen Hallie lying there, could see her now?

Oh, yes. I could, indeed, imagine.

"The fellow's clearly an egoist," I said, pulling myself away from the orchard and back to them all. "He—excuse me, Thomas— He/she can't bear to face the truth of the deed. Makes death look pretty. Wants to kill and keep his—or her—self-esteem intact."

"Or possibly to see his victims as he himself would wish to look after death." Eddie's voice was small and quiet, and I remembered his words of that morning. *If I were to choose suicide,* he'd said. Only once before had he been so upset about a real-life mystery, and that was a deeply personal involvement. Had he known one of those women better than I realized? But now was not the time to corner him.

"All right, then," I said briskly. "Sublimated suicide may be a thought. Lot of suicides at Christmas, it's a proven fact. Depression, loneliness, nostalgia for a lost childhood. But it doesn't give us much to go on."

"And—forgive me, Sarah—" began Merriman, "but I demand druids. Point being a certain personality type, you see. Mystical, symbolic. Sort of person who likes to play about with elemental truth."

I knew, of course, precisely who he had in mind. "Well, the best candidate for Archdruid in these parts is old Piers Ambrose," I said.

"Who was mucking about Elsa's orchard this afternoon. Who knew all four victims quite well."

"There's Geoffrey Swan," said Sarah. "He's rather a romantic figure. A loner, a drifter. That soft voice, and he never talks about himself at all. An Englishman turning up here, working in the greenhouse. And his accent, Win, you know? It's odd. The slang is Cockney, but the accent's upper-class, I'm sure of it. He's like a sort of exile, really. He was in the orchard with the body this morning. For all we know, he could've been there since he killed her, at—what was it? Two A.M.? And now he's run away."

"Or somebody's gotten rid of him," I said. "But you lot of flaming romantics are overlooking the alternative. What about somebody like my cynical self? There's a cool, sarcastic strain in Piers the Druid, too, you know."

"If you're looking for a cynic, somebody cold as ice, let's not forget Macauley." Sarah eased herself up onto the couch beside me. "I wouldn't put murder past him. Especially killing women. He hates us all, you can hear it in his voice when he talks to a woman. Condescension. Scorn. I'll bet he beats that wife of his, he's just the sort." She sighed. "But if you're looking for chilly cynics, there's also Madam Max, for pity's sake! Oh, phooey, what's the use of all this stirring round in personality types, when the thing that matters is the timing and the means of death? Where were these people when Hallie and the others died, and could they get hold of digitalis?"

"As for Macauley, Piers *did* see him out in Elsa's orchard this afternoon while the cops were there. Or claims he did." I'd been a bit uncomfortable with that handy revelation.

"Terribly dramatic, that scene in Piers's dressing room, wasn't it, Winnie?" There was a flicker of mirth in Eddie's weary baby blues. "Smashing the whisky bottle, all that. Perfectly staged. I was mistrustful, frankly. So convenient to divert suspicion from himself onto a man we'd all be delighted to hang from the yardarm. I wouldn't put it past old Piers to muddy the waters from sheer devilment, just to put our unbeloved chancellor in the hot seat. But murder? In this way? I think not. Not Piers Ambrose."

I had to agree. "A crime of passion, maybe. An overpowering impulse. But these deaths had to be planned, and if he were doing the planning, he'd hardly select four victims he had connections with himself."

"Not unless they all knew something about him and he had to shut them up." Sheffield polished off his toddy and gazed wishfully at the brandy bottle.

"Horseradish, Thomas. If he wanted them out of the way, why start now when he's known them all along?"

"But that assumes the killer does actually *want* to kill," he said. "Consciously, I mean. Aren't most serial murders more or less obsessive? The murderer acting from some deep level he's hardly aware of?"

"There *is* something ritual about it," said Sarah. "Such careful attention to detail. Like a performance, done the same way every time, as Eddie said earlier. But if it's a mental case—"

"Let's face it," I told them. "Anybody who can kill four people in cold blood couldn't be anything *but* psychotic. But there's certainly method in the fellow's madness. We'll just have to concentrate on that."

"The digitalis? Well," said Sarah, "Piers certainly hasn't got a heart condition, not the way he pushes himself. Teaching all day, the *Othello* at night. Does he still do that magic act of his in Manhattan at the weekends, too?"

"Indeed he does." Eddie fiddled with his pipe, tamping the tobacco carefully. "At a small magic club on the edge of Little Italy, I believe. What was the name of the place, Winnie? Palace of something, was it?"

"Castle," I corrected him. "The Castle of Wonders. As for the heart condition, I doubt it. But there are other ways of getting hold of a digitalis solution to inject."

"Diginox," said Merriman. "Terribly specific sort of stuff, though widely used," he explained to Sheffield.

"Mrs. Macauley takes digitalis." Tommy loped over and filled his glass, then went to stand by the ice-frosted French windows.

124

"Hilda Costello told me. Helen Macauley was getting a prescription filled at Castlebury's, and they had to call her doctor in Manhattan. Hilda heard them on the phone."

"I'll bet she did," I muttered. "With those matching microwave dishes she calls ears, the woman could tune in Tibet in a high wind. But is Mrs. Macauley's medicine diginox?"

"I don't know," said Sheffield, "but I can find out."

"And how do you plan to do that, Thomas, break into Castlebury's Drugstore on the dark of the moon and fiddle their computer?" I snorted and lit a Turkish Delight. Obviously the liquid courage had gone to the man's head.

"The Harvest Tea," he said smugly, and I'll swear his jaw seemed to recede less than usual and his eyes lost that watery look for a minute. "The annual Harvest Tea the chancellor gives for the department heads. It's only four days away, on Sunday. Diana's going to Manhattan tomorrow to buy a hat at Bergdorf's." He gulped, and I could sympathize, recalling the plumed battle helmet Lady Di had worn to Macauley's welcoming reception. "The medicine bottle has to be somewhere in that house." Thomas shrugged blithely. "All I have to do is find it and read the label. Childishly simple."

Eddie cleared his throat, barely able to suppress a grin. "But, Thomas, isn't your lady wife liable to blind and stiff a bit if you go waltzing round the chancellor's rancho rifling the medicine cupboards?"

He had that part right. The Ride of the Valkyries is nothing to Lady Di Sheffield with her dander up.

"I'll have a talk with Diana," said the new, masterful Tommy. "She'll just have to lend a hand, that's all. Diana can keep a lookout, while I toss the joint," he said. He knocked back the remains of his brandy like Duke Wayne at the brass rail of the Last Chance Saloon, and wheezed.

But then the truth came out, and so did the old, familiar Sheffield. "You see," he explained, "she can't stand Macauley. She never wanted us to hire him, and I was on the search committee. Diana's convinced he's out to ruin everything her father worked for.

125

Ever since he announced the new curriculum proposals, she hasn't given me a single minute's peace," he whimpered.

"By all means, then, Tommy, turn her loose," I said. "See what's in Macauley's closet."

"We know nothing much about this fellow Swan," said Merriman, "but Madam Max has a heart condition, you remember, Winnie? Always complaining about being deprived of life's little comforts by the quack. We could ask Elsa, or nose about a bit. Swan may have broken in, stolen some of the pills, if they're the proper sort."

I glanced at Sarah, who was frowning into the fire, and didn't say that Jaffer Swan would have no need to break in anywhere. All he'd have to do was get up out of Elsa's bed and nab the stuff.

"I keep feeling there should be *something,*" murmured Sheffield. He stood with his palms against the icy windows, looking out into the dark. "Something I ought to find. Some answer. To think of Hallie, out there in the cold. And Krishnan's face when he ran past us tonight. If it had been Diana . . . Or one of my girls . . ."

"Go home." Sarah got up and went to stand beside him at the windows. "Go home and be alive. It's all there is."

He turned to face her, his eyes wide and blank. "Six weeks," he said softly. "It's so little time."

"But it will have to be enough," I said, and poured myself another scotch.

The trees in the orchard wept ice.

He had begun by running, but now he came slowly, his feet crunching on the frozen grass. The ice turned back to rain almost as soon as it struck the bare branches, falling in a thousand small cascades onto the grass and leaves below the trees. His overcoat was soaked with it, and his hair where the branches caught at him. His face was scratched and bleeding, but he hardly noticed. Somehow, he had no idea how, he made his feet keep moving through the grass, searching the dark ground under the trees for her.

Surely, he thought, she was still here somewhere. If he looked long enough, carefully enough, he would find her. If he were quiet, he would hear her laugh above the rustle of the branches, the sharp pelting of the falling sleet.

Back and forth he went under the dripping branches, his eyes burning with the cold, one hand shoved into the pocket of his overcoat, the other still holding the broken birdcage he had bought for her.

She was nowhere here. Someone had lied to him cruelly. She was at home where it was warm, waiting for him to telephone and tell her how his day had been. He would give up, go home, wait for the sight of her in the morning.

But something held him. He circled in a small clearing where two old, dead pear trees had been felled. Turning and turning in the vortex of the dark and the bitter cold, enclosed by an invisible trap he could not fight free of, he spoke the word aloud at last.

"Dead." His voice was loud in the wet darkness. "Ahhhhhnnnnnnn . . . Dead."

The trees seemed to spin around him and he took a step, tripped on a piece of one dead stump, fell, grappled with the old, decaying wood. When at last his eyes could focus, there was something bright an inch beyond his nose. Something that gleamed like metal in the cold. His freezing fingers grasped it.

A steel knife, small and thick-bladed.

The taped hilt fit into his hand, and Krish rocked back onto his heels, staring down at it.

Dead. The desert future threw the word straight back at him in blinding waves. *Dead.*

He dropped the birdcage to tear loose his foolish necktie, rip open the button of his shirt. The knife was very sharp; it glistened with melting ice as he raised it, his arm stiff, his hand shaking. He had never wanted anything so much.

Suddenly strong fingers grasped his wrist, steadying him. The knife slipped from his own hand into that other, and he could feel support behind him, an arm around his chest, the warmth of another human shape that pulled him back to rest.

127

And then the blade of the knife was at his throat, cold, cold. "Like *me* to do it, mate?" Jaffer Swan's voice was soft and kind. "Up to you, see."

The arm tightened around Krish's chest and the warmth, the strength of it went straight through the bitter cold. The ancient fire at the heart of the world it was, so deeply disguised, so constant. And the blade of the knife, sharp and cold, barely nicking the skin of his throat.

"Way I see it," said Jaffer. His lips were close to Krishnan's ear, his breath warm, like an animal's, heavy and damp. "Way I see it, you got two choices. Life, which is generally shit. And the other. From whose bourne no traveler gets a two-way bloody ticket, see. Your toss, mate. I'm here, either way."

For the first time Krish was deeply, consciously cold. "She— She—is . . ."

He began to shake, the sobs great tearing cataclysms racking him like deep shock. Swan's slender body, too, shook with them; now he had lowered the knife and held Krishnan back against him tightly, swaying, riding the grief like a sailor in a storm. Rocking this total stranger in his thin arms, soaked with freezing rain, ice dripping from his sandy hair, his blue eyes pale in the heavy dark. Until at last the sobbing stopped.

"Alone," whispered Krish, half to himself.

Jaffer brushed a slim hand across his own eyes, wide and pale as ice.

"Makes a pair of us, mate," he said, and threw the knife away, into the dripping dark.

Eleven

There were more than a dozen bars on River Street, and Lloyd Agate made them all that cold November night. It wasn't till he got to Smitty's, next to the abandoned boatyard, though, that his copper's luck began to turn.

Smitty's Harbor Inn didn't really close till three, but it was after two already and the sleet was pelting harder than ever on the corrugated tin roof and walls as the lieutenant stepped inside. Only one couple, deeply absorbed, lingered at a far table. A loner hunched on a stool at the end of the bar by the till, and Irene Ransom, the tiny lantern-jawed bartender, her jeans shoved into scuffed cowboy boots, her outsized chambray shirt protected by a black apron with a white sailboat on it, pulled him a Rolling Rock and slid it down. When she looked up and spotted Lloyd, her pinched features lighted up.

"Hey, Supercop!" she cried, and slid out from behind the bar to meet him. "Long time no see. They bust you down to foot patrol, honey, or did Bev boot your ass out of the house? If you came in to get juiced, you better hurry up. It's almost witching hour!" Irene motioned him to a table and fell down in a chair herself. "I'd get you a drink, baby, but my feet are killing me. You know where the beer is, help yourself."

Agate shook his head, knocked over a couple of empty chairs with his backside, picked them up again, and parked. Last time he'd seen Irene, she'd had two black eyes and her face had been swollen twice its normal size. Drunks she could handle fine, but husbands were something else again. A complicated thing he'd never understood, but some guys staked their claim on life by doing women harm. Hell, why qualify? Maybe just by doing harm.

"No beer, Reeney," he said. "I could use a little talk, is all."

Irene frowned, searching his big, open face. "Hey, baby, I didn't mean to make a lousy joke before. You and Bev on the outs, or what?"

He grinned. "Not yet. But if I don't get home pretty soon, she's liable to kick my ass out for real. This is business."

"Cop stuff, huh?"

Lloyd fiddled with a laden ashtray on the table in front of him. "Reeney, we got trouble right here in River City. Four women, honey. If I don't find the creep, it'll be five, as sure as I'm sitting here with the roof leaking on my bald spot."

He moved his chair a foot and Irene, swearing under her breath, shoved an empty paint can under the slow drip. "God, why did I ever pay Smitty the down payment on this old sieve?" She paused, sat down again. "You said four women. I thought there were just the three?"

"You didn't see tonight's paper, right?" He glanced at the loner over at the bar. One of the regulars, Ray-Something. Not Swan. Agate sighed. It couldn't have been that easy. "Woman found the latest one early this morning, up at Worthing's Greenhouse. Know the place?"

Reeney shook her head. "I'm not much for the birds and bees, baby. I'm an indoor type, myself. Who was it this time?"

"Harriet Glendon. Graduate student, commutes into New York for classes three, four times a week. Went to Clinton, planning to marry one of the teachers up there. Pretty girl. Mother was from Pakistan, died young. Father ditched the kid, I guess, long time back. Know her?"

130

"Nope. Sorry. I did know the Cody kid, though. God. She was just a baby, Lloyd. She cleared tables for me, washed glasses now and then. And quit looking at me that way, Supercop. She was underage to serve booze and I never let her near the taps, okay?"

"When she worked here, she ever pick up anybody? You know, hang out and talk at the tables, make time with some guy?"

"Angela was a good worker, never screwed around much with the customers." Irene sat back, thinking. "Sorry, baby. All I remember is, she played in the high school band, because she had to work her schedule around band practice, and she had a kid brother named Peter she couldn't stand and she played video games in her sleep. Real Nintendo nut. Game Boy. That crap. She was a kid, goddamn it!" The shrill voice rose angrily, then dropped. "I'm sorry, hon'."

"Sure thing," he said softly. "Reeney, you ever get a guy in here, little older than me, sandy hair—thinning out a little, you know? Pancho Villa cookie duster. Kind of skinny, but— Not scrawny, just not much meat. Talks with an English accent, plays the clarinet?"

"Swanny?" Irene's face lit up even more brightly than it had when Lloyd came in. "That couldn't be anybody else, babe. Sure. Old Swanny comes in when the spirit moves him. Helluva good type, y'know?"

"He got a regular room someplace, apartment maybe?"

Reeney's small, bright black eyes squinted at him. "You want him for something, Lloyd? He spit crooked in front of the goddamn mayor's house, or what?"

"I just need to find him, is all." She was getting edgy, the way people always did when questions came too close. He'd have to give her room. *Time,* he thought, *time going to waste.* "On second thought," Agate said, "I guess I'll pull myself a brew."

He left her to think it over, got a Budweiser from the bar, and came back, forgetting to dodge the leaky roof. He sat down again, wiping his dripping forehead.

"Lemme get this straight," said Irene. "First we talk about these murders. What do they call this creep—the Heart Specialist?"

"He uses heart medicine to kill with," Lloyd explained. It wasn't quite that simple; even the lab boys hadn't really figured what was being used, not yet. The heart pills were combined with something, something else. They had to be. But nothing else was in the bloodstream. He sighed. "Digitalis," he told Irene.

"Okay. So then you start in pumping me about Swanny. Look, baby, if you've got the idea he's the guy, you better think again."

"How's that?" asked Agate, sipping at his beer.

"Because you're full of shit, that's how! The guy's just— He's straight, okay? I know he's not your ordinary bozo. He drifts around. He sleeps wherever he can find a flat rock, he's got nothing he can't lug around in that duffel bag of his. He doesn't seem to want a life, not what you'd think of. But he's—" Irene paused, hunting for a word. "Look, Agate. Most cops are real twenty-four-karat pricks, okay? Fulla crap, everybody oughta kiss their ass? I got no time for 'em. Fuck cops. You're different, baby. I could tell the first time you opened your mouth. Straight-arrow. Same badge, same cop rules. But solid. Swanny's that way. Seems just like all the rest of the pond scum unless you look close. But underneath—solid as a goddamn rock. Okay?"

"Okay," he said gently. Irene's hand was gripping the table edge too hard. She was past her middle forties, three times divorced. Men would have come easy in her job, but she'd had enough of them, or so he'd thought after the beatings, the stitches, the punched-out teeth. Maybe this guy Jaffer Swan was different. Or maybe she was just making the same old mistake again. "I don't want to bust the guy," he said. "Nothing like that. Only he works out at Mrs. Worthing's greenhouse, Reeney. I thought he might've seen something, heard something."

"He works a lot of places," Irene said. "Part-time, nights, weekends. I don't know what the hell he does with his money. Drinks some—not much, though— Maybe he plays the horses, I don't know. Doesn't spend it on his wardrobe, for sure. Goodwill Store specials, that's Swanny. I gave him an old pair of The Lousy Bastard's boots." This was the one who had used her for a punching bag, the last and worst of her three, whom Agate had arrested in his underwear and with whose wardrobe Irene had been supplying drifters ever since.

"You know any of the other places he works?" Agate wiped a small moustache of foam from his upper lip. "See, the thing is, we can't seem to find the guy. He's disappeared."

Her hand gripped the edge of the table again. "Maybe the creep that killed that woman— If Swanny saw him, I mean, maybe—"

"I don't think so," Lloyd assured her, and watched the small fingers heavy with dime-store cocktail rings relax a bit. *Jesus Christ,* he thought, *she loves the guy.* Women amazed him. After her losses, most men would have said Irene was just a fool. But maybe, thought Agate, that was what the weak had always said about the strong. "The woman who found the body saw him. He was out there, playing his horn in Mrs. Worthing's orchard, but by the time we got there, he'd taken off. We've been looking for him all day. I figured, if anybody could keep tabs on a guy like that, it'd be you, Irene."

She smiled faintly. "He's got a couple other jobs I know about. Likes the outdoors, so he always looks for something he can get his hands dirty. He told me once he worked for that lawn-care place, All Seasons Lawn Service. Trims hedges, rakes lawns—like that. And he's got some kind of job up at the college, too, I think. Groundsman, maybe?"

Odd, thought Agate, that Doc Sherman hadn't seen Swan over there. Maybe guys who grubbed around in the dirt for a living suffered from invisibility where professional types were concerned. Or maybe Swanny worked at being invisible. There was no rap sheet on a Geoffrey Swan, but these guys changed their names every time they hit a new town. The reasons weren't always criminal, though a lot of them were running out on bad debts, child-support payments, alimony. Mostly, though, they sloughed off old, used-up selves to start out new, to stay alive, to reinvent their chances one more time. Lloyd sighed. He wouldn't mind starting over himself right now, with a clear head and a good night's sleep.

"He ever stay here, Reeney?" Agate asked her suddenly. "I mean, you said he crashed wherever he could find a spot. Ever let him stay here?"

She snorted and swiped a sip of the remaining beer—now mostly flat—in Lloyd's glass. "If you mean, did I ever let him fuck me, let's just say he never asked, okay? He may have dossed in the back room a time or two. You know how that is."

Smitty's back room, under Irene's gentle stewardship, was famous among drifters, river bums, and hard-core homeless as a last resort, where you could go when the shelters were full and your pockets were empty, wipe the tables, push a broom in the morning, get a cup of coffee strong enough to walk and maybe a fried-egg sandwich for your trouble, and fall down on the two old mattresses back in the storeroom, in between the cases of Seagram's and the Johnny Walker Red.

"Mind if I have a look?" Lloyd asked her, and Irene shrugged. Swan had been there, all right, he thought, seeing the dismay on her narrow face, and not just once or twice.

The couple at the far table got up and paid their bill, and while Irene rang up the sale, Agate strode back beyond the bar, through the door marked EXIT. In back was a narrow, brownish hallway, stained with the damp and smelling of the river that ran roaring past them, down to Manhattan and the sea. There was a pay phone in the hall, numbers scribbled on the peeling paint of the wall in pencil and smeared ink, a sign taped to the receiver: OUT OF ORDER. Beyond the phone were the bathrooms, and at the far end of the hall the door that led outside, to where the booze deliveries were made. The storeroom was between, a narrow, low door the delivery guys always griped about because they cracked their heads. Lloyd—miraculously —remembered to stoop as he entered.

There was a light on somewhere in the room. The overhead fixture had no bulb, but a dim glow crept up the far wall from beyond the stacks of cartons. Lloyd held his breath as it played unsteadily in the dark. A flashlight, it had to be.

Agate stopped in his tracks, sniffing the dank air like a hound, listening, hand on the off-duty special in his pocket. He'd never carried a backup gun until these killings began. Now, working extra-long shifts and checking out every speck of possibility, he was tired and off his game; he felt naked without some metal on him, vulnerable to every crackpot.

The gun in his hand, he squinted at the faint moving light. You couldn't see beyond the heaps of packing boxes, the racks of wine bottles, and the piled-up twelve-packs. Last time he'd been back here, the mattresses had been just about where the light was, over the furnace ducts where it was warm.

The sleet was still hitting the tin roof with spatting noises, like an army of tap-dancing mice gone nuts. The heat pipes rattled, too, and the loner at the bar had punched the jukebox, a schmoozy Barry Manilow number. He couldn't be certain, with all that interference. But Lloyd was almost sure that someone else was with him in the storeroom.

"Swan?" he said steadily, not moving from the door. The gun in his hand was cocked, ready. The guy would have to get past him if he bolted, there wasn't any other door. Was there a window? Lloyd could not recall. Maybe, back behind the mountains of booze. Maybe. But shut this time of year, and if he was in luck, maybe swollen from the damp and hard to open. Maybe. "That you, Swan?" he called again.

Nothing but the goddamn mice, and Manilow. Lloyd took a step toward where he thought the mattresses would be, holding his breath.

"What time was the girl killed, baby?"

He almost went straight up through the rusty tin roof when Reeney spoke from right behind him. Coming down, he turned to look at her. "Early this morning."

"Swanny was here for a while," she said reluctantly, staring at the gun in Lloyd's hand. "He comes in sometimes, real late, hour or

135

so before closing. Has a drink. Plays something on that horn of his. Old stuff, you know? I like the old songs. Last night he played 'Georgia,' right? 'Georgia on My Mind.' Cool . . .'' The Manilow was grinding slowly uphill to its anticlimax. "Swanny came in around one o'clock last night, played Hoagy Carmichael maybe—I'd say an hour and a half. Left just about half an hour before closing. Yeah.''

"Any other customers in the place?'' It wasn't that he didn't believe her, it was just that he didn't believe her. The alibi was too handy, and it had stopped him going back to investigate that sound he'd thought he heard. Agate strode back through the canyons of piled-up beer cartons, Irene at his heels.

"A couple, yeah. 'Smatter, Supercop, you think I'm making up fairy tales? You gonna shoot me, or what, baby? Look, I got no reason to lie for the dude, you know? I got no stake in him.''

There was a scrabbling noise and the crash of breaking bottles and Lloyd took off at a run, to fall headlong across a carton of Gallo pushed into the aisle, the dark red burgundy seeping already through the cardboard from the broken jug. Agate picked himself up and forged ahead, but it was too late. The man was gone. The window onto the parking lot had been pushed open and the rain, laden with ice, was blowing in.

Lloyd pulled the window shut and turned on Irene Ransom. "He was back here all the time, wasn't he? When did he show up? This morning, right after he offed the girl, or did he cover his tracks first?''

"Eh, man, whoever the hell that was, they didn't register at the desk, okay?'' Irene backed away a step or two. "I'm a mark for these guys, you know that. They pull in, the weather's too lousy to crash in one of the parks, they come over here, I leave the back door unlocked till closing time. It coulda been anybody, for Chrissake!''

"Lot of your clients read this stuff, do they?'' Agate bent over the stained, morning-glory patterned mattress shoved up against the inside wall and picked up a tattered leather-bound volume. *"The Poems of William Butler Yeats?''* He leafed through the book. Poetry had never exactly been to Agate's taste, and who had time for reading anyway? Doc Sherman might make something of it, once they'd processed it for prints. "Your pal Swan was quite a reader, wasn't he, Reeney?" he said, looking up from the book. "Carried around a whole bag of books, that's what I hear."

He checked the flyleaf and the inside cover for a bookplate or a name, but there was none. *There wouldn't be,* he thought, *if it was Swan's.* He didn't sound the kind of guy to write his name on every surface of the world as he wandered by, like Kilroy. But readers, real ones, had a lot of habits, they made themselves at home with books, stuck clippings in them, and the reminder cards for dentist's appointments, and shopping lists.

Lloyd took the book by its spine and shook it and a flimsy piece of paper fluttered to the floor. He picked it up. It was parchment, a double-fold greeting card with a bouquet of tulips on the front. Inside was a verse, printed in fancy calligraphic script: " 'The world is charged with the grandeur of God,' " read Agate. " 'At Easter, celebrate the spring.' " It was signed with rounded, childish handwriting in purple ink. " 'Love to Geoff from Hallie.' "

The lieutenant's eyes closed and he took a deep breath of gratitude, then opened them again. It was the first slender thread that had connected anything to anything in this strange, brutal case. It was a place to start. For Irene's sake, and Mrs. Worthing's, he was mildly sorry it seemed to lead to Jaffer Swan. He flipped the greeting card over, hoping for some further message on the back, but there was none, only the printed name and emblem of the maker. A small crested coat-of-arms showing a lion and a five-petaled flower above a naked sword, that was the trademark.

It was the name printed in tiny Gothic letters underneath that made Lloyd Agate bite his tongue. Something made sense at last, and for what was left of that night, he could go home and sleep.

The name beneath the coat-of-arms read "Glendon Greetings, Birmingham, U.K."

As for Yours Truly, Winston Marlowe Sherman, Ph.D., Sarah herded me up to bed as soon as Eddie and I and gravel-voiced Frieda Fritz had stowed a well-squiffed Sheffield into Frieda's trusty Yellow Peril, Ainsley's one and only taxi cab. By then it was nearly two A.M., and Lady Di was sure to be waiting for the poor goop with war paint on and tomahawk in hand. But even Diana in full cry was no match for old Frieda at two in the morning, and Tommy's scalp—what was left of it—was safe for now.

My sleep that night was strangely deep—an effect, I decided afterward, of Hortense's sedatives. My own mortality had jumped up and bitten me that morning, then changed its mind and plunged me back into life once more; however deeply I might choose to delve into the mystery of Hallie's death and those of the other three women, *I* was still alive, and more or less as good as ever! The euphoria of that incredible fact had lent a sharp perspective to the rest of my day—to the meeting with Graham and Elsa in the orchard, to the *Othello* rehearsal and my talk with Piers, to poor Krish's figure disappearing into the night. The moments in themselves had been dramatic, yes; but I had seen them with a unique tunnel vision, like a watcher in a small dark room, spying on secrets played in brilliant light beyond a distant open door.

Eddie, Sarah, Lloyd, David, Alex—my pals had all been watching, too, but they could not, I felt, have seen what I saw, heard what I had heard. I didn't have the foggiest idea what it was, you understand. But I felt in my bones that I *knew* something, that somewhere in my memory lay that answer Sheffield had spoken of, the one that would make the six weeks until Christmas time enough to stop the Heart Specialist before he killed again. The problem was to drag it up into the light from wherever the hell I'd shoved it while I was lying in that hospital bed with an oxygen tube up my nose.

Had I really almost died that morning on our kitchen floor? I didn't feel like it, certainly. All the old equipment seemed to be running smoothly, and from the time I left the hospital that afternoon until I hit the bed at half-past two, I felt a surge of excess energy, my adrenaline on overtime, making up for lost time. If Sarah

1 3 8

hadn't made me, I wouldn't have turned in even after Sheffield was gone and Eddie had retreated to his parlor and his volume of Trollope. I wanted to hole up in my Cave, the three upstairs rooms that are my private lair in Sarah's father's ramshackle old mansion, have another Turkish smoke, put my dogs up on the desk, and think things out.

Instead, I did as I was told and lay down beside Sarah, figuring to wait till she'd gone to sleep and then sneak out and down the hall. But as it happened, I zonked out about five seconds after my noggin hit the pillow. When I woke up I felt a tugging on my arm, but my eyelids seemed to be stuck down with Super Glue and my tongue felt like it was wearing a furry mitten.

"Grrrrrr," I growled, and tried to lick my lips. I couldn't seem to find them with my overdressed tongue, so I gave up and squeezed my eyes tighter, ignoring whoever was shaking me by the shoulder.

It was Sarah. "I can't wake him!" There was a note of panic in her voice. "Win! Oh, please, Win!"

"Let me try," said Merriman.

I heard them talking, I knew they were close to me, but I couldn't seem to be bothered to respond. I had been somewhere else all night, traveling in bleak dreams that still dragged at me like treacherous current. I wanted to wake up now, I was even working fairly hard at it. I just couldn't quite summon the energy.

And then I felt something tickling the bottom of my right foot, which was sticking out of the covers. My foot shot up with a will of its own, there was a crash and Sarah gave a sort of squeak.

"Damn and blast!" said Merriman. I got my peepers pried open at last and there he was, plonked on the floor next to the mortal remains of a lamp table, rubbing his jaw and blinking. "Blast and double-blast! Serves me right for trying to rouse a hibernating hippopotomus! Not only has he kicked me in what is left of my front teeth, I do believe the man's broken my bifocals, blast him!"

"They're under your knee, you old knucklehead," I grumbled, lugging myself to a sitting position. "Anyway, serves you right for tickling a sick man."

139

"Sick? Ha!" Eddie grabbed hold of the bedpost and Sarah helped him to his feet. He put his glasses—well, half of his glasses—back on his nose and peered down at me like a disapproving owl. "Any man who can kick like that is no more sick than I am. He's malingering, my dear," he told Sarah. "Doesn't want to go to that faculty meeting on Friday, so he's playing sick, that's my guess."

"Well," I growled, sitting on the edge of the bed, "just guess again. I *am* sick."

Sarah sat down beside me and put an anxious hand on my forehead. "What is it, Win?" she asked me tenderly.

"The pip!" I roared. "Merriman gave it to me!"

Sarah pursed her lips and glared at me. "Fine," she said. She got up and marched primly to the bedroom door, then turned back to me with that look in her eye. You've probably seen one like it. I expect Mrs. Attila the Hun and Genghis Khan's beloved had it down pat. It means she's about to issue an edict with no reprieve, and all resistance will be in vain. "I'll make you an appointment at Dr. Pennington's for this afternoon. Perhaps there'll be a cure."

She flounced out, and I looked over at Merriman. "This is all your fault," I told him. "I hope you get bunions, confound you."

He frowned and ran his tongue along his front teeth, taking inventory. "You *were* remarkably sound asleep just now, Winnie. One usually sleeps lightly toward morning."

"How would you know?" I grumbled. "You're like Dracula, you never sleep at all."

He cocked his head on one side, considering me. "Were they bad dreams?"

"Not exactly. Confusing. But clear as the pictures on a Union Pacific calendar." I got up and paddled over to the window and opened the blind. The morning was clear, too, the sun melting the ice from the night's squall of sleet. "I suppose you were out in the hall all night with your ear to our keyhole, didn't want to miss out on the excitement if I decided to hand in my dinner pail on the spur of the moment?"

"I did come trotting up once or twice," he said sheepishly.

"Thought you might've slithered out of bed once Sarah'd drifted off. 'There he'll be,' I said to myself, 'sitting in that drafty old Cave till sunrise, snarling over the chancellor's new curriculum proposals till he gets pneumonia.' So. I came upstairs to see, and—"

"Got a water glass and held it to the wall," I said, nodding. "I was talking in my sleep, apparently. I hope I was my usual scintillating self?"

"You did not babble o' green fields, if that's what you're hoping, nor even recite the 'it is the cause, my soul' speech from good old *Othello*. Much as you love the Bard, your subconscious has not yet become iambic. But there was a certain word you muttered. 'Blackbird,' you said, over and over again. It's that old blues, of course, that Sarah heard Geoffrey Swan playing out in Elsa's orchard this morning. I expect it ran through your head all day, as old tunes will."

" 'Blackbird'?" I blinked, trying to concentrate. "Why would I pick that to yammer about? Doesn't seem to mean much. He could just as well have been tooting 'The Battle Hymn of the Republic.' He was there, that's what—"

"Aha," said Merriman, "as Sam Newlin would say, 'I perceive the gleam of elucidation in your fishy eye, Hyde.' You've remembered something. What?"

"It's not the song," I said. "It's Swan. He was in my dreams last night. I couldn't focus it at first, but now I'm sure. Those nice clear photo images I kept getting in my sleep? Jaffer Swan's was one of them. He was with somebody, but at first I couldn't remember who it was, what the setting was."

"Elsa's place, I expect," suggested Eddie. "When we've seen him, it's mostly been on our way past the greenhouse for those Sunday night soirees of Madam Max's."

"It wasn't there. That would be waking logic, and dreams carry a logic of their own. The bits connect at odd angles. No, I know now exactly where I saw Jaffer Swan in my dream." I shrugged into my bathrobe and headed for the door. "You know that escape trick of Piers's, the one he calls The Spanish Maiden?"

"Of course. Bloodcurdling article, that cabinet he uses, all lined with spikes."

I nodded. "A hinged cabinet shaped like a human body, with spikes in both halves. Invented by the Spanish Inquisition, that's what Ambrose told me once. It's worked by trick hinges, easy enough to get out of if you know the way they operate."

"And absolutely fatal if you don't. In your dream, Winnie, did Piers—"

"Oh, Piers was nowhere in sight," I told him, my hand on the doorknob. "But Jaffer Swan was inside the Spanish Maiden. And Old Ironpants Macauley was slamming it shut."

"But that means—" Merriman rubbed his chin and blinked. "What the dickens *does* it mean, Hyde? I'm baffled. Dreams, I admit, are not my line of country."

"Nor mine," I told him. "But I damn well know what this one means. It means I'm going to know our chancellor a whole lot better before that faculty meeting on Friday."

"And," said Eddie, frowning, "it means we'd better locate Jaffer Swan, before he winds up shish-kebabbed!"

Twelve

"Doc, where'd you put your buddy Ghandour?" It was Agate on the phone and he sounded worried. "I just checked with his landlady and she says he never made it home from Manhattan last night."

I shoved down one more lump of the oatmeal Sarah had insisted on making for me, "for the sake of my health"—the idea being, I guess, that if I could survive an entire bowl of those glutinous globules, I'd be proven fit for whatever other trials were in store. She'd had her beady eye on me all through breakfast, so I'd brought the loathsome stuff with me to the phone, hoping for a chance to nourish the spindly geranium on the counter with it. At Agate's news, I shoved the bowl aside and swallowed air instead.

"Have you checked his office at the college, Lloyd? Krish has a key to the arts and letters building, we all have. We met him at the station last night and broke the news to him about Hallie, and he took off, wanted to be alone. I assumed he'd walk it off eventually and go home, but he may have preferred his office." I myself would've spent that rainy night on a park bench rather than confront Blanche Megrim's brand of sugary sympathy. "Krish has too many brains to do anything stupid, Lloyd," I told him. "He'll turn up, when he's ready, I'd stake my hide on it."

"I talked to Miss Comfort." This was Hannah, our faculty secretary. "She says he hasn't come in yet. Doesn't have a class till this afternoon." Agate sounded weary. "Look, Doc, if he turns up, tell him to give me a call, okay? I need some background on the Glendon girl. Looks like there was a connection between her and Swan, and I gotta know what the hell it was."

He told me about the book of poems and the greeting card he'd found at Reeney's bar. "Glendon Greetings? Never heard of it," I said.

"It's only the biggest stationery firm in Britain, my lovely old duck." Alex breezed in the back door with daughter Gemma in tow and paused by the wall phone to give me her traditional peck on the cheek. "Sir Matthew Glendon was an institution. Died suddenly. Car crash, I think. The heirs are still going at it over the pickings."

"You hear that, Lloyd?" I said. "Krish's Hallie seems to be connected to the gift-wrap-and-greeting-card king of Britain. Minor nobility, and a lot of bucks to provide a motive. If Hallie was the heir—"

"Swan's an Englishman. The card in that book was signed 'Love from Hallie.' Glendon Greetings. Hallie Glendon. Doesn't give him a motive, but it sure as hell gives him an inside track."

"No luck getting your hands on Swan, I take it?"

"Not yet. Closest I've come is that book of poetry." He pronounced it 'poitry.' I winced. "Reeney says Swan's got a part-time job up at the college, Doc. Grounds crew. You ever spot him up there?"

"Not that I remember. But I wouldn't, necessarily. Clinton's a small campus as far as buildings are concerned, but the grounds are spread out all over these bluffs. There's the arboretum over by the theater building, the pond, the fountain and the planters in front of the student center—if Swan was assigned to any area except the arts and letters building and the library, I'd never have seen him. Of course, there's the theater, but those rehearsals are all at night, and the grounds crew doesn't work nights, naturally. I can check with the superintendent, find out what I can."

"Thanks," he told me. "It'll save some time." Lloyd paused, and I thought he was ready to hang up.

"Okay, kiddo," I said. "I'll be in touch when I—"

"It's a fucking worm!" It came from Agate like an explosion in a tunnel. I'd never heard him use the f-word before. In a minute it came again. "What kind of fucking fish does the bastard think I am, anyway? He hands me the bait and I'm supposed to swallow it. That goddamn book with the card in it. Shit!"

"Whoa, kiddo. You mean whoever it was back in that store-room at the bar last night, whoever left that book for you to find—"

"It damn well wasn't Geoffrey Swan," Agate said. "Somebody's playing games here, Doc. Swan's disappeared. Now Krishnan Ghandour's missing, too. All those women. Swan may have had a motive, he must've known Hallie Glendon somehow. But there's somebody else involved here. Somebody working the wires."

"Or the hinges," I muttered as I hung up, thinking once again of all those deadly spikes inside the Spanish Maiden.

I poured myself a cup of coffee—decaffeinated, thanks to Sarah —and parked beside Alex at the kitchen table. In the living room, I could hear young Gemma battling her way through "Long, Long Ago" on the Steinway, as she and Sarah launched into this week's piano lesson. The kid hit a pink one and Alex gritted her pearly whites.

"Oh, well," she said. "It's better than last week. I think."

"Time will tell," Merriman told her. "Not to be sententious, naturally."

"You always are, you old boot." I lighted a smoke, taking my chance while Sarah was too busy to spot me. We now had a scoreboard taped to the icebox, with an X for every Turkish Delight she saw me puffing on. I ask you! "But in this case, I hope you're right. Maybe time will tell us where poor old Krish has tucked himself away all night."

"I'd rather have Krish tell us," said Eddie with a sigh. "I kept an eye out the window for him during my nocturnal peregrinations, hoped he might turn up on the doorstep, you know. He didn't." He paused, studying the tabletop. "But Winnie—somebody else did."

"What? Why didn't you tell me before, confound you? Why didn't you wake me up? Was it Swan?"

"Don't know. Couldn't see. It was dark, of course, and raining. But I don't think so. I only saw his back. Standing out in the garden, beyond the French windows, as though he'd come up the path from the river. A big, wide shape, broad shoulders. Geoffrey Swan is slight, weedy—like myself. Couldn't have been Swan."

"What was he wearing?" asked Alexandra. "What sort of color?"

"An overcoat. Raincoat, probably. Lightish, I think. Tan. Possibly gray."

"That lets out Piers Ambrose," I said. "That greatcoat of his is black wool, with a black velvet collar."

"But he wasn't wearing the greatcoat last night, Winston," Alex announced triumphantly, her eyes glittering with excitement and her fingers fiddling nervously with a lock of red hair that fell along her cheek. " 'Piers is out of uniform,' " that's what David said to me as we were all leaving last night after notes. He had on a grayish tan Burberry and that slouch hat, the Irish tweed one just like D.'s." She was quiet for a minute, sipping at her coffee. Then she looked up, her small face sober and direct, her eyes on mine. "I'm afraid of him, duck," she said softly. "Not just nervous. Dirty scared."

"Nonsense," said Merriman. "He's an old rake, and all that magical claptrap of his is just, well it's—a sort of protective skin, that's all."

"I don't mean the magic." Alex frowned. "I know he's a friend of yours. It's probably nothing. But when I'm onstage with him, and he touches me— He hates women, Winston. Not just me. All of us."

"But Piers Ambrose has had more lady friends than—"

"I don't believe it!" Her small hands were fists, and she brought them down on the tabletop in front of her, then sat staring, surprised

146

at her own vehemence. "I don't doubt he's *had* a lot of women. Some men are like that, you know, men who hate women. Have it on with as many as they can, making fools of the bloody lot of us. Piers Ambrose may have taken a lot of women to bed. But not one of them was ever his friend, in or out of bed. I'd stake my life on it."

I hope to God you won't have to, I thought, but didn't say it.

"And the really awful part," she went on softly, "is that I *could* love the man, you know." She looked me in the eye again, then looked away. "I really could. That absolute despair . . ."

"Piers the prankster? Despair?" Merriman thought it over. "Perhaps you're right. There is something in that Iago of his. An undercurrent that's a bit more than acting."

"It's *not* acting, that's just it!" cried Alex. "David's acting when he strangles me, I'm not afraid of that. But Piers——" She paused and caught her breath. "He hates D., too, you know. You ought to watch his face when David's giving notes, after rehearsal. He resents any sort of control, that's what I think." She sighed. "I thought, coming up here to Ainsley, getting out of New York for a while, taking that old house by the campus with the yard and the trees—well, I'd hoped it would be a sort of idyll, really. Nothing to be afraid of. A little peace. But here I am, worrying about David all over again, a murder every time I turn round. I suppose I wanted paradise."

"And Piers turned out to be the snake?" I said. "I don't know, Alex. I don't know anything at all. Can't pretend to understand Piers Ambrose, but I've always rather liked him, in a casual sort of way, and we all have our darknesses. Frankly, everybody in this town's beginning to look like a suspect to me."

"But I did *not* see everybody standing outside our French windows in the driving sleet last night," said Merriman briskly, breaking the mood.

"Getting back to the famous raincoat," I said, relieved to see Alex's face relax. "Jaffer Swan hasn't got one to his name, I'd bet my socks on that," I said. "But I'll bet Graham Worthing has, a nice pricey designer specimen to wow the clients with on rainy days."

147

"What about Macauley?" said Merriman. *"He* has the build of that shadow I saw out there. Ever seen him wear a raincoat, Winnie?"

"He's probably got half a dozen lackeys to hold umbrellas over him," I growled. "But if he wears a raincoat, there's one person who's sure to know what color it is, who made it, how much it cost, and whether anybody in the Western hemisphere has one like it!"

"Hilda," I said, "I don't want a crash course in networking, I just want to know what color old Macauley's raincoat is!"

I'd cornered La Costello in the faculty lounge, hoping to tap into her legendary tittle-tattle memory bank. She was looking even more like Chairman Mao than usual in her latest fashion conquest, a sort of dark blue pillowcase with a Chinese collar. "I'm trying to tell you," she said. "Vera Beegleman over in the business office was telling me at lunch. She saw him buying it, when she and Frankie—you know Frank Beegleman, in biology? *Well.*" She paused to gasp for breath, then careened downhill to the punch line. "They were in Manhattan, looking for a dinner jacket because Frankie's got to go to some convention. They stopped into that designer place—Nino Somebody's. Nonno? *Any*way, they were trying on this jacket, and it didn't fit and they couldn't possibly have afforded it anyway, not on Frank's salary, and they were just about to leave, when there *he* was."

"Frank, Nonno, or Nino?" I said.

"Ma*cau*ley," she groaned. "Haven't you been listening? God, Winnie, you're such a *lump! Macauley* was in there, trying on a raincoat. Pale blue-gray, with a button-down cape in back."

"And impeccable Mechlin lace at the cuffs," I grumbled, my brain sorting the possibilities.

Pale gray. A light shape, Merriman had said. But what could Macauley have been doing at our French windows in the middle of the night? Now, if it had been Piers Ambrose. Piers who hated women. Piers who could lock himself inside the Spanish Maiden and escape without a scratch. Piers who was still my friend . . .

"Thanks, Hilda," I told her abruptly, heaving my aching backside off the old oak church pew that now passes for a couch in our lounge, part of Sheffield's redecorating program, aimed at making sure nobody lounges long enough to exchange damaging information about him over Hannah Comfort's dreadful coffee. "That's all I wanted to know. Pale gray raincoat. Expensive. Thanks a bunch."

"No, wait!" The woman was in spate. "He didn't *buy* that one, Winnie."

"Oh, my aunt!" I spluttered. "Then what the devil—"

She lowered her voice as a couple of our colleagues drifted past. "He wasn't *alone,*" she whispered. "That's what I've been trying to tell you. Macauley was in Manhattan *with* somebody."

"You interest me strangely, Hilda," I said, and plunked back down again. "So give, already. Produce!"

Of course, I might've known. The woman never passes up a chance to scratch a back or rub an elbow, and her little black book of favors-owed is fatter than the Manhattan Yellow Pages.

"Okay," she said, "let's talk deal. You take my film studies class the week after Thanksgiving. They're on *The Thin Man* and *The Maltese Falcon.* I give you her name. The woman Vera saw with Ironpants in Manhattan." She looked at me like Chairman Mao inviting Khrushchev to a tea party. "Deal?" she purred.

"Deal, confound it," I growled. "But I warn you, Costello, if you say it was Mrs. Macauley, I'll have a billboard made of that snapshot Merriman took of you chasing Sheffield with your hooter last New Year's Eve!"

"Oh, it definitely wasn't Crazy Helen," Hilda said smugly. "It was that girl who was murdered."

My breath caught in my throat and I coughed. "Hallie Glendon and Macauley were—"

"Not Hallie. It was the Cody girl! She wasn't even out of high school, but some guys like them young. Macauley's just the type for kinky stuff, if you ask me." Hilda nodded. "There he was in Nonno Ricci's, bold as brass, squiring little Angela Cody. And ten days later she was dead."

I leaned back in the pew and sighed. Just when it looked as though the light was about to dawn in this terrible business, it got curiouser and curiouser. Everybody was connected to somebody, nobody liked anybody, everybody had a nasty secret and nobody knew what it was. Piers would've made a trick of it, I thought, like the one he called Lights and Mirrors, in which the magician walks straight through a full-length mirror and disappears, to materialize a moment later in the front row of the audience. It was, I thought, exactly like the writing of one of my Winchester Hyde mysteries, the clues coming not single spies but in battalions—except that in the books I always knew where the clues were leading and I was certain to find my way out.

Well, almost certain. Unless I screwed it up, unless I missed something and had to trash a chapter or so and start again.

But this was not so easy. If I should fail to notice something here, misjudge a character, if my old brain should overlook some crucial bit of truth, then another woman was almost certain to die at Christmas. I bit my lip and frowned, as I noticed that, although it was still almost two weeks before Thanksgiving, our baleful mascot, Alvin the stuffed moose, already had a string of tiny Christmas lights draped over his antlers and a sprig of holly up his nose.

"Christmas gets earlier every year"—how often had I heard people say it, out of frustration, weariness, or just a sense of aging and the loss of those long childhood weeks of excited waiting?

This year when I heard it, I would be afraid.

I snapped out of my thoughts as Hilda got up to go off to class. Something she'd said had suddenly set off an alarm bell in my head.

" 'Crazy Helen'?" I said. "What makes you call Macauley's missus that? Aside from the fact that she's married to Old Ironpants, that is."

"Haven't you heard, Winnie?" Hilda paused to yank down her girdle. Hilda's girdle—probably the first one ever produced in North America—is the stuff of legend in our department. "Helen Macauley's a genuine space cadet. The woman's so far out of it she's barely sure what street she lives on half the time. Why'd you think the old boy moved her to that development house way out by the cemetery instead of living in the chancellor's residence? She wanders off sometimes. Memory lapses, breakdowns. Neurotic as hell. Drugs, that's the poop."

"I'm surprised Mr. Rochester doesn't keep her locked up in the west wing," I muttered. The whole thing was beginning to sound like one of those gothic romances Merriman smuggles into the house and reads under the covers when he can't sleep.

"Rochester? Oh, you mean *Jane Eyre,*" said Hilda. "Helluva movie. Who was in that? I forget."

"I couldn't tell you, Hilda," I called after her as she quick-marched off across the lounge, the girdle making tiny pinging noises as she went. "I only read the novelization, myself."

I had never been inside James Temple Macauley's office, until my appointment with him at eleven o'clock that bright, cold November morning. Chancellors' offices are pretty much alien territory to the rank and file of higher education, old war-horses like myself steer clear of administrators so long as they leave us in peace in our fusty offices and our classrooms smelling of chalk dust and cheap disinfectant.

Which is why, when I stepped through the sleek hammered-chrome double doors into J. T. Macauley's outer office, I felt a bit like Neil Armstrong going for a stroll on the banks of the Sea of Tranquillity.

The far wall, behind the receptionist's black lacquer desk, was glass from floor to ceiling, the panes set at angles to form a sort of huge prism that caught the light a hundred different ways and made the view of the Hudson and of Maxima Bergner's two wooded acres down below seem a picture puzzle, cut into a myriad tiny, jagged pieces. There was a rank of shiny black filing cabinets along the inner wall, the one that partitioned off Macauley's private office; on the opposite wall stood a long black leather couch with chrome arms, behind it—oh, my prophetic soul!—a wall of mirrors, smoked deep gray and gleaming in the broken light from the prism window. The floor was laid with deep, wine-colored carpeting, and the ceiling had been covered with some fabric or other in the same shade. The illumination spilled down the liquid, light-enchanted walls as though from nowhere, and in the exact center of the room, on a chrome stand as tall as I was, stood a moth orchid in a black pot, its cascades of fragile white bloom as unreal—almost—as the secretary at the reception desk.

I couldn't testify as to the lady's bottom, which Piers had found so noteworthy. She didn't get up from her chair to greet me. She sat perfectly still at her desk, eyes fixed on the screen of her word processor, fingers stroking the keyboard, the small, shallow keys barely clicking as she sped along them. She was very, very young, and I couldn't help thinking of Angela Cody. What had Macauley been to her, why had they been together in Manhattan? This secretary—the sign on her desk announced her name to be Marla—wasn't more than nineteen herself, some dropout business major raised to high office by virtue of her skill with Maybelline, her overplus of crimped, bottle-blond hair, and presumably her famous bottom. She was no secretary. This was Pluto's palace, and she was its queen.

She nodded me to the leather couch, and as I waited I thought fondly of prim, aging Hannah Comfort, who has ruled the arts and letters offices for more years than she would care to name, whose idea of makeup is a dash of lily-of-the-valley toilet water behind the ears, whose hair would make Clairol weep and Toni gnash his teeth, and whose bottom—praise the saints—could not have been much to write home about even back before the glaciers melted, when she was twenty-five or so. I thought, too, of my own narrow, coffin-shaped office on the third story of our creaky-floored old red-brick building across the campus, of my splintered woodwork, cracked gray rubber tile, and battered tan steel desk and chair. A large portion of my life has been lived there, and when I am finally forced to leave, a piece of me will stay behind, a cranky old ghost to grumble in the ears of overeager young professors who might otherwise think they are unique.

"You can go in now," said Queenie, barely glancing at me. I stood up and when I did I caught a view of myself in the smoky mirrors, a lumpy old Tyrannosaurus Rex in flannel trousers that bagged at the knees, a sport coat rewoven so many times the reweaving was rewoven, and a yellowish white shirt whose front had so many holes burned in it by the ash from my Turkish Delights it seemed to have been hit by shrapnel. I did not fit, I knew, in that sleek, cold, perfect room. Pride lived there, and ambition, and the strut and trade of charms. I saw no print of kindness on the place, nor fallibility, no trace of homage to the human past a place like this purported to be all about. The past, with all its stumblings and unevenness, its passions and its failures, lived down there, nestled in Madam Max's tangled orchard and her aging house full of casual and unsung treasures. No wonder, I thought, Macauley was so determined to level it. He was not a stupid man, and to look out his spotless windows and see the place down there, a silent, constantly galling reminder of everything he had called worthless and determined to discard because its price tag was too high for ignorance to pay—it must have kept his anger sharp as a scalpel, fed his scorn with secret admiration.

For, I thought, looking down at the vista of it as I passed the windows, the place was very beautiful. An idyll such as Alex had hoped for, and had not found. It had, in James Macauley's scheme of things, no right to exist. What he and his huge and growing tribe were building round us all was a sleek and profitable prison for the human germ, the nameless yeast that lets the spirit breathe and keeps the species whole. I felt it closing on me in that vain, gleaming office where nothing real survived, I saw it in my mind's eye invading the orchard down below, the tangle of briar roses, the small jewel box of the house. The Macauleys of the race were building us a lightless, airless, solitary cell. I had, I knew, no place in the world he aimed to own, nor had Merriman, nor Piers, nor Madam Max, nor even

David, whose values, thanks to Sarah and Yours Truly, were the wrong sort altogether to survive that cell, once it was finished.

Macauley the keeper, we the kept—that was the scheme of things to come. I would have done better, I thought, to die on the kitchen floor.

James Macauley, though, seemed to find an empty room congenial. He sat in the high-backed office chair behind his glass-topped chrome desk, looking out the long window, high and narrow as an arrow slit, at Elsa Bergner's orchard and the ribbon of the Hudson winding through its bluffs. His back was to me, and I caught his reflection in the window glass, a stolid face covered with old scar tissue, but not the great red welts crisscrossed with suture lines I still saw when I looked at David's rebuilt face, the aftermath of the slashing he'd survived. Macauley's scars were smaller, a years-long trauma like a thousand tiny cuts that slowly healed and thickened— acne, perhaps, or some kind of dermatitis that recurred. They gave his face a peculiar density, robbing it of expression. When he spoke, the mouth barely moved.

"Winston," he said, and whirled the chair around. On the desk in front of him was another pot of orchids, the kind they call lady's slipper, a single stalk rising from broad leaves, a strange hooded blossom with a deep, mottled throat. "Come in," said the chancellor. "I've been expecting you." He attempted a smile, and failed. The small blue eyes were red around the rims and he seldom blinked, though his bullet-shaped head with its cap of white hair nodded with every word, as if somehow it lent him credibility and made him accessible inside his iron mask. "I hope you've come to tell me you're directing the committee to approve my suggestions for changing the curriculum."

"I've come to talk, Chancellor," I told him. "That's as much as I can say right now. I'm still thinking, and the final vote won't be until after the faculty meeting on Friday."

"You've gone over the presentation?" His hands lay on the desk in front of him, side by side like a cat's paws, the fingers stroking the blotter pad. "Is there anything in the packet I can clarify for you? All

154

the feasibility figures seem pretty self-explanatory. Our intent is to keep some of the current offerings in place on a maintenance level, and to put in the more cost-effective tracks at growth speed, cut out anything that doesn't channel.''

"And what about Krishnan Ghandour? Does he 'channel'?" I studied the heavy face, hoping for reaction. There was none on the features, no glint in the eyes. But a dull, purplish flush began at his expensive collar and crept slowly up along the scarred jawline. "How about me? Do you receive me on any of your channels, or am I getting interference? What about Shakespeare, for that matter? Dead air, I expect, but I'll bet Tennis One-oh-one is coming in loud and clear, and so's that course of Mrs. Costello's. Soap Operas: An American Art Form.''

He tried once more to smile and failed even more miserably than before, the furious flush overwhelming him. He was bitterly angry now. Or was it shame? "It's actually a very inventive course, good motivational strategy. Begin with something the student understands.''

"Don't you mean something the student doesn't have to understand? And what do you mean, 'begin'? What does he move on to, Introductory SitComs and Game Shows, Intermediate and Advanced?''

"I'd think you of all people would respect the value of popular culture. Those mysteries of yours are hardly weighty tomes, after all.'' He sniffed and the corners of the thin mouth lifted just a bit in mild amusement.

"They're books, at least,'' I said. "You have to turn the pages. You have to read the words. The plot demands some rudimentary logic if you want to get to the end. You need a mind, Macauley, and even if the food isn't as nourishing as it used to be, it's food, not cardboard soaked in wine.'' I took out a Turkish Delight and puffed at it, raining ashes on the shiny desk and showering the handsome carpet. "You never answered me about Krish Ghandour. I'm told you're intending to give him the chop. Surely you've changed your mind about that now.''

He lifted his chin, and though I hadn't thought the flush could intensify, it did. "It's imperative to reduce the number of untenured faculty. Junior staff must remain expendable, no matter how much we may like them personally. We've drawn up our list of cuts based on the student evaluations from last term. Ghandour was on that list." He tried another smile; this time he managed a smirk. "As a matter of fact, Winston, your own evaluations were a bit questionable, but of course you're tenured. Until your current contract runs out."

Of course, he knew damn well I had no contract. Since I passed the official retirement age, I work from one term to the next, at the pleasure of Sheffield and anybody who's bigger and tougher than he is. Which James Macauley certainly was.

"Of course, you're more or less a tradition here at Clinton," he said. "But traditions sometimes have to be sacrificed to more important things."

"Like cost-effectiveness and Introduction to Soap Operas?"

He actually laughed, softly and with slightly parted teeth showing. "As chairman of the curriculum committee, you could be invaluable in putting the new tracks on their feet, smoothing the transitions. You're very much respected by the other faculty. But not indispensable."

"Only God is indispensable, Macauley. Do try to remember that." I flicked the butt of my smoke onto the rug and ground it out —with considerable gusto, I might add—with the heel of my Hush Puppy. "But of course you're not going to fire Krishnan Ghandour now. Surely he's got enough problems."

He raised an eyebrow. "Dissertation problems? I'm told he isn't making much progress."

"Murder problems," I told him. "Nobody's seen him since last night. His fiancée was murdered. But I assumed you knew. After all, you were at the scene of the crime not too long afterward."

He didn't blink, and when he spoke the voice was flat and without expression.

"It doesn't change a thing," he said, and whirled his chair to face the window again. "The man is dead wood. Whatever his personal problems, he has to go."

"Didn't you hear me?" I said, my voice ringing in the empty expanse of the office. "I said you were seen snooping around in Elsa Worthing's orchard yesterday. Was that you in my garden during the night as well?"

The face reflected in the glass was lifeless, the deep flush gone now, the plastic features almost pale.

"I think we're finished," he said, the steady voice hammering out the words like a machine. "Good morning, Winston."

He leaned back and closed his eyes. At that moment, I agreed with Piers Ambrose. The man deserved to be executed. In fact, I could cheerfully have murdered him myself.

Thirteen

When the dull old fool Sherman had gone, James Macauley wanted to relax, but he could not. Whatever key had wound him tight, it had done so at birth; with the first breath he drew, the moment when his mother died, the lock had sprung that might have freed him. He grew in spirals, in upon himself. He could not reach for comfort. Who would have heard him? His father's shouts and farts and belches would've drowned out any childish voice—a decent man who filled his son with food instead of love, proud of his ignorance, besotted by cheap religion, delighted by his own vulgarity to thumb his nose at anyone who did not sweat and strain his back to earn his bread. Pimps, he called the schoolteachers who tried to befriend young James. Pansies and pimps and white-faced whores.

The boy looked up the word in the old coverless *Webster's* he had found among his mother's few books. A prostitute, it said. A harlot.

''And there came one of the seven angels which had the seven vials, and talked with me, saying unto me, Come hither; I will shew unto thee the judgment of the great whore that sitteth upon many waters:

''With whom the kings of the earth have committed fornication, and the inhabitants of the earth have been made drunk with the wine of her fornication.

"So he carried me away in the spirit into the wilderness: and I saw a woman sit upon a scarlet-colored beast, full of names of blasphemy, having seven heads and ten horns.

"And the woman was arrayed in purple and scarlet color, and decked with gold and precious stones and pearls, having a golden cup in her hand full of abominations and filthiness of her fornication:

"And upon her forehead was a name written, MYSTERY, BABYLON THE GREAT, THE MOTHER OF HARLOTS AND ABOMINATIONS OF THE EARTH."

The preacher was short and round as a rubber ball. His voice rasped like a rusty saw, and his scarlet face dripped sweat. The boy sat beside his father, both of them in disguise, or so he felt, wearing the suits they never wore except for Sunday church and funerals like his mother's. He hunched down on the hard bench, his shoulders soaked with sweat and sticking to the cheap varnish as he dreamed the woman who had died when he was born. His father had no pictures of her. The preacher said that photographs were graven images, against the will of God. Instead, the boy would stand before the cloudy, wavering mirror where his father shaved and stare into his own dense milk-blue eyes the color of cheap crockery, searching blindly in his unstocked memory, summoning her.

The whore. The mother of harlots. Mother.

Until he was seventeen, James Macauley had never touched a woman, nor been touched by one.

He and his father shared a small house of unpainted, weathered boards at the edge of Tagg Harbor, an iron-ore town on the Lake Superior shore. The men, like Butch Macauley, were mostly sailors on the lakers, the huge ore boats that plied the lakeshore down to Detroit, up to the Canadian ports. There weren't many women in Tagg Harbor, and almost no girls of James's age at all.

But there was one. She was fifteen. He never knew her Christian

159

name. He never asked. They called her Simiak's Girl, and that was quite enough.

She was a miracle. From the stuffy classroom of the Tagg Harbor High School, James watched her lope along the street. She never bothered with sidewalks, not Simiak's Girl. Her Russian father was a laker, too, and always gone, and there were stories about her mother, who would sleep, they said with anyone. Simiak's Girl had knowledge in her long, lithe limbs, the breasts that swelled under her too-tight cotton shirt, the buttocks that jiggled slightly, unconfined by panties, underneath her straining jeans. She never went to school, and no one made her. She never went to church, but a strange cross —St. Basil's Cross, she said it was—dangled between her naked breasts that baking-hot June morning in the woods beyond Macauley's house.

She found him sitting cross-legged there, a crouching, fleshy gargoyle in the cool deep shadows of the pines, staring at the choppy water of Superior that stretched, gray and mysterious, out beyond.

"They say the bottom's paved with sailor's bones," she said, a soft voice behind him. She stood very close, her rich young thighs pushing against his back and shoulders where he sat. " 'Of his bones are coral made; those are pearls that were his eyes.' "

The words meant nothing to him. He read no books. He was his father's son. Her round hands, damp in the palms, cupped his face, the fingers locked beneath his chin. Then they released him and he felt her moving, heard the press of her small feet on the carpet of pine needles where he sat. He turned, and saw her naked, the round, small, tight breasts with the great pewter cross between them, the soft curling hairs below her belly, the white thighs open as she knelt to him.

She took his hands and put them on her breasts and squeezed them tight, and he could feel her nipples tense and harden under them, a sudden surge of power he had never known he had. He hid his round face between her breasts, the great cross sharp, scraping his acne-battered cheeks, cutting into the soft flesh of her though she made no sound as her fingers found his shirt buttons, the zipper of

160

his trousers. She knew her business, Simiak's Girl did. She pulled him into her darkness suddenly, before he could think, before he needed to feel, and he emptied into her the seventeen years of blinded, dreamless silence.

Carried away into the wilderness. Those are pearls that were her eyes.

He arched above her, alone in the universe, pouring himself into the dark solar system. Caliban had at last achieved Miranda.

He knew he had the means to punish her. He wanted suddenly to hurt her, and he did. Strangely, it seemed to please her.

"God," she moaned. "Jimmy, God."

"Yes," was all he said.

His mother was the first. Then Simiak's Girl, though he did not mind much when she died. Neither had touched the center of him, though the first had given him life, the second power.

The core of him remained, nerveless, sexless, hopeless, as insensible as wood.

There was the woman at Belmont College, thought Macauley, looking out the window, and now these others, four of them. Death lived in him like the bloody flecks in the deep throat of the orchid on his desk. He had never been free of it. Perhaps it was over now. Now there were seven.

Full of names of blasphemy, having seven heads.

Something inside him seemed to stagger from a blow, to cave him in upon himself. Not finished. Not yet.

It might be his own wife, Helen. Or the German woman down there in the orchard.

Macauley got up from his desk to stand at the long slit of glass above the wooded acreage of Sorrowheart. He could see, if he strained his eyes, a small figure, like a moving dot that wove in and out, in and out, between the trees. He turned and reached into his second drawer and took out a pair of high-powered binoculars, aligned them, aimed them at the dot.

Elsa was gathering the bittersweet that twined and wound and almost choked the trees it grew upon to death. She would use it to make wreaths and ship them to the Manhattan flower shop that sold

161

things for her on consignment, baskets of dried herbs and flowers and everlasting wreaths and nosegays. Now and then she stooped, her ankle-length blue skirt whipping in the cold wind, to cut a clump of dried meadowsweet or fine-bladed grass now gone to seed, the seed heads dancing in the wind like earrings on the stalk. Her strong arms pushed aside the branches, tugged the tough vines of bittersweet free, and her back, curved as she bent and labored, seemed to feel no strain.

Macauley trained the glasses on her face. There were tears on it, smearing her cheeks. Desire for her clutched him and he looked away, as he had often done. It was she who made him want the house, the orchard down. What right had she to life without him? He despised her clean, honorable selfhood, walled into her garden.

They had had a garden at home in Michigan, he and his father, and the boy would spend long hours in it, hoeing, weeding, tending the cabbages and early peas and carrots and the rich, milky sweet corn. Earth and water, those two elements his father knew. He taught the boy the names of all the weeds that grew along the roadsides and in the dark places of the woods, the medicines you made from them, the parts a man could eat and what would do him harm. In those cool, damp woods they had found the first orchid James had ever seen, small and greenish, springing out of nowhere in a tangle of hip-high ferns, like a tiny, inscrutable wizard peering out to taunt the world with secrets. His father had no use for flowers, but James collected it, pored over books in the Tagg Harbor Public Library, tramped the woods and fields greedily, till he had gathered everything the region offered. He never thought of raising them. He knew already he would be a man of clean hands and starched white collars and expensive suits. He would become the thing his father hated most. But the startling beauty of the orchids was the only thing he loved.

He adjusted the focus of the glasses. Two other figures had joined Elsa in the orchard. One he recognized—the pianist, old Sherman's common-law wife, her graying dark-brown hair braided as she wore it day to day, in one thick plait that fell halfway down her back. A

162

short scarlet cape was draped round her shoulders, flapping in the wind that shook the bare branches.

MYSTERY, BABYLON THE GREAT, THE MOTHER OF HARLOTS.

The words were ancient, and the voice in which he heard them was the soft moaning whisper of Simiak's Girl, found dead in the Tagg Harbor woods. The wilderness.

He squeezed the binoculars tight in his two fists and looked again, and it was then he saw her. An orchid of a woman, small and perfect, her red hair tumbling around her shoulders, catching the cold light, her face freckled like an orchid's throat. A slender, surprising woman in the shadowed garden where the trees grew thick. She would be bright, he thought, like fire in the dark.

She strode away from the two older women toward the tree in the middle of the orchard where the other one had died. There were still the narrow yellow tapes around the place, and the sprayed marks on the sodden grass. The red-haired woman walked to it boldly, her arms swinging, the careless walk he remembered so well, the walk of Simiak's Girl through the Michigan woods. If she had ever been afraid, it was never for herself. She knelt down and the loose sweater she wore fell open, and under it the shirt pulled tight across her breasts as she leaned toward the ground, examining, searching for something.

The chancellor did not hear the door of his office open, then shut softly again, did not hear the footsteps move toward his desk, pause, then move off again toward the door and pause again. He took no notice of the visitor who listened, who watched the silent, sinewy figure at the long window, the spyglasses motionless, trained on the small acreage below.

"Of her bones are coral made," whispered James Macauley, following Alexandra's slightest move. "And those are pearls that were her eyes."

He seemed to crumple, clutching at the window frame. Shame and isolation beat him down like fists, and he raised the glasses, needing to see her once again. The delicate face, the subtle promise of the body, the slim, confident thighs where the wind whipped her

163

split skirt round them. He had forgotten Elsa Worthing. It was this bright mystery who mattered now.

"God," he whispered. "God, my love."

"Yes," said the voice of James Macauley, "yes," as death drew close to him on silent and inexorable feet.

Fourteen

"You damn well *do* know where Jaffer Swan is, Elsa, and you've got to tell me!" Sarah spoke urgently, her voice low enough to be certain that Alex, who'd gone nosing around the crime-scene area, wouldn't hear her. "The man's gone missing, dear heart. He may be hurt somewhere, or dead. He may be frightened and alone. You love him, don't you? Tell me where he is!"

Elsa stooped down to put a dry stalk of fall aster, its starlike blooms long gone to seed, into her basket. "The sleet knocked off so many berries from the bittersweet," she said. "A shame. But still usable, if we're clever. My girls will have a good time fooling with it anyway."

Sarah had had enough of pleading. She took her friend by the shoulders and marched her backward until Elsa's head hit the overhanging limb of a pear tree.

"Listen here," she said, fixing her friend with a steady glare. "This is *me!* Sarah! Not one of those silly women in your flower-arranging classes. *Me.* I know you sleep with Jaffer Swan. Why can't you just admit it? You think I give a damn? Sleep with the Devil, and may he show you a good time. Who knows, he might even wake you up, for pity's sake! I can't, that's obvious." She considered. "If you don't care about Swan, what about Krishnan? He's disappeared, too, Elsa. Maybe Swan knows where he is, maybe he's seen him, or knows *something!*" She grasped the straight shoulders and shook them, hard. Elsa Worthing only blinked as though the sun were in her eyes. "Damn you! If I promise not to tell the police, or even Win? If I promise to go and find Swan myself?"

Sarah felt she was walking through an unmapped landscape. What had become of the woman with whom she could communicate on instinct, without bothering to speak? With that Elsa, a flick of the lashes, a catch of breath would be enough. She had always seemed to have not merely a sixth sense, but a seventh, an eighth, all tuned as finely as an animal's and constantly registering what they recorded to a mind compounded equally of passion, cool logic, and the common sense born of dirt under the fingernails. There was no nonsense in the woman, no matter how much she might fib about her age or invent sugary memories of the sad vanished mother she had barely known.

But all that had gone now, or been driven into hiding. Or maybe Jaffer Swan had taken it away.

"Countess," said Sarah gently. She had not called Elsa by that name for years. It came from one of the wildest of the fabricated stories, in which the lost mother had been a German aristocrat. At the word, Elsa looked up at her, blinked again, half smiled, then looked away, as though she had glimpsed something through a fog and then lost sight of it. "Where is he, Countess?" said Sarah. "What's he done to you?"

Elsa squinted, seeming hardly to recognize her. "Who?" she said.

"Why, Swan. Jaffer Swan, of course."

"I don't know where he is, I tell you," said Elsa at last. She slipped easily out of Sarah's grasp and went on with her work, tugging a vine of bittersweet, still heavy with berries, out of a clump of alders along the fence line. "He works for me, that's all. What else he does with himself, how do I know?"

166

"But you *do* know!" Sarah spluttered. "You love the man, of course you know!"

Elsa laughed. She paused to pull off her heavy canvas gloves and push back the tangle of curl that fell over her forehead and stuck to her damp skin. The morning sun was warm, and work—or something else—had brought a gleam of sweat along her forehead, in the hollow of her neck.

"Oh, my darling girl," she said. "Such a goose-girl! If I sleep with him, I must love him. If I love him, I must care where he goes when he's out of my sight. If I love him, he must write me little notes. 'Liebchen, I'm spending the night at the bus stop. Don't wait up.' The sleeping, I don't deny, not to you—though I wouldn't tell your Mr. Police my bedtime stories, naturally. Why should I?" She shrugged, put on the gloves again, and went back to her work. Carmine berries rained down upon her as she tugged at a stubborn vine above her head. "Graham is no longer interested to speak of. I was hungry. My wandering Swan was there, a picnic lunch. As for love—do you love food once you've eaten it?"

"She's horrid, isn't she?"

Maxima Bergner's sour, clotted syllables rang on the bright air. She moved well for her age, with some stiffness but none of the timorous unsteadiness with which Sarah had seen so many old women walk, as though the hands of the dead might reach up any minute from below the ground and trip them. Madam Max came strongly, her head held high, her thin legs in their neat blue trousers moving like scissors, the heavy wool cardigan wrapped close round her, buttoned tight. She put a bony hand on Sarah's arm as she joined them, and a thrill of energy seemed to pass from her.

Eleanor of Aquitaine, thought Sarah, might have walked so through her gardens, or the first Elizabeth, laden with Drake's pearls, ridden out to count her waiting ships. Wherever the fragile membrane lives that guards the wholeness of the human riddle, keeps it from perversity on one side and despair on the other, it had, in Madam Max, survived for eighty-four long years inviolate. The clear old eyes looked out from a tough mind that had never tricked itself into delusions, that needed no invented memories. The aged body, too, was tough, like the vines of bittersweet. She had married for love, a man of courage who kept her whole and strong, left her to grow as she wished, built her no loving prisons.

Like Win, thought Sarah suddenly. But Alois Bergner had died before his wife. Yesterday, seeing Winston in that hospital, those tubes and wires . . . How had she borne it, Maxima, to be alone when her Alois was gone? How had he dared to leave her?

He's old. The thought came like a brutal blow against her throat and she tried to swallow and could not. *Winston is older than I am and will die before me, and I will be alone in my house like Madam Max in hers.*

Danger and violent death were one thing. She could fuss and scold and rage against the risks he took, and in the end, because they were equals, she could share the odds with him and if he died, they both would die. But this episode—that's what he called it, now that it was past—this seizure, heart attack, reaction, fit. It might happen again at any time, and smash him. There was no raging against it. There was only what he had guarded with her, as Alois had guarded it for Madam Max—the freehold of herself. Sarah grasped the thin old fingers with their scarlet nails and held them tight.

But Maxima was not alone. She had Elsa and her secrets. If anyone knew them, surely it was Madam Max.

"Her father would be scandalized, you know," the old lady said. "Alois was an idealist, like yourself, Sarah dear. Straight through the bombing in the war. Civilization would not have existed, he used to say, without men of absolute ideals." She cackled softly. "But then, Herr Hitler had them, didn't he? Elsa and I are realists. We have our house to keep. Haven't we, my dear?"

" 'A picnic lunch'?" Sarah shook her head. "That's not what I call realism, Madam Max. It's just cheap, garden-variety cynicism, calculated to put me off whatever it is she's hiding." She kicked a shriveled pear out of the grass with a vengeance and sent it flying. "Does Mr. Swan realize he's only a convenience so far as you're concerned?" Nothing else had touched this veiled and hidden Elsa. Maybe anger would. Sarah fairly spat the words at her. "Does he know he's only something you fell down with because he happened to be handy? And what, my dearest girl, does that fact make of *you?*"

What happened next was so sudden that even Madam Max was stunned by it. Elsa had been winding the rope of bittersweet she had just freed into the deep collecting basket at Sarah's feet, bent over from the waist, her face invisible. At the question, she straightened suddenly and when she struck, her aim was true. It was no open palm that connected with Sarah's face. It was a fist, hard as a man's inside the heavy canvas work glove. Sarah reeled but didn't fall, and in another blink it came again.

"Fools!" cried Madam Max. Sarah heard the acid old voice as she fell, and from among the trees she saw the shape of Alex running toward her, arms fighting back the branches.

Then suddenly she was in Elsa's arms, both of them on the cold, wet ground.

"My dear," crooned Elsa softly, "my lovely dear. I didn't mean it, darling. Why did you push so hard?"

Sarah shoved her away and sat up, her head pounding. There was blood all over her, the bright red cape stained dark as wine. She passed a hand over her face, found where the blood had come from. The bridge of her nose was swollen, maybe broken, and two of her teeth seemed to be loose. She struggled to get away, to get up. She couldn't bear to look at Elsa now, to be touched by her. The voice was familiar, the great sorrowing eyes, the mass of wild curls escaping from the pins. But it was a clever disguise, that was all. This was nobody Sarah knew.

"Alex," she mumbled. She hardly heard herself, forced the words out louder. "Where's Alexandra?"

An arm grasped her. "I'm here," Alex reassured her softly. Her eyes never left Elsa's face as she helped her sister-in-law to her feet. "Can you walk?"

"Walk? Of course I can walk, I—"

Alex's voice was low and urgent and her grip was strong although her fragile features were taut with fear. What she had seen through the orchard trees was like the scene that had played over and over in her mind since the rainy night in another autumn when her husband's face was slashed by a madman—sudden, surreal, unstoppable. But in some way, this had been even worse. They were all women. They knew each other and were friends. Women did not strike at women as men struck other men.

"The car's by the greenhouse," Alex said. "Back away. Don't move too fast."

The words didn't seem to make sense to Sarah. The woman who had hit her was not Elsa. Whoever had worn that disguise was gone now, and Elsa was herself again, looking worried, biting her lower lip, tears pouring soundlessly down her face.

Elsa got up from the ground and took Sarah's other arm. The grip was hard but not angry, only meant to support. Her voice when she spoke was barely audible, an inner monologue like Jaffer Swan's.

"He's gone," she said. "Jaffer is gone. And Graham, too."

"The fool's gone, too? Thank God," breathed Maxima.

"When?" Sarah could feel the grip on her arm relaxing, and she slipped away and backed a step or two, with Alex at her side.

"This morning, early. Off he went in his fancy shiny car. Maybe he drives over a cliff, how do I know?" Elsa sank down beside the basket full of dead weeds and tangled vines. "He's finished with me. Now I can be alone."

So she is, thought Sarah. *Nothing I am has reached her. Nothing I have ever done or said.*

Maxima brushed a hand delicately over Sarah's bruised face. "Some women have potent roots. You can drive nails into us and we survive and thrive. You and I, my dear—we can lose anything, and live. But Elsa—" She paused and her red-tipped fingers drifted to Alexandra's cheek, then down her arm. "Elsa, and this lovely one here? One wonders. Doubts and wonders." The old woman let her hand fall to her side. "Do *you* think Swan murdered Harriet Glendon and the others?"

It was Alexandra who answered her. "How can we think at all? We barely know the man. But you do. Don't you?"

Madam Max smiled. "I know a voice, a sad, silly tune played on a clarinet. A pair of hunched shoulders under a cheap jacket. I liked what I saw. A fine way of speaking, a way with other people's words. He might've been anything. He chose to be nothing. Always a tenuous equation, and difficult to trust."

"You think he's a murderer because he lacks ambition?" Alex could feel Elsa's eyes on her, but she forced herself to concentrate on Maxima.

"I think he's one of God's fools," the old woman said softly. "There are two sorts, you know. God's and the Devil's. Macauley is the other kind."

"You won't need to worry about him for a while, at least."

Maxima looked up. "Won't I, indeed? Perhaps not. But someone should. Someone should certainly worry about James Macauley, and soon."

"You know where Swan is, don't you, Max?" said Sarah gently. "Were you awake in the night? What did you see down here?"

"Go home," the old woman told her, an edge of impersonal disgust on the acerbic voice. She had had enough of the human race and was weary of it. "Go home and wash the blood off, Sarah," she said with a soft laugh. "What a fearful aspect you present, my dear! The Angel of Death could hardly look worse."

"Max." Sarah's voice compelled attention. "If you need help. If you see Swan again. You must call me. A promise."

"I have made only one promise in the whole of my life, girl, and that was to my husband." Madam Max's voice rang on the cold air. "I will do what *I will do,* and that is all."

Alexandra put her arm closer through Sarah's and they had turned to go, when suddenly Elsa stood up and walked quickly forward, to stop on the path in front of them. For an instant they looked at one another, the trio of women, one face battered, one tear-stained, and one—Alexandra's—clear and perfect and so intense with concentration and emotion and the ghosts of private

171

memory it seemed to shimmer in the light. She was scarcely certain what was happening when Elsa darted forward and kissed her, softly, lips barely brushing her cheek.

"Please," she said. "I am— I am—"

Elsa stopped there, pulled away shyly and stood with her head down. *It is how her mother must have looked,* thought Sarah suddenly, the image blinding her mind's eye. *When they took her away, she must have stood and looked down, so, trying to remember what crime she had committed unawares. Trying to remember what it felt like to be whole again. Death,* thought Sarah, whose own mother had left her when she was a girl. She remembered the slender, elegant woman in expensive furs, poised at the end of the drive where the taxi waited, remembered the pale face that turned, wide-eyed, to look back at her father's house and the child with long dark braids in the upstairs window.

The death of the heart is long, she thought, *and slow.*

She put both arms around her friend and held her tight, and Elsa did not move nor speak nor reach out to hold her in return.

"Schande," she whispered. *"Schande, mein Herz."*

"What does it mean?" asked Alex as she got behind the wheel. Sarah had not spoken all the way from the orchard to the greenhouse, since Elsa had kissed her and they'd parted at last. "What does the word mean, the German word she said? *Schande,* was it?"

Sarah stared out the car window at the figures of Elsa and the old woman, now walking hand in hand along the path toward Sorrowheart. "Shame," she said. "The word means shame at heart."

"What do you mean, why don't I get counseling?" I was garbed in a snappy little number that resembled an outsized green paper napkin, and Hadley Pennington, our family quack, was tickling my manly chest with the coldest stethoscope north of Miami. "How long have I been doing *what?*"

"There's no need to cover it up with me, Winnie," said Penny in that tone of omnipotence they issue with the black bag and the white coat. "I've seen it often enough, this sort of thing. Sexual dysfunction, is it? Not unusual at your age. Crumbling self-image, doubting one's manhood. Out with it. I *am* a doctor of medicine, you know."

"Could've fooled me," I growled. "I thought you were The Iceman, who Cometh. Can't you breathe on that blasted thing and warm it up? No, on second thought, let me. You'd probably ice it over." Then it hit me like a left-hand punch. "Sexual WHAT? What the hell are you babbling about, Penny?"

"Trouble in bed," he said. He folded up the frigid instrument of torture, and I grunted down off the table and put my pants on. My attire seemed to be giving the man ideas. "A lot of men have it, at your age. They take it out on their wives. In your case, not-wives. I've recommended she call the Center for Battered Women, and you ought to go in for counseling yourself, you old ass."

"Battered—" I sat down and began to put on my shoes. "Are you talking about Sarah?"

"She came in this morning," he said. "The nose wasn't broken, but there was a lot of bruising and some damaged tissue. She'll heal. You were lucky. But obviously, there's a problem somewhere, and I can't find any physical cause for your collapse yesterday, either. You're still taking the blood pressure pills, you say. So, it's stress, I assume. Emotional problems. And, naturally, you need to lose weight."

"So do you, you old fake, you've got thirty pounds on Orca, the Killer Whale," I said. From the neck up, old Penny looked like one of those jumbo California grapefruit that make me dizzy in the produce aisle at Red Apple—round and bald and shiny and a nauseating shade of yellow, like Charlie Brown with a hormone problem and jaundice. "But do you mean that Sarah came to see you this morning?"

After my meeting with Macauley, I'd had a class to teach, then lunch with Merriman, who was taking Krish's students till he surfaced. Neither of us had been home and nobody had phoned. Sarah had meant to go out to Elsa's for a talk. If Swan had been waiting for her—

173

But Doc Penny was like a dog with a bone. "It's probably just transitional stress, Winston, facing retirement, old age. A bad self-image. Naturally, Sarah doesn't admit what's happened, she's a proud woman."

"What *did* happen, for the love of Pete? Is she all right?" I pulled on my jacket and jammed my old touring cap onto my head. "Is she in pain or—anything?"

"She's fine, but she must come to terms with what's happened. How long have you been beating her, Winston? She simply can't accept it, you see. I suppose it would alter her whole attitude to you, all her definitions. She might even have to leave you, find a new life-style—"

"You sound exactly like that Barbie doll who does the Minute for Your Health segment on the Seven O'Clock News—the one who looks like a panda bear in drag? I tell you, I DIDN'T HIT SARAH! I've never laid a hand on her in my life. Well, not *that* kind of a hand, anyway."

"Things will only get worse if you don't confront the problem. I mean, really, Winnie! She actually told me she ran into a door!"

I was about to walk out *his* door, when the old quack coughed slightly, which is his idea of an emotional outburst.

"You haven't got the number of that counseling center," Penny said primly.

"No," I said, "but I've got yours, you aged twit! 'How long have you been beating your wife?' I tell you, Pennington, with a brain like yours you ought to run for president. Your country needs you, and it might save countless lives. Including yours!"

"He actually asked me how long I'd been beating you up." I squeezed the ice water out of another washrag and laid it on Sarah's jaw.

"What did he say about your heart?" Her voice was muffled by the cold compress, her jaw was bruised and swollen, her nose was turning black and blue, and she'd ordered one of my jumbo eggnogs

174

for dinner, but otherwise she seemed her usual self. As for me, I'd beaten the land speed record getting home on my old bike, and if there'd been anything the matter with my pumps and hoses, they surely would've played out on me going up that last hill to the house. "Did Penny check everything?"

"The old poop checked things I'd forgotten I had," I told her. " 'Sexual dysfunction,' indeed."

"What!" She exploded in a snort of laughter, then groaned, holding her nose. "What did you say?"

"Never mind. He says I'm working too hard and I ought to take a banana boat to Tahiti. Want to join me? Don't pack clothes, you won't need them."

I laid another cold cloth on her jaw and she winced. "Don't make me laugh. I feel as if I've been to George Washington's dentist."

David came in from the kitchen with a bowl of ice, a refresher for the cold cloths. "Alex is still shaking," he said. "What the hell happened?"

"And what does the other guy look like? That's what I want to know," I said. "What on earth did you say to Elsa? She's the last person on earth I'd ever have expected to fly off the handle and bust you one. And you, of all people. I mean, to be honest, I've always been just a tad jealous of the bond between you two. Sort of thing that never really happens between a man and a woman."

"Piffle," said Sarah. "You know me better than any woman ever could, you old ninny."

"Maybe," I told her, still dubious, "but it's a cinch neither of us knew Elsa as well as we thought we did."

"I can't make her out at all, Winston," said Alexandra. She came huffing in and dumped an armful of firewood into the box beside the hearth, then dropped to her knees to lay the blaze. "I've been going to those classes of hers since we've been here. You know, getting into the rural spirit, rather. Herbs and flowers, all that. And I've admired Mrs. Worthing from the first. She's always in control, all those gossipy ladies interrupting and dropping things, and we've no taste at all, most of us, not compared with hers. She has a flair, you know. A sureness of touch with line and color. An eye. Trained by all those treasures in the house, I suppose. And there's nothing she doesn't know about plants and herbs—old myths, stories, history back to the Egyptians. I know it sounds idiotic, but I've thought, listening to her, that she's a sort of earth spirit, you know? There's some crucial thing in her that seems to have died out in most of us, something that heals and preserves and restores, and stays bound to the earth. Three hundred years ago, she'd have been burnt for a witch." She lit the fine sticks of kindling and sheltered the tiny blaze with her hands until it caught. "Until this morning, I'd never seen her the least bit impatient, and certainly not angry. She went off like a land mine."

"Maybe more like a pressure cooker," suggested David. "From what you tell me, it sounds as though her life's coming down around her ears. Lover ducked out on her. Marriage pretty much a sham. And living with good old Madam Max must be something like being a lady-in-waiting to Catherine the Great. The old woman even owns the house. Elsa's only got her plants, her gardens."

"And Macauley will have those, once Lloyd Agate figures out who murdered Hallie Glendon out there and the legal shackles are off." I sank wearily into my good old sagging armchair and watched Alex's fire mount and grow. "I don't blame the woman for exploding. But at Sarah, for pity's sake?"

My battered unwife sat up, dumped the cold cloth into the basin of water with a resounding plop and blinked, letting her assorted aches level off. She bit her lip thoughtfully, and regretted it.

"Winston?" she said.

"Kiddo?"

"Will Macauley really get Elsa's place? The house and the orchards, everything? Will Mayor Tebbs and the council just—just take it? I mean, after you pointed out the lack of precedent, the legal risks—will they?"

"Anything's possible," I said. "But if I know Tebbs, he'll go with the big boys. Macauley's given them a whole file of dandy facts and figures all doctored to say exactly what he wants them to say. The college brings thirty-five million a year to the town, employs six hundred people. It's a smoke screen, naturally. The thirty-five million is padded with government grant money the town never sees; three quarters of the six hundred employees are part-time, like me. But when Macauley and his pal Stormin' Norman get up to address the council, they're talking to the same boys they tee off with every Saturday and tip a couple with on Friday nights."

"The game's fixed, then," said David. "The old-boy network."

"It's not a game. Not to Elsa." Sarah spoke with absolute certainty. "It's a war. Oh, don't you see? That old place is a tiny country of her own. If she loses, she's a displaced person all over again."

"Oh, come now, kiddo. There's been a murder in her backyard, naturally she's not herself. And anyway, she'll be paid for the place, she and Max. There are other pieces of land with trees on them."

I wanted to make her feel better, but since I didn't believe what I was saying myself, it didn't work. I knew Sarah was right. Hallie's death might've been the catalyst, but the strain on Elsa had been intense during the past few weeks of struggle with the city fathers and the college. Macauley's assault on her small haven of fields and woodlands must have thrown Elsa Worthing straight back into her wartime girlhood. She had come out of broken Europe to this tiny sovereign kingdom where Madam Max ruled; old Bergner, like Prospero on his island, pondered the paradox of history; and no invader ever threatened the calm of music, books, and growing things. Even when Elsa married Graham, she had contrived to stay there, as though the world might drop off suddenly at the boundaries of the place and fall away in chasms and tempests.

"I wish somebody'd kill him," said Sarah suddenly. "I wish some public-spirited citizen would just walk up to James Macauley and shoot him in the head."

177

It was Pluto's Queen who found him, the receptionist called Marla. She had left her office for only a few moments, she told Agate later, to get a soda from the machine downstairs. When she returned, she found the door to James Macauley's private office ajar, and stepped inside to see if he had wanted something.

She found him lying in front of his desk, the afternoon light from the long slit window striking like a spotlight at him. The top of his head had been blown away.

On the desk, the pot of lady's slipper orchid had been shattered by a bullet. Beside Macauley's appointment book lay a hypodermic needle and a vial of cloudy liquid, tangled in a long necklace of gleaming, jagged black coral dropped carelessly on the blotter.

There was a smell, too—a fragrance, rather. Marla knew Macauley's musky after-shave, but that was not the scent. It was sweet and edged with sharpness, and hung heavy in the air.

Through all this, the girl Marla did not scream, nor even gasp. She was very young, and to the young death, so long as it is not theirs, remains a fiction, no matter how close it comes. It was only when she saw the man covered with Macauley's blood step from behind the door, only when she looked into the hungry mouth of the gun he pointed at her, that the girl began to scream and scream and did not stop until there were police and doctors and another sort of needle in her arm.

The gun was a nine-millimeter Webley automatic, and the man who held it was Krishnan Ghandour.

IV.

Lights
and
Mirrors

Fifteen

The autumn sun through the narrow slit of window in Macauley's office was almost gone when I got there. Lloyd had phoned me with the news of Krish's arrest, and David ran three red lights driving me over to the administration tower. But when we got there, Krishnan was nowhere to be seen, and neither was Agate.

From a neighboring office I could hear a woman's voice, sobbing.

The forensics team were still taking photos, and the medical examiner, a starchy middle-aged woman who might've been Hortense's mother superior, was squatting beside the thing on the floor in front of the chancellor's huge desk.

I do not use the word out of disgust nor disrespect for the dead nor lingering rage at what the man had been. A thing is simply what he had become, that's all. Macauley's nature had been secretive, wrapped in suspicion and self-defense. None of us had really known him. None of us had wanted to, least of all myself. Old Ironpants, I'd called him, and the Iron Chancellor, cheap labels that made of him in life what he had so brutally become in death—a thing.

Don't get me wrong. The fact that he was dead hadn't made me suddenly wish I'd known him better. It only made me wonder why the labels had been enough.

I forced myself to stare head-on at what was left of James Temple Macauley. There wasn't much. The face was almost completely gone, the top of the head blown away. The desk and the ceiling were spattered with what I knew must've been fragments of skull and brains. His body lay flat on the carpet parallel to the desk, the shattered pot of orchids not far away.

I had seen the dead before, some drifted off in the peaceful confusion of old age, some caught in the great mindless bitter gears of greed and crushed to death. I had seen men—and women— stabbed, hit by cars, shot to pieces, beaten until they were unrecognizable. No one who lives as close to any city in the modern world as I do to Manhattan could avoid such sights, and in the past few years, I had begun to study them, to seek them out and enter them like a man with a candle in his hand picking his way down a windy tunnel of horrors. Death and I had gotten fairly well acquainted, long before my collapse on the kitchen floor.

But James Macauley was like no other dead man I had ever seen. With all the others I had felt something—pain, anger, compassion. Something. As I looked down at the shattered body on the office floor, I tried to imagine his grieving widow. I could not. I felt nothing, as I'm sure he had intended, and it scared hell out of me. Even now, he was in control.

My eyes glazed and watered as though there were a fire in the room and I stumbled to a chair and sank down. It was only as I sat mopping my face with my pocket handkerchief and taking deliberate deep breaths that I realized what David was up to on the other side of the office. He was exercising his charm on the tough little steam engine of a medical examiner.

"I don't know how you keep your objectivity," he told her, "in a job like yours. But then I suppose you've seen every means of suicide there is. This one is more or less unique, though, wouldn't you say?"

"Barrel in the mouth?" she said, sounding bored. "Nothing unique about it, except that he didn't screw it up and just wind up brain-damaged, like half the jerks who try it. Wish they'd use a little imagination."

"I assumed it was murder, to tell the truth," Davy said. "The man wasn't well-liked, and I understood they'd arrested Krishnan Ghandour."

The lady medic was positive. "Has to be suicide. Powder burns on the victim's fingers. Angle of the shot. He must've done it right here on the floor. See how the bullet went up through that pot of flowers on the desk after it passed through the skull?"

David followed her gesture, then closed his eyes for a moment. I could see his long body sway slightly, and he reached out a hand to brace himself against the corner of the desk.

"Here, on the floor?" I said. I got up and forced myself to come close to the thing again. "Why would he do that? Why not in the chair, where he'd have been sitting anyway? What sense does it make for him to walk around the desk and sit down on the floor and *then* shoot himself?"

The ME shrugged. "Suicides do weird things. Maybe he didn't want to mess up his desk. Maybe he didn't want to risk shooting out the window. You'd be surprised the goofy stuff you run across in these cases."

"What can you tell us about the time of death, Doctor?" David asked.

"He couldn't have been dead more than fifteen, twenty minutes when the secretary found him," she said. "Four-ten, four-fifteen, that'd be my estimate."

I noted she had not said "my guess." Dr. Betsey Garwood, as her official police badge proclaimed her, didn't look the sort of woman who'd ever taken a flyer on anything.

She snapped her medical bag shut and stood up, pulled a Kleenex out of her sweater pocket and began to wipe her eyes, just as I had done a minute before.

"What *is* that smell in here, Doctor?" I asked her. "Some kind of smoke, is it? But Macauley didn't smoke, he was a real crusader. Not an ashtray in the place."

"You're right, Winnie." David was standing beside the long, narrow window where the last of the afternoon light fell past him into the room. "Switch off the ceiling lights, will you?"

I did, and it became plain enough as the thin beam of dusky light fell in at the window and cut like a sword through the haze of smoke that still hung in the airless room.

"Somebody's burnt *something* in here," I said. "Anything in the wastebasket?"

Davy peered into the elegant chrome bucket. "Nothing."

"Probably the secretary's herbal cigarettes," said the ME, trotting toward the door. "They're a helluva fad these days."

"Was she the woman I heard crying down the hall?" David asked her softly.

"God, I hate a weeper," said Dr. Betsey. "No, this one works in the registrar's office, end of the hall. Swears she heard two shots, but the elevator repairman was crashing around right then. She's been bawling in there ever since they found the body. I offered her a sedative, but no. She likes to cry, right?" She looked down at Macauley's ruined body. "Who the hell knows? Maybe she was in love with him. Poor sonuvabitch. I suppose somebody must've been."

When Dr. Betsey had gone, the body lay covered and only the shattered pot of orchids remained in view, the long, slender shaft with its hooded blossom wilted now, and dead. One of the forensics boys, Sergeant Dennis Milman, who'd been digging the bullet out of the office ceiling, came down from his aluminum ladder and almost put his hoof into the broken plant.

"You wouldn't have to have an ashtray," said David quietly. "You *could* burn something in that flowerpot."

"And if you *happened* to fire a bullet into it and the pot broke and the bullet and the ashes got thrown away with the wreckage—"

He finished the equation. "Nobody'd ever know what it was you burned."

Milman was about to sweep the broken pot into the wastebasket, when his boss, Lieutenant Agate, came in from the outer office.

"Hold it, Denny!" barked Lloyd. He strode into the room and

184

swooped up a king-size evidence bag, shoving his puzzled sergeant out of the way. Then Agate knelt down beside the ruined flowerpot and lifted the fragments, with potting soil and roots still clinging to them, carefully into the bag. He glanced down at what he'd got, then up at me. The medics with the stretcher came in for Macauley's body and I had to step aside. When they were gone, Lloyd stood up and frowned, the bag of dirt and shards still in his hands. He laid it on the desk. "You sure you want me to look in there, Doc?" he said. "If there's a bullet, that means the suicide was rigged."

I considered. "What you mean is, if it looks like suicide, Krish is in the clear. If it's murder, he's your chief suspect."

Agate nodded. "Secretary found him in here staggering around with the weapon in his hand. He can't account for himself since he left you guys at the depot last night. Some weird story about knives and ice. No alibi, not even a memory of where he slept. On the other hand, the means of death and the angle of the bullet aren't all that makes it look like suicide. There was a note. Kind of."

He pointed to a plastic-sheathed piece of typing paper lying on the desk beside two other evidence bags. The note was typed, probably on the word processor in the outer office. It looked exactly like the print on Macauley's edicts to the faculty that appeared in our mailboxes each week.

The note consisted of a single, resonant word, in glaring capital letters.

GUILTY.

David was peering at the label on one of the other bags. It contained a hypodermic needle and a vial of vaguely cloudy liquid. "Diginox?" he said.

Agate nodded. "Betsey says it's been diluted from capsules. Not quite all dissolved, see that?" There was a puddle of grainy sediment at the bottom of the vial. "'Course, we'll get a regular lab job on it, but it's gotta be."

Davy raised a skeptical eyebrow. "Pretty neat, wouldn't you say? A cryptic confession anybody could've typed out, a bottle of the poison that killed four women?"

"And naturally," I said, "the necklace in that bag is Hallie Glendon's, the one Sarah saw around her neck out in that orchard."

Agate nodded, poking at the thing. "Coral's sharp, even when it's polished like that, but those marks on her neck weren't just from wearing it. Somebody pulled it off her in a big hurry, between the time Miss Cromwell saw it on her and the time we got there."

"Swan? He was in the orchard." David frowned.

"And so was Piers Ambrose," I reminded them, "and according to him, so was this poor fellow here. Not likely you'll get any good prints off those skinny little spines of coral, is it, Lloyd?"

"Can't tell. Some of the pieces are big enough." The cop studied the necklace with a skeptical eye, and heaved a sigh of frustration. "We wasted half a day out in that orchard looking for this thing, and all we found was a couple ladders and an old pruning knife of Axel Engstrom's. Now here it is, all wrapped up with bows on."

I nodded. As usual, we seemed to be thinking on the same track. "A handy-dandy frame-up kit, neatly packaged, and with all the ends tied up, since the fellow in the frame happens to have his head blown off at the moment," I grumbled.

"So we're meant to believe Macauley murdered those women, including Hallie. Took her necklace for a souvenir and then was overcome with remorse and shot himself to death, after selecting a propitious spot in front of his desk?" David shrugged in disbelief.

"Even *I* never wrote anything *that* bad," I said.

"I gather he was a pretty strange guy," said Agate. "And he *did* fire that gun not more than an hour ago. It's just far-out enough to be possible, you know?"

I nodded. "I have to admit, I could see him using those orchids for target practice, all right." I didn't say it, but the single word on that confession was consistent with what I knew about Macauley, too. I thought of Sheffield's story of the woman at Belmont College years ago, and wondered how many other victims there had been since. Certainly, from what I remembered of her face, the chancellor's wife, Helen, was one.

Still, though the egoism and the guilt might be true enough, the suicide was not. I couldn't have been more certain. If there had been a seed of death in those dull blue eyes, it was not Macauley's own.

"I could *almost* buy it, Lloyd," I said. "I really could. Except—"

"Except for *that*," Davy was bent over the desk, squinting at the bag of potting soil and wilted lady's slipper orchids. "See there? It must've lodged against the drainage shards and the root ball."

He was right. Almost hidden by the tangle of roots and the muck of soil was a bullet, its blunt nose flattened still more by its collision with the pot.

No matter how much I might've wanted to ignore it, there the damn thing was, staring at us, right where all three of us had known it would be.

And Krish, I thought, was where we'd all been afraid *he* would be, where we'd just helped put him—up to his neck in trouble.

Lloyd Agate glared down at the array of evidence that might be turned against my friend. Then he looked me straight in the eye, his broad face angry and confused. "Remember what I said before, Doc, when I found that book with the Easter card in it out at Reeney's? I'm being had, goddamn it, and all I can do is play along till I figure out who's pulling my strings! This guy isn't just a murderer, Doc. He's a fucking con man!"

Lloyd and his boys loaded the dubious evidence into their car and headed for the station, where Krish would be questioned. Marla, Macauley's secretary, had been taken to Ainsley Memorial and the tender ministrations of my old buddy Hortense, and was too deeply sedated to be any use in interrogation until at least tomorrow morning. Helen Macauley had been told about her husband's death, and out of regard for her nervous condition, questioning had been put off for her as well. My bereaved and frightened colleague, it seemed, was the center attraction of the evening.

We found him in a small, bare room two doors from Lloyd's cluttered office, a cliché of a room you might've seen on television, with one of those two-way mirrors that was a sort of picture window when you looked into it from the dark, narrow hallway outside. By the time David and I got there, Agate was already inside asking questions. Watching and listening, seeing Krish's stricken face without being able to speak a word in his defense, was one of the hardest things I've ever had to endure.

"Where did you go when you left Dr. Sherman and Miss Cromwell at the depot last night?" asked the lieutenant.

Krish sat at the end of a longish rectangular table, its pale oak scarred by a million cigarette ends and scored by another million pencils. Lloyd sat around the corner of the table, a file of papers scattered in front of him. The light in the room seemed very bright from the dark hallway where David and I stood, and it lent the scene an eerie unreality, as though we were living out one of Piers's magic tricks.

"When you ran out of the parking lot at the train station," Agate repeated, "after you'd heard your fiancée was dead, where did you intend to go?"

The woman officer taking the notes sat with her pencil poised, but Krish said nothing. He did not seem to understand.

"Would he like an interpreter?" said the steno cop.

Lloyd shook his head. "Give him a minute."

Krish had been sitting with his hands in his lap. Now he lifted them up as though they were very heavy and laid them flat on the grimy table in front of him. He was a slight fellow in his middle thirties, a bit taller than men of his heritage often are, but with something of fragility in his cautious step, his way of searching a room with his great dark eyes before he could be comfortable. As though, I thought, he knew something was waiting for him in innocuous disguise and would one day single him out without warning.

Wherever he had spent the night, he hadn't had an easy time of it. The black-rimmed glasses he always wore were missing. One sleeve of his tasteful dark suit was ripped and his tie was gone, his shirt collar open and several buttons pulled off. His face was scratched and so was his throat where the collar fell open, a strange level scratch that had barely marked his tea-colored skin exactly over the crucial vein.

"I had some idea to find her," he said at last, so softly that if the sound system in the room hadn't been sensitive, I wouldn't have heard him at all. "Hallie had simply gone, you see. To my mind. I thought, if I only looked hard enough—"

"Where did you look for her?" Lloyd spoke gently, over the scratching of the steno's pencil. "Did you go to her apartment? Did you have a key?"

He knew the answer to that, of course, and so did I. When Krish went missing, we'd called everybody we could think of, and Agate had questioned Hallie's landlady shortly before we did.

"I ran," said Krishnan. "Very fast. There was, I think, rain on the street, and it was cold. Ice. I went to Hallie's house, yes, but there was no light in her windows, and I did not have the key. No. She offered me, once. But I felt I had no right. I thought to protect her—her—"

He broke off and sat staring at his own reflection in the two-way mirror. I could've sworn he saw me, there in my safe, dark spy-hole. His eyes seemed to search for me, and when at last, through that barrier between us, they met my own, I looked away as if he had really been able to see me. I felt guilty of what was happening to him, ashamed that I could not stop it. I was furious at kind, careful Lloyd Agate, who was doing only what he had to do. We had been turned into weapons against the very thing we stood for, like honorable soldiers drafted into the army of some tyrant, performing horrors in the name of duty.

He will never be the same, I thought, looking at Krish's ravaged countenance. Wherever wholeness lives, and open trust, and the unviolated atom of human energy that gives courage to imagination, that spurs the mind, gives birth to civilizations, weeds them like a garden and keeps them strong, wherever the secret center of a man or a race of men may be, this battering had found it in Krishnan Ghandour and ripped a piece away. It was a violation like the bombing of helpless cities, and I in my dark hall was helpless, too.

He will learn to be nothing. The words rang in my ears. *He will learn to endure until he dies, like prisoners of war.*

I had to stop what was happening to him, put it right. I was not fighting now merely to help out a friend. The war was mine now. I had seen my future in his face.

"Like a smoke?" Lloyd offered Krishnan a packet of cigarettes, the cheap generic kind he always carries for prisoners and suspects.

Krish stared at them, puzzled. "Smoke? No. It is proven to be unwise for the—health. I—" He paused, looking at his hands on the table. "I went to the trees. Through the campus. I ran through the parking lots. This I remember. The ice. I fell on the ice. Like skating. I have never learned to skate."

"You went to the trees? You mean the Grosvenor Arboretum?"

"No, no. The orchard. Mrs. Worthing's orchard. Where Hallie—"

"You knew where Hallie was killed?" Agate's voice was suddenly sharp.

"Winston had told me, surely?" Krish began to be afraid. "How else would I have known?"

Agate took a deep breath and sat fiddling with the cigarette packet. "It was raining. Turning to ice. You were in the orchard alone—"

"Ah," said Krish. "Not alone. I could not find Hallie, you see. I was— I had begun to understand that she was— That she would not be found." He paused, the hands on the table cupped slightly, relaxed again. "There was someone else. I was distraught. It was very dark, the rain, the sleet. I found a knife beside a tree. I had an idea of death, you see." He looked up at Agate. "He took the knife from me. It was very cold. I had become— I remember his hands, very strong, under my arms. I remember walking. I remember a long narrow room that was warm, and I lay there a long time.''

''The man,'' said Agate. ''Who was the man you met in the orchard?''

Krish's big eyes were brimming with tears. ''I don't know. How do I know he was even real? When I woke up, I was wandering around the halls of the administration building, empty halls, all but a few of the people gone home. I found a door open, I walked in. He was lying there. Macauley. The gun was on the floor. I picked it up. Then the screaming. So much screaming.''

''Let's get back to the man. Did you get a look at him? Can you describe him?''

''He knew,'' said Krishnan softly, ''how to live without hope.''

''Was he a big man? You said he had his hands under your arms. Did he lift you?''

''Yes. Oh, yes. A long way, in the dark. He was very strong. Not large, but strong. A pale face. The eyes very clear.'' Krish paused, thinking, trying to remember. ''How can I explain? It was— Could you recall clearly a dream once you have waked up? Images, perhaps. Flashes of memory. But a careful description? A name? It is not possible, not for me. Perhaps I lack discipline.''

Agate said nothing. ''Okay, Dr. Ghandour. Now, you were out of town at the time Miss Glendon was killed, right?''

''Mr. Ghandour,'' said my friend ruefully. ''Only Mister. I was in Manhattan, certainly, the conference of the Linguistics Society, Columbia University.''

''You put up at a hotel, did you?''

''The Empire Regency, yes. A new establishment on Eighty-sixth Street and Amsterdam Avenue. A great deal of glass, but furniture extremely uncomforting.''

''What time did you check in?''

''I went into the city on the afternoon before the meetings, when my last class had finished at four P.M. Hallie— Hallie saw me onto the train. I have a confusion concerning trains. I checked into the hotel before six. The check-in hour is six. I am careful to be on time."

"But the meetings didn't start till the next morning, right?"

Krish nodded. "Say it aloud, please," demanded the steno.

"The—the next morning, yes." Krish, being Krish, obliged.

"So what did you do that evening? Anybody with you, you see anybody?"

I glanced at Davy and sighed. If Agate was hoping Krish had spent the night crawling the Manhattan pubs with an old gin buddy, he was talking to the wrong guy. The alibi wouldn't come that easily.

"There was a film I wished to see, at a small revival house near Carnegie Hall," said Krish. "Mrs. Costello had recommended it. One of the films of the great Sikh director, Ranjid Khan. Remarkable."

"Did you go with anyone?"

"Alone," he said simply. "Without Hallie, I preferred to be alone."

I saw Agate bite his lip.

"I have, however, the ticket stub," said Krish. "If that will be of help?"

"Bless his old-maid habits!" I cried, unable to hold my tongue a minute longer. "Only Krish would save a stub from a movie ticket!"

"We'll take a look at that stub later, if you don't mind." Lloyd sounded relieved. "What time did the movie end?"

"Are you familiar with the films of this Khan?" A flicker of smile crossed Krish's weary features. "It ought to be recommended to bring a picnic lunch. Excellent, but elaborate, based on the old Hindi epics. It lasted until nearly midnight."

"And the new commuter schedule puts the last train out of Manhattan for Ainsley at just after nine!" I said triumphantly. "He couldn't have killed Hallie at two because he couldn't have got that train when the movie was over at twelve!"

Sarah and Eddie had joined us in the hallway, a regular support group. But Sarah's next remark didn't support me a heck of a lot.

"Win, don't be such a blockhead. He could've ducked out of the movie early and still caught that train."

"All right, then, ask him how it came out!"

"It's based on a Hindi epic, Goopus," said Merriman, sucking hard at his pipe. "How it comes out is a fact of cultural life to several million people in Krish's neck of the woods. And anyway, he might've seen the thing before."

Inside the room, Agate went on with the questioning.

"Did you meet anybody when you got back to your hotel? Talk to the desk clerk? Meet somebody in the elevator who might remember you?"

Krish fixed him with a puzzled stare. "Excuse me, please. You wish to know where I was when Hallie—" Suddenly he realized the reason for Agate's questions. His hands lifted slightly from the tabletop, then fell down again. "Oh," he said.

"Is there anybody who could vouch for your being at the hotel later than midnight?" asked Lloyd again. Hallie had been killed around two. Even if Krish had ducked out on the Hindi epic and taken the last train up to Ainsley, he couldn't have got back to the hotel before three or three-thirty A.M., even if he'd driven his car. "Did you stop in the bar, maybe? Stop to buy a paper from the desk? Speak to the doorman?"

"Nobody," said Krish. "I went directly to my room, you see. It was late, and the conference was to begin quite early in the morning. Also, I was hungry. I had eaten no dinner before this film began."

"Room service?" said Lloyd hopefully.

"Oh, no. I cannot afford these hotel meals. I stopped at a small shop near the hotel, a grocery open all night. I bought milk, a packet of crackers, a chicken sandwich. I believe chicken. Not particularly distinguished, but convenient."

"So somebody in an all-night deli sold you food and you took it back to the hotel to eat it? Could you show us which deli, where it was exactly?"

"Oh, yes! I see! If this clerk remembers me—"

Agate went on to get the description of the young Korean sales clerk and the approximate location of the deli, and I knew he'd be checking it out before morning.

"Well," said Merriman, relighting his pipe for the fifteenth time, "that's one thing out of the way. If the police are certain he didn't murder Hallie, they may be less inclined to treat him as a serious suspect in the chancellor's death."

"He was found with the murder weapon in his hand," said David. "And so far he hasn't explained where he materialized from."

Lloyd got up from the table and stepped out into the hall to join us. He stood looking through the two-way mirror at the man he'd just been questioning.

"A decent little guy," he said.

"So you're not intending to charge him?" I began to feel a little relieved, as Agate turned to reenter the interrogation room.

"You'd be surprised how many decent little guys commit murder," he said, and closed the door firmly in my face.

The questioning wore on, far into the night. No matter how many times Agate asked him, no matter how ingeniously he tried to get at the truth, Krish simply had no clear memory of what had happened in Elsa's orchard, or of where he had gone after that, where he'd spent the night, how he wound up in Macauley's office, how the gun got into his hand. The lapse of memory wasn't a complete blackout. He remembered having encountered the man in the icy rain under those trees. He remembered kind hands in a warm place, wrapping him in something rough and dry, giving him whisky. But the hands had no face, certainly no name attached to them. There was a warm room, no more.

Still, Agate—bulldog that he is—didn't give up, and neither did I. It was almost three in the A.M., and even the drunks in the holding tank had hit the hay and were snoring it off peaceably. I talked Sarah into going home and leaving me in David's capable custody, and I thought Merriman had gone with her, but when I turned round, there he was, perched next to me on the moldy vinyl-covered bench in the drafty waiting room.

I gave him one of my looks. "I figured you were headed home to your little trundle bed," I said, "or have you had some kind of microchip installed that makes sleep obsolete?"

"Where's David?" he said, ignoring me.

"Still back in the hall, playing Alice in Wonderland through that damn looking glass."

Eddie shuddered. "Bloody sort of thing, isn't it? Absolutely demolishes one's humanity, gawking through it, watching those poor fellows in the hot seat as though they were insects in a glass box. My admiration for Lloyd Agate increased by the hour, managing to do this dreadful work without losing himself utterly."

I couldn't take my eyes off Eddie. His hands were clasped together hard, the knuckles white and the fingertips deep red, and the double fist they made was shaking as if two halves of him were wrestling with each other.

"What do you know about this business, old sport?" I said. "Are you going to tell me what's going on, or not?"

I have spent thirty years writing mystery novels, and when their hero, natty old G. Winchester Hyde, comes up against a reluctant witness, he always manages to maneuver and cajole and charm and manipulate the story out into the open. But Hyde is a fiction, and I made him everything I am not. He is a master of gamesmanship, and I play by no one's rules. He is glib of tongue and elegant of figure, and I am plain and blunt, built like Mount Rushmore and dressed for comfort, as I damn well please. Hyde would have drawn the truth out of Merriman over a glass of mulled wine sipped beside a convivial fire in some Morocco-bound smoking room, and afterward they would have remained firm friends.

But friendship has an end, as all things have. It can be pushed too far. I have never had a better friend than Eddie Merriman; I never wanted one. He is too bright not to recognize manipulation and resent it. He is unseducible by charm, and when it comes to games,

195

he makes them up faster than I can learn the rules. Though he looks weedy and delicate, he is stronger, I often think, than any of us, and if I pushed into that secret place marked NO ADMITTANCE we all must guard against invasion all our lives, I knew he was strong enough to turn in self-defense and walk away from me for good.

I did not push.

Instead, I went over to the coffee machine and drew off a cup of the milky, pissy-warm stuff and brought it to him. Not exactly mulled wine, but the best I could muster.

"I haven't spoken before," he said at last, turning the foam cup round and round in his hands, "because I simply wasn't certain. I thought if we poked about a bit, we might find something that would confirm or deny what I thought I'd seen, but now, with Macauley dead, and Krishnan—"

He broke off, and the coffee cup slipped from his hands and fell with a splat onto the mucky tile, as he sat staring at the astonishing figure of Maxima Bergner, moving with that purposeful, almost mechanical walk of hers across the lobby to the sergeant's desk, like a small, unstoppable machine. She was wrapped in an opera-length coat of rich black fur, expensive in its day but now—though perfectly kept—a relic as brittle as the woman inside it. Madam Max was carefully made up, her taut, narrow mouth laden with deep red lipstick, slightly smeared, her wiry gray hair draped in a scarlet chiffon scarf whose ends streamed behind her as she walked. She looked tiny in the big empty room, and when she stopped at the high reception desk, she could barely see over it.

She didn't seem to notice Merriman and me at all. She looked straight through us, as though we were that trick mirror of Agate's.

"I have come to ask," she said in a ringing voice that seared like acid, "whether it's true."

The stunned desk sergeant looked down at her and blinked. "Whazzat, ma'am?"

"I have come to find out if James Macauley is really dead."

The sergeant rocked back in his desk chair and gave her the once-over. It was quite an apparition that had blown in out of the cold at three in the morning. The small bright eyes in the rouged and powdered face might've been doll's eyes, blinking mechanically in the light. Her breath was uneven, drawn heavily through the lip-sticked mouth. She pulled the coat closer around her thin body and put a red-clawed hand on the edge of the desk.

"Are you a dolt, man? Answer a simple question! Is the bastard really dead, or not?"

Her voice echoed, irresistible.

"Yes, ma'am," said the Sergeant. "He's dead all right, but I'm afraid that's all the information I'm at liberty to—"

"It's enough!" she said. I saw her stagger slightly and catch with both her hands at the desk. Then she straightened and drew a deep breath, forcing her equilibrium under control. "Now, then. Now I can die," she said.

Sixteen

But not yet, thought Maxima. That would simply have to wait its turn. She had work to do now. She had to find Jaffer Swan.

Of course she had seen Winston and Eddie, the old busybodies, sitting there in the station, taking everything in. So much the better. Let Winnie try to read *her* mind! He was far too proud of his famous intuition; a lesson in humility would do him good.

She straightened her scarf, pulled the sable Alois had chosen for her on their last trip to Paris close around her, and marched out of the police station without seeming to see Winnie at all. Whether she did or did not see him come toddling at top speed out of the station to follow her is a matter for conjecture. Even if she knew he was there, Madam Max would not have bothered to elude him.

It was the coldest hour of cold nights, that time when dark deepens and gathers strength for morning. Maxima would have preferred to walk in spite of the cold and the dark, but the pavements were still patched with ice from the squall of sleet two nights before, and the heart her quack kept maundering about was beating wildly in her, shaking her whole body.

She hadn't driven a car in years, but she still knew how. Once Elsa had come up to her room and closed the door and the only

198

sound in the small house was the creaking of the old boards on their nails as the world spun and settled, Maxima crept out and down the stairs, wrapped in her sable coat, found the keys to her stepdaughter's rusting, rattling delivery station wagon, and went out.

She had to know the truth, and act on it. She had sat by her upstairs window too long, and seen too much.

The news of Macauley's murder had been brought to the house by that silly Costello woman, who always heard everything before anyone else. She had turned up just after dinner, a good hour before the other women were to gather for their so-called class in fiddling artistically with weeds and brambles. Madam Max sat in her husband's study, pretending to read a satire of Juvenal, that ancient reprobate. She hadn't the concentration for Latin verse these days, but even the pretense was a discipline of sorts, and her eyes, seeking refuge from an interior landscape full of trolls and goblins, played over the cool hexameters with relief. Alois's study, always her refuge from pesky visitors, was dim and warm and lined with books, and the voices of Elsa and Hilda Costello drifted to her from the kitchen like the wind in the vines that scratched the study windows.

"So, my dear, you came anyway!" cried Elsa, simulating delight. She didn't like Mrs. Costello, and Max was surprised she had the energy for feigning. It had been a terror of a day.

The explosion with Sarah in the orchard had exhausted Elsa. She had gone into the house and slept all the afternoon in that strange way of hers, like some hibernating animal. Maxima had looked in on her once or twice, frightened both by the intensity of Elsa's anger and the suddenness with which it was spent. When she woke, late in the afternoon, she had seemed quite her usual self, energetic and eager to work on the designs for Thanksgiving centerpieces she was making in her shop at the back of the greenhouse. She had gone there for an hour before dinner, and Madam Max slipped out to watch her weaving the bittersweet she had gathered into a wreath for table candles, tangling it with the silvery dried herbs that hung in dense, aromatic bunches round the shop—rue, rosemary, lavender, thyme, bergamot, lemon verbena, tarragon, tansy. Elsa hummed contentedly to herself as she worked, a melody from *The Magic Flute.* The tension that had brewed in her since Swan's defection was entirely dissipated, now that the explosion was over. There was always an explosion, had always been, ever since Elsa's girlhood, but lately, since Swan's coming, they had been less predictable. It was the unpredictability that frightened Maxima. That, and the sense she had of panic carefully covered up but undispelled, not even by the bursts of rage.

Dinner had been like old times, fond and sentimental, Elsa laughing and talking about Piers's silly magic tricks and giving imitations of Winston at his most curmudgeonly, heaping portions of the grilled salmon Maxima loved onto her plate and granting her the boon of a cup of steaming, strong black coffee as a special treat.

Hysteria, thought Madam Max, closing the volume of Juvenal. The girl was imitating herself like a child dancing before a mirror. Under the dancing image, the great round unconcealing eyes were terrified.

"So, my dear," Maxima heard her say to Hilda, "no rehearsal tonight for that play of yours, your *Othello?* Pretty Desdemona does not die tonight?"

"Oh," said Hilda Costello, "rehearsal's been canceled. The whole college is pretty much on hold, now that Macauley's gone."

Maxima dropped the book from her lap and stood up, her heart racing, her pulse slamming against the roots of her eyes. She hung there, listening.

"Gone?" Elsa's voice was too loud. "What is this, gone?"

"I knew you'd want to hear about it, honey," said the Costello woman, her voice warming and eager, relishing the spotlight. "That's why I came over early. They found him in his office late this afternoon. You can probably get the dope from Winnie, he's always stirring around in stuff like this."

Elsa did not seem to comprehend. "Found him? Found him gone?"

"Dead, honey," said Hilda, sounding delighted with herself. "Shot himself in the head, the way I heard it. And that's not the best part. Wait'll you hear this."

She paused, partly for breath but mostly for effect, and Maxima moved somehow toward the door, unable to feel her feet, unaware of her body's existence. *Dead. He is dead. God is alive and he is dead.*

"He left this note, right on the desk. The necklace that Glendon girl was wearing the night she got killed. A hypo and everything. He was the guy, honey, don't you get it?"

There was silence from Elsa. Maxima drew closer, passed like her own ghost through the darkened dining room where the dishes still stood on the table, leaned silent and unnoticed against the door-frame to look in at the brightly lighted kitchen. Elsa sat at the table, where she had been working on the greenhouse ledgers. She looked at Hilda Costello as though she had never seen her before, with a vague disdain such as you might turn upon a hawker of cheap trinkets on a busy street.

Her reception of Hilda's news had been unsatisfying. The woman persisted. "Macauley was the Heart Specialist," she said. "He was the guy the cops have been after! He offed all four of those women." She got up and paddled over to the stove, poured herself a mug of coffee and sat down again. "I always knew the bastard was a chauvinist pig. I guess it doesn't really surprise me, you know?"

"Do they—" Elsa struggled to collect herself, played for time, fiddling with the account books on the table in front of her. "Do they think it's over, then? The women, the killings— They stop looking? That policeman—he means to arrest nobody?"

"Oh, well," said Hilda, "Winnie probably thinks it's murder, hell, he sees murderers in the woodwork, the old boot, he's written too many of those goddamn books of his! Over? Yeah, I'd say it's over. I heard they took Krish Ghandour down for questioning, but that's probably just routine."

"Who?" snapped Elsa. "Took who for questioning?"

"Krish. Krishnan Ghandour. You know Krish?"

"Get out!"

Elsa was up now, marching to the door, her long, full skirt swooshing, her tangle of gray-gold curls wild and pulling out of the clip that held them.

"Go home," she commanded. "No class tonight. Go home!"

For probably the first time in her life, Hilda Costello was speechless. She stood up uncertainly, her lips parted slightly in surprise, staring at the Boadicean figure holding the door open for her departure. There was power in Elsa she had not expected, control of a kind Hilda, who dished the dirt on half the faculty and used her gossip mills to grind some up and others down, had never seen before. Elsa Worthing was not issuing her orders out of anger. She was infused with purpose.

"If it's something I said—" babbled Hilda, on the defensive for once.

Elsa seemed to know she'd gone too far. She strode back to where Hilda was standing, a bulgy, dowdy middle-aged housewife, her self-important delusions punctured. Everything about her seemed to droop, as Elsa slipped an arm through hers and led her gently toward the door.

"My dear, forgive me," she crooned. "I'm a brute, you know, but the strain has been terrible, the past two days, since Hallie—"

Hilda relaxed, relieved to be given an excuse for pity, which reduced the stature of the other woman to a manageable size. It was stress, that was all. It had nothing to do with the inconsequence of Hilda, after all.

"Oh, honey," she said, "that's okay. You get some rest, now. I'll call you in the morning. Get some rest!"

And she was bundled out almost without being aware of it.

"Idiot!" spat Elsa as she slammed the door. "What has the idiot done?"

Maxima stepped into the lighted kitchen. "Which idiot would that be, dear? Graham hasn't the bottle to murder anyone, or he'd have killed you and Swan some time ago—or me, for that matter. If you mean Swan, I'd hardly call *that* one an idiot. You think he's murdered Macauley for you? My word, you bear a good opinion of yourself!"

"Swan?" Elsa lifted her head, her face framed by the tendrils of hair, Medusa-like against the light from the Tiffany-glass shade on the hanging lamp, its colors falling over her face like fine veils of ruby, amethyst, sapphire, emerald, and golden topaz. "Let him kill them all if he wants to! What does she care for Swan, that bastard? He takes and takes and takes, and then he goes away. The hell with him. The hell with all of them! She wishes him the plague!"

She.

The pronoun puzzled Maxima, but she said nothing. It was not the first time she had noticed the solecism, and it had been more frequent in the past few weeks, but a lifetime of translating even her dreams into another language for Alois's benefit and then for Elsa's had taught the old woman the limits of grammatical precision.

Elsa's iron control was slipping. She sank down onto the braided rug before the kitchen door, hugging herself and humming softly, some unrecognizable tune.

"Mutti," she whispered.

Maxima took a step toward her and Elsa looked up. The old woman slipped painfully, awkwardly down onto the rug beside the aging woman who had been a child when life still held chances for them both, still held hope and the love of Alois, beside the girl who might have been—but never was—her daughter. She took Elsa in her arms and for the first time in many years, she wept, that old woman distilled of pride and anger, in great catching sobs dragged from the marrow of a lost and precious world, discarded now, ridiculous as the scarlet paint upon her fingernails. Maxima held her never-daughter, and wept her life good-bye.

Elsa held the old woman close, her own arms strong, her body still rich with unused and unwished-for life. But Elsa did not cry. She sang, under her breath, a familiar melody.

> Redwing blackbird, flying bright,
> Fire, fear, and candlelight.
> Sometimes tossed and sometimes torn,
> Make my bed on the cruel thorn.

Seventeen

When I charged out the Cop Shop door after Madam Max with Merriman close on my heels, I didn't have much of a plan in mind. I suppose I'd hoped to head her off at the pass and give her a little third degree of my own. But the old girl was too fast for me. She marched straight to Elsa's station wagon, parked a space or two ahead of David's Olds, got in and began to fumble for her keys.

"Well, that's that," I grumbled. "I thought Grendel's mother lost her driver's license years ago." I might've caught her on foot, with a little luck, but cars and I have never been formally introduced.

Merriman cocked his head on one side and looked at me. "You don't need a license to make the beastly thing go, you know, Winnie. All you need is an available vehicle and a bit of pluck."

" 'Pluck'?" I said. "Have you been reading those Horatio Alger books again?"

"Pluck," he repeated firmly. "And a car key."

Madam Max began to back out of the parking spot. I had to think fast.

"You *do* have David's keys, don't you?" nagged Eddie.

Well, of course I did. David has a habit of losing car keys, and the pockets of my voluminous old overcoat were designed by the same Johnny who mapped out the cargo hold of the QEII. When David's with Alex or Sarah, his keys go into the lady's pocketbook. In my case, it's my carryall overcoat pocket. I could feel them clinking around in there now, tempting me.

"Confound it, Merriman!" I said, as Madam Max pulled away from the curb, "let's throw caution to the winds! She's getting away!"

If you have been a regular reader of these annals of my ventures into what is called "true crime," you know that so far as locomotion is concerned, I stick to my trusty old bicycle when I can't hitch a ride with some legally constituted carrier. Not that I *couldn't* have driven a car if I'd wanted to, mind you. It's not the mechanical stuff that fazes me. It's the other drivers. Stuck in traffic behind a female fiddling with her hairdo in the rearview mirror or confronted with a macho lane-hopper, I wouldn't be satisfied to swear and mumble and honk my horn.

I'd ram the suckers.

So up till now, though I'd been watching Sarah drive for years and was absolutely certain I'd be a natural, once I got the wheel in my paws, I'd abstained from cars. Putting a tail on Madam Maxima, though, was a very special case. Besides, Davy's Olds had automatic everything, and little Gemma probably could've tooled around the block in it if she'd wanted to. I figured I was a cinch.

"Not *that* key! The round one!" cried Merriman as I fumbled with the ignition. "Hurry up, Winnie! She's almost at the stoplight."

"Keep your eye on her," I said. "I've almost got it."

I turned the key and the thing squawked at me ferociously. I believe it's called stripping the gears. Finally, though, I got the little handle into line and the gauge on the dash said DRIVE.

I did.

Merriman shot back in the seat as I tromped on the gas pedal, and we lurched ahead. I took my foot off and tried the brake and Eddie snapped forward again, halfway to the windshield, blinking like an owl.

205

"I think I'm getting the hang of this," I said. "Okay, fasten seat belts. Ready for takeoff!"

"Gas, gas, gas, gas!" cried Eddie, "step on the confounded gas, not the brake! Your motor skills leave something to be desired, you old ass, and that is *not* a pun!"

I hit the gas and the thing bucked once or twice and took off down the street. Well, I suppose I ought to say down the sidewalk.

"Turn the wheel," cried Eddie. He was fairly quivering with excitement. "Wheel, wheel, wheel, wheel! Oh, my sweet Aunt Edna! Get it off the curb!"

In my rearview mirror, I saw a hulking black sedan pull up in front of the station where the Olds had just been parked. A man got out the driver's door, and I was surprised to recognize Tommy Sheffield in the bright lights of the station entrance.

"My hat," I said, "if it isn't Sheffield! Look there, Merriman. Right behind us. He must've been worried about Krish."

I craned my neck for a better look and the front of the car seemed to get ideas. It veered off to the left, mowing down Old Bess, the plaster cow in front of Weatherby's Steak House.

Merriman grabbed the wheel and the thing straightened out again. I was really getting the feel of driving.

"A fellow could get hooked on this," I said. We had leveled off by then, and were headed through the hilly middle of town toward the river bluffs.

"It looks like she's making for home," said Merriman.

But he was wrong. Maxima turned the rusting station wagon in at the gates of Clinton College and up the main drive toward the administration tower, deserted now and bleak in the predawn cold.

"I've got the wheel-turning part down pat, Merriman," I said, as we entered the campus in Madam Max's wake. After all—not counting Old Bess, of course—I'd only nicked *one* tree, and that wasn't a very big one. "But pretty soon now I'm going to have to come in for a landing in that parking lot, and to be honest with you, I haven't got the foggiest idea how to stop this thing. The chair is open to suggestions."

Merriman drew a deep breath and I could hear him muttering under his breath. "One, two, three, four, five—*Ten.*" He exhaled and almost fogged up the windshield. "Now, then," he said primly. "Lift your right hoof off the infernal gas pedal and do NOT slam it down on the brake!"

"What shall I do with it?"

"Tuck it in your pocket for all I care, just don't put it down on anything on the floor!"

I obeyed instructions and the car began to slow as we coasted into the huge, empty lot behind the administration tower. "Okay, now what?"

"Gently, gently, GENTLY, put your right foot, which you have been reserving for the purpose, onto the brake pedal. Don't push! Just put the blasted thing there, that's all."

I did. The weight of my Hush Puppy seemed to soothe the thing further and we slowed again.

"Now, gradually, with the tip of your tootsie, push down on the brake."

I did. The thing squealed and squawked, and stopped dead. Eddie shot forward and then back into the seat again.

"By George," I said. "It's stopped."

"No, don't take your foot off the brake, you ninny, put the lever into Park first. Yes, that's it. All right. Now switch off the key and give it to me!"

"Why?" I said, taking out the ignition key. "What're you going to do with it?"

Merriman grabbed the keys and pocketed them before I could protest. "I am going," he said, "to drive home, naturally. I have no intention of risking life, liberty and the public weal with you in the cockpit of this thing again!"

"Oh, horseradish," I said. "Anybody can be a backseat driver and give a lot of orders. You've never really *driven* a car in your life."

He got out and stood waiting for me. "What did you think I did in the War, Daddy? I drove troop trucks over half the state of Kansas, thank you very much!"

"Well, I'm damned," I said, amazed.

"And I," he said, "am constantly underestimated. Ever the fate of true genius. Hello, Maxima, my dear. What's up?"

In the excitement of my maiden voyage, I'd almost forgotten why we'd made it in the first place, until Madam Max came clacking across the parking lot toward us, like a small, bony horse with a mind of its own, the black fur coat flapping, her breath steaming in the cold.

"I assume," she said, "that you're following me. Well, come on, then! This way."

The old woman led us across the huge, blacktopped parking lot, and a strange procession we made. Maxima stalked ahead, aimed at the service door of the building in a perfectly straight line that might have been drawn for her alone across the gleaming surface of the empty lot. She looked thin as a sliver inside the huge old coat, the red scarf floating behind like a flag from a ship's mast as she sailed purposefully along. Merriman, nervy and frazzled by the ride and the lack of sleep, trotted behind her with his careful step, as though he were afraid of disarranging something invisible in his path. And I brought up the rear, my hands in my commodious pockets, run-over Hush Puppies squeaking on the patches of ice, collar turned up against the cold, and eyes scanning the night from under John L. Lewis brows.

I saw nothing, no clue to where Maxima was leading us.

"Max," I said, stopping and digging in my heels, "enough. I know you like to hold the reins, but I'm not going any further till I know where we're headed, and why."

"Why did you follow me?" she croaked, squinting at me from under the wiry bush of steel-wool hair. "What did you expect to find?"

"Me, old love," said a soft voice behind us.

He had come out of nowhere, which seemed to be his natural element. When I turned to look at him, he was simply there, hands shoved in the pockets of his thin windbreaker, sandy hair haloed by the parking lot lights, eyes shadowed, fixed on the ground at my feet.

He stood apart from us, in the barren center of a ring of intense pinkish light, absolutely motionless and utterly alone. Guns, I thought, might've been trained on him, the command to fire given, and he would not have moved nor flinched. Jaffer would merely have looked up, as he did at me, and smiled slightly, alien and bemused.

"I guess you want to know if I killed her, eh?" he said.

"You mean the girl in the orchard? Hallie Glendon? I want to know. Yes."

"Answer's no," he said, more loudly than before. "Your cop hear that, you think?" He whirled round once in the lights. "NOOOOOOO!!!" he shouted, and the echo came back from the enigmatic face of Macauley's tower. "NOOOOOOOO!!!!!" Jaffer stumbled, ran a step or two, and fell, sprawled on the parking lot. Eddie and I started toward him, meaning to help, but Maxima hissed suddenly, "Let him be!" and we waited. He was agile and he got up easily enough and turned to me, stepped closer, until his thin hands rested on my shoulders, fingers clutching in a tenuous hold, like a climber on a sheer cliff. When he spoke, his voice was hoarse from the shouting and I could barely hear him. But I saw his eyes, clear and shining, incapable of lies.

"Hallie," he said. "Christ, she was my daughter, wasn't she?"

Though I had no way of knowing it, Jaffer was right. Agate *was* out there in the dark, and so were David and a quaking Tommy Sheffield.

From his post in the dark hall outside the two-way mirror, David had heard Maxima's voice and stepped out to see what was up. When she left, he'd turned back to speak to Agate, who'd just emerged from the interrogation room. They went out to find Merriman and Yours Truly just revving up the Olds, and it was then that Sheffield pulled up in front of the station in Lady Di's precious jet black Lincoln, a parting gift from Daddy.

Tommy nearly collided with Davy as he charged out the front door after us, with Lloyd Agate thumping along behind.

"I couldn't sleep," moaned Sheffield. "I thought I'd just come down and see if Krishnan—"

"That your car, the black job?" snapped Agate.

"It's my wife's actually, terrible gas-guzzler, but impressive, don't you think?"

All the squad cars were parked in the small lot out back, but the royal coach was here, and the keys were dangling from Sheffield's suede-gloved fingers.

"Borrow your keys," said Lloyd, nabbing them. "Police business! Come on David."

They piled into the car and Sheffield stood staring after them. "But you can't!" he whined. "If it gets scratched, Diana will have my guts for garters! Please, couldn't you—"

The engine started and the car shot backward, with Lloyd at the wheel, driving as only a cop can drive.

"Wait for me!" cried Sheffield, and piled in the back.

Which is how it came about that the three of them—Lloyd, hunched over the cushy, padded steering wheel; Davy, slouched down in the seat to keep his head from bouncing off the roof when they went over bumps; and Thomas Van Doren Sheffield, chewing his lower lip and praying to every saint he could think of, including some who'd been demoted for years—arrived in the parking lot of Macauley's tower just as Jaffer Swan was leading us to the service door for which, to my surprise—but not to Maxima's—he had a key.

"What else do you know about this elusive gentleman, my dear?" Eddie murmured to the old lady as we entered the building.

"Courage, resource, and distinction," she said. "My father's list of cardinal virtues. I've always found them irresistible." She turned, gave Merriman and me the once-over, sniffed disdainfully, and marched on, following Jaffer.

"What Eddie was asking you," I said, "is how the hell you knew the man was hiding out here, in the bosom of the enemy, for the love of Mike?"

"I followed him one night," she said. "Naturally. Did you think you were the only snooper God ever made?"

210

"No," I said sweetly. "Just the best."

Swan said nothing more until we were all inside. When Agate and the others came huffing up behind us, he barely glanced over his shoulder. He led the way down a short hall to another door, then down three concrete steps into the basement of the building, where the furnace room was, and the delivery elevator. We entered a fairly large room next to the furnaces, lined with shelves that held bottles of insecticide and spray guns and flowerpots and bags of yeasty potting soil and indoor plants in varying stages of health. There was a desk and a time clock and a couple of tottering discarded office chairs, a couch of a similar species made up with a pillow and a couple of ratty blankets, a coffeepot, and a smattering of tattered paperback books. On the desk lay Jaffer's famous clarinet.

If the man could be said to have a home, this was it. I hadn't had a chance to follow through on my promise to phone the grounds superintendent, but from what I could see, it wouldn't have done much good, anyway. The grounds crew headquartered in the big shed near the stadium where the snow plows were kept. This place was something else again.

"Old Jackson take a shine to you, did he?" I asked Swan.

Louis Jackson, a fixture on the campus for longer than I'd been there, minded the furnaces and served as a resident watchman, and when the new administration building went up, room had been found for the old boy down here. He was more or less the campus mascot, and even Macauley hadn't had the nerve to throw him out on the street. Patches, as we all called old Jackson, liked to talk though he rarely made much sense, and when Jaffer Swan turned up to look after the collection of sickly jungle fauna that decorated the lobbies and lounges on campus, Jackson apparently offered to share his bijou residence down here with the temporary help.

It was blissfully warm in the room. Jaffer yanked the pillow and blankets off the couch and flashed me a smile as we took places gratefully. "Patches is cool," he said. "Yeah. I watch the furnace for him some nights. Got a lady friend, old girl keeps a bunch of cats. Fancies cats, does Patches."

2 1 1

David stood in the shadow of one of the racks of tin shelves, silent and thoughtful, studying the face of Geoffrey Swan. As for Madam Max, she took the position of power behind the desk and instantly assumed control—naturally.

"Now, then, Geoffrey," she began. "I know you're capable of running rings around the lot of us, but I am too old and far too dignified for a footrace. I know you are no murderer. You have too much self-respect to soil your hands on that reptile of a man. So suppose you simply tell us everything."

Swan, like Davy, was still on his feet. He turned to look at the old woman, ran two fingers through his fine, sandy hair, and laughed softly.

"Everything? Better be sure, lovey," he said. "Might get what you ask for."

"You said outside that Hallie Glendon was your daughter," Merriman began. "Which means that either her name was not, in fact, Glendon, or yours is not, in fact, Swan."

Jaffer picked up his clarinet and ran his fingertips along its gleaming length. It seemed to steady him, and he sat down, cross-legged on the floor, dead center of the lot of us.

"Spot-on. Got me in one. Glendon." He shrugged. "You'd have got it from Immigration in a day or two, anyway."

"Why Swan?" asked David.

Jaffer smiled up at him. "Named meself after a pub, didn't I? The Black Swan, Peasholme Green, York. So, what else you find out? Let's have a quick obituary now, shall we, save time later on? 'Geoffrey Edward Glendon, Esquire, Eton, Oxford, and the Slade Bloody School of Art, son of Peter Geoffrey Glendon, cut down in his prime by booze and boredom, and the Lady Harriet Burnshaw Glendon, batty as stewed owls. Mr. Glendon the Younger was also the only grandson of Sir Matthew Albert Effing Glendon, life peer and shit-merchant, deceased. Also husband of Marian Lady Enfield, who ditched him as a bad job after producing in his company Joanna the Beastly and Freddie the Unendurable, a pair of young thugs about whose nurture and education he had damn-all to say. Subsequently husband of Halima Rashdie, with whom Harriet. Hallie.''

He fell silent, staring at the clarinet in his hands. Then he put it to his lips and began to play, an unidentifiable riff that grew and climbed and traveled, and in the end became the title bar of the old Duke Ellington number, "I'm Just a Lucky So-and-So." When he'd finished, he sat silent.

"Is there whisky?'' Maxima spoke clearly, the edge of distaste entirely gone from her voice.

"Don't need it," Jaffer said.

"Speak for yourself, fool."

He smiled, without looking at her. "Drawer," he said.

Madam Max searched the desk and found a half-empty bottle of Canadian whisky, poured a healthy belt into a coffee mug and gulped it down. Then she filled the mug again and nodded to David, who handed it to Jaffer. He drank it in one long swallow, whether he needed it or not.

"Did Hallie's mother leave you, too?" David put a hand on Jaffer's thin shoulder.

Swan looked up at him, a long look, taking stock. "In a manner of speaking," he said. "She died, didn't she?"

"What happened to your daughter?" Davy was thinking of his own Gemma.

"She was okay," said Swan. "She was with her aunt in Wales. Nice place, Wales. Clean place, by the sea. Smelled like life. Didn't need me mucking her up, did she? So I took a walk, see."

"You mean you ran out on the kid?" Agate spoke with deliberate brutality.

"Actually, I booked a coach tour," Jaffer glanced up at him. "Gardens of Britain. How I wound up in York, right? The Black Swan? Thirteen cities in fourteen days. Travel Britain with Glendon Tours."

"Tours? I thought Sir Matthew was a greeting-card mogul."

I liked the look of the man, the feel of him. Whatever else he was, I didn't believe he was a killer. But would anything he said convince Agate of that? I could see my friend the cop wasn't favorably impressed with Jaffer's peripatetic approach to fatherhood, being a loyal and loving dad himself.

"Glendon Greetings, Glendon Package Tours, Glendon Home-from-Home Hotels. Not many pies old Granfer didn't stick his green thumb into."

"You inherited the money, too, did you, along with the green thumb?"

Suddenly Jaffer was on his feet. "I inherited piss. It was the most worthwhile thing *he* ever made!" He began to pace back and forth across the empty middle of the room. "Okay, let's get to it, right? I ditched the academic bullshit years ago. Gentleman and scholar, me? What a giggle, right? Knocked around Canada and the States awhile, found out my daughter was in this country. She came over with another auntie who'd emigrated. Rang up me old mum. She communicates with this planet now and then. Found out Hallie was living in this pearl of the Hudson Valley. Came here. Wanted to see her. Felt guilty. Felt old. Felt love. Felt dead. Christ knows. Came here and couldn't get myself nearer to her than standing outside her apartment house, playing 'Blackbird' on my stick one night. Went out to Elsa's because Hallie went there sometimes, fooled with the flowers. She got that from me. I got it from Granfer, the only thing he ever taught me. Had a whole bloody greenhouse full of orchids, brought them in from Singapore. That's how I got the gig here, the orchids. His Majesty fancied them. Macauley. The Victim, see? Didn't fancy getting his hands dirty. So." He stopped, breathing hard, then stood isolate, lost in memory. "I taught Hallie how to plant things when she was little. Beans in a tin can of dirt. Her face—"

He broke off and stood with his eyes shut, arms limp at his sides. David was beside him in two long steps.

"She couldn't stick me," whispered Swan. "I went back once, when she was eight, nine, maybe. She took one look at me and started screaming." He looked up at David and smiled, a brief flicker of self-ridicule. "Tends to sap the confidence, that sort of thing," he said.

"She sent you a card, though, didn't she?" Lloyd asked him. "An Easter card. 'To Geoff from Hallie'? You couldn't throw it away. You used it for a bookmark."

Swan snapped to attention. "Where did you get that? You got no right to that, man!"

David gripped him by the shoulders. "Listen to me," he said. "There are only two things that matter. Where were you at two o'clock the morning your daughter was killed?"

"I was with the Countess most of the night," Swan said. "Her Ladyship. Elsa. I guess *you* know that." He looked over at Maxima, who sat like a statue at the desk. "Not bloody much you *don't* know, is there?"

The old woman's face was impassive. For a long moment she hesitated, saying nothing. When she spoke at last, the cutting edge had returned to her voice.

"I was asleep," she said flatly.

"Piffle, my dear," announced Eddie. "You don't sleep any better than I do, and you know it. Surely you heard or saw something that night besides the ringing of the telephone at two A.M.?"

"And where has the other star witness gone?" I shoved my own oar in. "Why did Graham Worthing suddenly decide to take a powder after turning up on the crucial morning? Sarah says he's left Elsa. Is that right?"

Swan's face when I published this bit of news was a complex mixture of emotions, chief among them pain. Some ancient harm had been done him, I thought, the same brutal kind that had been done to David, but not so overt as that slash of the knife across the face. Sarah's kid brother was still standing very close to Jaffer, seemed drawn instinctively to the man, and Jaffer did not move away. They knew each other on a silent, invisible level, as survivors of a cancer ward can recognize each other instantly, though they have never met, never spoken one another's names.

Madam Max, though, did speak. "Graham Worthing is a drone

and an idiot. If he never comes back, it will be the best thing that could happen to Elsa. If she had married another sort of man . . ." She snapped her mouth shut like a turtle and pursed her bright-red lips tight. "Good riddance to him," she declared, and that was that.

Lloyd's focus was still on Jaffer. "Were you with Mrs. Worthing all night? What time did you leave her?"

"Not long after midnight," said Swan. "I like to walk best at night, when nobody gawks at you. Know what I mean? Just dogs and that, and cats out prowling. Helps me think."

"Where did you go? Might anybody have seen you?"

"Went to Reeney's, didn't I? Go there most nights. Good old girl, Reeney. I went in, all right, but I don't think anybody saw me. I went straight out again, didn't have a beer or anything."

"Why would you go all that way down to the river and into a bar, and then turn around without even having a beer or saying hello to Irene?" I asked him.

I felt the need of a shot of that rye myself, though it doesn't hold a candle to my usual Haig & Haig. I got up, toddled over, poured a healthy tot into a slightly grubby foam cup by the coffeepot, and stood beside Jaffer and David. They seemed to have formed some sort of instant alliance, and I felt like an intruder and sat down again beside good old Merriman.

"*He* was in there, wasn't he?" said Jaffer. "Didn't want to tangle with him. Thought he might be looking for me, wanting to come the heavy husband, see? So I ducked out again."

I wasn't quite following his drift. "Who was in there?"

"Friggin' old Graham," he said.

"Graham Worthing was at Reeney's?" Lloyd's big ears pricked up instantly.

"Like I said." Jaffer began to riff on the horn again. This time it turned out to be "I Got It Bad and That Ain't Good."

"Okay," Lloyd said. The stubborn look of dislike he'd begun with had eased a bit. The man was winning him over, too. "Okay, so where was Mrs. Worthing when you got back to the house?"

"In bed, wasn't she? Just like I left her."

"You went back to her even though you knew Worthing was in town?"

"Yeah. I went back." Swan smiled. "He might've come for me at Reeney's, to show off, see? In front of strangers. Wouldn't have the balls at home. 'Cause of her. Elsa."

"What time was it when you got back?"

"I walked around a bit. Came over here, did a bit of reading. Must've been three-thirty. Maybe four."

By which time, I thought, his daughter, Hallie, was already lying dead under the trees.

"How did you come back? Did you come through the orchard?"

Jaffer shook his head. "Walked straight up the drive past the greenhouse, into the house. There's an old wicker fernery on the front porch. She keeps the key in that. Let meself in and out, don't I?"

"Did you see any sign of Graham Worthing? Did he ever show up at the house?"

"Not so long as I was there. When it got light, I took off. Through the orchard. She was— Hallie was out there. I ''

He broke off again and sat silent, intent on the memory of the little girl he'd taught to plant bean seeds in a tin can. After a long moment, he looked straight at Agate.

"Look, mate," he said. "I didn't plan for an alibi. I lie to women, sometimes. I cheat on them. Sometimes. I take their brass and I take them to bed and I take away their dreams. Sometimes. I mean well, I always do. Swear to God. But things tangle up on me, fall to hell. I let them down a lot, women. I prove a disappointment. But Jesus. I don't kill them."

"No," said Agate quietly. "I don't think you do."

Lloyd would, I knew, have been much less inclined to believe Jaffer, were it not for the very first part of that speech. He *hadn't* planned for an alibi, and a killer, especially as methodical and careful a killer as the Heart Specialist, would certainly have planned ahead. But the deaths of Hallie and the other women weren't all our cop had to deal with now.

"You know Chancellor Macauley was found dead this afternoon?" Lloyd went on. "Where were you around four-thirty?"

"Doing the plants, wasn't I? That's what I do around here, see. I do all the indoor plants, the orchids up in the old boy's office, and the fig tree—poor old sod's on its last legs—down in the atrium next to the meeting rooms. I don't usually go in the offices till everybody's gone for the day. Start with the atrium, stuff in the hallways, reception desk. Move on over to the library and the theater lobby later. Work down here on the trauma cases." He pointed to a limp philodendron in the corner. "But it was quiet today. And *he* was down here, see, sleeping on the couch."

"Who was here?"

"Hallie's fella. Poor old sod. Krishnan Ghandour."

"He was *here?*" Tommy hadn't spoken until now, until Krish entered the story. His concern for the quietest, most disciplined, most genuine and untrendy member of our department was patent, as though he saw there every aspect of personal and professional life he himself had long since sold or thrown away, and had somehow to save it. "But, if he was *here,* if you saw him and he saw you, then neither one of you could've killed Macauley!"

"Still out of it, though, wasn't he?" said Jaffer. "See, that night, night after Hallie— I went back to the orchard, late. It was raining. I kept thinking I might find something. See something. He turned up there, pretty bad shape. I lugged him back here, made some herb tea for him. Lemon balm, lobelia, some other stuff. Elsa taught me. *She* uses it." He indicated Madam Max, who pulled a corroborating face. "Any road, I had some of the stuff in my pack. Gave him some. Good for the nerves. Made him sleep. Poor bugger slept all day, right there on the couch. I was in and out. Never tried to hide. Just didn't go back to Elsa's. Round four, off I went to do the plants. He must've come awake and followed me."

"Did you go up to Macauley's office? Did you see his body on the floor?" David had begun to pace now, in a crooked path among the shelves and clutter. He had one of Jaffer's raggedy books in his hand.

"I went up all right, but I heard the little tart from the office yelling, and I took off. Made meself scarce. Rule Numero Uno. When hassle threatens, disappear."

"Why did you take your daughter's black coral necklace from her body?" Agate's question came out of nowhere and Jaffer spun round, dazed. "Why did you leave it on Macauley's desk?"

"I took nothing from her," the man I could still only think of as Swan replied. "I gave nothing. I took nothing. Nothing you could see."

"Did you think Macauley killed her? Is that why you took the necklace and planted it on him?" Lloyd was like a dog with a juicy bone between its teeth.

"Macauley?" Swan gave a soft, throaty laugh. "I hardly thought of him at all, mate."

"Did anybody else see Krish down here?" I asked him. "Did Patches Jackson know he was here?"

"Patches came in, yeah. Saw I had company. Figured he was sleeping it off, gave me a big grin and jived off. Like I say, the man is cool."

"What time would that have been?" Agate was making notes like crazy.

"Afternoon. Two, maybe two-thirty."

"So now that you know why Krishnan was here in the building," said Sheffield hopefully, "surely you'll be able to let him go?"

"I already did. I sent him home in a squad car." Agate frowned. "It's a helluva mess. Nobody's got an alibi, but there's not enough evidence to hold anybody. Yet." He scowled in my direction. "Except for reckless driving, that is." He sighed. "All we can do is keep digging, and wait."

"And hope we don't wait too long," I said, thinking of that time schedule we'd figured out, thinking of the Christmas lights that would be going up downtown in another week and the body of some unknown woman, beautifully dead in some other lonely grove of trees.

"Swan," said Lloyd, "I won't take you in tonight, but tomorrow morning, I want you down at my office. I want some prints from you, and I want some straight answers."

I had my doubts about those answers. Whatever the cataclysm that had ended the life of Geoffrey Glendon, artist and scholar, and given birth to Jaffer Swan, drifter, it wasn't likely to come to light easily or willingly, and certainly not with a Cop Shop steno writing the whole thing down.

Maxima stood up and pulled her fur coat tight round her thin form. "I assume we are all free to go now," she said stiffly.

Agate faced her. "What is it?" he asked suddenly. "What are you keeping to yourself?"

"Oh, torture, Lieutenant," she said, her voice ringing bitterly in the cavern of the basement room. "Torture and poison. But I'd gladly share them with *you*."

She marched out, hard little heels clacking on the concrete floor of the hallway, as Jaffer raised the clarinet.

The song was "Smoke Gets in Your Eyes."

Eighteen

Sheffield generously offered us a lift in the Black Beauty, but I made David drop Merriman and Yours Truly off at home instead, extracting an oath that he'd go straight back to Alex and the kid in the rented house near campus, and not head off on his own to nose around, as he is often wont to do. I'd seen that look in his eye when he met Jaffer Swan, or Glendon, or whatever the hell his name was, and I didn't care for it at all. The only crime Davy was supposed to be dealing with was the murder of one Desdemona, and I was determined to keep him on the sidelines—or at least on the stage, where I could watch him.

He drove off without saying much—never a good sign with David—and it was the first hour of a cold, clear November dawn when Merriman and I at last retired, not to bed—we were long past that—but to my cluttered lair upstairs, Prospero's Cave of blessed memory, where I grade student themes on "Social Relevance in the Novels of Mickey Spillane," hatch plots for my Winchester Hyde mysteries, clean my antediluvian brain of the muck splashed upon it by Civilization As We Know It at the *fin* of a highly equivocal *siècle,* and sip my Haig & Haig amid a cloud of decadent smoke from my beloved Turkish cigarettes with no one to prophesy doom or discuss my wellness profile. Even Sarah does not venture to advise me there, and entrance is by invitation only.

Not that I wouldn't have invited her, mind you, but she was stacking up the z's in our bedroom down the hall, the poor old eye swollen and sore. I looked in on her, but I hadn't the heart to wake her, and I tiptoed down the hall again to the Cave and rejoined Merriman, who was already comfortably ensconced with his scuffed opera slippers propped up on one of my convenient stacks of unfiled files, a glass of the Highland elixir in his hand.

I lit a Turkish Delight and settled back with a creak of complaint from my ancient, springless swivel chair.

"Out with it, old friend," I said. "What's been eating you?"

"Give me one of those confounded cigarettes," he demanded.

"You don't smoke cigarettes! What's the matter, your old pipe finally give up the ghost, did she?"

"I am in the mood for self-disgust. Give me a cigarette, or would you like me to buy one from you?"

"Touchy, touchy!" I said, and handed him a smoke. He struck a match, inhaled, choked, and put the thing out in my ashtray. "Feel better now?" I asked him.

"No. I do not." He sipped his scotch and frowned. "All right. I saw something. Back in August. The seventeenth of August."

"The day they found old Mrs. Ten Eyck in Vandenberg Park?" That sequence of fatal dates was burnt into my memory by now.

He nodded. "I was out sketching. Beastly day, dog days of August and all that. Heavy and breathless, but the only time of year the water lilies in that pond at the west end are blooming. I was planning something rather in the Monet-at-Giverny line, and I'd set up my things under the big mountain ash tree on the rise above the pond. They didn't see me at all, but I certainly saw them."

"Oh, for the love of Mike, saw who? Whom?"

"I saw Isabel Ten Eyck, poor soul. She seemed happy, very much at ease and breathing quite easily in spite of her asthma. Wearing that old straw sun hat she always sported in the summertime, bunch of yellow flowers stuck in it.'' Merriman looked across the desk at me, his face set, determined to have it out, now. "Elsa was walking with her. Arm in arm. Carrying a basket full of late roses, deep red ones. Laughing. You know that wonderful laugh of Elsa's. 'What a lovely image,' I thought, 'those two women, delighted with the force of life in them.' Something from an Impressionist picture, the summer light on their faces, broken by the leaves of the trees. Their images in the pond as they passed, with the water lilies. And yet—'' He sat silent, sipping his scotch.

"Something about it worried you?''

"Only mildly. I convinced myself, as one does. Decided it was nothing to be concerned about. But her face. Elsa's face. It was lovely, of course, as always. That richness, quickness of hers. But there was a—an absence. Sense of dissociation. I've noticed it before, of course, at Madam Max's Sunday sherry parties and so on, but I suppose I put it down to pressures, to thinking about several things at once, which I'm guilty of myself, naturally. If Isabel Ten Eyck hadn't been found dead in that park, on that very day, I shouldn't have thought another thing about it. But—''

"But Merriman! Four women?'' I was stunned, partly because of the vague misgivings that had been lurking in the back of my own head since our meeting with Agate in the orchard. "Surely you don't seriously think that Elsa—''

"No! I don't know *what* I think!'' he snapped at me. "I'm damn sick of thinking at all! I'm not especially good at it, this hour of the morning. I only know that I've been in a very dark place for the last three months, and I'd like to see a bit of sun breaking through, but the weather seems to get gloomier, what with Macauley and poor young Krishnan, and this fellow Swan, and old Piers—'' He heaved a sigh. "And then there's the matter of the figure I saw at the terrace windows the other night.''

"Elsa?''

"That I could *not* say, I'm delighted to admit. But it *might* have been a woman. And Elsa isn't tiny. Not the size of our Hilda, of course, but large enough to simulate a man, if she were dressed like one, in a man's coat and cap.''

"But why? That's what I don't get. What reason would Elsa Worthing have to kill Isabel Ten Eyck, or Hallie, or any of the others? I could understand her killing Macauley. He was a threat, may he rest in whatever peace he can. And obviously, she knew at least two of the women who've been killed. I don't know about the Godowski woman, but we could check.''

"I did. Mary Ann Godowski only worked part-time at the supermarket, Winnie. She had a second job three days a week, doing housework for that maid service, Happy Helpers. She came in twice a month to help Elsa with the heavy cleaning.''

"And Angela Cody?''

"Delivered flowers for Elsa on her bicycle in the summers.''

I paused, my pooped-out gray cells struggling to gain a little strength from the whisky. "Look,'' I said at last. "Piers knew all four of them, too. If they all knew Elsa, then probably Swan knew them, too, or at least might have seen them, followed them. Elsa knows half the women in this town, thanks to those flower-arranging classes of hers, the herb-growing. She's a fixture in Ainsley, she does charity work, she serves on the library committee, the hospital auxiliary. Sarah knows her, too, and Alexandra goes to those classes. What you saw in the park that morning—it doesn't prove a damn thing, Eddie.''

I heard the words I was saying, but I didn't quite believe them. By itself, Eddie's image of the two women walking through the park on the day that proved fatal to Mrs. Ten Eyck might have been merely poignant, and no evidence at all. But taken with the obvious lies Elsa and Graham had told, taken with Elsa's strange explosion of violence against Sarah, taken with whatever secret Maxima was keeping—it was unsettling, to say the least.

"Still,'' Merriman continued, "I feel I ought to have said something. Those other two women—''

"Lloyd doesn't buy the idea that Macauley was the murderer. He thinks it was a setup. The murderer wanted a patsy for the crimes and he also wanted Macauley out of the way, so he zapped two birds with one stone."

"And if he's right and Macauley wasn't the Heart Specialist, then someone else is. And before Christmas, if our killer sticks to schedule—"

"You could go to Lloyd, tell him about seeing Elsa with Mrs. Ten Eyck."

"And put the dear creature through the same torment we saw Krishnan going through this evening, probably for no reason at all beyond my overactive imagination? A woman who underwent horrors as a young girl, a woman who—"

"Or we can muddle through on our own," I said. "Keep this whole business under our hats and poke around a bit more. Try to find out what's really going on with Elsa. Probably has nothing to do with either Macauley or those dead ladies."

"It may just be a string of unfortunate coincidences—marriage failing, Graham's being away so much, the trouble with the council." Eddie's high tenor was breathless and eager.

"I think I'll have a little chat with the chilly Mrs. Macauley," I told him. "And get my nose into that file of Sheffield's."

"And perhaps," suggested Merriman, "we can manage to lay hands on Graham, wherever he's sequestered himself."

"So," I said, trying my damnedest to sound reassuring, "even if we can't figure out who killed whom and why, we may just clear up this suspicion of Elsa, so that if Lloyd happens to draw a bead on her himself—"

"We can head the good fellow off at the pass!" Eddie drew a deep breath and let it out slowly. "Winston, you have no idea the relief. Now, then, what's next? We're *not* investigating Macauley's murder."

"Not exactly . . ."

"We're *not* looking for the Heart Specialist."

"Unless we happen to trip over him . . ."

"We're merely trying to help a friend." Merriman paused for breath and sat staring at the rising morning beyond the row of long

225

windows of my Cave. The optimism ebbed out of his weary face and he frowned at his whisky glass. "Help," he said. "A kind impulse, but I've seen it turn into a wicked weapon."

I considered him, my eyes narrowed under beetle brows. "There's something else, isn't there? Something more than that Monet painting that came to life in the park last August?"

He looked at me and opened his mouth. Then he closed it again. "Go to bed, Winnie," he said. "We are old men, you and I, and ought to know when to close our eyes."

"You'll tell me in the end, you know. You always do."

I held the bottle poised and offered him another glass. He only shook his head and walked away.

It was broad daylight when I slipped into bed beside Sarah at last, being careful not to wake her. I might as well have saved myself the trouble.

"Have you done anything I ought to know about?" she said, turning over with a grunt. "Or have you just been batting your hard old bean against the same old wall all night?"

"More or less," I said, pulling her against me.

"Ouch."

"Sorry. How's the trophy?" I peered over at her. The eye was at least four different shades of blue and purple. "I haven't seen a shiner like that since I was twelve and Raymond 'Attila' Hunsecker belted me with a sucker snowball that had a rock in the middle. I was in my glory for a week, with everybody asking me whether it hurt or not."

"It does," she said. "It feels like hell."

"Mmmmm." I stroked her hair a bit, waiting.

"Win?"

"Kiddo?"

"Nobody ever hit me before."

"Not even Erskine?"

"*My* father? I don't think he ever had an emotion honest enough

226

to explode. If he'd wanted to sock me in the eye, he probably would've hired somebody to do it. The way he was, devious and cold and— Well, I almost used to wish he *would* hit me, so I could hit him back.''

"Did you hit Elsa back?''

She was quiet, and her hand found mine. "I don't understand it, Win. I was nothing to her, nothing at all. I could see it in her eyes. As if I were a piece of wood, a thing to bang her anger out on. She had no human memory of me at that moment. I didn't exist. I feel— as though something's broken in me, and I can't find what it is. I love her. That's what's horrid. I still do. But there's that break, and I can't find it and fix it. I can just feel it, hurting and hurting. In time I'll pretend it doesn't hurt anymore, and maybe it won't. Maybe it will heal.''

"But breaks that aren't set straight don't heal true,'' I said. "There'll always be that weakness in you. That little crooked place where it's dark and dangerous.''

"Like David,'' she said. "You know, even now, I'm never quite sure what he'll do, how he'll react. Neither is Alex. The ruin never goes away, does it, not really? I never understood that before.''

"Will you go back to Elsa's?'' I said, holding her hand to my lips. "Will you see her again?''

"Oh,'' she said. "Yes. Yes. I must. Mustn't I?''

What damage, I wondered, had been done to Elsa Worthing? What terrors lived in the part of her that had never healed, the part that had exploded at Sarah?

"I don't know what I'll say to her. Nothing, probably. You see, it's extra difficult, because she's a woman. I don't quite know what to do.''

"Suppose *I* had hit you,'' I said. "What would you have done?''

She was quiet for a long, long time. She reached up then, and kissed me gently.

"I'd have killed you, I think,'' she said, absolutely serious.

Then it was my turn to lapse into silence. She was right, of course. We have weathered hard words and separations and minor infidelities and illness and catastrophe, and never seriously thought of ending things between us. But some things, some mindless, sudden acts of folly strike at the human bond, the glue of self-respect and private honor that holds the self, evanescent at the best of times and vulnerable to attack, upright and whole. "I was nothing to her," Sarah had said, and from Elsa, she could bear it and not strike back. But, thank the gods, I was more than a friend or a lover. I was part of her, and the betrayal would have been unbearable. I would have deserved to die.

"Make love to me, Win," she said softly. "I don't care if it makes my eye hurt."

I did, and it didn't. In the midst of the proceedings, she suddenly said, quite calmly, as I was nuzzling her neck:

"I do think we'd better get another doctor. Sexual dysfunction, phooey!"

We all slept most of that day, Friday. I had no classes, the faculty meeting was canceled, and Sheffield had agreed to teach Krish's two sections himself—a thing unheard-of in the annals of arts and letters, from a man who avoids actual classroom time at all costs. He'd probably ship them off to the library, but since most of them had only heard of libraries from their grandmothers and never actually seen one, it could only do the young blisters good.

I woke sometime in the middle of the afternoon and toddled down to the kichen to squeeze myself a glass of anything sour enough to make my mouth stop feeling like an old washrag, and as I hit the bottom step of the back stairs I spotted the hulking figure of Lloyd Agate just leaving our back door and headed for his cop car, which was pulled up under the portico.

I threw open the door. "Come on in, Lloyd," I said. "Sleeping Beauty's wide awake now. What can I do for you?"

He shambled in looking exhausted and slightly gray around the eyes and mouth, and sat down at the table, his huge frame hunched and comfortless. I found coffee and made it and dug out some old swaybacked graham crackers, all without getting a word out of the man. Then I poured the coffee and sat down opposite him.

"Okay, kiddo," I said. "What's the latest? Did Swan come down for those fingerprints?"

He nodded. "They matched the prints on that book and the card I found, but we did paraffin tests on him, and got nothing. Nothing on Ghandour, either. The prints on that gun were smudged. They almost always are. But we did get two fairly clear ones, a thumb and an index, two different sets overlaid. The lab did a batch of reconstructions, and we got them pretty clear."

"And?"

"The thumb was Ghandour's. The index finger was Macauley's. Nothing on the needle, the bottle, or the string of beads. Weird."

"Well, if Swan passed the paraffin test, at least you know he didn't shoot Macauley. And neither did Krish."

"I'll go along with you about Ghandour. We got his test fast enough to be accurate. But with Swan, it was too damn long a time lapse. Might've found traces after that long, but it'd be dicey. He's still a candidate." He dug in his pocket for a box of Fisherman's Friends and popped one. "By the way, your pal Krish is clear on his girl's death, too. That deli where he bought his supplies after the movie? NYPD tracked it down this morning. One of those new cash registers that practically print out the color of your eyes, right? The computer called up a copy for us, and it tallied with everything he said he bought, and it had the time on it. Must've taken him longer to get back uptown than he thought. It was after one when they rang up that sale, and he couldn't have made it back here that fast unless he had a helicopter. Besides, the Korean kid on the cash desk remembered him, said almost nobody's that polite in the middle of the night."

At least Krish was in the clear. I breathed a huge sigh of relief, as Agate went on.

"I talked to Helen Macauley this morning, Doc. We traced the serial number and the gun that killed the guy was registered to her. Funny woman. Still pretty much in shock, I guess. But I don't know— You ever meet her, get to know her? What do you make of her, Doc?"

"Not much. I've only met her once. But I had a mind to pay a little call of condolence on the chancelloress, maybe take a colleague or two along." I'd been thinking of Sheffield's offer to toss the joint, and there couldn't have been a better front woman than Lady Di. Between the three of us, we might just find out something.

"I'd appreciate it if you'd take a crack at her," said Agate. "This whole damn business is getting to me, Doc."

"You haven't hit a bed in days, have you?" I asked him. "You look like hell warmed over. What does Bev say?"

"Unprintable." He grinned, more or less. Mrs. Agate is a tough cookie and has been through more than one crime spree. "She thinks Macauley did it. Thinks he did kill himself after he killed those women. She went to one of those council meetings about Mrs. Bergner's place—you know Bev, she wants to run for councilwoman —anyhow, she said Macauley gave her the willies. He got up to talk, and he didn't make any sense, didn't have a single good reason for what he wanted. Just wanted it because he wanted it. Power, you know? Ego." He sighed. "Maybe she's right. It's beginning to look like that suicide might just be the real thing." He drew a breath through his adenoids. "I feel like hell. I think I'm catching a cold. I hate November." He pulled a bottle of nasal spray out of his pocket, tipped his head back, and snuffed mightily. "Sinus really gets me. We did some lab work on that pot of stuff with the bullet in it, right? Same caliber as the shot that killed Macauley. Nine millimeter. Fired from the same gun."

"Were there any ashes in the pot? Anything at all?" I said.

"Not much that we could isolate from the dirt," he replied. " 'Vegetable matter,' that's all the report said. We sent a slide to the FBI lab in Manhattan. Maybe they can tell us what the hell it was." Lloyd sat thinking. "That smell in there, Doc. You know, when I was a kid, back in the Sixties, we tried everything there was to get high on. Remember Mellow Yellow? Bananas were big. I even knew a

230

damn fool who shot up on peanut butter, like to killed himself. You know how it was—long hair and camel bells and incense."

I have to admit, I had a hard time picturing Lloyd Agate with a camel bell around his neck and a joss stick in his mitt, but what the hell, we were all young once.

"We used to buy this incense at a little place in Chinatown, got you higher than a kite and all you had to do was light the stuff. Poofed right up, like gunpowder," he went on.

I had a funny pricking in my thumbs. "Like the stuff magicians use?" I asked him.

"Yeah! Yeah, and after a while the customs guys must've got onto it, because you couldn't buy it anymore. But I was thinking—"

"Lloyd," I said, "that little place in Chinatown? You think it's still there?"

"I don't know. The guy sold imported teas and souvenirs and junk, little jade, some rice bowls—you know the kind of joint. And herbs. All those Chinese shops sell ginseng, herbs to make your fortune come true."

"Can you get me a pinch of those vegetable ashes from the flowerpot in Macauley's office, Agate?" I said. "I'm feeling the urge to shop for a bit of ginseng root."

He grinned. "They do say it keeps you virile."

"Oh, goody," I grumbled. "Let's send some to Dr. Pennington, shall we? It can't do the old behemoth any harm."

Agate dragged himself off to confront the grim blank spaces of the job at hand, and I took my coffee into the living room, figuring to settle into that somnolent transitional daze that passes for consciousness when my regular hours of sleep and waking are rearranged by fate. And a helluva fate it was, too. It was only Friday, and since Wednesday two people I knew had been found dead, Sarah had been bashed by her best friend, and several of my own pals had turned into suspects. Not to mention the fact that I myself had staged a car chase worthy of James Bond—well, a sort of geriatric Bond, at least— been accused of spouse beating, and collapsed in an interesting heap on the kitchen floor.

The last three days had been surreal, an upside-down universe in which nothing was what it seemed and no one could quite be taken at face value. Sheffield had turned out to have a gleam of human conviction, and Elsa a vein of blind rage that made her dangerous. But how dangerous? That was the question that had been nagging Eddie, and now the old blister had passed it on to me.

I sank down in the familiar contours my unique physique has molded into the living room couch over the years and sipped my half-cold coffee, wishing I could drift off to sleep again and wake up to find that I was back in that torture-chamber hospital bed of Hortense's, that I'd been under the influence of her intravenous goofer dust for the last three days, and nothing that happened had really happened at all.

I closed my eyes for a minute, hoping that when I opened them, the whole business would've gone away. I opened them. It hadn't.

What I saw, on the coffee table in front of the couch next to my bedroom-slippered hooves, was a manila file folder. I picked it up— with some trepidation, I might add—just as Merriman toddled into the room, blinking and yawning.

"This yours, Eddie?" I asked him. I hesitated to open it what with one thing and another. Surprises did seem to keep exploding in my face, you see.

"What's that? File? No. My file on the Heart Specialist is in my parlor, on the writing desk. I put things away, you see. Don't leave them scattered about piecemeal like some people who shall remain nameless." He perched on the arm of the couch and peered down at the file. "What's in it?"

I took a deep breath and opened the cover, glanced down the first page, then sighed with relief. The phone in the hall was ringing, and I heard Sarah answer it. Life seemed to be getting back to normal at last.

"It's only Sheffield's file on Macauley," I said. "Why didn't you tell me he dropped it off yesterday?"

"I didn't tell you, Goopus, because he *didn't* drop it off. Thomas was never here, to my knowledge." Merriman frowned at the thing.

"Then how did it get here?" I said. "I've been trying to get this file from him for weeks, ever since Macauley started the campaign to condemn Madam Max's place. Now all of a sudden it just materializes on the coffee table?"

"Perhaps the same person brought it who delivered Swan's book and the greeting card for Lloyd to find at Smitty's," he suggested.

"Perhaps." I mused for a minute, listening to Sarah's voice on the phone. "Or maybe it's magic."

"Piers, you think?"

"If you can get out of a locked cabinet full of knives, you can damn well get into a locked office and a locked living room," I said. "Besides, he probably knows where we hide the extra key, under the planter. Whoever it was—"

"Damn the man!" Sarah hung up the telephone with a crash and came rushing in. "That was Alex," she said. "David came home last night and went to bed and when she woke up he was gone!"

"Oh, my tail and whiskers," I groaned. "He's on the prowl again, confound him!" I hefted myself up. "I was afraid of this. He got entirely too interested in that fellow Swan last night. Why can't the kiddo just work with *us,* instead of dashing off like the Lone Ranger?"

"Because," said Eddie, "we are a team, and David is not a team player, bless his anachronistic heart. He functions best alone and in control. Let him be, you two, and stop worrying."

"No," said Sarah, "you don't understand! He didn't take the car. His shoes were still beside the bed, where he took them off. He didn't get dressed, his pajamas were nowhere in sight. None of his coats was missing. He isn't just gone, Win! David's vanished!"

Nineteen

Now you see him, now you don't.

David Cromwell, star of stage, screen, and television, director of the college production of *Othello,* sometime sleuth and silent partner in the private detection firm of Julian Stockfish Associates in Manhattan—Davy is the "Associates"—had indeed vanished, but hardly into thin air. He had done what he usually does when something's eating him; he'd changed his shape.

He didn't wear his usual shoes because they were too clean and respectable. Instead, he dug a pair of worn-out tennies with a gaping hole in the side and broken laces out of the box in the mudroom of the old house he and Alex were sharing. He'd joined in his wife's idyllic delusions to the extent of buying a rake and raking the front yard when the leaves were falling, and when he ditched the muddy tennies on the back step, the neighbor's Yorkie had waltzed over and used them for a chew-bone. They'd been headed for the next trash pickup by the Boy Scouts, who seemed to be able to recycle anything, but they were just the thing for the little job David had in mind that morning.

With bare feet in the old tennies, he moved on up his lanky pajama-clad frame, building the role as he went. His oldest jeans went over the pajama bottoms, and the light blue top impersonated a chambray work shirt. Over this went a baggy fatigue jacket Alex wore when she went out to Elsa's to muck about with the plants. It was grimy and tattered, and big as a tent on tiny Alexandra, but it more or less fitted her husband.

David studied himself in the long mirror on the hall closet door. The beard hadn't been shaved, the eyes were shadowed from lack of sleep and a bit red around the edges, the hair hadn't been cut in a while because he'd have to curl it for Othello when the show went up—all in all, he looked sleezy and broke and completely untrustworthy.

It was just what he wanted. He closed the back door silently behind him and made for the riverfront.

Irene Ransom was on a stepladder with a caulking gun when he got to Smitty's, trying to smear waterproof caulking around the old patch on her leaky roof. She squinted down in Davy's general direction. "Shit," she said. "You know how to use a caulking gun?"

"Hell, yes," he told her with a grin.

Now, as you might expect, they don't teach you a lot about fixing roofs at the Royal Academy of Dramatic Art. David had absolutely no idea what a caulking gun was, let alone what you did with one, but he figured he could wing it. He held out a hand and Reeney climbed down.

She dusted herself off and gave him a long, hard, unembarrassed stare. "How you like 'em?" she said at last.

He gulped. "Like what?"

"Your eggs, honey. Over easy, couple sausages, fries, coffee? That do you?"

That'd do Paul Bunyan, thought David, but what he said was, "Great."

That was all he said. He just followed her silently to the bar and watched as she did the eggs and sausages, fixed the fries, and poured the strong, oily-looking coffee. Under the gaze of his tired dark eyes, Reeney's movements were tense and uncertain. Men made her nervous and she didn't trust them. That was because she was a sucker for every damn one of them, bar none.

"So," she said, "you wanna work a couple days? I can use somebody to clean out the back room, maybe paint it. Fix this goddamn roof. Jeez!"

David ate hungrily, though he'd stopped for an Egg McMuffin on the way. He nodded, his mouth full of sausage. "Right you are, ma'am. I been out of work awhile."

Ma'am, she thought. *That's nice. Old-fashioned and nice.*

The liberated broads nobody ever took it out on could afford to throw away gentle words and call them sexist. What did they know? Sexist was a sonuvabitch ex-husband who broke into your trailer two years after the divorce and cracked three of your goddamn ribs and stuck himself in you like you were made out of plastic, like you were make-believe or brain-dead, without a memory or pain or need of hope, who broke you and left you spraddled on the floor with a death inside you, a whole black universe of hurt and cold and made you nothing Christ nothing that could even any longer cry, because tears belonged to human things and you were none.

No. Ma'am isn't sexist. Ma'am is cautious and tender and a little bit afraid.

She looked down at the guy's feet. He was barefooted in the mangy tennies. "Look, honey," she said, "I got some shoes and socks in my trailer, across there." She nodded toward the other side of the parking lot. "Used to belong to my ex, The Lousy Bastard. Might fit you. You'll get the shivering shits trying to get through the winter in them things you got on."

"Thanks," he said, stuffing in the last of the breakfast. "I kinda wore the suckers to hell, eh? Long way down here from Canada."

"Oh, yeah? Whereabouts?" He had the accent, all right, he said "reet" and "oot" and "eh." He had the Canadian way about him, too. A little Brit, a little careful. Must be all that snow up there, she figured, and the long dark nights. The Canucks knew how to keep their counsel.

Jaffer had been in Canada. Reeney felt a spasm of loss when she thought of him. She could've loved the guy. After everything, she was still strong enough for that. He had been kind and friendly, in his way, but not really interested. He had a woman somewhere, that was why. The good ones always did, like this new guy here, still wearing a wedding band he could've hocked for a decent pair of shoes but wouldn't part with.

He, too, would drift away like Swanny. Where the hell was he now? she wondered. What wind had blown him suddenly off track?

"I'm from Toronto," said the tall, dark-bearded guy. Actually, he said "Toronno," like a regular native. "I worked the grain boats at the Soo a while, but I got canned. Company sold out and went to shipping by rail. Thought I'd check out the weather down here, eh?" He smiled, a nice smile, not too sure of itself.

Reeney nodded. "Okay," she said. "I got a mattress in the back room where you can crash. No juicing, no hitting on the customers, no getting high, no cute stuff with the cash drawer."

"No, ma'am."

"Irene," she said. "My name's Irene. People call me Reeney. You?"

"Ian," he told her, picking the first Canadian name that jumped into his mind. Must've been all those Ian and Sylvia records. "People call me Jack."

Irene went off to her trailer to find The Lousy Bastard's shoes, leaving him to take his best shot at the caulking gun, but David had other ideas. He made his way down the dingy back hall to the storeroom for a little reconnoitering.

The boxes that had tumbled over on Lloyd Agate had been restacked, and everything was neat and tidy, except for the two stained, lumpy mattresses in the far corner of the room, where a square, unlocked window looked out on the back of the parking lot.

David examined the window. It was fairly large, big enough for a reasonably bulky frame to squeeze through, even in a hurry. Whoever had been here planting that book and the card that would turn

Agate's eye in Swan's direction had probably been halfway out the window when Lloyd opened the storeroom door. Whoever it *had* been, it couldn't have been Swan, David was sure of that. Jaffer said he'd found Krish in Elsa Worthing's orchard and taken him to the furnace room at the school to rest and warm up. If only Krish had been able to confirm the story, Swan would've been home free. But so long as it looked like he was sneaking around, evading the cops and running away, Swan looked guilty as hell of something, even if it wasn't the murders of those four women, the last of them his own daughter.

David dropped to his knees and crawled the space around the window, found nothing and got up again to survey the rest of the corner. There was a stack of worn, neatly folded blankets, a few old magazines and comic books in a cardboard box, a muddle of assorted junk—roller shades without springs, a spineless venetian blind, the bottom half of a percolator—piled near the mattresses. David gave the venetian blind a nudge with the toe of his sneaker and the thing unrolled like a Slinky all over his feet.

It was when he bent down to free himself that he saw the small square of tan card stock, printed in bright red, that was caught between the slats of the blind.

It was a ticket from a parking garage in Manhattan, EZ-PARK, just off West End Avenue on Seventy-ninth Street. David knew it well; he lived in that part of town himself, and he might have thought he'd lost the claim ticket out of his own pocket, if he'd been dressed as he usually was.

But it wasn't his. Whose, then? Somebody climbing out a window in a loose jacket or a raincoat, falling behind him as he clambered up in a hurry, might've lost a slip of paper without noticing.

Somebody with a car. Most of the guests at Reeney's back-room motel, he figured, traveled by thumb, but they didn't drive and they didn't use parking lots. The card had a license number scribbled on it: OKK 8759. It had been stamped with the hours of entry and exit to the lot, and the date. November 12, twelve-thirty A.M., was the final checkout time. The night Krish had spent in Manhattan, and less than two hours before Hallie Glendon had died in Elsa's orchard. You could drive from Manhattan up here to Ainsley in two hours, easily, at night when the roads were quiet, if you pushed it a little.

David stuffed the thing in his pocket. According to Blanche Megrim, Krish hadn't taken his own car, but he could've rented one, come up here, killed his fiancée and driven back to his hotel in Manhattan after that Indian epic film was over.

But he hadn't. Krish couldn't have killed anybody, not even to save his own neck. It was somebody else who had come here to cast suspicion on Jaffer Swan, somebody who had access to his books, somebody who hated him enough to want him out of the way. Somebody who had been here, in Reeney's place, on the night of November 12, when he said he was tucked up in bed with his wife. Somebody who had taken off the next day and hadn't been seen or heard from since. Somebody Eddie Merriman might've seen at the terrace doors in the same light raincoat from whose pocket that parking stub had been lost.

Graham Worthing.

It hit him suddenly, and it seemed to make perfect sense. David knew he ought to give that parking stub to Lloyd Agate, let him dust it and check out the license plate number. He also knew he wasn't going to. Agate was a good cop, but the rules a good cop played by put up walls that sometimes shut the wrong people in. Krish was one of the wrong people. So was Geoffrey Swan. Until he heard Graham Worthing's story, David could not be sure he wasn't putting still another of the wrong people in that small square of rigid, necessary, suffocating blank walls made of rules and duties that could crush you as they closed.

He made for the pay phone in the hall and was just swearing under his breath at the OUT OF ORDER sign, when Irene came up behind him, a pair of long, narrow black wing-tips, slightly scuffed, in her hand.

"You need a phone, you can use the one behind the bar. No charge for local, I'll take the long-distance out of your salary." He nodded, and she studied him quizzically. "Any luck with that roof?"

"We'll get it, ma'am," he said, and with a sigh, he followed her out to the bar again. He fiddled with the tube of caulking and loaded it in the gun, then climbed up the ladder to take stock of the job. Irene perched on one of the high bar stools, counting last night's take and recording it in a battered old ledger.

"Got enough caulk, you think?" she said, looking up at David.

He ground his teeth, wishing he knew what to do with the stuff. "More than enough," he told her, and meant it. He fiddled with the job a bit, thinking, an idea taking shape at the back of his mind. At last he dived in and took his best shot. "There was a guy here while you were gone," he said, "fancy car. Executive type. Kinda glassy-eyed, right? Big guy, a little red in the face. Muscles like a fighter." He was describing Graham Worthing, whom he'd met once or twice up at Elsa's. "Said he was in here a couple nights ago and thought he lost a credit card."

"Oh," said Irene, "that's old Karl. It's Charlie, really, but he likes Karl better. Go figure. Charlie Graham, he's a salesman. Real estate, I think. On the road a lot. He stops in here when he's bottomed-out and needs a little liquid energy. Always comes in real late at night, doesn't talk much. Just drinks straight bourbon and watches the regulars get pissed and stumble out. I never let 'em go out and drive juiced-up, though. You watch that, too, Jack, okay? Just steer 'em to the back room, let 'em sleep it off."

David forged ahead. "Some car he was driving, eh? Jaguar, was it?"

"Hell," said Reeney, "what do I know from cars? A Jag, a Merc, a BMW. That's it, though, a BMW. 'Cause I kidded him about it, you know, called it his Yuppiemobile."

David smeared the last of the caulking around the leak and prayed. "That'll hold 'er," he said, with considerable bravado, and climbed down.

Irene squinted up at the roof. "Not bad," she said with a grin. "Not too shabby. Now you can sweep out and then the tables need swabbing. First try on the shoes, though."

He had been hoping to slip out the back door, but her eyes held him, wide and pale and almost colorless within the penumbra of willow green mascara. He saw no greed there, no lies, no ego, no cheap and patronizing write-offs. Irene took the human race one face at a time, keeping each new riddle clean of the pain and anger the last had left behind.

You will give away your life, he thought, *an inch at a time, in quenchless hope. You will be used and battered and discarded and left alone. To die alone.*

He could not leave her yet. For two cents, Ian would've stayed the night with a lonely lady. But David sighed and smiled and sat down to squeeze his bare feet into the long narrow shoes of The Lousy Bastard.

"They don't fit, do they?" said Reeney anxiously.

"Appreciate your trouble," he told her, wishing he could fake a different shoe size and make her smile. It was impossible. The things were at least an inch too narrow for him. "They don't fit. Not really."

"Figures," she replied with a shrug and a soft smile. "I shoulda known a guy like you wouldn't fit into that freako's shoes." She stood up and brushed a hand delicately across his sleeve. "How about some lunch?" she said. "I make a helluva cheeseburger, hon'."

It was six hours later, after the sweeping and the swabbing and a hefty lunch and a stint of window washing, that the telephone in our front hall began to ring. I was up in my Cave with that file of Sheffield's that had mysteriously appeared overnight, and was about to trot out to grab the upstairs extension, when I heard Sarah beat me to it down in the front hall. She'd been working out her worry and her battered feelings on a Chopin polonaise at the old Steinway in the living room, and she rushed for the phone the minute it rang. I made do with listening in on the extension.

241

It was Davy.

"You idiot!" she cried. "Where have you been? Alex is worried sick, and if I could get my hands on you, I'd throttle the life out of you! Haven't you any consideration at all?"

"Listen to me," he said calmly, "and stop grandstanding. I've been working, that's all. I'm perfectly all right. And *I* haven't *got* a black eye."

"Phooey! You're the one who's grandstanding, you—"

"Filibustering, then. Sarah, I need to know something. What's Graham Worthing's middle name?"

"Why," she said, "that's easy. It's Charles. Graham Charles Worthing. Elsa always calls him Karl."

"Do you know where his office is, the ad agency?"

"Madison Avenue somewhere, that's all I've ever heard. Why all the interest in Graham? Has he turned up at home again?"

"His car, sis. Is it a BMW? What's the license number?"

"It's blue, for pity's sake! I can't even remember my *own* license number. David, what's going on?"

"What have you found, kiddo?" I chimed in from the extension.

"Hello, Winnie," he said. "Maybe nothing. Maybe a couple of answers. Possibilities, at least. Don't wait up."

"Kiddo, hold on!" I hollered into the receiver.

But it was too late. He'd hung up.

"Hell and damn!" I heard Sarah say, as she hung up her phone.

I hung up, too, and flipped through the address book on the phone stand till I found the number of Julian Stockfish, David's partner in crime. I dialed and got the confounded answering machine, then waited for the tone and began my message. "This is Winston Fish, Sherman," I said, ill-at-ease as usual with our technological masters. "I mean, Winston Sherman, Fish. Just wanted to warn you. David's on the rampage again and headed in your direction. He—"

"Doc?" Stockfish came on the line, live and in-person. "Sorry about that, sport. I'm avoiding my ex-wife. What's Dave got?"

"A bee in his bonnet, kiddo. It's this serial killer on the loose up

242

here. Davy's nosing around it, and he's out looking for a man named—"

"Graham Worthing?" Stockfish chuckled. "I know. David phoned me right after the guy ditched his wife and took off from Ainsley. I spent most of yesterday checking the dude out. Tyrone's staking out his apartment."

"Worthing would be at his office this time of day, wouldn't he?" I suggested

"He would if he still had one. From what I hear, the ad agency went belly-up six weeks ago. The office is for lease, no forwarding address. He's got a place on West End Avenue up in the Seventies, but it's up for sale, phone's disconnected, doorman told Tyrone the furniture's been sold and hauled away. We're keeping an eye on the place, but it looks like the guy's dived, right? Creditors nipping at his heels and he just did a good old bunk."

I didn't say it, but from what I knew of him, I wouldn't have thought Graham could pull off a disappearing act. He'd always seemed to me utterly honest, not so much from moral fiber or conviction as from want of imagination, the kind of man who chooses his road and keeps plodding down it, even when the road falls away under his feet.

"Fish," I said instead, "keep an eye on Davy. I'm not sure he's really good enough at this to go poking around on his own."

Julian Stockfish laughed softly. "With serial murder, pal, nobody's ever good enough."

I hung up the phone, feeling raw and sore and vaguely angry, not so much at Davy as at the muddle of oblique information and surmise and innuendo, of guilty appearances without a solid fact to hang them on that surrounded most of those touched by the deaths of Hallie Glendon and James Temple Macauley.

It wasn't as if I'd forgotten the other dead women. Mrs. Ten Eyck's trek through the park with Elsa and Angela Cody's visit to Manhattan with Chancellor Macauley kept flickering like television

243

images across my mental retina, my imagination investing them with vivid color and stereo sound. I could hear the laughter of the two women, I could see the teasing smile on the young girl's face as Macauley tried on clothes and postured to impress her.

But in addition to landing the whole thing in my lap, the last two deaths seemed to have brought the business to a head. If Macauley really was the killer, then he was dead by his own hand and we could all relax. If he wasn't, we had more tangible clues than we'd ever had, and the real Heart Specialist was running scared, trying to hide his tracks.

Or somebody was trying to hide them for him.

It hadn't occurred to me before, but even serial killers have wives and children and parents and lovers. Could anyone with a shred of humanity, I wondered, cover up four murders to save the life of a killer, no matter who he was?

I didn't have the answer. In fact, I wasn't even sure I had the right questions.

Sarah had gone back to her Chopin as I dragged my weary feet into my Cave and the recruitment file on Macauley that lay on my desk; I still nursed a shred of hope that I might find something there, some sudden revelation that would put an end to the killing.

What I found, to my surprise, was Piers Ambrose, his big, energetic body parked in my desk chair, his feet up, and a glass of my best scotch—a hefty one, at that—in his hand.

"Hocus-pocus-dominocus," I growled at him. I absolutely refused to be a prey to prestidigitation at my time of life. "This is getting boring, Ambrose. Get the hell out of my chair, and a plague upon you!"

He just laughed. "Sarah was punishing the Pole when I knocked, so I just let myself in."

"Let yourself in last night, too, didn't you, with that file of Sheffield's? Do you magicians use regular picklocks, or do you just dematerialize and then reassemble yourselves the other side of the door?"

"Speaking for myself, I prefer a nice plastic credit card. Works

244

like a charm," he said. "I wanted you to have the file before things went too much further. You never know about men with Thomas's peculiar brand of self-interest. He might just decide that since he helped hire the bloody bastard in the first place, he'd be smeared when your Keystone Kop got hold of the file and started putting two and two together about Macauley. I was afraid Sheffield might get a fit of the vapors and decide to burn the thing to save face."

I nodded "Interesting theory. But it assumes that Sheffield has put two and two together himself and knows the implications of what's in this file. I haven't had a chance to read it yet, but obviously you have. Care to fill me in? That is why you came, isn't it?"

Why was it that at that particular moment I remembered one of my big scenes from *Othello,* the one where Iago comes to Desdemona's daddy (played by Yours Truly) and says "Guess who's coming to dinner" in his best blank verse? I lit a Turkish Delight, and sat back to enjoy Piers's performance.

"I didn't have to read the damn thing," he said. "Helen told me."

"Helen?" I choked on my cigarette and grabbed a swig of Piers's scotch. "You mean Helen Macauley? You know her?"

He smiled, one of those smug ones that make me want to pop him one. "I do," he said. "I know her rather well."

The lines of that scene rang in my ears.

> Your heart is burst, you have lost half your soul;
> Even now, now, very now, an old black ram
> Is tupping your white ewe.

Piers shrugged. "Helen's an intelligent girl, and Macauley bored her. I wasn't busy. We had some interests in common. She's a bug on Arthurian literature, it seems. The world is full of unemployed English majors. I happened to meet her at old Pennington's office, in the waiting room."

I curled my lip. "Not much of a recommendation. I suppose you

245

pulled a couple of rabbits out of your hat and seduced her on the spot, did you? What were you doing at the doctor's office, anyhow? You're healthy as a horse. Or should I say stallion?''

"Just a checkup," he said casually. "Helen has a little heart condition.''

"Wouldn't know what she takes for it, would you?''

He laughed. "Sorry, old Sherlock. We don't spend a lot of time discussing the ills our flesh is heir to, Helen and I. I expect she'll be able to throw the damn pills away, anyhow, now that her pig of a husband's dead." His broad, affable face was transformed at the thought of Macauley, the dark, slanting brows dived down into a scowl. "He was a brute, Winnie. Without exaggeration. Oh, not in the predictable ways. He never struck Helen, never. He preferred subtler humiliations." Piers closed his eyes, then opened them again and fixed me with a stare. "He fancied little girls. Never touched them. Took pictures sometimes. Got them interested. Fancied them. Did you know?''

I didn't give him the satisfaction of being surprised. "I know he'd been squiring young Angela Cody.''

"Yes!''

He pounced, Iago-like, on the image, and something about his description of Macauley's perverse amours reminded me of the character he had drawn that night on stage, his lips so deliberately on David's, his hands exploring Alex without intent. Or perhaps, I thought, the intent had been the fact that I was out there watching, just waiting to be put off the scent by a bit of fancy footwork.

"Helen was terrified, she came to me in the middle of the night. He'd been out all day and most of the night, his secretary had no idea where he was. Then the Cody girl turned up dead. Helen knew Macauley'd been watching her. That's what he did. Watched them, sometimes in person, sometimes through spyglasses. Moved in, struck up a friendship. I don't know all the details. Helen couldn't bring herself to tell me everything." He tapped the file on my desk with a long, hard index finger. "And it isn't the first time a woman's died because of him. It's all in there."

I glanced at the page in front of me. "You mean the lady professor in Wisconsin followed the same pattern?"

"Belmont College, yes," he said. "It's Minnesota, actually, up near the border. The professor of music history who died suddenly after Macauley had hounded her for almost two years."

"But Piers," I reminded him, "that woman committed suicide, didn't she?"

"That was the official version. The college hushed it up, as colleges will—with the help of Norman Shumaker, naturally. But Helen's convinced her husband did it."

"Stormin' Norman was with Macauley in Minnesota, too?" Apparently they were a tag team.

"There was a real brouhaha when the woman died," Piers went on. "Another professor—art history, I believe Helen said it was—made a fuss, insisted the police charge our late chancellor with murder, not suicide. The art professor was forced out of his job and Macauley wrote letters to other colleges smearing him, impugning his degree, his qualifications. He disappeared into oblivion, and the police settled for the tidy expedient—death by suicide."

"How?" I said, with a sinking feeling in my tummy. "How did this lady supposedly kill herself?"

Piers lifted one of the Mephisto eyebrows. "Overdose of diginox," he said.

I half-expected him to go up in a puff of smoke.

When he had played the scene and made his exit, it was getting dark in the Cave and I switched on my desk lamp for a clear look at the contents of the file. Everything Piers had said—without the embroidery—was there: the accusation against Macauley, the verdict of the coroner's jury. But there was one thing old Ambrose had failed to mention. Perhaps he'd overlooked it, or perhaps he knew me well enough to know it would make more of an impression if I thought I'd found it by myself.

The file didn't list the name of Macauley's accuser, the vanishing art instructor. But it did contain the name of the music professor who'd been hounded into her grave—or helped into it with diginox.

The lady's name was Elizabeth Swan.

Twenty

She did not believe he was dead. On the night they said he had been killed, Helen Macauley went to the big hollow room in the court-house where they kept them, stripped and cleaned and bagged and filed and labeled, photographed with instant cameras and stored in drawers that ran smoothly, silently in and out. The big clumsy policeman hesitated to show her the one who had been her husband. He tried to appease her with a snapshot instead, like some fond, embarrassed father showing off his newest child. But it was not enough. She still did not believe, and even when he took her at last into the cool, quiet room where the dead waited, guiding her kindly with his arm as though she might collapse, even when she made him roll out the silent drawer and unzip the body bag, even when she stared at the ruin of some man who might have been James, or might not have been, Helen was not convinced.

As certain patients, cured of long and grievous illness, wake from the anaesthetic painless but afraid; as a man who has bent too long beneath a heavy weight, and, finding it lifted from him, can no longer straighten his back and walk upright; as a blind man given new eyes will open them to a terror of nameless shapes and colors, so Helen Macauley, confronted with the loss of her long fear, found new ones even worse.

She had resigned choices when she married. She might have been an English professor; she had trained for it, she knew Old and Middle English, she had studied the ancient stories of the race in their originals, she read easily in Latin and Old French. The academic power structure, though, appalled her; before interview committees —almost entirely male, in those days—she lost her nerve and gibbered. She took a junior-level job at the University of Michigan while she worked on her Ph.D., wrote careful papers on the ballads and the alliterative romances, attended conferences, piled up an impressive dossier. It was then she met James. He was a graduate student in sociology—a trumped-up excuse for a discipline in her opinion.

But it wasn't sociology James Macauley was really studying. It was power. And Helen, being powerless herself, was irresistibly drawn to him.

He knew how to seek out friends who were useful and discard the idealists, the eccentrics, the too-kind, and the too-honorable. The women he squired to faculty functions and student parties were a poised facade. Helen herself had once been beautiful, she recalled vaguely. She remembered the face of a photograph somewhere, a laughing woman with thoughtful, musing, lazy eyes. That confused beauty was the woman James had married.

It had nothing to do with the face upon which she laid her long almost skeletal hands, her own face now. Looking into her mirror— she did so only when absolutely necessary—she saw the skull beneath the skin. Food disgusted her and she subsisted on vegetable drinks, vitamin pills by the handfuls, soda crackers.

Now she lay on her bed, the ceiling spinning over her, a record playing softly, an ancient plainsong of an order of monks high in the Pyrenees, disciplined, clear, emptied of human connection by the search for something to call God.

Helen locked her fingers over the death's-head that was her face and tried to weep, forcing the tears painfully from her dry, burning eyes. It was no use.

In the same year that James Macauley married Helen, he selected Norman Shumaker to be his friend. The word scarcely conveyed the facts. Norman was pasty, pudgy, hopelessly stupid, an education major who would probably have ended up a high school coach in some tiny town, without James to use him. Too much a fool to find any other purpose for himself, Norman was delighted with his new vocation. He slouched around the faculty room egging the professors on to bitch and gossip, then reported what he heard to James, who calculated, engineered, rode the main chance. When they were finished, James was president of the Student Senate, then student adviser to the board of governors. When at last he got his Ph.D., his list of credits was three pages long. He had a dozen offers of jobs in college administration to choose from.

As for Helen, she sidestepped her degree. She delayed, finding still another fine point of research to be cleared away before the actual writing. She taught classes, rode out the seven years of assistantships the university allowed its doctoral candidates, hedged and dodged, afraid of her powerless future. Even if she got a degree, the most she could hope for was a junior-level job, teaching the classes the male professors wouldn't bother with. That was what academic women were for, after all.

At the end of the seventh year, she married James. She was then thirty-two, and he some months past forty.

They began at a small college in Colorado, but it had no scope. They stayed four years; when the offer came for the presidency of Belmont College, James snapped at it, taking the ubiquitous Norman along as administrative assistant.

When James wanted a rumor spread, Norman spread it. When he wanted a lie told, a character assassinated, a career destroyed, Norman saw to it. When he wanted the goods on some recalcitrant faculty member who opposed his watered-down cost-effective curriculum, his job cuts, his frontal attack on academic standards, Norman got him the goods. When he wanted someone watched, Norman watched him.

And he watched her, too.

Shumaker had been with Macauley for two years before Helen realized he was spying on her. She knew it was not in his own interest; Norman's only interest was his collection of Elvis Presley records.

He was following orders, she knew that. It was James who was having her watched. When she went to the hairdresser, she spotted Norman's small white car parked in front of the coffee shop across the street. When she went to vespers at the Catholic church, the white car would circle, watching the worshippers file in, and be there waiting when they filed out again.

"Do you seriously believe I'm cheating on you?" she screamed at her husband when he came back from a faculty meeting one night. "How could I? Even if I wanted to, who would there be in this ridiculous town?"

It was a tiny rural community in which the college was the only glimmer of formal culture, and the prospects were few enough. But the truth was, Helen had had enough of husbands and of lovers. She felt she had committed a great sin against her own soul by marrying, the sin against the spirit which is the only unforgivable sin. She wanted to do penance for it, confess and be told the myth of universal mercy. If only James would help her.

She asked the question again. If she provoked him, perhaps he would knock her down, punish her as she felt she deserved. She did not want a divorce; it was too late for that. She wanted to be new again.

"I asked you a simple question, James," she cried, her pale face white as wax. "Why have you got that fucking Norman following me?"

Macauley set down his expensive briefcase in the front hall and walked over to where she stood. Staring at her with those glazed blue eyes of his, like some badly-painted figurine's, he stepped very close and put both hands on her temples, his fingers catching in her hair and pulling it.

"Why, James?" she moaned.

He did not answer. His hands slipped down behind her ears,

onto her shoulders, then downward again, cupping her breasts, rousing her deliberately. Under her belly, along her thighs he crept, his body pressed against her, until he knelt at her feet. She was fully dressed, but she might have been naked, standing there before the big front window, convulsed with useless desire.

Outside on the street, Norman Shumaker sat watching from the window of his small white Chevy. At her feet, James looked up and smiled.

He had not made love to her since the night of their marriage, and even then he had failed in all but the crucial detail of consummation. He delighted in exciting her, knowing he would leave her burnt and helpless. James Macauley was impotent as a stone. His only desire was for power, over her and over Belmont College.

Helen Macauley lay on her own bed in which her husband had never slept. The room looked out onto the Ainsley Memorial Cemetery. She would not bury him there, she decided, if he were really dead. She would not bury him anywhere. The earth did not deserve the insult. She would burn him, instead, and give him to the wind.

She got up and switched off the plainsong record she had been playing to calm herself. The slow, unmelodic chanting of the monks was like rain on rocks, wearing the sharp edges smooth. She felt in control.

Helen went out into the hallway and down the basement steps to the room her husband had fitted out for a study. There were no windows, and she switched on only the swing-arm lamp at the desk. A television set glared at her from the bookshelf opposite the desk, a video player beside it. The shelves beneath the player were lined with tapes.

She selected one and put it into the machine, touched the controls, and sat down, switching off the light. The player whirred and the picture materialized on the screen.

Materialized. It was a word of magic, and it made her think of Piers, whom she loved. An old man who could afford to set no price on tenderness. Piers who had absolved her, fed her at last. It was he who had come to tell her her husband was dead, even before the police, long before Norman Shumaker's pasty face, stained with tears, appeared at her door. How he had known she did not bother to wonder. Piers knew many things in odd, secret ways, and stored them away for eventual use. It was his kind of power, and it did not stink of pettiness and greed as James's had. It was Piers who had frightened her with freedom, as he frightened her often with the startling truth of his tenderness.

The tape sputtered and began to play. It had been remade from an old home movie, and like all Macauley's tapes, it focused on a woman. She was tall and dark-haired and slender, walking through a woods or a park of some kind, beside a clear lake whose water was almost black with depth. The woman carried a guitar slung across her back on a strap, and as the camera jerked and bobbed unsteadily, following her, she sat down on a rock under a tree and began to play. There was no sound. Her music was lost, as the camera zoomed into close-up. Her thick dark hair fell across her face as she played, and suddenly a hand brushed it back and held it for her.

The camera danced away, trying not to catch the man whose hand it was. But that was impossible. He bent and kissed her on the forehead and his face was there, the wide, dark-blue eyes, the soft sandy hair, the drooping moustache that disguised a mischievous grin.

Did you know he was watching you then? thought Helen Macauley. *Did you know he took the pictures? Did he let you know on purpose, to weaken you, to control you better?*

She had been only mildly surprised to see Geoffrey Glendon here in Ainsley when they arrived. He called himself by another name now, by the name of Elizabeth Swan. But she knew him the moment he set foot in the house, sent by the college to tend James's orchids. Grotesque, devouring plants they were, and Helen hated them, but the house was full of them, and James only wanted them to look at, not to labor over. Already some of them were beginning to wilt.

Glendon had not come again and she herself refused to go near them. Soon they would all be dead.

The lovers on the tape were kissing now, sweetly, in the darkening afternoon. The camera jerked away, fanned the treetops like machine-gun fire, dodged back again, tormented, then went black.

There were a dozen other tapes of Elizabeth Swan, some with Geoffrey Glendon, some without. James had begun them when he first took over at Belmont College. Some of them Norman had shot, but most, almost all, James had made himself.

He had other tapes, of other women: Angela Cody; Sarah Cromwell; that Marla girl, his secretary; Hallie Glendon. What her connection to Geoffrey Glendon had been Helen had never considered, but perhaps James had. Perhaps he had found some link between them and determined to play on it, pretend he did not recognize the man who came to tend the plants, insinuate himself with the girl, and punish Geoffrey. More probably, though, he had erased Geoffrey Glendon from his mind without a trace, like one taped image replaced by another, newer one.

Many, the most recent of the videotapes, were of Elsa Worthing. Helen had looked at them all, over and over, each new face another sin to expiate.

She felt she should have warned them, but she had not. When Angela and the others died, she had been secretly glad, had gone to mass and prayed forgiveness and been glad again.

In some hidden corner of her battered mind, Helen Macauley hated every undamaged woman in the world. If she had had the courage, she might have killed them all herself.

Helen did not know if her husband had killed Elizabeth Swan, as Geoffrey Glendon had said. What did it matter? There were many ways of taking life, and some of them were legal. However the woman had died, James was responsible.

Piers said so. Piers had seen all the tapes. It was Piers who had given her the gun to protect herself with. Someone had taken it from her dresser drawer and used it to kill James. Piers was not afraid and he had hated James, believed him to be guilty of the string of murders. If Geoffrey Glendon had not taken the gun and murdered Helen's husband, it must have been Piers. It was a kindness he would have done her.

Helen sat in the dark cellar room, the dull red glow of the clock on the video player mocking at her like fox fire. Before her the fearless future loomed, huge and unsettling. She tried to take stock of what she knew, and found only one thing certain. The big policeman had said her husband killed himself. This, she knew, could not be true.

James Macauley had been murdered.

"Requiem aeternam dona eis, Domine." Helen knelt in the dark and began the prayer for the souls of the departed, her emaciated body shaking with hate.

Twenty-one

After Piers left me—by the usual route, mind, no puffs of smoke—I dug out my copy of his novel *The Sorcerer King* to refresh my memory of its hero, a trickster called Lancelot Mortimer. On the surface, he was a rather dowdy, entirely ordinary professor of mathematics, but in his front parlor he performed elaborate illusions that lured eager ladies to his bed, world-famous magi to his feet, and enemies to his gates.

It was the ladies, though, who interested me at the moment, and among them there was one in particular. Call her the one who got away. In the book she was named Marya, a Polish Jew who had survived the camps. She drifted into Lance's parlor one day, come to do the cleaning before the usual Sunday afternoon magic soirée. From the parlor, she drifted into his bed as most women did, and then was gone.

Lance never touched Marya again, though he came tantalizingly close. She disappeared from the small town where he lived and taught, and most of his life from then on was spent searching for her. As soon as he thought he'd found her, she would change her shape again. She was a Lilith of a woman, a Lamia, a Circe with a dozen personalities that were all strangely the same, had the same center, damaged as it was. Forgetting Marya was the one escape trick the great magus never could perform.

I'd wanted to reread a passage near the end of the novel, one I'd underlined when I first read the book without really knowing why at the time, one I remembered almost word for word, even now. It had been gnawing at the back of my mind ever since I saw Piers in Elsa's orchard, and once I got the words in front of me in black and white, I began to understand why:

Lancelot Mortimer has followed his lovely illusion, his Marya, in and out of nunneries, brothels, theaters, and luxury hotels on three continents, and he hits bottom at last when he glimpses her in the back alleys of Paris:

> Marya turned at the end of the Rue St. Sebastien, her confusion of wild brown-gold curls a cobweb in the greenish glow of the neon from the bar beyond her. Her face, as always, was expressionless, and if she recognized Lancelot, her wide, bottomless dark eyes gave him no sign. He began to run, stumbling over the rubble of the earth, old cans and bottles, newspapers blown into dirty, brownish paper blossoms by the wind and rain, discarded rags the beggars had refused and left behind. A man slumped beside a trash can moved and groaned in drunken sleep, cursed Lancelot as he tripped and fell, crashing on the broken glass and jagged paving stones underfoot. His hands were bleeding, the palms pierced by slivers of glass, but still he did not give up. He began to crawl toward Marya, who remained there, a motionless silhouette. There was still perhaps a yard between them—a yard of ancient chaos—when she turned and looked down at him. In the neon glow he could see great tears falling silently down her cheeks.
>
> But then she laughed, a full-bodied, honest, robust

laugh of genuine amusement. "A new trick, my dear?" she said. "What shall we call it, do you think? I know! The Fool Fooled!"

"I love you, Marya," he croaked. His heart, at last, was failing him.

"Ah my poor darling," she crooned from the darkness. There was music from the bar, played on a tinny piano, and she danced to it, moving in and out of the greenish light, dancing as she had danced beside his bed. "What is love," she sang, "but another way to torture butterflies?"

Then she was gone. Lancelot lay back on the sharp stones, slippery as afterbirth. The rhythm of his heart was jagged as the alley where he lay, and when his death came, it had the shape of Marya, dancing on his grave.

I closed the book and poured a glass of scotch and drank it down. There was no mistaking the woman—the wild mop of brownish curls, the throaty laugh, the wide dark eyes. Even the words were Elsa's, the cadence of her speech was there. I couldn't imagine how I had missed it when I read the book before.

Now, I've written enough books myself to know that you can't just go round playing pin-the-tail-on-the-donkey with any author's characters, figuring out which one's based on which pal or wife or lover or enemy the fellow happened to want to get even with. But I also know that life feeds art, especially the kind of art Piers had created. He wrote close to the bone, out of a well of emotions his usual jovial manner masked almost perfectly. I'd always believed there *was* a Marya in his life, some unattainable love that all the bedded ladies in the world hadn't been able to replace for him, no matter how he tried. He had made her a symbol of a brutalized humanity made brute in its turn, capable of torture as it had been tortured; in Mortimer's love for her, death and birth took on the stature of an artist's gesture. She led him deliberately to that Paris alley, wore down his damaged heart with fruitless search. She killed him equally for death and birth, gave him in that last moment the only thing he really wanted—an end, an utter silence. That was the ultimate, the infinite magic.

For some reason, it hadn't dawned on me until now who that semimystical, untouchable woman was, the original of Marya.

It was Elsa Bergner Worthing. Of course it was.

Even that wasn't so surprising. They knew each other, after all, though I'd never noticed any special bond between them—but that, too, was true to Piers's novel. Perhaps I had never quite identified her as Marya because I'd never seen the other Elsa, the one capable of inflicting damage, until I looked at Sarah's battered face.

What puzzled me, though, was the heart condition of Lancelot Mortimer. If the novel were enough of a roman à clef to be based on Elsa, perhaps Mortimer and his unsteady heart were more than literary symbols, too. Ambrose didn't look it, with his rosy cheeks and broad-shouldered physique. But appearances could be deceiving.

Could hyperactive Piers, the man of many careers and endless energy, suffer from a heart condition like his sometime lover, Mrs. Macauley? They had met, he said, in old Penny's waiting room. Had Piers been there for a refill on his *own* diginox prescription?

The idea opened up a whole new nest of vipers, and I had quite enough to be going on with. I polished off my scotch and turned in, to dream of a huge white rabbit with tailcoat and magic wand, who pulled a smiling Piers Ambrose out of a silk hat.

Next morning, Saturday, I found myself confronted at the breakfast table with yet another bowl of glutinous porridge, and began to wish I were still dreaming.

"Look, Goldilocks," I told Sarah, "I appreciate the thought, but my oatmeal slot is full up. Isn't there any of that liverwurst left? Just give me a cup of java and a sardine sandwich, that'll do me dandy."

"We're out of sardines," Eddie piped up. "I fed the last can to one of Mrs. Megrim's customers yesterday evening."

The Widow Megrim, who dumps more cans of tuna fish into more nauseating concoctions than anyone living or dead—viz., her tuna and Cool Whip mousse—is renowned among the local pussycat population for the cans she leaves on the back porch to be licked clean. Eddie, like old Patches Jackson, is always a sucker for a well-turned tail, and he often depletes my cache of kippers on their behalf; usually I give him a hard time about it, but this time I knew he hadn't gone to Blanche's just to feed the lions.

"Did you see Krish?" I asked him. "How's the kiddo doing?"

"I phoned Blanche just before you came down, Win," Sarah interjected. "She said he was still asleep. She heard him during the night, pacing around in his room."

"I saw him only briefly myself," said Merriman. "Still weary from the interrogation and the shock. A bit battered. But weathering." He shook his head. "I have never had the misfortune to be caught in a hurricane or a flood, nor to be standing on a fault line when the earth decided to scratch itself a bit. But what our friend is going through must be something like that. And Swan, too. A daughter found, and lost in such a way."

"Just imagine, Win," said Sarah softly, "if it were David. If I had found *him* lying there instead of Hallie."

"Don't you really think Macauley *might* have been the killer?" Eddie sounded hopeful. "It would mean the whole thing's over. A consummation devoutly to be wished, I must say."

I shrugged. "It would mean the whole thing's wrapped up in a nice neat package, certainly."

"But you don't believe it?" Sarah frowned and nibbled at a soda cracker, avoiding her own bowl of porridge.

"Neat packages, in my experience, rarely have anything very interesting inside," I replied, and, gritting my teeth, I dug into my oatmeal with a vengeance.

When I'd got the stuff inside me at last, washed down by a half gallon or so of insipid decaffeinated coffee, I climbed the stairs and settled down at the phone in the hall with a list of numbers. The first was Sheffield's, but it was one of his interchangeable daughters—either Frick or Frack, the distinction escapes me—who answered.

"Sheffield residence," she said. "Who's calling please?"

"This is Doc Sherman," I told her. It was a little like talking to an answering machine, except the machine enunciates better. "Is Thomas up and at 'em yet?"

"I'll see if he's available," she said coolly.

There was a sucking noise as she clapped her paw over the receiver, and I could hear a muffled shout of "Hey, Dad! The Rogue Elephant's on the phone!"

Then she was back. "He'll be with you in a moment. Please hold."

I heard shuffling footsteps and Thomas was on the line, breathing hard.

"Winston?" he quavered. "Is that you?"

"Just call me, Dumbo," I growled. "Look, Sheffield, I've been going over that file of yours on Macauley, and there are a couple of points—"

"But I never gave you that file!" He paused. "Did I?"

"Didn't you?"

"I didn't think I did."

"Then maybe you did. Didn't you?"

"Yes, I suppose I did. The last few days have been such a—"

"Oh, a muddle, I know. Forget which way your head's screwed on next. Listen. You remember our little talk about Helen Macauley, when you volunteered to help me toss the joint in search of her heart medicine? Well, how's about tomorrow? You and Diana, Merriman and me, a little visit of condolence?"

"I'd really like to, Winston," he purred, "but tomorrow is Vanessa's dance recital and I can't miss it."

"Come before. Come after. Surely the child can impersonate

262

Isadora Duncan without you. Bring Diana. She can wear one of her hats. Tell her a woman's touch is needed."

"But why can't Sarah—"

"Sarah's under the weather." I didn't figure she'd fancy a visit to Mrs. Macauley with that shiner, and we were fresh out of eye patches. "Let me put it this way, Thomas. Now that Macauley's gone, you may think you have nothing to fear from job cuts and curriculum changes. But I beg you to remember who's chairman of the curriculum committee this year. I have the power to bind and loose, Sheffield. I could get up in front of the faculty senate and reduce the Department of Arts and Letters to a shadow of its former self, and you along with it."

"You wouldn't!"

"What have I got to lose? I'm headed for pasture anyway. Why be sentimental? Might be rather fun to level the place before I leave."

"Winston! You're a man of conviction, you've always been—"

I had him where the hair grows short. "Take your pick, Thomas, old sport. You can rule over a department of shreds and patches, or you can beg off Frick's dance recital—or is it Frack?—dammit *Vanessa's* dance recital. And come with me to Mrs. Macauley's tomorrow afternoon. Which is it? Well?"

"Hell," muttered Tommy. "I'll pick you up at two."

"Fine," I told him smugly. "And bring Diana's car, not that Japanese fruitcake tin *you* drive. I can't even get in that thing, you'd have to pull me with a tow rope."

"It would serve you right, you old eohippus," he said, and was about to hang up when I yelled at him.

"Hold the phone, Sheffield! I'll ignore the fact that you just called me a prehistoric pony, if you answer one more question. When you interviewed Macauley for the chancellor's job, who was your contact at Belmont College? Can you give me the name of somebody out there I can phone for information?"

"You won't pester him, will you?" he asked suspiciously. "You won't stir up anything embarrassing?"

263

"Embarrassing? Look, Thomas," I said sternly. "Murders are going on here, Macauley's among them. I thought you understood that the other night. I guess I was wrong."

When he spoke his voice had lost its whine. "I thought—Vivian from the registrar's office phoned me, Winston. She told me what they found on Macauley's desk. I thought it was all over. Those women, the whole terrible mess. I thought Macauley had confessed and killed himself. But now you say *he* was murdered?"

I leveled with the man. "I don't know, Thomas. I think so. I can't prove it yet."

"That means you think the Heart Specialist is still out there?"

"I do." I could hear the big case clock down in the front hall ticking, ticking. Christmas, I thought. Already the signs were up in the downtown shop windows—THIRTY-ONE SHOPPING DAYS TILL CHRISTMAS. "Which is why we mustn't waste time with our usual game of Gotcha," I said. "You and I can resume business as usual when this is over. You can try to force me off the faculty and I can keep helping you stick both feet in your mouth. But for now, we're partners in crime. Give me that name."

He did, and the home telephone number of Professor Bob Hendricks, an old Yale classmate who taught history at Belmont.

"How the hell is old Guppy?" he said. He was one of those hearty, cheerful academics designed by nature to be early-morning disk jockeys.

"Guppy? Do you by any chance refer to Our Mutual Friend, Thomas Van Doren Sheffield, Ph.D.?" I said.

"Hell, yes! Used to call him Guppy. Something around the eyes. Looks just like a goddamn fish. Guppy Sheffield, helluva guy. What was it you wanted again?"

"It's this way, Professor Hendricks," I began.

"Hell, call me Bob. Bobby or Bob. Some people like Rob. Guppy used to call me Touch. Always broke, you know, typical undergrad. Touched old Gup for a five-spot almost every weekend. Always plenty of scratch, Guppy. Call me Touch."

"What I need, Professor Hendricks," I forged on, "is the name of the art professor who accused James Macauley of murdering Elizabeth Swan back in the Seventies."

There was a tense silence. Touch was getting nervous. He and Sheffield had certainly gone to the same school, all right.

"You writing a book, or what?" he said. "Some kind of an exposé?"

"No fear, Touch," I told him. "Nothing in print. Just want to locate the man. I might have a job for him."

"Oh, hell, that's different," he said. "That's great. We all figured Geoff got shafted. Of course, he was torn up when Elizabeth killed herself. Accident, naturally. Accidental overdose of digitalis. Somebody probably screwed up the prescription, too strong a dose. God knows. Anyway, he went over the edge for a while, poor sonuvabitch. Lot of wild accusations. Lost his job here, never got another one. Figured he might be dead by now. I didn't know he ever got out of the bin, matter of fact."

"Bin?"

"Minnesota Psychiatric," he replied. "That's where they took him. Same route as Elizabeth. Helluva looker, that girl, but she couldn't take the pressure. Artists like Geoff, musicians, writers— lousy academics, I always say. Personally, I don't even think the arts belong in the curriculum. Put 'em in some kind of special schools, that's what I say."

"Or camps," I suggested. "How about concentrating them in camps? Keep them all together, where they won't cause trouble?"

"Right! Nice woodsy places, they dig that stuff. But keep them the hell out of here. Can't play by the goddamn rules, you know?"

"Geoff what?" I said. "What was the art professor's name, Touch?"

"Art history, yeah." He took a gulp of something and I'd have sworn it wasn't decaffeinated coffee. "Englishman, Oxford man. Geoffrey Glendon." He took another swallow. "Listen, pal, what did you say your name was again?"

"Winston," I told him. "Winston Sherman. Just call me Sherm. Oh, and Touch?"

265

"Yeah, Sherm?"

"Get stuffed, Touch," I said, and hung up.

Next on my list of phone calls was Alex.

"Any word from our wandering parakeet?" I asked her.

"He phoned last night," she replied. "And Julian rang up as well, told me he's keeping an eye on David." She sighed. "Now if only somebody were keeping an eye on Julian, I might feel a bit better. By the way, no rehearsal till Monday night. Apparently he intends being back by then."

"I might've known," I growled. "He doesn't mind driving the lot of us nuts, but he wouldn't dare miss rehearsal. Listen, Alex. If he calls you tonight, give him a message from me, will you? When he finds Graham Worthing, tell him he can look, but not touch. Don't make direct contact. We don't want to spook him. Just follow him. If he looks like he's taking off on a long-distance jaunt, then we can intercept him. Otherwise, we'll learn more by watching than by trying to ask him questions now. He's gone underground for a reason, and if we push him, he'll dive so deep we'll never find him."

"Winnie," she said thoughtfully, "could it *be* Graham? The Heart Specialist, I mean. Hallie *was* found in that orchard on the day he turned up unexpectedly. According to David, he *was* lurking around town, that bar by the river, a lot of times when nobody knew he was here. It looks awfully suspicious, and it explains the way Elsa's been acting. The pressure would be tremendous, if she knew."

What she was really asking me, of course, was whether David was just tailing a disappearing husband or putting himself in range of a multiple murderer.

"I won't fudge, kiddo," I told Alex. "I haven't got the goods, not yet. I think the Worthings and Madam Max know something about all this they're not telling, for whatever reasons. I think we've got to find a way to get the truth out of them. So far, I don't have the foggiest idea what the way will be." I thought for a moment. "If you knew David was a killer, that if you didn't tell someone, he'd kill again and again and again, endlessly— If you *knew,* not just feared or suspected, but knew—would you tell the police?"

She was silent, her breath soft and steady against the receiver. "No," she said at last.

"Would you do anything?" I asked her.

"Die," she said.

The Macauley house was a low brick-veneer built cavelike, halfway into a hillside, one of those energy-conserving experiments that never quite caught on. Its front faced a treeless development street of square, earth-toned boxes with tiny yards designed for the minimum of upkeep. It was Sunday afternoon, but there were no people around, no cars moving. A lone dog, a big setter, was chained to an iron hook beside one of the front doors, his great eyes watching us as Diana Sheffield pulled her shiny black Lincoln into Helen Macauley's drive. Beyond the house the expanse of Ainsley Memorial Cemetery reached into the distance, a vast stone forest of the dead.

"Whose car's that?" I asked Merriman as I eased myself out of the roomy backseat. "The Pontiac. Looks familiar."

"It's *his,*" whispered Tommy. "Norman Shumaker's."

Diana snorted. *"I'm* not going in if that overweight lizard is in there!"

Lady Di was wearing her black Bill Blass suit, a pair of pumps that made her tower over Sheffield in graphic illustration of the nature of their relationship, and a hat—how to describe that hat? Well, let me put it this way. If Zsa Zsa Gabor, the Queen Mother, and Boris Karloff got together and designed a black-felt light fixture with a feather on it, Di's hat would be it.

"I will not dignify that man with my company," she sniffed, and started to get back into the car. "Tell Helen I went to the dance recital. Where, by the way, I ought to be, because I was supposed to pour at the reception and they had to call Lana Ellsworth's mother to do it and she has liver spots on her hands and she never has the sense to wear a pair of gloves—'' She glared at me and gasped for breath. "Tell her I've got rickets," she said to Sheffield. "Tell her I've got a black eye."

Thomas took a deep breath of his own and drew himself up to his full height—which was almost as tall as Diana's ear.

"You're here and you're going inside with me and you're going to ignore Norman Shumaker as he deserves to be ignored," he said. "Or I may just give you a black eye myself!"

Diana gulped. "I—" she began. She was silent for a moment, studying that interesting stranger, her husband. "That's the most sexist thing I've ever heard," she said, amazed. "I quite enjoyed it. Just don't make a habit of it. Come along, then, what're you waiting for?"

She grabbed Tommy's arm and they marched off down the walk and up the steps.

"So, Stormin' Norman's here to offer his sympathy, is he?" I chuckled in spite of the solemn occasion. "Poor old lump of dough's likely to be out of work soon. When a chancellor pegs out in office, he's succeeded by the vice chancellor for academic affairs, not by the administrative assistant."

Merriman frowned. "I hadn't thought of that," he said softly.

I glanced at him sharply. He had that look again. "Why? Who the hell *is* the vice chancellor for academic affairs, anyway? I don't keep track of those minor administration jobs."

He didn't answer, just looked in the direction of the front door, which was opening to admit the Sheffields.

"Oh, my tail and whiskers," I said, staring at the man who was ushering Tommy and Diana inside. "You mean, Macauley's replacement is the Sorcerer King?"

"Helping the Widow with the funeral baked-meats, are you, Piers?" I asked him as he took my coat. "Or should I call you chancellor now?"

He laughed out loud, uninhibited by the formalities of a grief neither of us felt. "I was wondering when you'd twig to that, Hyde," he said. "I'm sorry to disappoint you, but as a motive, the chancellorship isn't much. There's an age limit on it in the by-laws of the college, you see. You can't become chancellor if you're older than sixty-five, and that lets me out by a good few years. Satisfied? The job passes to the head of the Faculty Senate, and that's Phil Crosley from biology."

I shrugged. "Ah, well, it was a thought."

Merriman, who'd been eavesdropping with his big ears flapping in the breeze, was grinning from ear to ear. "Of course, the job's not much of an attraction to a man like you, Piers, is it, even if you were a young tadpole of sixty-five? Being one of the stars of the literary firmament, I'm surprised you haven't simply whizzed off to a penthouse in Manhattan and left the lot of us to our lowly toil and strife."

"Perhaps," I said, shooting one of my looks in Ambrose's direction, "there's something else keeping our friend in Ainsley. Or somebody."

Piers looked indulgently at me down his long, beaked nose. "Obviously, you think you know something, Winnie. But I beg you to remember that a shot in the dark can bounce off the walls and hit the best of marksmen in the eye."

"Is that some kind of a warning?"

"Do you need one?"

"Not from you, Iago," I muttered, as he led us into the living room.

As it turned out, I didn't have to toss the place. The lady of the house, now that her husband wasn't around, turned out to be anything but the drugged-up crazy woman Hilda Costello's gossip mills had turned her into.

I was stunned by the thinness of Helen Macauley. I tried to imagine her brittle body in the strong, muscular arms of Piers Ambrose, but it was somehow a perverse image, like making love to a scarecrow lady, a woman made of sticks and straw. Her eyes in the thin face were huge and circled with dark hollows, the color smeared unsteadily along the narrow line of her lips. She rose and came to meet me, a bit uncertainly, I thought.

"Dr. Sherman," she said in a soft, clear voice. "It was kind of you." She stood in the center of the room, turning round like a music-box figure, as though she were looking for something that ought to be there and wasn't. "I thought—" she began, then stopped, her thin hands half-extended, cupped slightly. She caught a glimpse of Shumaker, who was slouching against the fireplace talking to Merriman. Helen Macauley's body jerked convulsively and she grabbed hold of my sleeve. "I'm sorry," she said. "Please."

She led the way quickly out of the room, and I followed, leaving Piers with Thomas and Lady Di to keep him busy. We ended up in a large room at the far side of the house, where a huge plate-glass sliding door looked out at the cemetery. Helen had opened the door and the cold November wind was blowing some loose papers like dry leaves around the darkened room, a sort of family room—if there had been a family.

Instead, there were orchids, pots and pots of them, some in hesitant bloom, some glorious with color, some ugly and grotesque, like half-conceived creatures of some nightmare imagination. Some —many, in fact—had begun to wilt and die from apparent lack of attention. That icy wind through the open doors, I thought, wasn't likely to help them much, but Helen didn't seem to mind.

"Does it help you?" I asked her. "Fresh air? It's your heart, is it?"

She nodded. "It's minor, really. The pills help. But when I'm nervous or upset, it gets worse."

"Your husband's assistant makes you nervous, doesn't he? Shumaker?"

She only smiled. "The pills help," she said again.

"If you don't mind my asking, what sort of pills?"

"You mean, were they the kind that killed those four women?" Her high voice was shrill with tension, but she wasn't angry or even

270

particularly surprised. The wind blew a paper onto her feet and she bent to pick it up, crushed it in her hands. "You want to know if my husband might have killed them with my medicine. Piers told me."

"I want to know if the medicine you take is called diginox," I said.

She turned and walked across the room and into an adjoining bathroom, returning with a vial of prescription medicine, then handed it to me. I stepped outside where the light was better and she followed me.

The label said digitala, not diginox.

"He might've got it somewhere else," she said.

"He might have. But I don't really think he did, do you?"

Her pale, colorless eyes stared out into the wind at the field of the monumented dead. "There won't be a funeral," she said. "I would have to lie and pretend, and I'm finished with that."

"I'm glad," I said. "Then you won't mind a few more questions. When you and your husband were at Belmont, in Minnesota, did you know an art professor named Geoffrey Glendon?"

"Not personally. I suppose I saw him at some reception or other. They dissolve, after a while, the faces."

"Did you know he was here in Ainsley?"

"I'm sorry," she said. "Can I get you something to drink?"

It was time to change course. I wandered over to the banked pots of lavender blooms against the far wall. "Interesting plants, orchids. Your husband an avid gardener, was he?"

"He liked having them around, that's all. He always found someone to do what he wanted."

"What about Elizabeth Swan?" I said, not turning from the plants to face her. "Did she do what he wanted?"

I heard her draw a sharp breath. "I suppose so. She died, didn't she?"

Now I turned suddenly, walked over to where she was standing, and took her by the hands. "You knew Geoffrey Glendon was here, didn't you, calling himself Jaffer Swan? Calling himself after that dead lady? Did he come here to tend these orchids the way he tended the ones in your husband's office? Did he find the gun in your dresser drawer and take it and shoot your husband with it, punish him for Elizabeth and for himself, the lives Macauley'd ruined?"

Her thin lips pressed tight and the wind burned tears from the wolf-pale eyes. "Does it matter?" she said. "James is dead. He deserved to die."

"Why do you say that, Helen? Why did he deserve it?"

"He did kill women," she said, the clear voice cracking. "The Cody girl, Hallie Glendon. Elizabeth Swan. What does it matter which?" She looked at me, a faint smile playing round the narrow mouth. "After all," she whispered, "he certainly killed me."

It was late that evening, as I lay stretched out before the banked fire in the living room listening to the wind rising outside, while Sarah toyed with one of Papa Haydn's sonatas at her piano, that the phone rang. I toddled out to answer it, hoping for David. It turned out to be Elsa.

"You did not come," she said. Her soft German accent was slurred and unclear, and if I hadn't known she rarely touched the stuff, I'd have said she'd been drinking. "Our Sunday evening, Madam Max's evening. You did not come. Always before, you and Sarah and Edward. I remembered you were ill. No return of the fainting spell, Winston?"

"Oh," I assured her, "nothing like that. Just got tied up with a little social obligation at the college. Sorry. Should've let you know." I paused, thinking, listening to the sounds in the background. I'd have sworn I heard traffic noises. "Did Piers make it?" I asked her, determined to keep her on the line long enough to figure out what the noise was.

"Oh, I don't know," she said absently, as if she'd hardly noticed whether he were there or not. "Maybe. Yes. A little while. Very late. Winston, I want to send you something, a package. Axel will bring it, some herbs for a hot drink. Strengthening and very good for you, and it doesn't even taste so bad."

The background noise swelled and grew and I was sure. It was traffic, heavy traffic—far too heavy for Ainsley. The woman had to be in Manhattan. She must've driven into the city after the sherry party. But why? Had she, too, gone looking for her missing husband? Or were she and Jaffer about to take a powder together? You could fly almost anywhere from JFK, even on a Sunday night. My suspicion of her deepened.

"What kind of herbs, Elsa?" I said. "Interesting things, herbs."

She laughed then, Marya's laugh. "Old woolly bear, what do you care with herbs? It's green, it grows in the ground, it makes you strong, like Popeye. You live forever!"

The background noise seemed to be changing. "Wait, Elsa!" I said. "Don't hang up yet!"

I wanted to hear that combination of sounds for just another minute. The woman I had always liked, the woman so much like my Sarah I might have loved her instead if things had been different, was assuming a sinister shape in my mind, and her sudden trip to the city seemed to confirm it. Those traffic noises couldn't lie.

"Winston," she said quietly, steadily, "tell Sarah the harpsichord is hers. I give it to her. Madam Max, too. We both want it. What good is a harpsichord to us? We have no music."

The offer set me back on my heels. The thing was priceless. Was I mistaking a contrite friend who'd suffered an unfortunate lapse for some kind of homicidal maniac? Surely Alex was right, and Elsa was just under a lot of personal pressure. Her generosity, her utter kindness was just as it had always been, and greater.

But there were those traffic noises.

"The following program is brought to you by a grant from Mobil Oil Corporation," said an unctuous male voice. The noise in the background had ceased, to be replaced by the familiar theme music of *Masterpiece Theatre*.

Elsa was in her own workshop, where she often watched television while she made her wreaths and nosegays. I was a suspicious fool.

"I am alone, Winston," she said suddenly, her rich voice heavy

273

with the darkness that often lived there, the huge cave of the past she could never escape. "Tell Sarah. I deserve to be alone."

"My dear old kiddo—" I began, feeling guilty of treason.

"Nah," she said, pulling herself back. "Go to bed, old woolly bear. And take your good green medicine!"

She hung up and I went back to Sarah, who had taken over the couch. "That was Elsa," I said. "Funny, I thought it sounded like she was calling from Manhattan, some booth or other. Cars zooming by, sirens, horns. Turned out to be the TV set. I think I'm getting jumpy. She was right here in Ainsley all the time."

Sarah looked at me, her head on one side. "They have television sets in hotel rooms, too, you ninny," she told me. "Even in Manhattan."

Twenty-two

The sun set; the dusk fell on the stream, and lights began to appear along the shore. The Chapman lighthouse, a three-legged thing erect on a mud-flat, shone strongly. Lights of ships moved in the fairway—a great stir of lights going up and going down. And farther west on the upper reaches the place of the monstrous town was still marked ominously on the sky, a brooding gloom in sunshine, a lurid glare under the stars.

"And this also," said Marlow suddenly, "has been one of the dark places of the earth."

Graham Worthing stood on the flagstone terrace of his ravaged forty-fourth floor apartment overlooking the gathering night of Manhattan, the soft, sober voice of David Cromwell speaking Conrad's lines through headphones clamped tight over his ears. He had been wearing them for almost two solid days and nights, listening to the same tape over and over, ever since he left his wife's house and drove away, to end up here, where he had meant to bring her, to live with her at last in a peace he himself controlled. David's voice was his pulse and if it stopped, life, too, would stop, whatever it was worth to him now. Graham could no longer put much value on it. He could barely perceive himself as a unique, functioning entity. His shadow drifted like dust through the empty place as the words fell upon him like steady rain.

It seems to me I am trying to tell you a dream—making a vain attempt, because no relation of a dream can convey the dream-sensation, that commingling of absurdity, surprise, and bewilderment in a tremor of struggling revolt, that notion of being captured by the incredible which is of the very essence of dreams. . . .

The only piece of furniture left in the apartment was his wife's bed.

Before he realized she would never leave Madam Max's, could not leave, Graham had bought Elsa a special gift, an antique Spanish bed for which he had paid nearly as much as a whole semester's tuition for Jordan. He didn't especially like the thing. Even with the most expensive mattress and box spring you could buy, it wasn't comfortable, and it was much too short for Graham's legs.

People had been smaller then, perhaps, he thought, looking out at the tiny lights just flickering on in the colossal buildings that surrounded him, like upended sarcophagi of some giant race. Far away he could see the huge rising spire of the Empire State Building, the red light glowing on its top.

It seems to me I am trying to tell you a dream. . . .

"Jesus . . ." he began to pray, his lips moving voiceless, the words of the tape washing over him, cool and perfect.

I am trying to tell you . . .

"Jesus," he mouthed again, and stopped.

It was very silent where he stood, the cold wind roaring round him. The noises from the street were swallowed by the distance and the wind, and looking down he could barely suppress a laugh at the dwarfish shapes that crept along the pavements, devoid from this height of ambition, of vanity, of human status. These were the tiny things that filled the huge stone coffins, cell after cell of them, like bees in a hive.

> But as I stood on this hillside, I foresaw that in the
> blinding sunshine of that land I would become acquainted
> with a flabby, pretending, weak-eyed devil of a rapacious
> and pitiless folly. . . . For a moment I stood appalled, as
> though by a warning. . . .

He remembered going with Elsa to The Cloisters, her delighted laughter as he squeezed through the tiny, low doorways, tried to squat on the child-sized chairs in one of the chapels. The tombs, too, were undersized, the effigies short-legged. Graham closed his eyes against the wind and the face of one effigy in particular returned from that long-ago afternoon, a young noblewoman with high bones, the smooth stone cheeks pitted by damage as though by tears. Elsa had stood a long while beside that pale, cool form, as her husband, mildly bored, wandered the room glancing casually at the tapestries and altarpieces and reliquaries. At last he came to stand beside her.

"Ready to move on?" he asked.

She looked up at him, her great eyes brimming. "She died in the wars, you see," said Elsa. Her voice, which was usually rich and quiet, rang shrill in the stone vault of the room. "Her face," she said. "Look. A soldier."

Graham looked at her, puzzled. "How do you make that out, my love?" He studied the brass nameplate, glanced at his museum guide. There was nothing.

"Empty," was all she said, and walked away.

The "she" of whom Elsa spoke—it was obvious even to her husband—was not the dead baroness, but herself.

That moment had been the dawn of a new knowledge of his

wife. He did not understand her; Graham knew he was not capable of that, had never expected it. But he had never before realized that she was almost a complete stranger to him. The hearty wife who had stayed with him for thirty years was a carefully fostered myth she usually believed herself. But the crucial part of her was isolate and unknowable, unreachable by the most fervent love he could invent.

Worthing pulled off the headphones, turned suddenly and went into the apartment, closing the terrace doors behind him. Dust bunnies drifted across the bare parquet like mice, and the naked frame of the Spanish bed stood in a corner of the living room like some ruined scaffold.

Suddenly decisive after two days and nights of utter confusion, Graham went to the telephone. He would call the police, he must. He crouched on the floor beside the elegant white phone and picked up the receiver. There was no dial tone. The thing was dead. The telephone company had disconnected it.

He sat down cross-legged on the floor and stared at the figure reflected in the glass of the terrace doors—a chesty, burly man, a man made for fighting off attack. No dreamer, no thinker, but a builder, ambitious, tenacious, tough enough to value nothing but winning, and to throw away the weak and damaged when he had to. If there had still been a continent to conquer, Graham Worthing would have marched out and taken it. If there had been railroads to build, he would've forged them through. If there had been a possibility, he would've seized it, shaped it, mass-produced and packaged it, made up a jingle and a logo and a catchy name, seen to its distribution, and worked out its obsolescence just in time to cash in on the next one headed down the line.

But there were none. All the options had run out.

"Oh, my love," he said softly into the silent telephone. "Oh, my love."

If he had only made enough money, he would have known what to do. When he began to suspect, after the boys went off to Harvard and her life narrowed and lost its bright gloss, that Elsa's complexity was deepening, he would simply have taken her to Europe, to Switzerland, bought her into the finest clinic, and paid for a remedy.

If you had enough money, there was always a remedy.

But even then the business had been failing. He couldn't pay the bill. He tried instead to get her away from that place of Maxima's, that dark old house full of relics. To Graham, it seemed a prison, not a kingdom. He ached to let light and air into it, to batter down the precious toys, to cut the trees and level them. Secretly he prayed that James Macauley would win, and take the place, set Elsa free. By then he knew she would not come by choice.

He blamed himself for having left her there. He was her balance; she often said so herself. Without him, she had fallen into bed with Swan, whose isolate nature seemed to have touched her peculiarly, raising all the old ghosts and terrors of her past. On the weekends when Graham came up from the city, he lay nervously beside her, floating in and out of sleep. One night in late summer, he had wakened to a strange keening that came up from the rose garden through the open bedroom window. Elsa was not in his bed and when he looked out, he saw her sturdy figure almost lost in shadows where the orchard trees began.

She was kneeling on the ground, her body hunched and swaying, the high stifled cry that was not weeping so much as the breathing-out of some deeply buried malignancy issuing from her in a predictable rhythm, like the pulsing howl of a dog in a storm.

"Elsa," hissed a voice, and the scissor-stiff figure of Madam Max came from under the porch roof and measured off the ground toward the kneeling woman.

Elsa's cry broke off in a gasp, as though she had wakened from a dream, and she sank onto the ground, her long-sleeved, high-necked white nightgown strewn over the grass. She lay still, and Graham, frozen in the window, could not move nor shout. She seemed to be dead, and somewhere inside him a thread of connection, perhaps the final thread, broke in despair.

The old woman bent, stiff-legged, and stroked the tousled hair that floated loose around the white shoulders, the briars of the rose-bushes catching at her. Maxima got painfully down onto the ground and bent over her stepdaughter and kissed her on the cheek, a hesitant, delicate kiss that cost the old woman dearly. Graham had never seen her demonstrate love in any form before. It seemed to have died out of her when her German husband died.

Maxima sat on the wet grass holding Elsa's hand, and in a moment the unconscious woman woke and sat up, puzzled, and suddenly the roles were reversed.

"Max?" she said to the old woman. "Prowling again? My dear, come in. The wet grass! I will make a pot of the lemon balm tea, to soothe you. Sleep comes easier with a little comfort."

And she was up and off toward the house. Maxima sat for a long moment in the darkness, the sweetness of the roses rising round her. Then, with a stifled grunt, she got to her feet and went inside.

It was nearly two weeks later that Mary Ann Godowski, the first of the victims, was found dead under an oak tree in Grosvenor Arboretum on the Clinton campus.

There were no more incidents like the keening in the rose garden. When he came up on weekends, Graham found Elsa her usual loving, warmhearted self, working with her flowers, teaching her classes, cooking special dishes to please him, fussing over Madam Max's numberless ills and her dicky heart. Of course, there was Swan, but he hardly showed his face when Graham was there, and it was easy to pretend that the woman he had thought he married, the mother of his precious sons, was just the same as always.

Perhaps that woman, unreal as she now seemed to him, had been his own creation, not Elsa's, a brutality imposed upon her by his incomprehension. Love and regret pierced him like a blade, doubled him over, and Graham crouched fetuslike on the bare parquet of his expensive cave. He felt he was guilty of murder.

Might be guilty. That was his only hope. No matter how racked Elsa was by her memories, they did not make her a murderess.

He pushed the possibility away, the vision his imagination conjured of her. Even what he had seen on the night of Hallic Glendon's death, when no one had answered his telephone call from Smitty's bar and he had come, as he often did, to watch the house from the silent orchard, even the figure of Elsa slipping naked, bright and pale as flame through the cold darkness—even that was not proof enough. She had not come from the orchard, after all, where the Glendon girl was killed. The girl must already have been dead when he had seen Elsa come from the workshop. He heard the door close and thought it might be Swan coming back; he had seen the man drift into Smitty's bar, then out again, wordless as usual.

But it had not been Swan. It was Elsa, her wild hair loose in the icy wind, her body naked to the November weather. In the light from the house door he could just make out the faint old scars around her throat and wrists, which she hid with the high-necked blouses, mostly for Graham's sake, because he could not bear the thought of how she had come by them, the wire they had bound her with.

He closed his eyes, burying his face between his knees. He seemed to feel the metal cutting his own flesh. Alone in the tomb of his ambition, Graham Worthing loved his wife more than at the moment of his first son's birth; then, ignorance and greed and foolish self-importance had made him too small to see her, small as those amoebic creatures on the street below.

He was more than that, now. He was capable of anything for her sake. He would shoulder the possibility of guilt that terrified him. He would tell nobody what he had seen. Perhaps it meant nothing. Or perhaps it meant she had done horrors in her soldier-sleep. Either way, he would share the truth with her. He was her husband, after all, in spite of Jaffer Swan.

He took the telephone receiver in his hand again and pressed it to his lips, kissed it as though it might somehow connect him to her, as though the kiss might reach her face and she might feel it, miles away at home in the squat shadowed house. "My dearest love," he said. "I'm here."

And then the doorbell buzzed, a harsh quack in the empty silence. Graham went to answer it, shuffling barefoot across the rooms. He opened the heavy front door to a tall, dark-haired man with a strangely handsome face that was not, somehow, quite the same on both sides, like a stroke victim who has been through years of therapy and almost recovered, but will never be quite the same.

As for David, what he saw was a ruin. He remembered Graham Worthing as a fairly splendid fellow, given to expensive suits and good colognes and hundred-dollar haircuts. The man who stood in the open doorway, the empty rooms gaping beyond him, hadn't shaved for days. His eyes were ringed with darkness and the graying fair hair fell dank and unwashed over his forehead; he smelled of old sweat and fear.

The cold in the place was deep, as if the heat had not run in days, though the rest of the building was almost too warm.

Graham said nothing, just looked at David, hollow-eyed, as though he recognized him. It wouldn't have been easy. David was wearing an old beard from *As You Like It* and a pair of black-rimmed glasses. He had on jeans and a Detroit Lions sweatshirt, and was equipped with a toolbox, and he was all but certain Worthing *didn't* recognize him, since even Tyrone, Julian Stockfish's all-purpose stakeout man, who could spot a mark a block away and not lose him, had let David slip past him down in the lobby.

He knew he wasn't supposed to make contact. It was better to let things run their course and keep an eye on Graham, only move when you were sure.

But David had never been very good at waiting, and he knew enough about Jaffer Swan from their one brief encounter in the furnace room to know *he* wasn't the kind to hang around long either. Everybody in this business was like unstable dynamite, impossible to calculate and likely to go off if you breathed wrong. David had no intention of doing anything in that empty apartment, he didn't even mean to question Graham. He wanted to see, that was all. To estimate.

282

"Sorry to bug you on a Sunday night, man," he said, "but the furnace is all screwed the hell up. Gotta check your thermostat."

Graham squinted at him, puzzled. The deep voice washed over him.

It seemed to me as if I also were buried in a vast grave full of unspeakable secrets, it said.

"Secrets," he mumbled.

David frowned. "Thermostat?"

Graham Worthing padded through the empty flat to a hallway beyond the dining room, pointed out the device to David. He put his tools on the floor and squatted before them, diddling, playing for time.

"So, you house-sitting, or what?" he said.

"This is my house," said Graham. "I own it."

"Just moved in, right? Waiting for the furniture. When the wife and I moved here from Rochester, took the fucking movers three weeks to bring the shit down here. We was camping out like a coupla goddamn bums for a month." He laughed and the laugh exploded in the empty hall like gunfire.

"I'm selling it," said Graham. He seemed to relax a bit, leaning on the blank wall. "I've sold the furniture, but the apartment— There doesn't seem to be much interest."

"Hell, you got it right there," said David. He stood up, a screwdriver in his hand, and pried off the cover of the thermostat. It was set at forty-five degrees, but Graham didn't seem to notice. David began to fool with the dial. "Real estate market's crapped out, man. Can't sell these big fucking joints for nothin' now. You try to ride the odds, try to make a dime, some bastard comes along and kicks you in the balls."

"Your wife—" said Graham suddenly, and then began again. "You have a wife?"

David almost dropped the screwdriver; he drew a breath, summoning his instincts, trying to read Worthing's mind. "Aw, shit," he said quietly, painfully. "She's long gone, man. I caught her with this bastard she worked for, shacked up in a room at the Doral one afternoon when she figured I was on shift.''

"What did you—" Again Graham broke off.

David glanced at him, then stared at the floor. "Do? Nothin', pal. Love's a piece of crap, right? But there it is. You can't just make it disappear. Some guys, they yell and punch and raise hell, and then they go out and find themselves a broad to lay and they feel lousier than the old lady that's been slippin' around on 'em, so they take her back just to forgive themselves.''

"Did *you*? Did you take her back, your—your wife?''

David was silent for a long moment. *I have seen with your eyes,* he thought. *I have fallen into the dark and wished to drown there. There was a peace in that endless fall, the calm of sinking ships beyond the sight of help.*

He reached out a strong hand and gripped Graham Worthing's wrist, held it hard. The other man stared at him, blinked, looked down at the hand, the tenuous connection.

"I don't believe in slamming doors,'' said David quietly.

"No matter what she might have done?'' Worthing's thick voice rose, a hoarse cry. Behind him the naked scaffold of the Spanish bed cast huge, brittle shadows on the pale walls in the almost-dark.

David released his grip and bent to put away his tools. He looked up at Graham, whose gaze had not left him. *"Ask* the lady,'' he said. "Sometimes they even tell you the truth.''

I should be loyal to the nightmare of my choice, whispered the voice of the tape in Graham Worthing's eager memory. His decision was confirmed.

It was late that Sunday night when David, who had slipped out again past Tyrone and spent the evening watching the high-rise building from a little coffee shop across West End Avenue, saw Elsa Worthing enter the lobby. She wore a cream-colored man's raincoat and a black felt slouch hat, her mass of curls shoved unwillingly inside it and tumbling out around her face. David knew her too well to miss her, her swinging gait, her European habit of walking with one arm behind her back.

He dumped far too much money onto the table and charged out of the coffee shop. In the lobby, he rushed over to a drowsy Tyrone and shook him by the shoulder.

"My man, what's happenin'?" Tyrone snapped awake and was instantly his usual jittery self. He stood up and jounced from one foot to the other.

David was out of breath. "Woman in a light raincoat just went upstairs, Ty," he panted. "Worthing's wife. I'm going up. If she comes down, follow her. Black hat, curly hair."

"Dave—" Tyrone began, but it was too late. David disappeared into the elevator.

When it opened on the forty-fourth floor, he made his way along the angled corridors that led to Graham's apartment, careful not to be seen.

He needn't have bothered. Neither Graham nor Elsa would have noticed him. They stood in the open door of the deserted flat, locked together, Worthing's head cradled against his wife's shoulder, she stroking the heaving, muscular back.

"You should have let me explain," she said tenderly. "My poor dear fool. What a silly Karl you are."

"Secrets," murmured Graham, and kissed her hand.

They went into the apartment and closed the door and David, with Tyrone beside him, went out into the chilly, exhaust-smeared New York night. The revival movie house across the street was just disgorging a small crowd from a rerun of *Breaker Morant,* and a knot of pedestrians, mostly past middle age, had stopped on the corner opposite the theater and stood clustered around something, their breath steaming in the clear cold.

"Come on, Ty," said David, "let's get a cup of coffee."

The kid was discouraged and too beat even to jive and wisecrack. He had just spent two days on what had begun to look like a false alarm, just another marital spat. The pair walked silently, hands in pockets, heads down, paying no heed to the little group on the corner. It was only when he heard the song, the sweet reedy notes of the clarinet rising in the cold, that David snapped to attention.

"Sometimes caught and sometimes chased," sang the wordless lines. "Blackbird got no time to waste."

David broke into a run, and beside him, Ty put on a spurt of energy and reached the small crowd first. The song broke off and there was a muttering from the onlookers and the sound of running feet on the pavement. A slim figure, the instrument gleaming in his hands, slipped into the darkness with Tyrone after him, headed for Broadway. David followed, but he had only reached the brightly lighted all-night video store on the next corner when he met Ty coming back.

"Damn, he's fast!" he puffed.

David threw his head back and drew a deep breath of the cold night. Somewhere above the fear-lights of the city must be stars, but he could not find them. He left the unhappy Tyrone and walked off alone into the dark of Seventy-seventh Street, headed for his own place a few blocks away. Wherever Swan had gone, he would only be found if he wanted to be.

David walked on, nerves on edge, eyes searching the parked cars and the stoops of the brownstones, all the well-trained defenses of the longtime New Yorker taking over by old habit. He was already fishing for his front door keys when he heard it, high and sweet and clear. It came from the shadow of a Dumpster across the street, in front of a building they were tearing down. As David turned, he saw the elusive gleam of the clarinet in the dark, as the notes climbed and reached.

It was Jaffer, playing "Show Me the Way to Go Home."

Twenty-three

After that night, the world seemed to slow its spinning more or less to the normal pace. It would soon be Thanksgiving break and I had term papers coming in from my mystery fiction class, a sheaf of stuff from the curriculum committee to wade through, and all sorts of formalities about the appointment of an interim chancellor which Tommy Sheffield, unwilling to risk picking another Macauley, had shunted off on me. I got out my old bike and pedaled over to the campus early on the Monday morning, scarcely able to savor the shrewd bite of the November air.

I made a detour through the housing estates some enterprising hustler made of the bulk of Sarah's father's property after he died, a depressing expanse of boxy houses, a dozen variations on the same floor plan, the same chunky redwood decks tacked on at back or side, the same treeless yards and borders of non-labor-intensive juniper bushes. Erskine Cromwell had been deep in debt and Sarah had had no choice about selling. We had managed, though, to keep enough woods and yard to let us pretend, if we closed our eyes and didn't look too far down the hill, that nothing had changed.

It was a myth, of course. John Donne, that saintly old born-again roué, was right; no man *is* an island. The very fact of being cut off had changed us. When we left our drive and ventured out into the maze of cul-de-sacs and dead ends of Erskine Estates, we were deep in enemy territory. The future I saw there raised the hackles on the back of my neck. It would be, I thought, pedaling through the place as fast as I could, a clean world in which almost no one lived, a house swept and garnished and kept for company, while the family splits apart and betrays its heritage, turns brute, and dies.

I drew a deep, grateful breath as I left the development, feeling temporarily reprieved as I entered the older streets lined with bare oaks and sycamores that creaked in the cold. Near the campus, I turned into Blanche Megrim's drive. Krish's famous relic of a Plymouth was still parked in the graveled area reserved for boarders, and upstairs, the curtains of what I knew to be my young friend's room were pulled to the sills.

I'd just begun to walk my unwilling old cycle up to the porch when a horn honked about five feet behind my posterior. I turned round to find Lloyd Agate in one of the department's unmissable unmarked detective cars, the motor idling and wheezing, the driver's window squeaking fiercely as he rolled it down. My bleak mood dissipated at the sight of him; so long as the earth has a little salt like Lloyd left on it, there's hope for the bunch of us. I parked my bike and propped myself against his car.

"What's up, kiddo?" I asked him a bit nervously. I'd heard nothing from David since my phone call to Alex, and when I'd tried Julian Stockfish that morning, he'd had his confounded answering machine turned on again. "Have you—um—heard anything?" I ventured.

Agate grinned, sneezed, and sneezed again. "Relax, Doc," he said through a pink Kleenex. "Your boy's home. Says he'll see you at rehearsal tonight. I was just over there."

He filled me in on David's visit to Graham Worthing, and the trail of Elsa and Jaffer Swan.

"So," I said, "the Worthings are once more a pair of turtledoves, and Geoffrey Glendon's done another swan dive." I didn't say it, but I was deeply relieved to hear about Elsa's reunion with her

2 8 8

husband. My suspicions of her looked a little paranoic in the bright light of day.

"Unless I miss my guess, Swan will surface again. I don't think he did it, but he knows more than he's telling. Like everybody else in this case." Lloyd reached for a Thermos in the seat beside him and poured out a cup of steamy, thickish stuff. "Want some?" he offered in an adenoidal monotone. "Chicken soup. Best thing for a cold." He took a slurp and lost a noodle down his cleavage. "Thing is, we haven't got enough to hold anybody. Everybody's got half an alibi, nothing's conclusive. I talked to Macauley's widow last night." He took another gulp of soup. "I gotta tell you, Doc. I did some calling around, talked to that kid's mom again."

"Angela Cody's mother?"

He nodded. "Seems Macauley used to hang around with her. Kinky, if you ask me, guy his age and a little kid like that. She was flattered as hell, guy picked her up at some pizza joint on the highway. Mother put a stop to it, but she works all day, the kid's on the loose—you know how it is."

I thought of those nice clean empty rooms again.

"Tell you the truth, Doc," Lloyd went on, "I think Macauley may have *been* the Heart Specialist."

"But his wife's medicine—"

"I know, I know. It wasn't diginox. But the guy had connections. You know how easy it is to buy drugs? Factory surplus, black-market stuff headed for World Health and the relief organizations, generics skimmed off the drugstore chains and sold on the street—anything you want, you got it if you know the right street dude. Macauley moved around a lot, and according to the wife, that Shumaker guy would've got him whatever he wanted, legal or not."

"All right, suppose Macauley did murder those four women—"

"He had Hallie Glendon's black coral. She was wearing it that night."

"All right," I said, "all right. Let's say he was the murderer. I still don't buy his own death as a suicide, confound it! The shot that was fired into that pot of orchids, that vague suicide note on the desk. 'Guilty'—it's a jury verdict, not a confession. The position of the body's all wrong. Nothing makes sense except that somebody put a gun in the man's mouth and blew the top of his head off, and fired at that flowerpot to destroy what was left of those ashes you found, probably with Macauley's fingers on the trigger, too. That would explain the traces on his fingers and his prints on the gun. It was an execution, Agate, I'm convinced of that. Somebody believed what you do, that Macauley killed those women and would kill again, was after a woman the executioner loved and was afraid for. He found a way to render the man unconscious without a fight and he waited until the secretary left, he hid in that office, waited his chance, and carried out sentence with Helen Macauley's gun—" I broke off. "That reminds me, where did she get that gun in the first place? She seems to me like a good candidate for suicide attempts herself."

"She says she bought it in Manhattan, right after Mary Ann Godowski got killed. Nervous, wanted to protect herself. We checked it out, and her signature's on the paperwork, little gun shop down on the Lower East Side, Little Italy, I think."

That magic place of Piers's, the Castle of Wonders, wasn't far from Little Italy. I bit my tongue as Agate continued.

"She kept it in her dresser drawer, so the husband would've known it was there. It all fits. Only way anybody else could get it would be if Macauley took it and kept it in his desk, but she says she never missed it till we told her how her husband died. Says it was still there until that morning."

But Piers could easily have taken it. Piers hated Macauley. Piers shared Helen's bed. Piers had a knack for popping up out of nowhere and not being seen when he didn't want to be.

And so did Geoffrey Glendon. Jaffer Swan might've been the caretaker of those now-deserted orchids in Macauley's house. He might've used the chance to search the place, to find anything he could use against his old enemy, the man who had destroyed the life of Elizabeth Swan, destroyed Glendon's own life.

But, goddamn it, I liked both of them. They both reached me; something in me was committed to them in some unknown, inexplicable way. We were men in common, as Sarah and Elsa were women in common. Cheap Freudian twaddle might invest such feelings with sexual dualities, the users and the pigeonholers of the world consign us to the grubby old-boy network or the easy sisterhood of the born-again feminists. The truth was far simpler. We saw the world in the same way at least part of the time; men, women—it mattered very little. We were kin, all of us. We would have known each other instantly, glancing at one another on a crowded crosstown bus or meeting in a supermarket queue. It was always there, in the eyes. I saw it in Jaffer's eyes, and Piers's and in Elsa's. I had always seen it in Merriman's and David's and in Sarah's, oh, long ago. And most of all, I found it staring back at me whenever I looked into a mirror or a window glass. The eyes that saw more than was good for them.

And so, though I knew I ought to say something, tell Agate about Piers and Jaffer and their access to that gun, I didn't. The words were on the tip of my tongue. But I didn't. Nor did I outline for Agate the short and spectacular academic career of Geoffrey Glendon.

"How about that sample you sent to the FBI, Lloyd?" I asked instead, "the stuff in that broken pot?"

He scrubbed at the remains of the noodle on his sweater. "I got it on fax this morning." Agate dug in his pants pocket for his trusty notebook. "Latin junk," he said, and handed the page to me. "Means damn-all to me. FBI said they'd never seen it before, it wasn't on the controlled substance lists, and the poison center doesn't list it either. Probably just some weed that came up from the dirt they had in the pot."

"Oh, no doubt. And Macauley decided to have a little bonfire in honor of the season," I said with a snort. "Give us a break, Agate."

"What's the name mean?" he asked.

I squinted at it. "*Reticulum diabolicum?* Latin was never my best subject, but I'd say it means 'devil's net.' Maybe 'devil's lace.' I'll look it up."

The library is always my home base, and there's not much you can't find there if you know the back streets of the card catalogue.

"And I'll also pay a visit to that Chinese herb shop of yours. Thanksgiving vacation's coming up. I'll take Sarah and make a weekend of it." I frowned. "There's one more thing that puzzles me, Lloyd. You said there wasn't really enough diginox in the bloodstreams of those women to kill them, and what was in that bottle on the chancellor's desk was diluted from capsules, not even entirely dissolved. Couldn't have been very strong. So there must have been something else. Now, I'm sorry, but I simply don't believe in exotic untraceable poisons, not in this day and age. What was it? How did they *really* die?"

He wiped his nose with another pink Kleenex. When he looked up at me, his big, plain features were stricken, the lines around his eyes deep furrows of regret.

"Jesus Christ Savior, man. If I knew, don't you think I'd have stopped it long ago?" he said.

When Agate had driven away, I went up and knocked at Blanche's front door and was surprised to be met by Krish.

"I saw you, of course, from the upstairs hall," he said as he ushered me into the plastic-slipcovered living room. "The police person, your friend." He raised an eyebrow. "Watching me?"

"Not anymore," I reassured him. "He's completely sure you had nothing to do with any of this, Krish. You're in the clear."

If I'd expected jubilation, or even obvious relief, I didn't get it. His face was calm as a mask.

"I see." He sat quietly, his short-fingered hands folded in his lap. For a long moment he didn't speak and I thought perhaps he wanted to be left alone, but then he spoke again. "Mrs. Megrim is very kind, but she talks too much. I am afraid I shouted at her this morning. Most inconsiderate of me. I heard sniffling, afterward, and then she went to do the shopping. I cannot countenance unkindness."

"Sometimes it's necessary," I said. "In self-defense. Do you mind if I ask you something, Krish?"

"About Hallie?"

"If you'd rather not just yet—"

One of Blanche's transient cats, a medium-sized yellow tiger with one white paw, came sidling in and bounded up beside Krish on the couch. He began to stroke the animal delicately, the tips of his fingers moving down the sleek back from nose to tail.

"Please," he said. "Proceed."

"It's about Hallie's black coral necklace," I told him. "She was wearing it. on—the night."

"She wore it quite often, yes. A striking ornament, and worth a good deal, I believe."

"Did she buy it herself or did somebody give it to her? Did you?"

"I? How could I afford such a thing? I believe she said it was a graduation gift. I have no other knowledge of it."

"Did she ever mention her father to you?" He was more collected than I had feared, more calm. "Did she tell you anything about Geoffrey Glendon?"

"Only that he had left her with her aunts and never came back for her. She disliked the memory of him. I believe she loved him very much, that was the reason."

I wanted to tell him who had found him in the freezing rain and taken him to that furnace room and gotten him over the worst of the grief, but to be honest with you, I wasn't sure I had the right. If Jaffer Swan wanted to remain an anonymous transient, elusive as the purring cat in Krish's arms, that had to be up to him. Krish raised his head just then and I noticed for the second time the odd faint scratch on his brown throat where his shirt fell open.

"What's that?" I asked him. "Pussycat biff you one?"

He put a hand to his throat. "In the orchard. On the night when—" He stopped and started over. "I have begun to remember a little, you see. I fell, and there was a knife in the grass, a tool for trimming the small branches, I believe. I looked for Hallie and I knew she was not there. I had not understood. The knife seemed— more attractive than—the future."

"And the man you met there? Did he take the knife away from you?"

"No." He blinked and rubbed his eyes. "He took my arm and forced the knife against my throat until I felt it cut me. 'Choose,' he said." Krish fixed his brown eyes on me. "I did."

I gulped. A picture flashed like a photograph across the retina of my mind, two figures, one half-conscious, the other holding a weapon to him, forcing a decision that had been growing there, perhaps, lifelong. There were no ice-laden trees in my picture, but there was a pot of lady's slipper orchids. And the weapon wasn't old Axel Engstrom's pruning knife. It was the gun that had killed James Macauley.

I blinked and stared at Krish. "Of course you would never have killed yourself, not really. Would you?"

"Perhaps. Perhaps not." He put the cat down and it trotted away, still purring. "I think he knew I would not. But he forced me to know it also. A man of perception. A kind man." He studied my face. "Do you think he was a dream?"

"I think," I said, "he was exactly what you needed him to be. And where."

It seemed to be the stock-in-trade of the shadowy Jaffer Swan. That image in my mind became less vivid and changed shapes, and I saw instead the figure of Piers Ambrose kneeling there. He had spoken of execution on that night of the rehearsal.

For two cents I would have backed off and left the whole thing to Lloyd, as I'd wanted to do in the first place. It was Eddie who'd got me into it, and I still believed he knew something he wasn't telling me. I sighed as I stalked out of Blanche's place, and thought again, more kindly now, of Jaffer Swan. I wondered where the wandering minstrel had spent the night, what corner of Manhattan he'd found to drag his books into and huddle down and wait out morning.

Manhattan? Old Jaffer traveled light. By this time, he could be in Borneo. And, to be honest with you, I wished I was, too.

From anything I saw of him in the next ten days, Borneo might've been exactly where he was. Julian Stockfish and the energetic Tyrone did their best to lay hands on him in Manhattan, and Agate called out the buddy-system of the NYPD, but though there were a dozen false alarms, no one even got a glimpse of the man.

Agate released Hallie Glendon's body for burial, and the funeral was held the Wednesday afternoon before Thanksgiving. There was a fine mist falling, and through it, beyond the cemetery gates, I could see the thin figure of Helen Macauley watching from behind the glass wall of her dead husband's house, like a stick drawing in white chalk, light against dark.

As we drove out of the cemetery past a huge old mausoleum surrounded with overgrown blue spruces, their heavy boughs glittering with the damp, I could've sworn I saw a figure moving, ducking into the protecting circle made by the low branches, which hung almost to the ground.

"Stop!" I ordered David, and we both got out. "I think I just spotted Swan in there!"

Despite his best dark suit, Davy charged through the sodden boughs and I could hear him thrashing around. In a moment, he ducked out again, his hair damp and the shoulders of the suit soaked.

"Nobody," he said, disappointed.

I walked over to the mausoleum. Something lay on the marble steps and I bent to pick it up, an odd-shaped piece of plastic like a child's whistle. Merriman got out of the car and came to join me, peering over my shoulder at the thing.

"So," he said, with satisfaction, "he couldn't stay away after all."

"How do you make that out? Some kid lost a whistle, that's all. Blasted kids play cops-and-hit-men in here all the time and this noble pile is usually headquarters."

Merriman sniffed and grabbed the thing out of my paw. "Winnie," he said, "your little gray cells may be just like mother made, but the density of your occiput never ceases to amaze. This isn't a whistle! For your information, it's the mouthpiece of a clarinet!"

295

It was only a small package, wrapped in brown paper, my name in Elsa's ornate German handwriting on the outside. I knew what was in it, of course—the strengthening herbal brew she'd promised on the phone, her version of Sarah's oatmeal-and-decaf cure. Axel Engstrom, her factotum, had brought it while we were at Hallie's funeral, and now it lay on the hall table, taunting me.

I tore the wrapping off and looked at the plastic bag of deep green dry leaves inside. Gingerly I opened it and took a cautious whiff.

"The woman expects me to graze on this?" I grumbled. "Do I *look* like a sheep?"

"Certainly not," bleated Merriman, coming down the stairs. "You look like a hippopotamus, but I'm fond of you and I hardly notice anymore." He stuck his nose into the bag. "What is it? Smells foul."

"It's Mother Worthing's Home Cure for What Ails Me," I told him. "Supposed to rid me of glanders, the botts, and tooth decay. You brew it into tea, that's what Elsa prescribes."

"Mmmmmm," said Eddie. "Dear Elsa again. And will you?"

"I might *brew* it," I replied.

"But will you drink it?"

I glared at the stuff in the bag. "Would you?" I said.

"I should think very hard about it. I should certainly brew up a cup." He nabbed the bag from me. "In fact, I'll do it right now. And then I'll pour it into a peanut butter jar and deliver it to Lloyd Agate for examination. Sarah can drive me, on our way to the train."

We were all headed into Manhattan that evening for our Thanksgiving weekend.

"We're behind schedule already," I said. "Anyway, Sarah will want to know where it came from, and she's upset enough about Elsa as it is. I'll just call Lloyd from the depot, tell him I've left the whole shebang in the mailbox. He can stop by and pick it up after we've left for town."

"Pick what up?"

Sarah came down lugging her carryall and my old gym bag, all packed for the excursion. My own supplies included one of Agate's evidence bags with a minuscule pinch of the ashes of devil's net, whatever the hell *it* was. Maybe some clever Chinese would be able to tell me, or failing that, fix me up with a shot of ginseng.

I was wearing down, and I knew it. Funerals are always bad enough, but all through this one I'd kept scanning the faces of the women gathered there—Hilda Costello, Diana Sheffield and her eldest daughter, Alex, Sarah—and wondering which of them might be next. Elsa had been missing from the circle of Krish's friends, though old Madam Max had amazed us all by turning up at the last minute in Frieda Fritz's taxi. Elsa and Graham—the drone, Max called him—had gone away together to sort things out, she said, and sent their love.

"Who's going to pick what up?" Sarah wasn't about to be put off. "We can take the luggage with us, there isn't much."

"Oh, just another part of Sheffield's paper chase," I lied, shoving the little bag of herbs in my pocket. "The file copy of my midterm grades. I forgot to leave it with Hannah in the office, and the poor sap's pining for it. I'll stuff it in the mailbox for him."

She scanned my face like an X-ray machine, eyes narrowed. "But I thought you filed your grades in the registrar's office, not with Hannah."

"New regime," I said blithely. "We all set? Merriman, where's your carpetbag?"

"For your information, goopus," he said, "it is referred to as soft-sided designer luggage." He darted into the living room and returned with a football-shaped article in purple paisley.

"Looks like a carpetbag to me," I said, "but I haven't got time to argue. Just hang the blasted excrescence around your scrawny neck and let's go! The train leaves in forty minutes!"

"Oh, Win," cried Sarah, as we were about to pile into the car. "Your blood pressure pills! I was going to pack them this morning and I found the bottle was empty. I intended to refill them before we left, but what with the funeral, I forgot!"

"Never mind," I assured her, "I don't need the damn things anyway."

"Nonsense! I'm not going anywhere until you refill that prescription. You won't be able to do it tomorrow, it's Thanksgiving. We'll stop at Castlebury's and get it done now."

"But we'll miss our train!" I groaned.

"Then we'll take the next one." She got into the car and sat there, tapping her gloved fingers on the steering wheel. You could almost see the smoke coming out of her ears.

I know when I'm licked. Merriman and I got in and Sarah took off for the prescription clip-joint like a bat out of You-Know-Where. We rounded the corner into Castlebury's parking lot burning rubber, and I got out, still grumbling.

It was crowded in the place, as usual. The horde from the doctors' waiting rooms had just pulled in and there was a line at the prescription counter and another at the check stand up front. I didn't even see Piers Ambrose at first among the blue-haired old ladies and the snuffling five-year-olds and the pregnant girls with weary, bored expressions. But he certainly saw me.

" 'What ho, Brabantio! Look to your house, your daughter, and your bags! Thieves, thieves!' "

His deep voice was no more than a muttering in my ear. Before I knew it, he was beside me, bending down confidentially from his height.

"What're you doing in here, Ambrose?" I said, trying to sound casual. "The rabbit in your hat got the mange, has he, or did you run out of sneezing powder? What *is* that stuff you make the puffs of smoke with, anyway, the ones you wizards disappear into?"

"The distillation of the spheres," he said, and I almost thought he meant it.

"Goofer dust, you mean," I growled, and we moved one space closer to the counter.

"Stop by the Castle of Wonders when you get to Manhattan," he said, that smug smile on his handsome kisser. "Catch my performance. You might just be surprised what a little goofer dust can do."

"How did you know I was going to Manhattan, you old—"

"Help you, sir?" nagged the owl-eyed kid behind the prescription desk.

I had to take my turn, then, and when I got my pills paid for, I played for time, shopping through the nearby bin of discounted off-season hay fever nostrums, my big ears standing up straight. Now was Piers's turn at the counter.

Owl-eyes took the empty pill bottle Ambrose handed him and scowled at it. "I don't think I'm supposed to fill this yet. It was only refilled last week, and there were twenty-five pills in it. You're only supposed to take one diginox a day. You're not following doctor's orders."

My famous blood pressure shot up a few dozen points, and I moved a step closer.

"I had a bit of an accident with the other bottle," said Piers. "Embarrassing as hell. You see, I never screw the damn lid tight because it's one of those child-proof things and I have trouble getting it off."

That, I thought, would be the day—Piers the Prestidigitator boggled by a child-proof bottle cap!

"I keep the bottle in the cupboard over the bathroom sink, naturally," he went on, "and I was shaving yesterday morning, had the water running. Cut myself—" He demonstrated a small gouge, now scabbed-over, just below his lip.

"Ridiculous, really. The pill bottle simply fell into the sink, and all the pills that were left—they washed away. I've been without one all day, and I really can't wait until after the holiday. If you could just—"

"It's too late to phone the doctor. The office will be closed by now." The kid sighed and nudged old Cass Castlebury, the boss. He grinned over his glasses at Piers and nodded. They'd been one half of a poker foursome for the last twenty years.

I dodged behind a rack of suppositories and lay in wait. When Piers went by, headed for the door, the hard-won bottle of pills in hand, I made my move.

" 'Avaunt, be gone!' " I hissed.

I hadn't really thought I could pull it off, but I swear to you, the man jumped as though he'd been skewered. I pushed my advantage home.

"Well, well, I see you got your diginox. Funny thing," I told him as I toddled past him out the door. "I wouldn't have thought you *had* a heart."

We checked into our favorite down-at-heel hostelry, the storied Battersea, and spent the night in quiet slumber, aside from a hard-fought game of pinochle with Bert, my old pal the night-desk clerk. Next day was Thanksgiving; we steered clear of Macy's and the arrival of Old St. Nick, which was far too early to suit me. Instead, I treated Sarah and Merriman to a slap-up feast at Hannibal's Grille, a little bistro popular among those in the know, that serves the kind of chili you can hardly ever find east of West Texas. (Eddie, who'd forgotten to refill his traveling supply of Maalox after the last faculty beano, played it safe and stuck to chowder.) It was a quiet day, a respite from the darkness and confusion and suspicion of the past weeks. We talked of movies, books, the price of cab fare, and the irreplaceable beauties that still lurked beneath the grime and terror of New York. We strolled, not uncautious but unafraid, along streets we had walked a thousand times before on other visits. We ate uncomplicated, unpretentious food that warmed and heartened and renewed us all. We traded wisecracks, ignored the sirens circling like nervous flies somewhere beyond us, and laughed together over nothing.

We were at peace, we three, in a slowly strangling America. On that one precious day, the Pilgrims could've taken our correspondence course.

We all slept deeply and well that night, and early next day, Friday, Merriman and I headed for Chinatown while Sarah went to see her friend Teresa, the symphony cellist. The herbalist Lloyd remembered had been on Mott Street not far from the Buddhist Temple, and the cab let us out on a nearby corner in front of a sidewalk fish market where live carp swam in one huge tank and crabs squirmed in another.

"Well," said Eddie, swiveling his noggin around like a barn owl, "the temple's certainly still there, all right. But I fail to discern an herb shop."

"Lloyd said they sold curios, rice bowls, tea— Let's try over here," I suggested, and we set off down the crowded street toward a storefront whose sign proclaimed "Wing Yee, Fine Tea."

Outside, the place wasn't much, but inside it was clean and rather elegant, the walls lined with tiny drawers labeled in Chinese and English, and the center aisle taken up with a long, low lacquered table on which was a beautiful deep-red Chinese teapot kept hot by a candle underneath. Beside the pot a half-dozen bloodred tea bowls stood ready; I didn't see any of that happy-hour incense Agate had mentioned, but the place was fragrant with the noble leaf of the East.

The temple bell fixed to the front door had bonged when we entered, and it wasn't a moment before a tiny Chinese girl with what appeared to be a shaven head and the tattoo of a rosebud on her slender throat came sailing through the curtains from the back room.

"Would you like to sample anything in particular? That's hibiscus flower in the pot there." She poured some into tea bowls and handed one to each of us.

I couldn't take my eyes off her. She was like the queen of a set of Chinese chess pieces I'd once coveted in an antique shop, although I've never learned to play the game at all. They were white and black jade, but it was the white queen I'd noticed most, pale and eerily lovely, but missing one arm and part of her head.

The girl must've noticed me staring. "It's the hairdo, isn't it?"

she said, and laughed. "The Sinéad O'Connor look, it's very hot right now. Dramatizes the victimization of women. Convict stuff, concentration camps."

"You look a little young to have suffered any of that," I said, sipping my tea. I hate tea.

She laughed again. "Me? Oh, I'm in a rock band, that's all. We call ourselves China Rose." She brushed a finger over her tattoo.

"Victimization, indeed," I mumbled, my mind on a tattoo of quite another sort. I pulled Lloyd's evidence bag out of my pocket. "Look, I wonder if you could help us? I see you do carry a few herbs here." There was a cabinet of the famous ginseng, all types and sizes, and another with glass jars of what certainly didn't look like tea. "The Latin name of it is *reticulum diabolicum,* and I need to know what its properties are. What it would do to you if you brewed it into tea, say, or munched it down."

"Or burnt it like incense," piped up Merriman, "and inhaled it deeply."

"Just a sec," said China Rose. "I'll get Ma."

She zoomed through the curtains to get her mother. At least that was what my occidental brain assumed. It turned out to be a very old man whose bright black eyes glittered within a net of fine wrinkles.

"Ma Yee," said the girl. She spoke rapidly to him in Chinese and he smiled and held out his hand for the sample. When I'd forked it over, he opened the seal, took a fraction of the pinch between his thumb and forefinger, and rubbed the fingers together. Then he licked his thumb cautiously, challenging his taste buds. He closed his eyes in concentration for a moment. Then he put his index finger first to one nostril, then to the other, and inhaled deeply. He wrinkled his nose. He closed his eyes again. At last he opened them.

"*Reticulum diabolicum,*" he said, in perfect Oxford Latin. "A curious herb. In China, it has another name with which I will not bore you. It translates to 'smoke of the gods.' We have a very different attitude than you Europeans to such things. A plant that induces sleep is from the gods, not the demons."

"So," said Eddie, "it's a sort of drug, is it? Anaesthetic?"

The old fellow nodded. "It has been used so. For tooth extractions, labor pains—that sort of thing. Not especially strong, and no good at all in teas or extracts. It has been valuable in herbal medicine because the effect can be adjusted by the age of the dried leaf. Like tobacco, it concentrates the vital oil over the course of time, providing it is stored carefully. Fresh leaves have very little effect. Old ones, stored for four or five years in glass, are very potent. A herbal doctor can use them in different strengths, depending upon the amount of pain to be dealt with."

"Mr. Ma," I said, "what if you used the stuff full strength, aged just right? What would happen if you gave it to somebody perfectly healthy?"

He laughed, a dry laugh that might have come from the small bronze Buddha over the counter. "That's easy," he said. "Sleep. A gift of the gods. How deep the sleep would depend on how much was inhaled, for how long. Sometimes it is given as anaesthetic for very precise, long operations, but they, of course, were experimental. It's not a common drug in this country. Hardly known at all, though it's familiar enough in Europe and Latin America, I believe. You Americans prefer to buy your cures ready-made. You have too much money. The rest of us must grow our own relief."

"Could you grow it around here?" I braced myself, hoping he'd say no, that it needed some special soil or more rainfall or a warmer climate—anything.

"Oh, yes," he said. "Many Chinese have plants of it, imported as seeds before the Department of Agriculture rules were quite so strict. I expect the same is true of other cultures, too."

"You could ask Señora Alzado," interjected the girl, "over at the Essex Market. She runs the botánica there, and she knows every herb there is."

"Let me get this straight," I said. "Could too much of this stuff kill a person?"

"Only if there were other circumstances. Trauma of some sort. Something that slowed the heart dramatically or dropped the blood pressure."

"And if I wanted to put somebody to sleep with it, how exactly would I do it?"

Ma Yee shook his head in exasperation. "I told you," he said. "Smoke of the gods. You burn it, of course. In a pipe, like opium, in a burner, like incense."

"Or in a pot of lady's slipper orchids," I heard Eddie say.

We left the shop and headed for the Essex Market some blocks away, both silent, neither of us willing to voice what was in our minds. At last Eddie broke the ice.

"So, whoever shot Macauley drugged him first with devil's thingamajig, and it might've been thriving in a pot on the killer's windowsill for years."

"Mmmmmm," I replied.

"Magicians have been using herbs for thousands of years."

"That puff of smoke business again," I said. "Good old goofer dust."

"And Swan. From what you tell me, he probably had access to Mrs. Macauley's gun. He's learned enough about herbs from Elsa to brew up that sleeping potion he gave Krish. And how he must've hated Macauley! He'd found a sort of refuge here, you know. His long-lost daughter within sight, that marvelous anachronism of a place of Elsa's. A lover, possibly the first since Elizabeth Swan." He smiled softly. "Even at my age, imagination permits me to speculate on the sort of lover our Elsa must be."

"And then Macauley turns up here as the new chancellor and threatens all of them."

"And once his daughter was dead—" Eddie shook his head. "If it's true, one could hardly blame the man." We walked along in silence for a moment, and then he said, "Of course, there is another possibility."

"If you mean Elsa killed Macauley," I told him, "you can quit barking up that tree right now. I did a little checking on my own as to her whereabouts the afternoon Macauley died. She was giving one of those flower-arranging chalk talks of hers to the hospital auxiliary that afternoon. Started at four o'clock and lasted right through dinner at six. Alex was supposed to go, but after the big punch-out in Elsa's orchard, she gave it a miss and came to our place with Davy instead.''

Merriman blew a sigh of relief that was gale force, at least. "Then she couldn't have killed Macauley. Praise be."

"Mmmmmm. But just paste this in your hat. If Macauley was sedated by somebody, whether it was Swan or Piers or somebody else altogether, then he certainly didn't commit suicide and he wasn't the Heart Specialist. He was set up, and the real killer is still out there with his handy little vial of diginox. Piers takes diginox. I told you what I saw him pulling on that clerk in Castlebury's."

"Flapdoodle, Winnie!" he cried. "I absolutely indemnify Piers Ambrose. I shall simply ask him this afternoon. 'Piers, did you murder four women with watered-down heart medicine?' "

We were all going to take in the enigmatic Ambrose's afternoon set at the Castle of Wonders.

"Do that," I said, "by all means. You'll get an answer worthy of the Delphic Oracle. But ask him. Oh, hell, Merriman. Just listen to that."

Eddie strained an ear. "What is it? Thunder?"

"My tummy growling," I said. "We were going to grab a bite in Chinatown, but I got so excited at Ma's that I clean forgot."

"I know what else you forgot," he said, diving in his pocket. "These."

He shoved my bottle of old Penny's blood pressure pills under my nose. "You didn't have your medicine, did you? I am solemnly sworn to see that you take one, or Sarah's curse will light upon us both. There's a soda machine right over there. Go!"

"Horsefeathers," I snarled. But I got a can of 7-Up from a machine outside a small grocery store and downed the thing. "Now, where's food?"

"It went thataway," said Merriman. He was pointing to the Essex Market.

We entered the old building that houses the collection of fruit stalls, bakers, jewelry sellers, fish markets, delicatessens, poultrymongers, and purveyors of assorted odds and ends, an institution tucked away at the crossroads of a dozen cultures, of Chinese and Puerto Rican and Cuban and Italian and Jewish and Vietnamese. There were flower stalls laden with showy bunches of lilies and mums, long spikes of gladioli and snapdragons, and gorgeous orchids that would've done Macauley proud. Huge whole salmon and halibut lay on beds of ice on the counters; chickens hung in squadrons on racks overhead; cats from Blanche Megrim's fondest daydreams, whole battalions of fat, sleek, suspicious, worldly-wise pussycats of every complexion roamed under the counters, closing in on the chickens and the fish and ogling the hamburgers frying on the grill at the fast-food bar.

"Let's get a burger," I said, "before one of those confounded cats gets too close and I scarf *him* down."

"There's the botánica," Merriman said. "Right over there!"

He made a beeline for a stall containing row after row of painted plaster statues of the Virgin Mary and the saints, crucifixes, rosaries, amulets of many sorts, and in the back, before a small window with a cash register where an old lady sat knitting, a long table full of odd-smelling potted plants. There was nothing beautiful about them. They were mostly foliage, and not very spectacular foliage at that, some of it needlelike and some round and flat. Many of the leaves were silvery gray, and although some smelled sweet, a number were positively stinky.

"There's rue," said Merriman. "That's for remembrance."

"*La ruta,*" said a voice. "*Para las mujeres.*"

It was the old knitter. She stuck her head out the cubbyhole window, keeping an eye on the merchandise.

"Señora," I said, "forgive me, but I don't speak Spanish. *No hablo español.*"

Mrs. Alzado—I assumed she was the woman China Rose had recommended—cackled richly. My ignorance seemed to delight her. I felt like Gulliver in the Land of the Horses, a gawping ninny.

"You call it rue," she said. "*La ruta.* A plant for women's troubles, you see."

I wondered sourly if China Rose knew there was a plant made just for women, and whether it would be any help with what ailed Helen Macauley. But I let it pass.

"I'm interested in a plant called devil's net," I said. "The Chinese call it smoke of the gods. Puts you to sleep if you burn it."

I handed her the minute remains of Agate's sample, and we went through the same routine as at Ma Yee's place, to the musical rumbling of my empty tummy. At last Mrs. Alzado completed what seemed to be the herbalist's ritual, and handed me back the empty plastic evidence bag.

"*Sí,*" she said, "*yo lo conozco. Se llama 'hierba del brujo.'*"

She stared at me, then she cackled again, whinnied a bit, and translated for the benefit of the lower orders. "We call it herb of— of— *Cómo se dice, brujo?* Ah!" Another cackle. "*Brujo, es* a man witch. Herb of the man witch."

"In other words, wizard's herb," said Eddie, as we walked away.

He left it up to me to say what both of us were thinking. "Or sorcerer's," I muttered. "Or maybe even Sorcerer King."

What with meeting Myra Fish, producer of *Bookends,* the literary talk show I'd taken over on public TV, and taping a show on location at the Stock Exchange during what should've been my lunch hour, in which I had to figure out semi-intelligent questions to ask Rupert Babbitt, the Mr. Fix-it of Wall Street, about his current recipe book for saving the economy, I never did get that breakfast, not to speak of lunch. My mind wasn't on the economy and it certainly wasn't on Rupert. It wasn't even on my growling tum-tum. It was on a poem that kept running through my mind. Well, not the poem exactly. Just the title.

It was called "A Ballade of Dead Ladies."

The taping ran late, and Sarah was already waiting for us outside the disused movie house that billed itself as the Castle of Wonders. By then it was past noon and I'd had nothing all day but a can of pop and that ridiculous blood pressure pill of old Pennington's. I toddled into a deli and grabbed an outsized pastrami sandwich, which I was still chomping as we bought tickets for the afternoon's magic extravaganza, featuring L'Empereur de Neige—the Emperor of Snow— otherwise known as Piers Mandeville Ambrose.

It wasn't an especially prepossessing joint. The lobby was papered with some sort of midnight-blue velvety stuff over which an enterprising magic-lover had stenciled zodiacs and star maps in silver fluorescent paint. There was a record playing over a loudspeaker and you'll just have to trust me when I tell you that the song was "Stars Fell on Alabama." Not wishing to waste the facilities afforded by the former movie house, the local magi had stocked the snack bar with munchies purveyed by a girlie in blue velvet pants and a halter top made of what looked to me like tin foil. We were about to go in and find seats when a weedy little fellow in black tie and tails that almost swept the floor oozed up to us, rubbing his pink palms together in unctuous delight.

"Welcome, welcome children," he said. (This Uriah Heep of a wizard must've been at least forty years my junior, but he probably would've said we were all children of the spheres.) "You, of course, are Professor Sherman. L'Empereur told me you were coming and of course I was *stunned. Utterly* stunned. I read all your novels religiously. A Henrietta Slocum fanatic, *absolutement!*" He whipped out three of my old paperbacks from somewhere—probably up his sleeve —and pulled a pen from behind my ear. "If you'd just sign them for me, I should be *prostrated, utterly* prostrated, with gratitude."

I obliged, as he fixed me with a beady and rather unnerving eye. I handed the books back to him and they disappeared into whatever orbit they'd come from.

"Now," he said, slipping his arm through Sarah's, "if you'll just follow me, I'll take you back. You want to see L'Empereur before his triumph, of course."

He pranced away like one of the Rockettes leading a limbo line, and Merriman and I followed. "What exactly is this triumph of which you speak, uh— Sorry, old thing, but I didn't catch your John Henry," I said.

"Moi? Oh, the Great Donaldo, charmed, I'm sure. I do apologize. I just assumed you knew. Our Emperor of Snow is attempting rather a coup this afternoon. He's doing The Marvelous Harmony."

"Musical number, is it?" It meant nothing to me.

Donald glared over his shoulder at me. "It's one of the tricks of the great magus, Belisarius, of course, a subtle illusion, a classic."

We had gone up some concrete steps to a sort of landing, what looked to have been the old projection room of the movie house. There were more stars on the door, and a photograph of Piers looking like an overdressed Jack Frost, in a long white robe and a white cape sprinkled with spangles and fringed as if with icicles—the Emperor of Snow.

" 'The only emperor,' " I intoned as we walked in the dressing room door, " 'is the Emperor of Ice Cream.' " I sniffed, and glanced at Merriman. He wrinkled his nose. "Whatever you've got on the stove, Ambrose, it's burning. I smell smoke!"

He bent over his dressing table, and I don't mind admitting he was quite a sight. The white hair, the long white silk gown fringed with silk and spangled with crystal beads, the white velvet cape that fell heavily from his broad shoulders—it was more than theater. It was true illusion. He seemed huge and invincible, and when he struck a match and an aureole of white smoke instantly surrounded him, I felt a shiver of excitement run through me. My heart was racing and the blood was slamming against my temples and the backs of my eyes ached. I risked a deep breath of the smoke, and grabbed Merriman's arm.

"It's *not* the stuff that was burned in Macauley's office," I whispered. "It's not the same smell at all. I—"

"Look!" cried Sarah. "He's gone! Oh, piffle. I don't believe it. There must be a closet in this room somewhere."

She began to poke around, and Eddie picked up something from an old couch in a corner. The white, fragrant smoke hung thick in the room, thickest near the dressing table where Piers had stood, and the full-length mirror beyond it. I stared into the mirror at my own unwieldy image, and saw behind me, where he could not have gotten without walking straight through me, the fractured reflection of the Emperor of Snow, the Sorcerer King himself.

"You!" I said. "Damn you, Iago! You—"

The image didn't speak. It swirled and broke and came at me in pieces sharp as mirror glass, cold and bright as snow, pieces that battered my chest and took my breath and tore the muscles from my legs. I grabbed for Sarah and she wasn't there, and I was falling, falling again, into the bottomless illusion, the game of lights and mirrors that was my death.

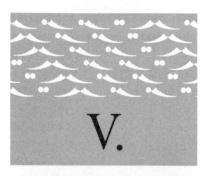

V.

Sorrowheart

Twenty-four

I woke up almost nine hours later in a dark cubbyhole of a room lined with tiled counters and mysterious drawers in which I could've sworn somebody must've put my insides for safekeeping, because I felt lighter than goose down. I wasn't a bit surprised that they'd had to strap my arms to the bed.

In front of me, up on the wall, a TV set flickered, and all around my bed electronic contraptions beeped and blinked and hummed. I seemed to be hitched up to most of them by tubes and wires that sprouted out of various portions of my anatomy. One was coming out my nose, another out my mouth, and one or two were hitched to my hands.

There was no sign of Merriman or Sarah, whom I seemed to remember having left someplace.

"Where the hell——" I tried to say, but it came out, "Rrrrhhhhlllll!"

Something white flapped past the end of my bed and I blinked. My eyes didn't want to focus.

"I'm here for your history," said a female voice.

"Rrrrrhhhhhhllllllggggggg!" I told her around the tube in my mouth.

"Don't fiddle with that tube!" she commanded. "Just answer these questions. Blink once for yes and twice for no."

My eyes came into approximate focus and I perceived a small woman in a white nylon uniform and a black sweater. She was wearing the veil of a Roman Catholic order and there was a stethoscope dangling from her sweater pocket.

"Rrrrrrng anh nah?" I asked her, wondering if I'd slipped into heaven when nobody was looking. It would've explained the nuns.

I must've enunciated more clearly than I thought. "You're in Mother of Mercies Hospital," she told me. "On East Twenty-seventh Street. You're still in intensive care, but you'll be leaving as soon as we get your history."

"You can let that go for now, Sister," said a gently authoritative voice. "We'll get him off the central monitor and just leave the oxygen for safety's sake. He's stable now."

"Yes, Doctor," said the little nun obediently, and rustled out.

"Doctor" was nothing whatsoever like old Doc Pennington. He was sleek and streamlined, with a white lab coat that fit him like a second skin and a neatly trimmed brown beard. It was his eyes that got me, though. There they were again. Those eyes. They were large and pale brown, and for an instant, as he deftly slipped the rubber tube out from between my tonsils, they met mine.

We saluted each other silently, and a smile flickered across his sober face.

"You put on quite a magical performance at the Castle of Wonders, so they tell me," he said. "When you came in here, your heart was going a mile a minute. Look at that EKG now." He pointed to one of the machines. "Practically perfect. Your—um—lady says you had another attack like this a week or so ago?"

"More or less," I told him. Just as it had the other time, the whole thing was wearing off, now, and I felt almost normal.

The little nun came sailing in again. "We've got a room ready for him on two," she said, and tacking to avoid Doctor, she weighed anchor and sailed off again.

"I don't want a room! I'm going home. I'm perfectly all right. Where's Sarah? Where's Merriman? Where are my shoes?"

The doctor let a grin escape him, then tucked it safely behind his beard and worked on looking stern. "You're not going anywhere, Professor. Not until I make some tests."

I squinted at him. Blast those eyes of his! "I hate tests," I told him.

"Good. Then you'll be glad to get them over with."

"What kind of tests? What for?"

"Let's just say I can't resist a mystery. Something's going on here, and I want to know what it is. It may be physiological, emotional. May be allergic, even. I've got to have more information before we can get any farther, and the tests will help me eliminate some things. We'll do a couple of scans, your lungs and heart, digestive tract. Brain scan."

"There is absolutely nothing the matter with my gray matter, thank you very much indeed!"

"I can believe that," he agreed. "In fact, I don't think there's too much wrong with you at all. I think it's very possibly something you're doing yourself, without even realizing it. Sister will take down all your medications and record your eating and sleeping habits. Anything that will give us a clue."

I liked the fellow's attitude, but I kept thinking of Christmas. It was less than a month away now. I couldn't afford the waste of time.

"How long is this going to take, all these tests of yours? I've got things to do, you know!"

"We'll schedule them as soon as possible. But you're not an emergency anymore, so it'll take some time. You'll have to bear with us."

"I guess that's why you fellows call us 'patients,' " I said.

The nun popped in again. "They're ready in O.R., Dr. Macklin," she said, and was off down the hall.

"When I was a kid in Iowa," I grumbled, "I had my appendix out in a Catholic hospital in Sioux City. In those days, all the nuns looked like Loretta Young in *Come to the Stable*. They smelled like peppermint and crackled when they walked.''

"Oh,'' he said, heading for the door. "New York City nuns don't crackle. They roar. And look out for that one. She carries mace.''

I was wheeled upstairs to my new bijou accommodations riding my lumpy bed like General Rommel in his jeep, reviewing the troops. The troops, I discovered were already in my second-floor room, waiting to mount a pincers attack.

"You old ninny!'' cried Sarah, as Dirty Harry, the nun with the mace next to her stethoscope, plugged my oxygen tube into a spigot on the wall and cranked my bed down a peg. "What do you think you're doing?''

"Palely loitering,'' I said. Sarah looked a touch gray around the gills herself, and as for Merriman, he stood outlined against the grubby window that looked out onto a warehouse, his eyes on his shoes. "Maybe the sister could fix the pair of *you* up with a bed each and a selection of tubes. You both look like hell.''

"Tcch!'' clucked Dirty Harry, and yanked the sheet up around my chin. "Watch your language, if you please! There's a *gentleman* in the *other* bed, you know.''

"Could've fooled me,'' I muttered, craning my neck. The curtain that divided the room was pulled back and there certainly was another bed in the corner nearest the bathroom. Something seemed to be thrashing around under the blankets, and then at last an egg-shaped head emerged. A pair of small bright eyes scanned the bunch of us. Then the head disappeared again.

"Mr. Friedenberg!'' Dirty Harry wasn't about to suffer any nonsense. "Mr. Friedenberg, come out of there this minute!''

"Ayyyyyyyyeeeeeeeee!'' A long, thin wail issued from under the covers.

"Come on, dear!''

"Ayyyyyyyeeeeeeeeeeeeeeeeeeeeeeee!''

"He's in pain!'' said Sarah. "Should I call someone, or do something?''

316

"He's quite all right," said Harry. She marched over to the old boy's bed and whipped the covers back.

Friedenberg turned out to be as long and thin as his cry of torment, with a gray-fringed bald dome and the countenance of a basset hound suffering from chronic depression.

"Mr. Friedenberg dislikes hospitals," said Harry, and began to shake down a thermometer.

"Join the club," I growled. "What's your problem, Friedenberg, or are they just practicing on you, too?"

"How I've suffered!" moaned the old fellow. "AAAaaa-yyyyyyyyeeeeeee!"

"It'll all be over after tomorrow morning," said Harry blithely.

I gulped. *"Tomorrow?"* Sarah bit her lip and Merriman's eyes came open very wide indeed. "I probably have no business asking," I said to Harry in an undertone, "but what's going to happen tomorrow?"

"Ayyyyyyyeeeeee!" wailed old Friedenberg.

"Oh, only his surgery." The nun shoved her thermometer in his mouth. "It'll all be over once that's done."

"Er, 'scuse my asking and all," said Merriman, looking mournfully at the old man, "but what exactly—"

"Oh, Mr. Friedenberg won't mind my telling you. Will you, dear? Such a bothersome problem. He has an ingrown toenail. Haven't you, dear?" And she whipped the thermometer out of his chops and sailed away again.

It was only an hour until Lights Out, and I was finding it hard to keep my peepers open. Sarah tiptoed out, headed for the hospital shop to buy me a toothbrush before the place closed for the night. But Merriman hung around, perched on the radiator under the grimy window. Old Friedenberg had been asleep since shortly after Sister Harry left, and the quiet was broken only by the nasal voice that came over the speaker system now and then outside in the long hall, summoning one doctor or another to some emergency. Merriman hadn't had much to say all evening, and not once had any of us mentioned the various deaths up in Ainsley. I

317

was almost asleep when I felt a light touch on my arm. It was Eddie.

"Winnie," he said, and the softness of his voice had nothing to do with the presence of the suffering Mr. Friedenberg. "I know this is neither the time nor the place for it. I'm ashamed of myself for bothering you now." He closed his mouth. "No, damn it all! Go to sleep! Get well, do you hear me! Forget everything!"

I licked my lips, which still tasted like Doc Macklin's rubber tube. "If you were intending to tell me what I've been trying to pry out of you for the last two weeks, then for pity's sake spit it out. I need something to keep my gray cells in condition while I'm lying around this joint, and if you think I've forgotten what's been going on at home, you're badly mistaken. Now, then. Out with it!"

He squinted at me, studying my face. "You don't think that magic smoke of Piers's caused you to keel over at the Castle of Wonders?"

"I didn't see any goofer dust that morning in our kitchen, did you?" I shook my bean, and instantly regretted it. I still had that oxygen tube up my nose, and it tickled. "Piers had nothing to do with this. More like old Penny and those damn blood pressure pills. Half the problems in this world are caused by pills, if you ask me."

He stared at me, openmouthed. "You know, don't you, Hyde?"

"Know what? What are you dithering about?"

"All this time I've been walking round like a secret criminal, and you've known about those damn pills—"

"Oh, my Sunday hat," I groaned, "will you please calm down and make sense! What pills? My blood pressure pills?"

By this time he was positively quivering with excitement. "No, no, no, no! You don't know at all, do you? You haven't a thing in your noggin. Pills! Heart pills!"

"Diginox? Are you talking about diginox?" Now it was my turn to stare. "Piers's, you mean? Did you say anything to him about it after I passed out? Because I don't think you should have—"

"Not Piers!" he hissed, as old Friedenberg's feet—ingrown toenail and all—began to flail again. "Maxima! Madam Max takes digi-nox, Winnie. I knew it before any of those women died, before Mrs. Ten Eyck. Before Hallie. I've known it for nearly five years, ever since the doctor prescribed them for her. Max has a severely irregu-lar heartbeat, and they were new on the market then. I can hear her now: 'The quack will put me in a wire cage next, like all the other guinea pigs.' " He avoided my eyes. "That's why I bullied you into investigating the business, don't you know. Hoped you might ferret out something to clear it all up. But it's only gotten worse, hasn't it? The very idea of anyone in that household—well, it's altogether mad, that's all!"

I tried to gulp, but there wasn't enough spit in my mouth for a swallow, let alone a gulp. "Get me a glass of water, will you, Merriman?"

Having something to do seemed to calm him down a bit. He handed it to me and ran the head of my bed up so I could keep from baptizing myself with it.

"All right, now," I told him. "That was five years ago. The prescription may have been changed since then."

He shook his head. "After that day in the park—Mrs. Ten Eyck's death, you know—I toddled upstairs to visit the facilities on one of our Sunday evenings at Elsa's and explored the medicine chest in the bathroom, just to be sure. It's diginox, all right. And there's some-thing else. The bottle had been refilled only three days before Mrs. Ten Eyck's body was found. And it was nearly half empty!"

"But you only take one of those pills a day. Unless—"

Eddie nodded. "Exactly. Unless somebody decided to make a nice little solution from those capsules and use it for injection. Swan. Graham. The pills were right there in the cabinet. I could've taken them myself."

I noticed he'd left Elsa off his shortlist, probably because hers was the name that headed it. "There are other explanations, you know, for why that bottle was half-empty. Maybe the pills were dropped. Maybe they fell in the sink." It sounded just as fishy coming from me as it had when Piers tried it on the kid at Castlebury's Drugstore. "Anyway, if Max needs the pills and she came up missing that many, she'd be dead by now, wouldn't she? Maybe they were in the wrong bottle. There are a dozen—"

"But she doesn't take them properly," he said. "You *know* Maxima—stubborn as dammit. Can't admit dependence of any sort, always the *grande dame*. Why, the only way she'll take anything at all—" He broke off and bit his lip.

I finished it for him. "Is if Elsa brings it to her on a silver platter. So if somebody wanted to take a few capsules when the bottle was full, it'd probably last long enough not to be noticed by the druggist when it was refilled a bit early."

"And if you garnered even a half-dozen pills from each refill and saved them up over a few months—"

"You could just dissolve them in a little distilled water. Elsa makes tinctures and extracts from those herbs all the time, out in that workshop of hers."

We both fell silent. I understood why he had withheld the information so long. It admitted a possibility both of us had been trying our damnedest to wriggle out of—the possibility that somebody in that wonderful house, the house of the treasured past, might be a killer.

We have to have more information before we can get much farther. The tests will help eliminate some things—Dr. Macklin's words came back to me as I drifted off that night to the vague half-sleep of hospitals. But what tests could I devise for the capacity to kill, when I still didn't know whether I was looking for one murderer, or two very different ones indeed?

Next day was Saturday, and the hospital testing center was booked solid. Sister Dirty Harry came whizzing in at the crack of dawn and spent almost two hours writing down everything she could drag out of me on the subject of my anatomy, habits, frame of mind, and

320

method of eating Brazil nuts. On Sunday, the labs shut down and I spent the day listening to old Friedenberg—who'd managed to get his stint in surgery postponed—nurse his toenail on the insurance company's time. Sarah and Eddie took turns keeping me company during visiting hours, and David and Alex made the trip in from Ainsley, but mostly they were all just nervous faces popping in and out while I was put through the hospital routine of rude questions, inedible food, a daily forced march down the hall to the showers—always ice cold—and the constant badgering of a small Japanese nurse's aide who seemed obsessed with functions of my physiology I'd been brought up to believe were best kept between me and the Prune Growers of America.

By then it was Monday, and the only thing that was good about it was that I could legally renege on my deal to take Hilda Costello's film class this week. Merriman had caught the train home that morning with orders to give my Mystery Fiction kids the exam on *Bleak House* I'd promised them after Thanksgiving, and I'd hounded Sarah into spending the day with Teresa, since I'd be incommunicado with Macklin's machines most of the time. The doctor had been in early that morning to tell me my tests would begin after lunch—a shameless euphemism for the chilly grayish wood-substitute that had arrived on my tray masquerading as chicken on Sunday—so I had nothing on my agenda until then except a nap.

Tamiko—the Eighth Samurai—had just scuttled off down the hall cursing my digestive tract in Japanese, and I'd barely closed my eyes, when I heard the door close and looked up to find Piers Ambrose standing uneasily at the foot of my bed.

I just lay there squinting at him and trying my darnedest to look sickly. It's been my experience that people of the coolest nerve get the collywobbles in the presence of a body in a hospital bed, and I wanted the man off his guard.

" 'My lord is fall'n into an epilepsy,' " said our Iago. " 'This is his second fit, he had one yesterday.' "

I capped the line. " 'Rub him about the temples.' "

"Damned if I will," he said, and sat down on the cracked plastic chair, a double for the one at Ainsley Memorial. "I must say, Brabantio, you pick a helluva way to get out of rehearsals."

I snorted. "Too bad I missed your trick the other day. What did The Great Donald call it? The Marvelous Harmony?"

"I didn't try it. After what happened to you, my heart wasn't in it. Lost my concentration. I couldn't have topped the act you put on, anyway." He frowned. "Winnie, that bit of nonsense in my dressing room, the disappearing act? Hell, man, if I'd known you had these medical problems—" He halted there and stood isolate beside my bed, his handsome face old and sagging and uncertain, full of genuine concern. We had been friends a long, long time. "That's why I came," he went on at last, "to say I'm sorry. First time in years I've said that to anybody. Don't believe in it, as a rule. But I had no intention of causing you to keel over. You've seen me do Lights and Mirrors before, for the love of Jesus!"

Of course I had. I knew exactly how he'd disappeared and reappeared behind me. You set off the stuff I called goofer dust, a combination of chemicals that consumed itself instantly when the final catalyst was added, making no flames, but leaving a nice cloud of smoke behind—the famous smoke screen. It wasn't at all dangerous, and it had provided just the right diversion for Piers to duck through that mirror—which was really a revolving door with mirrors on both sides—come out through a hallway or an adjoining room, and turn up behind me, his image in the mirror once again. He'd performed the trick at the Christmas Revels on campus a year or two before with great effect.

I thought a moment and decided to try one of those "further tests" Doc Macklin kept talking about.

"Lights and mirrors?" I said. "Is that how you got into Macauley's office without anybody seeing you, on the day you killed him?"

He never blinked. He never batted an eye.

"Winnie," he said soberly, "I've had a long life. Sometimes I think it's too long. I've met a number of people who deserved killing, Macauley more than most. I told you that. And if I did, it

322

wouldn't be with lights and mirrors. But I have never killed anybody. To my regret, not even him.''

He sat frowning at a stain on the rug beside my bed, his blue eyes set, his mouth grim and fixed. My old fondness for him rose and I felt the ache of sympathy behind my eyes. Alex had been right about one thing. The man had long ago despaired of himself. His casual beddings, his games of illusion, his too-late literary fame could not reach the dark, still-vulnerable heart of him. At that moment, I believed absolutely in his innocence.

The man was one hell of an actor.

I spent the next four days in the tender care of Sister Dirty Harry and the Eighth Samurai, Tamiko, being steered hither and yon in a wheelchair too narrow for my backside even though I now felt perfectly capable of hiking all the way home on my own steam. Instead, the Terrible Twosome poked, punched, and pried me into that wheeled excrescence and then complained because they couldn't get it to move with me in it! I could have been to Paris and back in the time it took us to get down to the testing center.

But down we went, not once but five times. I had brain scans, CAT scans, and mouse scans, too, for all I know. Strange mechanical pincers grabbed me, wires attached themselves, electronic eyes probed my every inch. Lights blinked, beepers beeped, and I learned how to hold my breath for as long as it took a camera to travel the length of my body a centimeter at a time, stopping to admire the scenery as it went. In small, cold, tomblike rooms I lay at the mercy of unknown machines that seemed to have minds of their own, while strange voices issued commands from behind glass walls. The voices were kind, most of them, and they wished me well. But I was less important than the machines, whose kingdom this was. The healing profession had done its best, from the noblest of motives, to make of me a less-than-human thing.

Someone or something had done the same to James Macauley. How long ago it was, how violent the wrench, I could not say. But he had emerged from it the creature I saw lying shattered on the office floor. Confronted by those machines and the blank, invisible souls who served them, I began to understand Macauley just a bit, to comprehend his anger and his cold facade and even his brutal incomprehension. I was furious—as he must, at some point, have been—with what was happening to me. I was helpless and alone. My last shred of dignity was gone. I was not permitted a personality. For all those machines and their servants cared, they might have been scanning and calculating and photographing my corpse. When tiny Tamiko, my samurai, wheeled me up to my room, the last test over, and made some Japanese crack behind my back, I felt my fist double and my face flush, and if I'd been able to pry myself out of the damn chair, I would have smacked her one, so help me.

It wasn't just medicine. We had built a universe of faceless modern monoliths on every side that dwarfed us into nonentity; in time, confronted with such impersonal punishments, the brutalized subspecies turned brute in its turn. We used others as we ourselves were used, and discarded them as easily. Anger swelled, crime turned random and ceased to be motivated by anything so predictable as greed or jealous passion. Wars exploded between sects, races, even sexes. An unspecified hatred grew and simmered, looking for an object.

I could feel it happening to me, battering away at the stubborn, quirky lifelong defenses of my self. It began with a sort of mental armor, a barrier that kept out some emotions at the risk of starving the rest to death. After that must come confusion, while the shreds and patches of oneself kicked and shouted and begged to escape, to take the gamble of complete humanity again. And then, finally, the submerged fury beneath the well-trained mask, a fury that could burst forth at any time, to bludgeon anyone it met without a qualm.

As Elsa had struck out at Sarah, I thought, and felt my own fist tighten once again.

And then, I thought—because underneath the armor and the mask, the mind ranges and strikes, to turn at last upon itself—and then, the wish for death. And final escape. As James Temple Macauley had at last escaped.

I could almost have believed in that suicide; knowing what I did now, it made perfect sense.

Except for that herb, the devil's lace. Wizard's herb.

My mind had been on the stuff all through the last of the tests, and I was just glaring at my dinner—if you could call a mealy baked potato and a couple of slices of what tasted to me like roast mule dinner—when Doc Macklin tiptoed in past the drawn curtains around the bed of pain of the famous Mr. Friedenberg, whose surgery was finally over.

"Toenail?" asked Macklin softly, jerking a thumb at the drawn curtains.

"Aayyyyyyeeeeee!" I said. The curtains thrashed around a bit and then were still again. "Okay, Mack," I told him. (We'd agreed on Day Two that he didn't have to call *me* Doctor if I didn't have to call *him* Doctor, either. I'd decided to call him Mack and he'd settled for Henrietta. My fans are everywhere.) "I'm braced. Give me the bad news. What did the tests say?"

He parked on the excuse for a chair and leafed through a pile of papers on his clipboard. Then he looked up at me with those damn eyes of his and grinned. "Not a helluva lot, pal," he said. "We've given you every test known to man and some they haven't even got names for yet. You're showing a little wear, but you know that. From what I can see here, though, you'll probably outlive me. I'm fifty pounds lighter than you and my blood pressure's twice as high, even with medication. Which, by the way, is the same as yours." He paused. "When do you take your pills, Henrietta?"

"Once a day."

"But when? Morning? Bedtime? What's on the label—the instructions the pharmacy puts on, the doctor's orders?"

"I don't know," I told him. "Nothing, really. 'One capsule per day.' Get the bottle, see for yourself. It ought to be in the drawer over there where Merriman left it."

325

He got it out and pulled a pair of glasses from his coat pocket, then held the bottle under my bed lamp and squinted at the label. "Shit," I heard him murmur between his teeth. He looked at me over his bifocals. "Nobody's put any instructions on this! Didn't your doctor tell you when these have to be taken?"

"All he said was, 'Take them.' "

Mack just shook his head. "Well, hell. When you passed out the other day, when did you take your pill? Before or after you ate?"

"Before. I usually take it *after* breakfast, right before I go to work. But that day I didn't get breakfast or lunch, and I took the pill on an empty stomach long before I got time to eat anything."

"Aha! And it was only after you finally did eat something that you conked out?"

"Yes, but—"

"Now we're getting somewhere! What about the first time, when did you take your pill that day?"

"Why, right after I got up, as a matter of fact. Sarah nagged me into taking it before she left, and then Merriman and I got talking. I suppose it might've been forty minutes afterward when I ate the pizza."

"Pizza for breakfast? What was it for lunch on Friday? Couple of tacos?"

"Well, it wasn't roast army mule, I can tell you. It was a pastrami sandwich, and a tasty one, too."

"Aha! Okay, Henrietta. This is it. That particular blood pressure pill is called Benedrolomine, and when it's prescribed, you're supposed to tell the patient not—I repeat, *NOT*—to take it on an empty stomach. You see, certain chemicals react differently in the body depending upon the sequence in which they're introduced. Because there was nothing else in your system to stabilize and help break down and digest the medication slowly, it went to work too fast, like dropping a bomb. When you ate spicy food, your insides snapped to attention, the signals got crossed, and everything went nuts. Your blood pressure went crazy, your heart rate did calisthenics, and finally you just passed out."

"So it wasn't actually the pills, and my old carcass isn't going to pot at all! It's all because the damn quack—sorry—the antiquated excuse for a medical practitioner didn't bother to tell me when to take the stuff?"

"Sequence," he said. "It's very important. For instance, you can do a lot of damage in the operating room if the patient has certain medications before instead of after he's sedated. The wrong body functions are stimulated and slowed down, the sensory messages to the brain get crossed up, the heart and the circulatory system rebel and don't respond correctly."

"Doc," I said, figuring I'd take my best shot, "what do you know about a heart pill called diginox?"

"You shopping?"

"It's for a book," I lied.

"Well, it levels off the heart rate. There are newer things that work better, but they're not as commonly prescribed, not yet. It's sometimes helpful, if it's taken regularly for a while."

"How long is a while?"

"Two, three weeks, probably. With cardiac medications, you have to keep monitoring. Works differently on different people."

"What would happen if it were given to somebody who didn't need it? Somebody with a perfectly normal heart rate?"

"Probably create an artificial arrhythmia. Sensation of heart racing at some times and weakness, lassitude at others. Might not do real heart damage unless it were taken for a long time."

"And what if a weak dose were given to somebody normal who'd been sedated—deeply sedated?"

"Any qualified anesthesiologist would control the amount of diginox in the patient's system very carefully before he administered a sedative," said Mack. The dose should be absorbed and the heart rate leveled before sedation occurs."

"*Before?* Not after?"

He shook his head. "Could be pretty dangerous."

"How dangerous?" I asked him.

"Deadly," was the reply.

327

Since nobody gets out of any hospital until the hospital is damn good and ready, it was already nearly dark on the sixth afternoon of December by the time David's commodious Oldsmobile pulled smoothly up at our back door with Yours Truly in the passenger's seat. Everybody was there waiting for me—Alex and Gemma, Merriman, Sarah, Lloyd Agate, and even a serene, though unsmiling, Krish. We began with a few rituals—my removal of Sarah's Turkish Delight scorecard from the icebox door, to applause as I tore it up and stomped on it; Eddie's appearance with a cup of the foulest, blackest, most caffeinated coffee I've ever seen, to more applause as I made *him* drink the muck; Sarah's gift of a quart bowl of slimy oatmeal and a plastic garbage bag into which I dumped it, to more applause. We feasted on piping hot pizzas, one of Alex's special salads, and plenty of normal-strength coffee, topped off with slices of the fruitcake Bev Agate had been soaking in rum since August. After dinner, Gemma favored us with a selection of fractured Christmas carols on the piano—a selection of two—and we all made an effort not to talk about what was on everybody's mind.

The Christmas season was in full swing now. The coming week would mark the end of regular classes and our performance of *Othello,* and after that would come final exams. Lights blinked and chased their tails and twinkled from trees and bushes all over town; we'd passed a Santa with a ratty cotton beard ringing the Salvation Army bell beside the red kettle on Market Street on our way home; our own tree, always Merriman's contribution to Christmas, was waiting in cold storage out in the garage; and the malls and downtown stores were jammed with frenzied shoppers.

Almost three weeks had already passed since Hallie's murder. Half our time was gone and though we'd amassed a wealth of confusing detail, we seemed no nearer to what Lloyd called "hard evidence," the stuff that indictments are made of. We knew Macauley hadn't committed suicide, and from what Doc Macklin had said and what I'd learned about devil's net from old Ma at the herb shop, it sounded to me as though the same thing might have been used by the Heart Specialist to sedate his victims before the fatal injection, just as somebody had sedated Macauley before shooting him. What we still didn't know was whether there had been two killers or one. Had Macauley known the identity of the Heart Specialist? Had he been killed to shut him up? Whoever the killer or killers might be, a knowledge of that herb was paramount.

Elsa knew herbs, was famous for it. She had taught Jaffer. Piers knew the herbs used by magicians and he was an expert in the life and history of the Middle Ages, when herbal healing had been a highly developed art.

But there was no evidence that any of them had access to devil's lace, and absolutely no way of connecting any one of them directly to any of the murders. All we could do was wait. Christmas was coming, the goose was getting fat, and all of us were dreading it.

Except little Gemma. The kiddo played her two carols over and over, the scrawny chestnut pigtail she now demanded in order to look like Sarah swinging in tune, the small hands struggling with both of the chords she could manage. At last David saved us all from yet another verse of "Jingle Bells," and swooped her up, to land her on the hearthrug for one of their monster tickling matches before the mellowing fire. Worn-out and delighted with herself, Gemma fell asleep there, curled like a satisfied cat in the crook of her father's arm. Sarah, Alex, and Merriman went off to clear the table and do the dishes, and David, Lloyd, Krish, and I sat in silence for a long time, watching the fire and listening to the wind that blew dead leaves against the French windows.

Suddenly David looked up. "What's that noise?" he said.

I shrugged. "Dry leaves against the glass. Fire cracking."

"I disagree," Krish said, getting up from his corner of the sofa to peer out the steamy windows. "Certainly not leaves. Perhaps a branch falling. Perhaps a stray cat. I cannot identify."

He gave up and sat down again, but I noticed that although David didn't move for fear of waking Gemma, he didn't relax, either. Neither did Lloyd.

"That stuff you wanted the lab boys to test, Doc? Stuff Mrs. Worthing gave you?" he said. "It was nettles. You make tea out of it. Mulhaney in the squad room says his grandma poured the stuff down him by the gallon when he was a kid. He was puny, believe it or not." Michael Patrick Mulhaney was now six feet three in his socks and built like a linebacker.

"So the brew was exactly what she said it would be." I sighed and scrunched down in the couch.

Lloyd smiled. "I think you're off base about that lady, Doc. Okay, she tells a fib or two, she's got a lousy marriage. Sometimes things don't work out, right? Women got ways of dealing with it." He kept thinking of Irene Ransom. "It doesn't mean she's hiding anything illegal."

"I sincerely hope not." Krish seemed to be coming out of his shell a bit, strange noises in the night or not. "A remarkable lady, Mrs. Elsa Bergner Worthing, a woman of much discernment. The cultivated evenings at Sorrowheart, the music and pictures. Such grace is perhaps old-fashioned, but—"

"What did you call Elsa's place?"

"Oh, yes," he said. "Sorrowheart. Hallie told me the story. She admired Mrs. Worthing greatly and confided in her. Sorrowheart was the name she and her father first bestowed upon the property when he and Madam Maxima were married. In German, of course. I have myself no German as yet. But the word means Sorrowheart."

"Funny name," I said. "Sarah's never mentioned that to me."

"How did Hallie know Mrs. Worthing?" Lloyd's basso was deeper than usual. "Did she go to those musical evenings with you?"

"Only once. Hallie had an early class at Columbia on Monday mornings and she was accustomed to study on Sunday nights. But she went to Mrs. Worthing's whenever she could, sometimes to the small groups that meet in the greenhouse workshop, often just for advice and conversation, to learn about the herbs and their properties. Hallie was a great believer in natural healing. Nothing artificial, not even an aspirin." Krish studied Agate's face. "Surely you cannot suspect—"

Agate took a deep breath. "I was going to keep this for a while," he said reluctantly. "But I've been checking alibis for the night of Hallie's death. Piers Ambrose spent the night with Helen Macauley, and they alibi each other." He shot me a dirty look. "Of course, *you* knew about that, didn't you, Doc? If you hadn't been sick, I'd land on you about holding out on me. I wouldn't know *now,* except I went back out there to ask the lady a few more questions, and I found Ambrose with her." He chuckled. "Talk about that ginseng root—the old dude must buy it wholesale. Anyway, I went out there because I found something in Macauley's desk. A pair of high-powered binoculars with infrared sights. What the hell were they doing in a college president's office desk? I couldn't figure it. So I asked the lady. She and old Ambrose sort of looked each other over and then he went trotting off and came back with this."

Lloyd dug down beside the couch and pulled up the nylon carry-all he used to carry to my Remedial English class when he was boning up for his lieutenant's exam. He pulled a videotape cassette out of it and handed it to me.

"This is a copy. Keep it, Doc. Take a look and let me know what you make of it." He got up, preparing to leave us. "I can't explain a lot of things about this mess. Everybody seems to have something to do with it, some kind of a private stake or a grudge. But that guy Macauley— Just look at the tape and gimme a call, okay?" He started out the door, then turned back. "Oh, by the way, the Worthings are back home, still claiming they spent the night together. I checked out Graham Worthing's story with the guy at the Esso station. Guy likes to jaw, knows Worthing, remembered telling him they'd found a body in his wife's orchard. Worthing never said boo, just got in his car and took off like a bat outa hell, headed home."

"What about Swan?" asked David.

"One of my boys spotted him in an old bait shack down by the river, but by the time he stopped the squad car and gave chase, Swan was long gone. I—"

"Shhh!" Krish bounded up and made a beeline for the hall. "Someone at the front door. Please, allow me!"

"Probably that cat again, out caroling," I grumbled as he trotted out to the hall.

"I heard something, too," said David softly. "Somebody rattled the doorknob."

" 'Rest, rest, perturbed spirit,' " intoned Merriman as he came in to park in the wing chair opposite Lloyd.

"You lot are giving me the willies," I said. "I didn't hear—"

"Win! Look there!" Sarah had just come through the door from the dining room with Alexandra behind her. "The French doors!" she cried.

I tried to see past the bright light of the room to the darkness outside, but it was no use. I heaved myself off the couch and made it to the terrace doors as quickly as I could, and in an instant David was beside me, leaving a disgruntled Gemma whimpering on the rug. I pressed my face against the cold, steamy glass and shaded my eyes from the light. What I saw was a sturdy figure in a long, belted, pale cream raincoat; it walked quickly through a drift of blown leaves to the edge of the terrace, then down the shallow steps to the back garden and the path that leads down our bluff to the Hudson.

Merriman knelt on the window seat nearby, looking out the peephole he'd cleared in the steamed-up glass. "That's him!" he said triumphantly. "The man I saw outside those doors the night after Hallie's body was found! The same light raincoat, the same—"

"Man, my foot!" cried Sarah, and before I knew what was happening, she had shoved me out of the way and charged through the French doors, leaving them to bang in the icy gust. "Elsa!" she shouted, and the wind tore the syllables apart like dry leaves and blew them back to her. "Countess! It's me! Elsa, wait!"

The pale figure on the path was almost in the woods when Sarah's voice reached it. It spun on the frozen ground, the long coat

332

tangling its legs, and a gust caught the man's hat it wore and tumbled it to the ground.

The tangle of her light brown curls fell loose around Elsa's face, then, and the light from the open French doors struck the wide, handsome features, void of all guile, childlike against the deep darkness of the woods behind her. Intent on Sarah's figure, now moving toward her down the path, the large eyes luminous in the darkness, sparked with gold by the light, she might have been Rembrandt's Saskia come to life.

Sarah stopped a few feet from her, hesitating. Elsa raised her arms, the hands palms-up, in the same gesture with which she had welcomed us that afternoon in the orchard. A sound came from her. At that distance I could not discern words, and probably there were none. The wind caught at her voice and carried it away, and she took a step toward Sarah. My breath stopped, and I thought she would turn and run, and then suddenly they were locked together, embracing like reunited lovers on the dark path, the wind whipping at them, Elsa's hair blown like a net around them both.

It was very late that night, when all the rest had gone and Sarah was asleep, that I slipped into the spare bedroom where we hide the TV set, and stuck Lloyd's copy of Macauley's videotape into the player. I sat in the dark, alone, and watched it.

The tape had been shot from a car window. Occasionally the camera caught the frame of the door or the outside rearview mirror, and now and then the sunlight burned the lens and blinded me.

It showed two women on a brilliant autumn day, their ankle-length dresses touched by a light breeze, their long hair loose down their backs, one like smooth black silk, the other crimped and tangled and wild, its brown turned golden in the sun. They joined hands as they walked, laughing in the sun beneath the maples just tipped with crimson and the black pines and the yellow mounds of the great old ash trees. Beyond them was a lake—Lake Tamarack, I was all but sure. They carried baskets, and as they walked they spied out plants and stopped to gather them, stalks of undistinguished grasses and roadside weeds.

There was no sound, but none was needed. The camera had a powerful lens and it zoomed in on one or another of the women now and then, as intimate as touch or breath. It slipped along the length of Hallie's silken hair and down her back to find her small feet, the feet over which Sarah had tripped in the orchard.

But it did not stay on Hallie Glendon. It was Elsa upon whose rich, energetic body the camera focused almost entirely, traveling up and down her shamelessly, lingering and exploring, tantalizing and tormenting the maker of the film until the camera itself seemed able to bear no more and the focus dived away among the treetops, bouncing madly, aimed at nothing.

At last it settled down again as the two women turned and started back the same way they had come, ending in a clearing among the trees where a car was parked. There was a man leaning beside the car, deeply absorbed in a book he was reading, a slender man of late middle age with thinning sandy hair and a drooping moustache. He opened the doors of Elsa's rusting station wagon for the herb-harvesters and stowed their baskets in the back, and all the while Macauley's camera ranged over him, closing and withdrawing and closing in again.

Jaffer Swan—Geoffrey Glendon—was about to get into the driver's seat, when he must have seen or sensed that he was being watched. Perhaps he saw the glint of the sun that burned Macauley's lens. He stared, then made a sudden lunge in the direction of the camera.

The picture went black and I was alone in the dark. Or I thought I was.

"He'd have killed her, too, wouldn't he?" said Sarah's voice. "He'd have killed Elsa, too."

I didn't reach for the lamp beside me. The dark seemed to suit us better. Outside, the December sky was pitted with stars. "Maybe," I said. "According to Piers, Macauley took pictures of a lot of women. Not all of them are dead."

"Only because *he's* dead. Because somebody—maybe Geoffrey Glendon—had the nerve to kill him first."

"A little rough justice?"

"The courts let murderers go every day. It may have been the only way."

"You think I should let it go?"

"Yes," she said. "I do. It's over. Macauley killed those women and Geoffrey Glendon saved more lives than he took." She was very close to me now, sitting beside me on the spare room bed. "I want to help *Elsa* now. She's my friend, and she needs help. I want to be finished with death."

"All right," I told her. "I'll do what you say. But be sure, old love. Be very sure Macauley was the one who killed those four women. Because if not, if there's even a flicker of a doubt—"

I felt her get up and heard her staccato footsteps move toward the door. She opened it and stood there in the dim light from the hallway. I hadn't even noticed when she came in, so absorbed had I been in the tape.

"What's the answer?" I asked her. "Is it over? Or not?"

"God damn you, Win," she said, her contralto a hoarse angry croak. "You know bloody well it's not."

Twenty-five

> Behold, I have a weapon;
> A better never did itself sustain
> Upon a soldier's thigh. I have seen the day
> That with this little arm, and this good sword,
> I have made my way through more impediments
> Than twenty times your stop. But O vain boast,
> Who can control his fate?

Some men are born to live backwards, thought Piers Ambrose as he stood in the wings of Gould Theatre, waiting for his cue to play the final scene. He himself was one such man, and David Cromwell, the evening's Othello, was another.

> Here is my journey's end, here is my butt,
> And very sea-mark of my utmost sail.
> Do you go back dismayed? 'Tis a lost fear;
> Man but a rush against Othello's breast,
> And he retires. Where should Othello go?

For David, birth had not really occurred until the beautiful facade that had brought him easy success was ruined by a maniac's knife. Oh, he had always had talent, no doubt, and used it well according to his lights. But some final choice remained unmade until he saw himself in ruins. There was power in him now, the courage to do anything he chose, without considering risk. It was an old man's courage, and its mother was despair.

Piers knew it well.

He let the backstage traffic thump and buzz behind him, his eyes fixed on the tall, lean, blackfaced figure in the crimson robe that bent over the huge bed on which his tiny, fragile wife lay, her red hair spread across the counterpane.

> Now; how dost thou look now? O ill-starred wench,
> Pale as thy smock. When we shall meet at compt,
> This look of thine will hurl my soul from heaven,
> And fiends will snatch at it. Cold, cold, my girl—
> Even like thy chastity.

Piers regretted that he did not love Helen. He could be sorry and kind and passionately tender with her. He could encourage her to go back to her scholar's life, he could infuse her with confidence, he could counsel her as he had counseled Hallie Glendon, as Abelard had counseled Heloise and brought her to second birth in order to make her whole and love her. Of course, he had always had his doubts about that romantic bit of history. Certainly Abelard had paid the price of his adventures, and no doubt the silly girl believed he loved her. But how did a mind like Abelard's find room for love?

Helen was sitting in the fourth row of the audience. He could see her from where he stood; even with the house lights down, the flickering glimmer of the stage torches in Desdemona's bedroom caught her thin face, touched her pale blond hair, fired the bright gold of the necklace he had given her.

He always gave them something, a token of some kind. A ring

bought in a tiny European secondhand shop, a carved bone Aleut bracelet from his Canadian visits. The necklace he had taken from Hallie Glendon's body that morning in the orchard was his gift to her, a graduation gift in more than one sense, when she was strong enough to leave him and find her own way, someone of her own to love. He had not known why he reclaimed his gift. He would not have thought himself capable of such a sentimental gesture as keeping mementos of the dead. He had carried the black coral necklace in his pocket until that final afternoon, and when Macauley lay dead, Piers had put it with the other things on the desk. It seemed the least he could do for them, for Hallie and for Helen, too. A gesture of infinite contempt.

But most of all, he had done it for Elsa.

She sat in the front row of the audience, between her dullard husband and Sarah Cromwell, her features motionless, lips slightly parted, her body hunched forward in the seat, the Medusa curls piled elegantly on top of her head, a pair of Maxima's diamond earrings glittering against her neck.

How beautiful, he thought, his throat aching with passion. *How beautiful you are. How I could have taught you to love me. I could have made you whole.*

"Iago!" hissed a voice in his ear. "You're on!"

And the student stage manager shoved him onstage, along with some of the minor players. It was always, he thought ruefully, the minor players who survived. Two of them seized his arms and dragged him on, captive to his inferiors.

Othello raised his head from his dead wife's breast, the bright sword still in his hand. He stared at Iago as though he had come up through the floorboards, hypnotized by the audacious eyes of his tormentor. Piers bent his head like a charging bull and fixed David's Othello with a terrifying stare.

And then he laughed. It was a demon's laugh, and it rang through the dark theater, a high, shrill crow of triumph that might have been a woman's scream, or the cry of some wild bird, hunting through the dark.

From the corner of his eye, Piers perceived a movement in the front row, and Elsa's figure rose from the seat and stood for a moment, frozen there, as he felt the stroke of the stage sword.

" 'If that thou beest a devil, I cannot kill thee,' " said David, and sent the point of the prop sword into the foam cradle built into Piers's doublet. The blade retracted, just as they had rehearsed it. Then the minor players, those eternal busybodies, pulled Othello away and yanked out the sword, whose point neatly popped back out again. The gooey stage blood, its plastic sack punctured by the sword, soaked through the pale green doublet on his breast.

" 'I bleed, sir,' " taunted Iago, and there was the laugh again, " 'but not killed.' "

Out of the action, Piers had leisure to look at Elsa. She was seated again, her eyes still fixed on the stage, a hand gripping Sarah Cromwell's arm with all her might. Not her husband's arm, but Sarah's. The thought pleased Piers, and he looked back to the stage again.

David had begun Othello's dying speech, his hands hidden, monklike, in the wide sleeve bottoms of the crimson robe. He looked like an amputee, or a man bound and about to be led to execution. Helpless, armless, he sat on the bed beside his wife's body.

> I pray you in your letters,
> When you shall these unlucky deeds relate,
> Speak of me, as I am. Nothing extenuate,
> Nor set down aught in malice.

Some men are born to live backward. They conceive themselves over and over, and the final birth will happen only when they die.

> I kissed thee ere I killed thee. No way but this,
> Killing myself, to die upon a kiss.

The knife flashed out of the crimson sleeve and David's body curved and sought the blade and buckled like a flame in the wind and fell softly upon that of his wife, a cruel lovemaking.

I want no more births, thought Piers as the applause rose and rose and the curtain fell. *This last was quite enough.*

The bright pain broke from his incorrigible heart and jerked him sideways as he smiled and laughed and took his bow, hand in hand with the Cromwells. The applause was deafening, and in the front row Elsa and the others were on their feet, smiling now, applauding with the rest. Elsa was smiling too, now, her hand through her husband's arm.

But her eyes sought neither the figures on the stage nor the face of her dull husband. As the curtain closed before him, shutting him from the sight of her, Piers could see what Elsa was looking at. It was Sarah.

The pain smashed at him again, and in the din of backstage clamor and the roaring chatter of the departing audience, only two people were near him—old Winston, who'd come trotting on to congratulate his boy, his almost-son, and the son himself, David, already rubbing Othello's blacking from his face.

Perhaps they took it for a cynical joke, or a cry of triumph. Perhaps they failed even to hear the sound the pain tore out of Piers.

It was Iago's laugh.

He had suspected it before and pushed his doubts away, but now he knew it, quite suddenly and without question. His last birth and greatest trick, the death of James Macauley, had been for nothing.

It was when David saw the raincoat that he understood. He saw it in the dressing room mirror as he was wiping off the last of the black-face—the pale, belted raincoat he had seen Elsa wearing that night in Manhattan, the same one she'd worn when she stood outside the terrace windows, needing Sarah and unable to ask.

David turned from his mirror to greet them, a smile on his face, the one he could put on and take off as a disguise whenever he chose.

"Terrific show, my friend," said Worthing, slapping him on the shoulder. "One helluva job."

The voice was hearty, but distant and removed. Perhaps he thought he recognized the man who had come to repair his thermostat.

No, thought David. That had been another man, a different Graham. Someone had given him back his life since then. Elsa had come to find him.

Sarah was there, and Winston, and Alex was pouring champagne, her face still pale from the emotion onstage. He could not rid himself of the memory of her eyes when he had strangled her, there on the bed. She came to him where he stood with the Worthings and put a glass into his hand, her arm around his waist under his loose dressing gown, her fingers dancing a ticklish tattoo on his back. He looked down at her and she smiled, very happy in spite of her recent demise.

"Such a pair!" cried Elsa, and squeezed her husband's arm. "Look, my dear! How lovely they are, as pleased with themselves as a couple of pussycats by a fire!" Her earrings danced and glittered, her eyes shone with delight.

"Plain smug, if you ask me," groused Winston, beaming from ear to ear. He was still wearing the striped robe and the wispy beard of Desdemona's father, old Brabantio, though his part had been over since the end of Act I. Something about the costume seemed to suit him, and he sailed around in it like a brightly painted battleship among a lot of smaller craft, not bothering with signal flags.

Suddenly he trained his guns and fired.

"Nice coat, Worthing," he said, looking the raincoat up and down. He'd obviously had the same idea David had. "That's the raincoat Elsa had on up at our place the other night, isn't it? Good practical roomy article, plenty of pockets. It does have pockets, doesn't it?"

Elsa laughed and shoved her hand into the one nearest her. She herself was wearing a black wool coat with a high collar, nothing like the raincoat at all. She pulled her hand out of the pocket and displayed the contents. "See? This is what he gets from lending his fancy raincoat to his uncivilized wife, my poor Karl! Acorns I found in the woods! Why should the squirrels have all the fun!"

Graham smiled. "Too bad they're not deeper, though. She stuffs them full, and then goes around leaving a trail of weeds and nuts and berries behind her."

"Like Hansel and Gretel," cried Elsa, and kissed her husband's cheek. "I leave a trail of breadcrumbs to the witch's house!"

Winston smiled and chugged away again, and David saw him a minute later out in the hallway, talking to Eddie. Of course, they'd both noticed, as he had, that the man's raincoat they had all seen Elsa wearing was really Graham's. The knowledge raised another question: had it been she, not her husband, who had left Jaffer Swan's book and the Glendon Greetings card in Reeney's back room, who had slipped out the window to avoid Lloyd Agate and lost the parking stub her husband had shoved into his shallow pocket when he left New York? Had she known Graham went to Irene's bar, suspected him, meant to protect him by laying down a false trail? Had she been willing to throw Jaffer to the wolves in the person of conscientious Lloyd Agate to do it?

Of course, she might be certain *Swan* was really guilty, might have chosen an indirect way of revealing his identity. It was subtle, and it would have given Jaffer—as indeed it had—a chance to get away. It was honest, yet kind in its tough-minded way. It was like the Elsa they had always known, the Elsa his sister loved.

Or had she been protecting herself?

"Where are you, love?" said Alex. Lost in his thoughts, David had hardly noticed her standing beside him. She reached up and brushed a hand over his eyes. "Not satisfied with it, were you? Didn't fancy me as a leading lady?" She stood fiddling with the belt of his robe, uncertain of him. She had never been really sure of herself, nor of him, even before the slashing. Robbed of her confidence and native buoyancy by a modeling career that underused and bored her, Alex was only now beginning to stretch and flap her wings a bit. "I'll never be what you are, will I?"

He took her by the shoulders and held her at arm's length, his eyes boring into her. "You're yourself, Red," he told her. "I've seen sexy Desdemonas who couldn't tell their lines from mine. I've seen virginal Desdemonas who played the love scenes like ice sculptures, with me as the heat lamp. I've seen intellectual Desdemonas who had the energy of a deflated party balloon and the emotional depth of a Frisbee. Once I had a Desdemona who wore invisible plastic lips in the death scene, in case I had any germs when I did 'I kissed thee ere I killed thee.' Don't get me wrong. You're not perfect. You stepped on my toe in the 'Welcome to Cyprus' scene. You blew the 'Poor soul sat sighing' bit to hell. But you were the sexiest, brainiest, most emotional former virgin I ever strangled in her goddamn bed!"

"Bravo!" cried Elsa, and she began to applaud. "I listen shamelessly, a wonderful speech, Mr. Director!" She planted a kiss on his cheek, then turned to Alexandra. "Alex, my dear, have you decorated your house yet for Christmas? Too busy with your play, I bet, nothing but a little tiny tree with electric lights. Phooey! I have holly, three or four bushes full, you ought to see the berries! I will send Axel with it. And some for Sarah, too, yes?"

She caught her friend by the hand and pulled her close. The marks of the black eye were almost gone now, except for a faint ring of abrasion where the blow had struck hardest, on the brow and cheekbone. Otherwise, thought David, it was as if the incident never happened. Sarah's forgiveness was complete.

"Holly you don't cut till Christmas Eve, though," Elsa went on. "These modern houses, the central heating. It dries out too quick, by Christmas nothing is left but brown sticks with prickles!"

Piers Ambrose, oddly subdued after his shenanigans when the curtain fell, stood sipping his champagne, his eyes never leaving Elsa. No chance of slipping out with him there, lounging right in the doorway. David had plans that did not include his sister, his friends, and his wife. They certainly didn't include the tall old magus in the doorway.

The energy of Iago seemed to have drained away from Piers entirely. He looked old and weary, and no threat to anyone.

Elsa was another matter. She was the center of the room, warming all of them, talking and laughing and telling stories, teasing Graham and Winston.

Unnatural, thought David, closing his eyes and listening to the rise and fall of her voice. The highs too high, the lows too low, like someone doing vocal exercises. And in between, when for a moment she came to rest, a vagueness, drifting off to loneliness. She ceased to be with them at all, and then an instant later she was back, joking and laughing, as though some invisible button had been pushed that worked her performance.

You are falling, he thought. *You have been falling a long time, into a place that is dark and narrow and has no bottom. Falling into your grave.*

He shuddered, his whole body convulsed. He was very cold, and he forced his eyes open wide and looked for Alex.

"I think we ought to go, my love."

Worthing spoke softly, and Elsa did not hear. She stood in the center of a circle of her friends, turning with quick, angular movements from one to the other, eyes very bright, hands reaching now and then for Sarah, who stood—somewhat uncomfortably, David thought—at the edge of the circle nearest Graham. Winston and Eddie Merriman were with Piers, who had moved from the doorway at last to a chair by the dressing table. Everybody seemed to be staring at Elsa, her unnatural brightness overwhelming everything else in the room.

Then Graham Worthing spoke again. "I think we ought to go, my love," he repeated. "Madam Max is all alone out there. We—"

"Stupid Karl, go away!" snapped Elsa suddenly.

Worthing snatched at her. "We're going now," he said, and caught her wrist.

She rounded on him, and her punch hit him in the chest, knocking him backward into weedy Eddie Merriman, who toppled against a folding chair. Graham righted himself, as Elsa paused in the doorway. No one else in the room seemed to remember how to breathe, let alone speak, but when Elsa did, it was as though nothing at all had taken place.

"I want the cold, Karl dear," she said. "It's so hot in here, and the wine makes me sleepy. I'll walk, you bring the car, hmmm?" She smiled gently at the puzzled faces. "Good night, my dears. *Fröhliche Weihnachten!* Good night!"

They could hear her footsteps, perfectly steady, moving away down the hall. Graham pulled the belt of the pale raincoat round him as if he were about to follow her, but he did not. He turned uncertainly in the hollow center of the room, glancing from one puzzled face to the other.

"She's — She likes to tease me with a punch now and then." He laughed. "I do a bit of boxing, you know. I taught her self-defense when we were first married." Another laugh that broke midway, a swallowed sob. "She's never connected before. I'm sure she didn't mean— It was a joke. A joke, she—"

It was a desperate sales pitch, and it didn't work. The faces around him were blank with disbelief.

A joke. It was a joke.

Sarah took Worthing's arm. "Oh, Graham," she said. "Let me come with you."

He embraced her, a reflex that came out of nowhere. Sarah looked stunned, and he held her very hard, a long moment, his face hidden against her shoulder his arms locked round her. "She loves you," he said at last, so softly that aside from Sarah herself only David, who was standing nearby, could hear the words. "She loves you more than anyone. Much more than me."

"Then let me come," repeated Sarah. "Of course I'll come! I'll—"

"No," he said firmly, and he let her go.

The others, embarrassed, milled and mumbled, and suddenly Graham was gone. Sarah turned to her brother.

"Go after him," she said, and being David, he was already halfway out the door.

The night was cold and very clear. The stars put the twinkling Christmas lights to shame, but the sign outside Irene Ransom's bar—the one that was supposed to say Smitty's—was mostly burned out, and all it said was mitt s.

Jaffer Swan lay in the warm dark of Irene's ancient Airstream trailer across the parking lot, a copy of Eliot's *Four Quartets* open on his chest. He had switched off the light hoping the darkness would help him think.

Made a helluva cock-up of it, haven't you, mate? he thought. *Spent your whole bloody life trying not to make a decision, and when you do . . . When you do. The roof of the world falls in.*

> Do not let me hear
> Of the wisdom of old men, but rather of their folly,
> Their fear of fear and frenzy, their fear of possession,
> Of belonging to another, or to others, or to God.
> The only wisdom we can hope to acquire
> Is the wisdom of humility: humility is endless.

Humiliation, more like. He had only stayed because of her, because he could not erase her from his mind, could not wash the print of her from his skin. Even though he had been nearly six weeks gone from her, the scent of Elsa rose from the pages of his books, the taste of her mouth invaded the food he ate. He had gone back to the orchard, hidden like a snake in the long grass the weather had matted into a blanket, and watched her moving softly with her shears and her basket, harvesting the last of autumn and storing it away, mulching the summer perennials against the coming snows and the Atlantic winds. He had watched her and bitten his tongue until it bled to keep from calling out to her:

You are the only thing I have left worth loving. Including God. Including me.

He wondered whether Elsa would have noticed if he had. She moved as though asleep; the soldier-silence of her sleep now claimed her waking, too. If he had stood up and spoken to her, she would have seen him as a stranger, smiled as she smiled at strangers. She had dismissed him from her life as soon as he was out of sight.

Humiliation. Jaffer Swan had had shit served up to him more ways than anyone he knew; it was an old familiar diet, and you got used to the flavor, after a century or so. But this was something else. Elsa was traveling in some strange country of her own, and she didn't want company. He understood that, being a man who traveled light himself.

> The houses are all gone under the sea.
> The dancers are all gone under the hill.

Elizabeth was gone, and Hallie. Now that the bloody bugger was dead, he had nothing to stay for. But Elsa bound him here like a dog on a leash. For the past week, ever since she and bleeding Graham got back from wherever he'd dragged her off to to make her forget what bed had been like with old Jaffer, for six days and seven nights he had watched her, followed her everywhere. She was doing it again.

It was a cycle like the moon, a buried frenzy that grew and grew and then was gone. It grew and climaxed and then was gone for a month or more, until he saw the early signs again, the brightness of her wide eyes, the tongue that slipped between her parted lips, as though she were enduring private pain. When you watched her unobserved, the soldier's passionless calm possessed her, but in company she was manic, laughing too much, talking louder than usual. She spun and danced and whirled away, out of control, and then, when the height of her fever had passed, she was normal again, working in her gardens, doing the greenhouse books, teasing old Axel or badgering Madam Max to swill some foul herbal drink. What she did with the panic that attacked her like the climax of love, where she chased it into hiding until the next time, Jaffer did not know.

He had seen it before, though, in the Weirdie Bin. His own confusion, which he now thought of as a sort of sabbatical from the universal shit-diet, had taken the form of utter silence for almost thirteen months after Elizabeth Swan's murder, after his own dismissal and the period of academic exile that ensued. There had been nothing mad about his silence. He had simply chosen not to speak. The reasons were perfectly clear to Jaffer—or Geoff Glendon, as he was then. He had trusted only himself, and so long as he didn't talk, he didn't run the risk of accidentally connecting anywhere, to come crashing down again. He wouldn't speak to grocery clerks, cops, librarians. Made up a sort of sign language, Tonto-style, convinced his snotty landlord he was deaf-and-dumb. Worked a treat till some twit saw him out on one of his evening rambles and decided he was the Peeping Tom who'd been having a look-see when she took her knickers off at night. Screamed bloody hell, cops came, old Jaffer wound up in jug, from which it had been a short hop to Minnesota Psychiatric.

Known to its more literate inhabitants as the Weirdie Bin.

When he got out, reluctantly verbal and laden with a new supply of books, he had taken Elizabeth's name and tacked it onto his own, his granfer's nickname for Geoffrey. He was Jaffer Swan, and it suited him.

But he did not forget what he had seen in the dear old Bin. The faces. The eyes, watching from corners. Now he saw them again, and they were Elsa's.

He heard her footsteps on the blacktop of the parking lot before he saw her through the steamy window of Reeney's trailer. She was wearing her own black coat, not Worthing's raincoat, and except for the glittering earrings and her own wild, bright hair, she was almost invisible in the dark.

She had on high-heeled shoes, and she was running. She charged through the door into Irene's place, and by the time Jaffer had crossed the parking lot and gone inside, she was squared off with little Irene Ransom, who had come out from behind her bar to stand, hands on her hips, head stuck forward in bulldog determination.

"Look, lady," she said. "I told you, Swanny took off about six weeks back, I got no idea where he went, I don't give a fuck what you want him for! He's not here, and I got work to do, so—"

Jaffer had come in behind her, and Elsa saw him before he laid a hand on Irene's arm. "Never mind, lovey," he told Irene. "It's cool. I'm back."

Reeney looked at him and blinked. So this was the woman who'd kept him from loving little Irene. He had slept with her, and he was kind, and maybe you ought to be satisfied with that. But Irene wasn't. He was no different than the rest of them.

A classy broad with diamond earrings, she thought. *High heels and goddamn diamond earrings.*

Irene's earrings were plastic mistletoe and her sneakers were run down in the backs from putting them on without untying them, and her black apron smelled like stale beer.

Fuck them, she thought. *Fuck the both of them.*

"Okay, out!" she shouted. There were three or four loners in the corners and they stared. She was screaming. "Out, goddamn it! Everybody out! I'm closing this goddamn hole in two minutes! Out!"

Jaffer caught her by one elbow and it hurt. She tried to kick him, but he was too fast.

"You lousy bastard!" she hissed.

He pulled her against him and she kicked and bit and finally she was still, her face against the zipper of his jacket. She could feel his breath, as she had felt it in bed, and he wasn't like the rest, had never been, and if he left her now she would not have been alone. For those few weeks, as the winter closed down on her like the tightening of a screw, she had not been alone.

"Okay," she whispered, her face still against his chest. "Okay now, baby."

Jaffer let her go and Irene shot one last look at Elsa, who was standing where Swan had left her, her face impassive now, and soldier-calm.

Not so much, thought Reeney. *She's not so much to look at. Maybe the high heels turn him on.*

"Okay, you suckers," she yelled. "Drinks on the house!"

There was a light in the upstairs bedroom when they reached Maxima's small, cold kingdom on the bluff. Graham Worthing had come home alone, and sat alone beside the window. His shadow was there, burly and hunched against the light.

It was freezing in the workshop, but there was an old heating stove; Elsa laid a fire when they came in and soon they did not notice the cold, nor the impossible positions into which the springless old chaise lounge forced them, nor the roughness of the wool coverlet they pulled over them when at last they had to sleep.

Jaffer woke with Elsa in his arms and slipped carefully out from under her, down off the edge of the chaise onto the cold bricked floor. The fire had burned to embers in the stove. He shivered, considered pulling on his clothes, then decided against it. She might, perversely, choose to wake, and for the time being, until he'd finished what he had to do, he wanted her asleep.

Birth-naked, he padded across the brick floor, wincing from the cold at every step. It was her desk in the corner he wanted, and he knew she kept it locked. Old Engstrom sometimes went looking for an order book or a bill and messed up her filing system, such as it was.

He could not afford a light, though when he glanced up at the house, he saw that Worthing's own light had gone out. Elsa was absent from him now, and even the desk lamp might not have wakened her. But he could not take the risk.

He made the mistake of sitting down on the cold, hard wooden desk chair, and instantly regretted it, but there was no help. He gritted his teeth and began to fumble for something that would open the lock on the center drawer which controlled all the others.

He found it. There was a roll of the wire Elsa used for wreath-making in her classes. It was thin enough, but tough. He unrolled a four-inch length and bent it back and forth until it snapped free. Then he began to work on the lock.

Not a very tough one, just cheap discourage-the-snoopers stuff. He felt the tumblers trip. Once. Twice. Jaffer gave the drawer a gentle tug, and it came open. He pulled it as far out as it would go without risk of dumping it with a crash. Then he used his fingers to feel over every inch of what was inside. There were pencils, pens, bobby pins, paper clips, rubber bands. Nothing else. God please. Nothing else God.

The top left-hand, the top right. God. Old Jaffer needs a break. Nothing.

The second left, the same.

Only one drawer remained. He opened it softly, his heart banging against his thin, cold chest.

It was there. He could feel it, and the shape was unmistakable. Suddenly the cold overpowered him and he began to shake, his hands banging against the sides of the goddamn drawer so hard he thought she was sure to wake and find him, his legs trembling, his head shaking like a man with palsy, his teeth chattering uncontrollably.

The houses are all gone under the sea.
The dancers are all gone under the hill.

Jaffer pulled his hand carefully out of the drawer, the smooth cold shape held gingerly between his thumb and index finger. It was a hypodermic needle.

His doubts had begun when the big cop asked him about the book of poems with the old Easter card in it, the card he'd treasured all these years because Hallie had sent it to him when she was a child, when she was still *his* child. Nobody but Elsa could have known. He had told no one but her about his daughter, and she had taken Hallie under her wing, invited her out more and more often to bring her close to him. He'd missed the book, but figured she might have borrowed it, as she did sometimes. She knew about Irene's place, too, that he sometimes went there for a pint, sometimes crashed there when he chose. He'd told her everything, given her every inch of him. She was the only one who could have planted that stuff for the cops to find.

He reached into the drawer again. It was the last drawer. If the stuff wasn't here, there was a chance. A chance he'd misunderstood. A chance she only used the needle for the plants, for fungicides, systemic insecticides. A chance he was a fool and she was Elsa, still Elsa. He felt carefully, an inch at a time, holding his breath.

There was nothing. No bottle of medicine. No pills. No diginox.

He stuffed the needle back into the drawer and sat there bathed in sweat in the freezing darkness.

"Where is my wandering Swan?" said Elsa. "Come to bed, my dear. I'm cold."

Jaffer gulped for air in great deep painful breaths of relief. "Coming, bossy-boots," he said, and slipped back under the scratchy cover next to her.

Elsa drew him to her. "Such a goose, you are. You would sweat at the North Pole," she said, and laughed softly.

"Pure unadulterated passion," he said, twisting his fingers in her hair as he found his way to her again.

When it was over, she lay quiet, at peace and with him, the old absence broken, or so it seemed.

"How I have missed you," she murmured. "Your voice, too, not just bed. I wish you could read to me. But it's so dark. You couldn't see the book."

"Who needs one?" Jaffer said, and began.

Where she stood in the dark outside the greenhouse workshop, Maxima could not make out his words, but through the thin walls she could hear the soft and steady music of his voice. She pulled her heavy old cloak closer around her, the forest green velvet cloak her father had bought her in Paris, the nap matted now and the color mottled by day, but in this darkness rich and beautiful. It was almost morning and bitterly cold and the stars were blinking out one by one, like ancient eyes closing. Maxima went round to the front door of the greenhouse and let herself in with her key. She wanted nothing so much as to hear the man's voice again, to hear the words as Alois might have spoken them, Alois who had loved her and was dead.

Maxima did not see Graham Worthing watching her from his window, as he had not seen David follow him home and wait in the orchard, shivering, while Elsa and her lover went into the workshop and did not come out again. The old woman saw nothing but the thinning dark and the dying stars through the cloudy panes of greenhouse glass, the tendrils of the plants and vines and the crooked branches beyond, etched against the clear dark.

She did not hear the raucous roar of the cars passing on the highway, nor the clack of the upstate freight as it passed over the points. All she heard was the voice of her dead husband, in the voice of Jaffer Swan.

> Love is the unfamiliar Name
> Behind the hands that wove
> The intolerable shirt of flame
> Which human power cannot remove.
> We only live, only suspire
> Consumed by either fire or fire.

Twenty-six

Christmas Eve dawned strangely warm, with a lowering sky and the rumble of distant thunder. The streets were bare of snow and ice and the evergreen wreaths in the front doors looked vaguely foolish, as though someone had forgotten them and left them up till spring.

It was barely eight o'clock when Sarah tugged Win's old bike out of the garden shed and wheeled it onto the drive. She was going to Elsa's again to play the harpsichord, her final Christmas gesture of reconciliation.

Of course, she had refused the gift of the instrument. Completely absurd, in the circumstances, to give away a priceless asset. Elsa was broke, Sarah was almost sure of that, and today she meant to find out for certain.

It was not her first visit to Sorrowheart—she'd all but forgotten the old name till Win asked her about it—since that day in the orchard when Elsa had blacked her eye. After her friend's strange behavior backstage at the *Othello,* Sarah had mustered her nerve and paid a visit late next afternoon to Madam Max, while she knew Elsa would be busy with the Christmas wreaths she sold. Aside from spring, with bedding plants and nursery stock, Christmas was the only really profitable season of the year at the greenhouse, and it kept Elsa out of Sarah's way all that afternoon.

While a wood fire crackled in the high white tile stove and Madam Max made hot chocolate laced with rum and did her best to pretend the punch-up in the orchard hadn't happened, Sarah was free to wander the downstairs rooms, taking inventory. Though other things had been rearranged to fill the space, lesser pictures hung to disguise the alterations, the fact was obvious. The treasures were disappearing, one by one.

"You miss them too, don't you?" The old voice was a curdled muttering in Maxima's throat. She stood in the parlor door, two cups of chocolate shivering on their saucers. "My Van Gogh etching. The little Seurat study. The silver potpourri bowl. Alois's first edition of *Buddenbrooks.*" She smiled faintly and set the cups down. "Have I left anything out, my dear?"

"But where— What's happened to them?" asked Sarah. The old woman's small bright eyes drilled into her. "Where have they gone?"

Max shrugged. "Pawn shops, I expect. A number of the antique dealers make a good thing of buying stolen rarities under the counter. Of course, you could hardly take them to Sotheby's or to anyone who would pay full value. That would require the owner's signature. Mine."

"Swan? Are you trying to tell me that that man Swan's been cleaning out your—"

"Little fool!" hissed Max. "Not Swan."

"Graham, then?" Sarah sank into a chair. "Dear Lord."

Maxima took a sip of her cocoa, a sardonic smile on her lips. "Not Swan," she said again.

On that afternoon, though she'd intended to, Sarah had not played the harpsichord. She hadn't had the heart. Instead, she stopped off in the workshop, bright with red ribbon and pine cones and gold and silver glass ornaments, frosted artificial fruits for the huge Della Robbia wreaths, Santas and elves for children's party trimmings. The warm room smelled of cedar and pine and fir and arborvitae, and of the great bunches of herbs that hung from hooks on the rafters. Elsa was just putting the hanger on a huge spray of Douglas fir and long-needled red pine boughs meant for a mantelpiece; there was music in the room, as there always was when she worked. It was the Bach anthem, *Wie soll ich dich empfangen,* delicately and amazingly played upon a lute.

Elsa fastened down the last bit of straggling evergreen and snipped the wire. Then she looked up at Sarah, her lips slightly parted, her breath steady and serene. She was nothing like the hysteric spinning out of control in the center of David's dressing room. That had been someone else.

Someone else. The same thought had come to Sarah as she reeled from the blow that day in the orchard. Another woman, one who did not know her. A woman who scarcely spoke her language, and who hit because she was afraid.

"She's afraid of me, I guess," said Elsa, echoing her thoughts. She stood back to admire the handsome spray of greens. "Your Alexandra. She started this in the class, but she never came back again, after—" She fell silent, fiddling with the red and gold ornaments on the spray, adjusting the huge velvet bow. Then she looked at Sarah, the dark eyes clear as cold water. "You, my dear. You are not afraid? You do not play for us anymore. The *Klavier,* your harpsichord. You punish me to keep your music still."

"It's not punishment, you ninny. It just hasn't seemed—quite the time, Countess. That's all." Sarah took a step nearer her friend. "Look, Elsa. I know you've been worried about Graham. All those things he's stolen from Madam Max, the pictures and books and things? If you'd like me to have a word with him . . ."

The music of the lute wove softly through the scented air. Elsa said nothing in reply to Sarah's question, merely sat listening, her head on one side, her unruly hair tumbling from its pins to lie in tendrils along her throat.

When at last she spoke, her voice was hushed by the music. "I think there will be snow before Christmas," she said. "Don't you?"

After that day, Sarah had been more determined than ever to get to the bottom of her friend's troubles. She remembered what it had been like when her own father died—the crushing, ridiculous debts he ignored to feed his vanity with spending; the beautiful things she'd had to sell off at insulting prices in order to keep the house; the sound of the great trees falling to power saws and bulldozers as the development crept up to her gates, built on the wooded bluffs that had till then been hers and David's to wander freely in.

She would not see Elsa go through that. If Graham was keeping them afloat by stealing Max's treasures, it would have to stop, that was all. If the greenhouse wasn't paying, there'd just have to be some other way, and she would help them find it whether they liked it or not.

Macauley had been bad enough, but this was worse. It explained everything—Elsa's submerged anger, her distraction, her pretense of good humor and happiness when Graham was around. Even her love affair with Swan might've been some unconscious way to punish her husband for the trouble he'd caused her, the threat to her safe haven.

Her Sorrowheart.

Sarah jammed her sheaf of music—Couperin's *Little Windmills* suite for harpsichord—into the bike basket along with a small, battery-operated tape player and began to walk the bike down the drive. She was careful to hug the paving where the unpruned hedge of bridal-wreath bushes was thickest; if she could manage it, Win wouldn't see her from the windows of his Cave, where he had disappeared just after breakfast to begin his annual ritual of wrapping presents and swearing at the Scotch tape.

He didn't like her biking to Elsa's alone, Sarah knew that. The six weeks were almost up. If another woman was going to be killed, it would be soon. Today. Tomorrow. Winston fussed and stewed every time she set foot out of the house alone, and David practically kept Alex and Gemma under lock and key. Everybody snapped at everybody, all their nerves on edge with waiting.

Win had even offered to go with her, but today she didn't want him, and Eddie, who was spending Christmas with a jar of Vicks and Lloyd Agate's cold, could certainly put him to better use. Now that he knew how to manage those damn blood pressure pills, Winston had been back in midseason form, and more or less normal.

"Normal as he ever gets, the old pot," muttered Sarah fondly as she pushed the stubborn creaky bike along the verge of the drive.

Since that night backstage after the *Othello,* Elsa had seemed perfectly normal, too, better than she had in a long time. Naturally, she didn't want to talk about her money problems, and she changed the subject whenever Sarah broached it. But there was nothing to be afraid of. Nothing at all.

The thunder was getting louder and a few drops of rain began to fall. A thunderstorm on Christmas Eve—it didn't make sense, and Sarah was a great believer in sense. The wind was up, too, and shifting to the northeast. She shivered, her confidence suddenly undermined.

Perhaps Win was right, perhaps she ought to stay at home, or at least drive the damn Bronco out to Elsa's place instead of riding the bike. She didn't like the car, which was the gift of Zachary Pasco, the spy, in payment for her poor old totaled Volkswagen. Every time she swore in traffic, she looked around for hidden microphones and wondered whether she were coming in loud and clear in Moscow. Besides, the thing started with a roar like a 747, and Win would hear it in a minute and come huffing out to stop her.

"Piffle," said Sarah to her own misgivings. She glanced over her shoulder at the windows of Winston's cave, stuck out her tongue, and pedaled off down the drive toward Elsa's.

"Blast it, Widdie," said Merriman. He blew his nose and tried again. "Blast it, Winnie, you must go straight out there and bring Sarah back! Neither of us has told her what we suspect about Elsa. We've been so busy protecting her feelings and trying to prove somebody else guilty that we may be letting her put her head in a lion's mouth. Well, what're you waiting for? Go on, why don't you!"

He was flapping his feet around under the covers with all the energy of old Friedenberg. Being confined to quarters with his annual Christmas cold had been the final straw, and he was fairly vibrating with the nervous fidgets.

"What exactly am I supposed to do, Merriman? Hitchhike up to Elsa's and drag the kiddo back here by her pigtail? I can't drive, you know—not legally, anyway—and besides, without you to tell me where to put my feet, I probably wouldn't stop till I bumped into Nova Scotia. Sarah phoned me this morning when she got there. She phoned me again after they'd had lunch. She phoned me an hour ago and said she'd wait for Axel Engstrom to get back from his deliveries and hitch a ride home with him. Axel hasn't even made it *here* yet! Look out that window. Little Eva wouldn't try to cross that ice, and neither would I!"

The morning's unseasonal thunderstorm had turned to a full-scale ice storm as soon as that northeast wind got going. It had rained and frozen most of the morning, and by midafternoon a thick coat of ice bent the spruces nearly double, turned the bare maples and sycamores and ashes to glittering fairy-tale sculptures, hung like pendants of a chandelier from the twigs of bridal-wreath bushes and lilacs. Out in the woods along our bluff, great branches broke with their own weight and crashed down on smaller trees, and the thunder of their dying boomed and cracked its way into the bright warmth of the house, a bitter, haunting Christmas carol. Icicles hung thick outside the windows of Merriman's bedroom. As the afternoon grew late, the wind dropped and a wet snow began to fall, clinging to the ice and loading the trees and bushes with still more weight, a cruel, beautiful burden that turned the world to magic. I half expected to see Piers Ambrose, the Emperor of Snow, come striding up our drive in his white robes and tell us the whole thing was his climactic trick.

"Sarah sounded as though the three of them were having a ball," I told Merriman, trying to sound reassuring. "She and Elsa and Madam Max. Like old times, she said. Anyway, she was out there a week ago and nothing happened."

"But it's Christmas Eve, Winnie! You know the time schedule as well as I do! And it's almost dark already. If anything happens—"

"Yoo-hoo!" crowed a voice. "Yoo-hoo, Edward!"

There was a stamping of feet and the sound of laughter from the kitchen, but that nasal twang certainly wasn't Sarah's.

Merriman dived under the covers, sneezed, dived out and grabbed his Vicks and the Kleenex box, then submerged again. "Damn and hell and double-damn," he said in a muffled voice from under the electric blanket. "It's Blanche! Tell her I've got bubonic plague. Tell her my doctors have forbidden me all visitors until the turn of the century!"

"Come out from under that electric blanket, you sniveling coward, before you sneeze again and short yourself out!" I commanded him.

David stuck his head in the door and grinned at the sight of the mound of blankets that was Merriman. "I stopped off with your beloved's fruitcake, Eddie, and she was about to walk over here with some soup for you. Can you imagine, in all this ice? True devotion, if you ask me. So Alex and old Gemma and I gave her a lift."

I heard a peal of childish laughter and Gemma's resounding soprano cried, "P-yew!"

"Gemma! Hush!" This, in mild chagrin and secret agreement, from Alex, to the accompaniment of rattling crockery.

"What kind of soup?" I asked Davy, my nose to the wind. "Smells like Blanche's Best Bermuda Onion to me."

There was a moan from the mound of blankets. Visions of Maalox were dancing through Merriman's head.

"Edward!" called the Bony Mrs. M from the kitchen. "I'll be in in a minute with a nice big bowl of my special onion soup. It'll fix you right up, you'll see. Nobody can stay sick with a bowl of this inside them!"

Merriman poked his head out and snarled. "Of course they can't stay sick," he said, between clenched teeth. "They'll be dead before they know what hit 'em!"

Lloyd Agate spent the morning and most of the afternoon of Christmas Eve locked in his office with the files of the Heart Specialist cases spread out on the desk in front of him. He'd tried everything; he'd been over the statements of all the principal players, the FBI lab reports, the medical examiner's reports, the autopsies, the findings of the coroner's jury. He'd pried everything he could out of Doc and David and little Krish Ghandour.

But there was still something he wasn't seeing, some piece that was right in front of him, like when his daughter Sylvia was a kid and they'd worked jigsaw puzzles. A piece would fall onto the rug and the colors would blend into the background and the thing would disappear, and unless you ran your fingers over it, unless you felt it, the goddamn vacuum cleaner would eat it, and it'd be gone for good.

He picked up the ME's reports on the four women and shoved them aside. Out in the squad room, there was a Christmas party going on, or what passed for one. It was after seven o'clock now; except for the skeleton crew that had drawn the short straw this year, almost everybody'd gone home, hoping to make it before the storm got worse and they were stuck at the station for Christmas.

Agate sighed and drained the dregs of a cup of cold coffee. Bev and Sylvia would be cooking the cranberry sauce for tomorrow's dinner and fixing the giblets for stuffing, and Sylvia's dog, Ninja, would be going nuts from the smell and wagging his tail off. The tree would be plugged in, and when he pulled into the driveway he'd see the lights reflected on the snow outside, and he could pretend for that one moment that things were as they ought to be.

To hell with death, he thought. *For one night, life ought to get a turn at bat.*

He had just begun to put his papers back in the file when the phone on his desk buzzed. He debated for a split second. If he let it ring and went home now, he might still have a Christmas Eve, the first one in a long time.

"Shit," he said, and picked it up.

"Supercop?" The voice was Reeney's, and she sounded scared. "I think you better get your ass over here, honey. There's this guy. I know him, he comes in sometimes. Name's Charlie Graham."

The name resounded in Lloyd's tired brain like a dinner gong. It was the name Doc and David had told him about, the name Worthing used when he went slumming at Reeney's place, looking for Jaffer Swan, looking to tie one on.

"Keep him there, sweetie," he told Irene. "I'll be there as soon as I can." It wouldn't be easy in all that ice, but he'd driven in worse. You could do a lot of things if you had to. "He drunk, or what?"

"Hell," she said. "If he was just drunk, would I be calling you? He's quiet enough. He just sits there in my back room on the goddamn mattress and talks to himself."

"Then what's the problem?" Agate was relieved. If Worthing was quiet, he'd have more time for the icy drive down to the riverfront.

"Oh, hell," said Reeney. "No problem, Supercop. Except old Charlie's got a gun stuck in his goddamn ear."

It was while he fought the lousy streets and the layer of ice under the mushy snow that kept him sliding sideways at every stop sign in spite of the department's best radial snow tires that Lloyd's mental fingers began to feel the shape of that missing piece.

Betsey's autopsy had said Macauley had smoke in his lungs and his nasal and bronchial passages, even though he didn't smoke himself. That made sense. The herb that had been burned, the stuff Doc had found out about in Chinatown—devil's lace—that had oils in it, and when you breathed it back, the oil stuck to your insides. That was why its effects lasted long enough to knock a guy out.

Or a woman. It didn't take as long to knock a woman out, usually.

The autopsy reports on those four dead women—had there been smoke in the lungs?

No matter how hard he tried, Lloyd couldn't remember. He'd read the damn files so many times the words hardly sunk in anymore. The little kid, Angela, had only been fourteen, but even fourteen-year-olds smoked; he'd caught Sylvia at it and paddled her butt, teenage or not. The old woman, Mrs. Ten Eyck? Would she be likely to smoke?

He was still guessing when he slid into Reeney's parking lot. Except for Worthing's fancy BMW, the place looked deserted, and when Lloyd got inside, he found it was. He could hear Irene's voice from the back room, a steady patter that was beginning to fray out at the edges as she worked at keeping Worthing calm, keeping him alive.

"Aw, baby," she said, "I been down that street. You ever been to Vegas, Charlie? They got this casino out there, you know? Casinos are shit. They call this joint Dream Street. That's old Irene's personal private thoroughfare, honey, you know that? I been blowin' up and down Dream Street since I got outa diapers, I ain't found a door on either side would open yet, and some sucker'd holler, 'Come on in, baby, I got a table waiting for you.' "

Graham Worthing said nothing now, not even to himself. The gun was a big one, a forty-five unless Lloyd missed his guess, with a barrel long enough for Marshal Dillon and a fancy silver-chased pearl handle. An old gun, probably valuable.

Lloyd couldn't help smiling to himself. The gun wasn't pointed at Worthing's head anymore. It lay cradled in his palm, the barrel aimed at the floor. Irene was making progress.

Agate came quietly into the storeroom. He could be almost soundless when he needed to be, though he was famous for his clumsy inattention to little things like chairs, plates, ashtrays, and stacks of file folders. He was standing right in front of Graham before the guy even saw him.

The gun came up a couple of inches, aimed halfheartedly at Worthing's face.

"Helluva night out there," Lloyd began. "Mind if I sit down?"

Worthing just stared.

Agate parked on a pile of twelve-packs and took out his plain-label smokes. There it was again. Smoke. Somewhere in the back of his mind, the pieces were coming together.

"Cigarette?" he said, offering one to Worthing.

Another stare.

"Quite a gun you got there."

It moved another inch. The aim was improving. Lloyd sighed. Maybe he ought to let Reeney take over again.

"Antique, is it? What is it, French, English?"

"German."

Finally, he talks.

"You in World War Two?" asked Agate. "You're not that old, hell, you can't even be sixty yet, can you?" Tonight, the guy looked older.

"Fifty-nine," said Graham. "The—the gun was my father-in-law's."

Irene came over and sat down on the other side of Worthing. "Charlie, honey," she said. "Can I see the gun a minute? I'll give it right back." It made her nervous, and Supercop was getting nowhere fast.

But Charlie Graham, whose name was really Worthing, pulled away from her. Reeney bit her lip. Another goddamn liar. Why did they all have to lie?

"Charlie," she said, her voice shaking with lousy memories. "I'm alone here. It's Christmas Eve and there's nobody here but you and me and you're trying to blow your head off and I don't want to mop your brains off my wall on Christmas Eve, goddammit! I don't want to be alone!" There were tears streaming down her face although she didn't seem to be crying, not like most women. "Is that so much to ask? What's wrong with me, I always gotta be alone on Christmas?"

Worthing looked at her, a small, hunched figure in the grubby storeroom, shaking with her anger at the useless past and the dreamless future. He hesitated, breathing hard, the burly chest heaving. He lowered his head, unable to look at her, and Maxima's heavy old gun, Alois's gun, which Graham had hoped to sell, had hope not deserted him at last, fell from his limp hand onto the floor. His other arm slipped round Irene and pulled her stiffly, clumsily against him. They were not lovers. They would never be. They were both here, and that was as far as it had to go. Irene grabbed Worthing as, one night some years back, her eyes blackened and her teeth loose and her clothes torn off her and her body shaking so hard he could barely hold her, she had grabbed on to Agate in the dark of her trailer. She hung on like a scared cat, and as Lloyd looked away from them he heard Worthing say something, but he couldn't make it out. He reached down and picked up the gun and stuffed it into his jacket.

"What did you say, pal?" said Agate softly.

Graham Worthing looked up from Irene's shoulder, smashed against his chest. "I said I killed those women, Lieutenant. All four of them."

He blinked and closed his eyes and began to stroke Reeny's wiry hair.

"The hell you did," murmured Lloyd Agate, and went out to use the phone.

He knew damn well Worthing wasn't the Heart Specialist, but if they wasted a lot of time dancing around with alibis and whereabouts and who saw who where on what night three months ago, another woman could die in the meantime. There had to be a quicker way, that puzzle piece he'd been fumbling around with in the car on the road up to Irene's. He grabbed the phone behind the bar and dialed the station.

"Merry Christmas, Ainsley Police," said Dot.

"It's me," barked Agate. "Cut the 'ho ho ho.' Go in my office and check my files." He told her what he wanted from the autopsy reports and in a minute Dot was back on the line.

"You got it, big guy," she said. "Smoke residue in the lungs, the throats, the noses of all four victims. The Godowski woman was a chain smoker. Cody kid's mom says she sometimes fooled around with it, trying to look sophisticated. You know. Nobody knows for sure about Hallie Glendon, but you could ask her boyfriend."

"What about the old lady? What about Mrs. Ten Eyck?" Agate was holding his breath. If it didn't pan out, he was looking at a whole night with Worthing, trying to prove false confession. *Time. Time shot to hell.*

"That one's the clincher, pal," said Dot. "Smoke in the lungs, in *her* condition? Come on, right?"

"What? What condition?" He'd read it probably fifty times, but his mind was blank as the snow outside. "What was wrong with her?"

"Asthma," said Dottie. "You ever hear of somebody with asthma smoking?"

Not by choice. Not unless they got caught in the devil's net, thought Agate.

But all he said was, "Merry Christmas, Dot."

"And a 'ho ho ho' to you," she told him, and hung up.

It was about the time Lloyd Agate got Irene's phone call that two more snowy visitors came stamping in our back door. Blanche Megrim's nosy cackle was still issuing from poor Merriman's sickroom as Krish joined us, wiping his feet carefully on the mat, and ushering before him a tall old man with a bushy white beard and a red stocking cap whose arms were laden with holly branches.

No, it wasn't Santa. It was Axel Engstrom, the old Swede who'd been mushing around in the ice and snow all afternoon, delivering the holly Elsa had promised her friends at the cast party. His cheeks were pink and his blue eyes were surrounded with crinkles, and if he wasn't St. Nick, he could've been his stand-in for the close-ups.

"By damn," he said, "this is one for the reindeer, Doc! My pickup, she's stuck in a drift, the corner of Elm Street and the Boulevard, she don't go forward, she don't go back. Mrs. Elsa, she's gonna chew my tail off, I'm gone the whole afternoon!" He chuckled.

"The holly's gorgeous!" cried Alex, gingerly gathering it into her arms and heading for the living room. "Come on, Gemma, love!"

"But Axel, didn't you get back to Elsa's place *yet?*" I said. It was going on for half-past seven, and she'd been up there all day!

"Hell, nah, Doc. Like I tell you. Stuck good and proper. This fella here, he give me a lift." He indicated Krish.

"I found Mrs. Megrim's note, saying she meant to walk here," said Krishnan. "Naturally, I was concerned. So easy to fall. The bones of the elderly, brittle as the dickens."

"Don't let Blanche hear you say that," muttered David. "Look, Winnie, why don't you phone Sarah out at Elsa's and tell her I'm on my way. It'll take a while getting up that hill—this one was bad enough an hour ago—but my Olds will make it."

I was already at the telephone. "There's no dial tone!" I said, rattling the receiver cradle. "It's deader than a doornail."

Krish peered out the window. "Oh, yes. The same all over the city as I drove up here. A tree branch down on the wires! You see?"

He was right. The backyard looked like a devastated area somebody had playfully frosted with whipped cream. Tree branches dangled from half a dozen old giants, and one as long as our living room had fallen across the phone line.

"I'll get my coat, Davy, and you go warm up the Olds," I said. "We'll make it to Sorrowheart, if I have to shovel us a path!"

Old Axel laughed. "Oh, yah, sorrowheart. All summer long I pull that stuff out of the flower beds, first thing I know she's gathering it up like it was gold. Herb, she says. Me, I say weed. I call a spade a spade, by damn."

I pricked up my ears. "Sorrowheart is the name of an herb—er, weed? What kind of a weed? Why does Elsa gather it?"

"Women, who knows?" said the tall old Swede. "My mama used to smoke it in a pipe when she got sick. Elsa's papa, too. A lot of pain, he had. Makes you sleep good, better than pills."

"Axel," I said, "this herb that grows up at Elsa's, the sorrowheart that makes you sleep—it wouldn't have another name, would it?"

"Oh, yah, sure," he said. "Us Swedes, we call it the devil's fishnet. Fine leaves, see, just like a net. The devil's net."

"David, for God's sake, let's go!" I cried, shrugging into my coat.

Out in the drive, the Olds was already revving up, with Davy at the wheel, and Krish was two feet in front of me, diving headfirst into the backseat.

Twenty-seven

It was always worse at Christmas. The Invisible Lady hidden away during the warm seasons came out screaming when the earth lay dead. Assailed by memory and loss as the cold deepened and the days grew short, the other Elsa lost the will to protest and pretend. At her center, the great dark hollow begun when she was fourteen, when her childhood should have had the time to linger and ripen and make her whole, the black pit of ruin where the Invisible Lady hid herself away grew huge and voracious, demanding Elsa's death.

But she could not die. She had tried seven times after she came back from the bomb shelter on the Alexanderplatz where the three Russians kept her. Some had never been visible, but some of the scars of her failures remained on her body—the marks she hid from Graham, telling him they came from wires, from Russian torture. There had been no torture, not as Graham understood it.

Other women had a worse time of it. She had heard the stories, mumbled between housewives standing in ration lines, gasped from ear to ear on busses, streetcars; at the few pumps where you could find safe drinking water, women laden with backbreaking buckets, their eyes set in caves of shame, would tell their stories. Seventeen times, twenty, twenty-five. Over the weeks, as 1945 settled into summer, then into fall, the comparisons grew ludicrous, a perverse game. The numbers soared. A thickset, furious woman at the washhouse in the Leibenstrasse claimed for her nineteen-year-old daughter sixty separate rapes as groups of Russian soldiers came to the broken-down apartment looking for radios, watches, fountain pens to send by military post to their families in Leningrad and Moscow.

Hearing them, the girl Elsa took it for nonsense, the same sort of game they had played with sons in the German Army. "My boy was wounded twice, mine four times, mine had his head blown off and the glorious German doctors sewed it back on, good as new." They hated the Russians, anyway. A lot of German kids had died on the Eastern Front. But Elsa's mother had been part Russian, her grandmother was born in St. Petersburg. The young girl liked the big, gruff, burly soldiers who sang in the dark around their fires. As for rape, it meant nothing to her. She was fourteen, and all her time was spent with her lonely, bookish father. She had no girlfriends; her mother had been taken to the camps, and being of suspect blood she had been denied formal schooling. Everything she knew came from her father, from Alois. She knew books and music, and such pictures as could still be found unhidden and unpillaged in Berlin. She knew plants; Alois took her to the botanic gardens, pronouncing the Latin names for her. He even taught her dancing, and French, and how to make soup from the bones of a dead horse, and swallow it, and smile.

But he taught her none of the meanings of the word "rape."

She began to learn it first at the beginning of December 1945. Their old house in the Essener Strasse had been bombed away two years before, and Elsa and her father had found a small flat in what was left of a building not far from the Anhalter Bahnhof, the train station in what became, during the Occupation, the Russian zone. The Russian bombardment had taken the top three floors off the building, there was almost never any power, and they cooked in a makeshift tin barrel out on the terrace, its length of stovepipe propped up with broken cement from the bomb craters in the street.

There was no heat inside; they both wore every article of clothing they had left, only removing it long enough to force themselves shivering through a weekly bath, the water lugged up four flights in buckets and heated on the terrace stove. The Russians had taken everything they had saved from the old house—the precious radio that contained the voice of Winston Churchill, the mantel clock with Frederick the Great on top, the silver frame that held her dead mother's photograph. To give them credit, they had left the photograph, and though they looked hungrily at the wide dark eyes of the young girl, wrapped in her layers of heavy clothes, they had gone off again, appeased by the few words of Russian Alois Bergner knew. When they'd tramped off, laughing and lugging their treasures away with them, Elsa's father had taken her to him and held her, all but smashed her, until at last he collapsed into one of his fits of coughing and let her go, no explanation offered.

The year was drawing toward another Christmas, but the war was over at last, and the young girl felt some celebration should be made. Early in the morning of the eighteenth of December, old Albrecht, their neighbor from downstairs, came wheezing up to whisper at the crack of the door, as Elsa stood shivering inside.

"Some fool went to the Spandauer Forest and came back with a whole truckload of Christmas trees, my girl! Can you imagine? Not just scrawny little cedars full of last year's blight, either. Real firs, four, five, six feet high!"

"Where?" cried Elsa. "Where are they? We ought to have a Christmas, just this once." The last one she remembered was the year before her mother was taken away, and Elsa had been five. A huge tree with real candles, paper angels touched with gold, tiny cornucopias filled with sweets, and molded Christmas cookies, fruity spiced *Lebkuchen* and anise-flavored *Springerle,* hung from ribbons on the branches.

"Yes," she said, "we must have Christmas!"

Albrecht shrugged. "Risk your neck if you want to. They're all the way across town, you have to take a train to get there." He poked her shoulder with a bony finger. "The Russians will have you for breakfast if they catch you. Your papers aren't right for that part of town, are they?"

"They're fine," she said. "Don't you worry about my papers, Albrecht. And when I'm back, I'll even let you come and trim the tree with us, you old woolly bear!"

All the trains at the Anhalter Bahnhof were late, and Elsa sat down to wait, only vaguely nervous as pairs of Russian soldiers walked by with their silly, stiff, stamping gait. When they had passed and she could relax, she noticed a girl lying on a bench against the far wall. Another woman, middle-aged, with set, emotionless features, noticed the girl, too, and went over to her. Elsa, curious in her child's way, crossed the waiting room to where the girl lay. She was nineteen or twenty at least, and she might have been beautiful if her face hadn't been swollen up with crying. She had been crying for a long, long time.

"Come on," said the emotionless woman. "I'll find you a doctor. There's one two streets over. You can't go on like this. He can stop the bleeding for you. Otherwise you'll die."

"You think I care?" said the girl. "Go away! Let me alone!"

"To hell with you," the woman told her. "You think you're the only one?" The pretty girl on the bench stared, and the woman laughed. "I'm ugly, I haven't even got my own teeth anymore—I see what you're thinking. They don't care. Ugly, pretty, young, old. How many times, you?"

"I— I—don't know," moaned the girl. "I hurt. God. Why? Why did they?"

The older woman shrugged. "To pretend there is something besides death in the world. Their officers treat them like pigs, they turn into pigs. To remember what women are like. To find out if they are dead themselves or not. To be bigger bastards than we are. Who knows why? Who cares? Come on. We'll go find that doctor."

"No!" said the pretty, swollen-faced girl. "I want to die! Let me die!"

"Be my guest," said the woman angrily. "Maybe that's the

372

reason they did it, who the hell knows? Men you kill with bullets, women you kill with love.'' She turned and saw Elsa watching, listening. ''You, too, kid?'' she said.

''What?'' said the girl.

''Ah, go to hell,'' the woman said, and shoved her out of the way.

It was that same night, as the Christmas tree she had dragged through the Berlin streets for miles stood fragrant in a corner of the icy living room, that the Russians banged on the door of Alois Bergner's flat.

This time his few words of Russian did no good at all. There were no more radios, no clocks or picture frames to distract them. One of them was the same man who had come before, a tall, broadshouldered Byelorussian with startling green eyes and oily brown hair he kept scratching. The other two were older, one almost bald with a fringe of sandy hair around his pate and government-issued glasses sliding down a bulbous nose, the third tall and thin and dark, with wiry black hair growing down out of the cuffs of his uniform to cover the backs of his hands, growing over the bridge of his nose to join his eyebrows into one.

''Stay in the bedroom, Elsa,'' ordered her father when the rifle butts began to bang on the front door. ''Push the chest against the door.''

She did as she was told, nothing more; she did not climb out the window onto the ledge or hide under the bed. They would have found her anyway. From the other room, she heard her father's futile efforts to convince the men to go, and then a sharp command, a cry, and the sound of something falling. As they pushed the door open, she saw Alois lying on the floor, blood streaming from the gash the rifle butt had made in his scalp.

The green-eyed youth had learned a few words of German, probably from other visits such as this. *''Schöne,''* he said, moving toward Elsa. *''Schöne Dame.''*

Pretty. Pretty woman.

''Nett,'' said one of the others, the bald one. *''Du bist sehr nett.''*

You're very nice. Nice.

They began to stroke her. They were not brutal, nor unkind. They did not hit her, throw her down, batter her unconscious. What they wanted from her had nothing to do with punishment. From the tangle of arms and legs and the great hands that explored her half-formed woman's body and the wet lips that brushed her breasts and thighs and from the moans, the shouts as though of pain, the girl who even then was becoming invisible learned one thing. They didn't mean to harm her. Harm is seldom a thing meant or consciously planned. They entered her half-child's body again and again, without passion but with terrible hunger, looking for the heart of her to take away and put into themselves, the center they had lost.

It took them five days in the breathless, too-warm bunker they shared on the Alexanderplatz. They wrapped her in thick rough blankets, fed her groats and powdered milk, sang Russian songs and rocked her as they might have rocked their children. They even tried, the fools, to make her laugh. They had not found what they wanted yet, the thing they lacked and had lost and would never, never have again. They searched for it over and over, for five days and nights, and all the stories she had heard came true.

And when at last they set her free, to stumble back to her father's house naked under the Russian Army blanket, her mass of pale brown curls crawling with lice and her body aching and her legs barely able to move, they had not found what they wanted, though they had taken it from her forever. It was hope.

By that time, it was Christmas Eve.

She found her father gone; he was out begging the authorities to help him find her, and by the time he returned, Elsa had washed herself, dressed in her old clothes, cut off most of her infested hair, and burned the Russian blanket in the terrace stove. Alois found her trimming the Christmas tree and singing carols as she worked, a pot of coffee-substitute steaming out on the stove. She told him nothing. He could not bring himself to ask. "Taken for questioning," they told the neighbors. "Because of her mother's deportation."

The old women raised their eyebrows and nodded and smiled. They knew what Russian questioning was for.

On Christmas morning, Elsa tried for the first time to kill herself. There were six other attempts, the last on the night after she had made love with Piers Ambrose in Maxima's orchard, when she was twenty-one.

She could have loved Piers Ambrose, thought Elsa. *But he wants the heart out of her, just like Swan. With Piers she had resisted. She had shocked the poor man with desire and withheld the only thing he really wanted. But when Swan turned up she had grown old and tired, and given him everything that was left of her. All the untried tenderness of the Invisible Lady, the child who disappeared forever in the cold Christmas of 1945.*

Elsa lay on her bed, the bed she had shared with her two husbands, Swan and Worthing, wishing it were possible to kill herself. She knew it was not. Even when she had been pregnant with Paul and thought about throwing herself down the stairs, Madam Max had stopped her. It had to be otherwise, another way for the Invisible Lady, as it had always been.

She lay listening to the music from downstairs. Sarah, dear Sarah, her other self, had come at last to spend the day and play her father's harpsichord. In this house, the storm outside, nothing could touch her. Elsa felt strong, intensely alive; she could feel the motion of the blood along her veins and capillaries, all the way to her fingertips.

She got up from the bed and went to the window, the tinkle of the harpsichord following her. It sounded odd, a hint of some other tone. Perhaps it needed tuning.

Outside, the roof of the workshop and the greenhouse beyond it lay blanketed with snow, the herb clumps in the garden small white tepees, the trees in the orchard cracking, groaning with the weight, and the great Austrian pines, like black soldiers in white uniforms bowing to the storm, bent halfway to the ground with their wintry burden. There was a peculiar, unnatural brightness to the night; the

375

crystalline world of the ice and snow reflected on the heavy clouds and kept the darkness vague, as though shades had been pulled around the world to make it dim instead of dark, while beyond them the sun still shone somewhere.

Elsa turned back to the room and went to the chest in the corner, an old cedar chest meant for bridal linens. Hope chest, that was how they called it. It had a key, and inside was another locked box. The music of the harpsichord rose to her and Elsa hummed softly as she turned the key. It had been a lovely day, with Sarah here. Laughter. She had not been sure she remembered how to laugh, except with Swan. But he had taught her how. He had forced her to remember. Now Sarah was playing, at last playing the harpsichord again. It would be a good memory, and she had few of those. She was so young, the Invisible Lady. Still so young.

She took from the locked steel box a small vial of liquid. She had prepared it with loving care, as always, the right proportions mixed with distilled water, just as she had mixed her father's medicine when he lay dying.

How could he have died here, in Sorrowheart? she thought. In this house, you had to live forever, whether you wanted to or not.

She took the other things she needed from the steel box, closed it carefully, and locked it into the hope chest again. The music of the harpsichord was dull, repetitious. Surely she had heard that same phrase before.

Elsa shook herself like a waking cat and went out into the hall. Across the way, Maxima lay napping, making up for the sleep she never got at night. She had enjoyed herself, too, that day, a day like all the Christmases that should have been and never were.

She pulled the old woman's bedroom door shut quietly and moved down the stairs, hardly making a sound, her broad feet in soft leather slippers with rubber soles. She wore a deep green dress, its long sweep of skirt brushing her ankles, its high neck touched with gold, her wild curls loose and falling round the pleated shoulders and the green silk scarf she had tied around the neck. In the deep pockets of the costume were the things she had taken from the locked box: the vial of medicine, the syringe, and the bag of sorrowheart.

The harpsichord music went on and on, the same monotonous phrase. Had she not heard it a moment ago?

She went silently through the dining room and into the living room, where they had lighted candles and a fire crackled in the white tile stove. There was no Christmas tree. This year, she had ceased to pretend.

Though the music of the instrument continued, Sarah was no where in the room. On the bench where she should have been sitting, a small tape recorder was playing the *Little Windmills* suite of Couperin. It came to an end, whirred, reversed automatically, and began again.

Elsa's breath caught in her throat and she tilted her head to one side, listening. A trick. A joke for Christmas.

A sound came from the kitchen and she slipped silently through the dining room again. The lights were on, the weight of snow on the lines making them blink dangerously. Soon the power would go altogether and there would be only the thin darkness of the crystal night outside, the veil of falling snow.

Elsa peered in through the half-open kitchen door. Sarah sat at the table, leafing through the greenhouse books, papers scattered around her, bills, receipts. She must have sensed the other woman's presence at the door, for she looked round, no snooper's guilt written on her handsome features though her eyes were wide with dismay.

"A cup of chocolate, my dear?" said Elsa, her long skirt swooshing as she marched into the room. "Max's papa used to say it was depraved, a cup of cocoa in the evening, but he was a stuffy old goat. A little depravity is anyway good for the soul, I think, and Max agrees." She went about making the chocolate, saying nothing about the books and papers spread on the table.

Sarah closed the ledger and put the other things back into their file. Then she came to stand beside her friend at the stove.

"It's you, isn't it? It's you who's been taking all these things of Max's and selling them off. Not Swan. Not Graham. You."

"Max's?" snapped Elsa. "If *my* father had not chosen them, Max's house would be full today of curlicues and gewgaws and old dresses made for eighteen-year-old debutantes. *I* dust them. *I* polish them. When they break *I* glue them back together. *I* pay for the tuning and the cleaning and the silver polish. Max's? When does Elsa get a little piece, please?"

"Only it's not going to help, is it? No matter how much you sell, you'll lose this place, with or without the college. Why didn't you tell me? Maybe I could've helped you, before things got this bad. All Graham's business debts, and the boys—they didn't have to go to Harvard, you know, there are cheaper colleges!"

"Enough!" Elsa's hand shot out and covered Sarah's mouth. She smiled. "What's done, is done. I'll manage. Maybe a miracle, who knows? It's Christmas, after all. Santa Claus is coming!"

She laughed, and turned to pour the chocolate into cups. As she led the way into the living room, the lights blinked again, stayed off for a long moment, then came back on. Elsa set the cups on a table and switched off the tape player.

"I'm ashamed of that," Sarah said suddenly. "It was a damn cheap trick, but you wouldn't have it any other way. You wouldn't trust me. Now you never will again."

"Ah, my dear," Elsa told her softly. "I might as well not trust myself." She set one cup of the chocolate on the harpsichord and settled herself in the love seat near the stove. "No more tape recordings. I demand for Christmas the genuine article. Play, my dearest Sarah. Forget money and bills and who should do what. Play for me."

"But—"

"Play!"

Sarah began, reluctantly, the same Couperin as on the tape, but more sensitively played, her fingers barely stroking the keys, her eyes closed and her back turned to Elsa. She was too absorbed in the

378

music to notice when her friend got up and moved softly to the stove, opened the latch of the fuel box at the front, and threw in a handful of the lacy, dried leaves of sorrowheart. She hardly noticed when the electricity went off, though she saw Elsa move round the room lighting more candles and the old kerosene lamps with colored-glass shades that hung from brackets on the walls. A sweet smell began to pervade the place, pungent as pine but softer, a hint of anise with it. She took it for a potpourri, some Christmas scent Elsa had mixed from her herbs for the season.

She hardly noticed when the sensation of heaviness began to come over her. It had been a long, happy day until she read the greenhouse books, and Sarah was tired. Her hands felt foolish and uncertain, and the keyboard kept moving farther and farther from her, as though her arms were yards long, miles long, stretched beyond capacity, and weighing more than her whole body. She was only barely aware of the nearness of someone else as Elsa slid onto the harpsichord bench beside her, the pine-green scarf pulled over her nose and mouth. She drew Sarah against her, and though she spoke in a normal tone, all Sarah heard was a whisper, as Elsa's deft fingers unbraided the long plait of her hair and stroked it smooth.

"Schöne," said Elsa. "Schöne Dame. Du bist sehr nett."

The lane that led from the highway to the greenhouse was clogged with ice and snow, and the windshield wipers could hardly keep enough of the stuff off to permit David to see. Halfway up the lane, the Olds slid sideways into a ditch and stuck fast, and we went the rest of the way on foot, plowing through knee-deep drifts in some places, breaking through ice in others and crashing down into water that soaked our shoes and socks and trouser legs and froze around us. The wind had dropped and the only sounds were the creaking of laden branches, the glassy tinkle of ice-covered twigs in the windless currents of the dark, and the occasional crash of some overburdened bough in the distance.

It had stopped snowing now. Beyond us, the house glowed with warmth and light, and all my sinister imaginings seemed once again absurd.

"If we're out here plowing around like Nanook of the North for nothing," I grumbled to David as I mushed along in his wake, "I'm going to give that sister of yours what for, I can tell you. I—"

"Look!" Krish was behind us, but he saw them first. His voice was very small in the darkness, and I thought for a minute I'd imagined that he spoke at all. "There! Just now coming out of the house!" he said.

It was a vision such as magic could not have invented. The two women seemed, from that dark distance, our eyes watering with cold, to have grown into one. Elsa carried Sarah's body lightly in her arms, as though she weighed nothing at all, as though she were a child. Sarah's long hair hung down and veiled the skirt of Elsa's dress, brushed the snowy bushes on the path. Her head dangling lifelessly, and her arms were limp.

"Christ," I heard David breathe.

We began to run then, or as close to it as we could. I tried to shout, but there wasn't enough breath for shouting, and my voice was gone.

Dead. The word hammered into my ears with every step. *Sarah. My Sarah. Dead.*

I heard a sound come from Krishnan, a cry that made Elsa look up for an instant, made her pause to look at us.

"Hallie!" he screamed, but the only answer was the fall of ice from the brittle trees.

I was sure Elsa saw us, but she didn't seem to care. She moved slowly, her friend held gently in her arms, picking her way through the snowy garden and into the orchard. I could still see them among the trees as we fought our way through the drifts. My feet were too cold to feel, but I kept them moving somehow. David was a few yards ahead now, almost on the orchard path.

Elsa laid Sarah's limp form down in the snow under one of the biggest apricot trees, its sharp spiny branches coated with ice that

380

slipped off now and then and fell glittering, to be swallowed by the snow beneath. Elsa knelt beside the body on the ground and I could hear her mourning, a high, thin keening cry.

The word struck me down again. *Dead.* I lurched sideways and felt Krish's arm grab me, pull me up. He was very strong, much stronger than I had ever thought he was, and I felt old and broken. *Dead.*

I never saw the figure come from the snowy pine grove, never saw it move like a shadow among the pear trees, never heard the footfalls plowing through the treacherous ice-covered grass and the heavy drifted snow. Before we could have reached the two women who were one woman, Jaffer Swan was there.

And so was the needle. I saw it glisten in Elsa Worthing's hand, saw the hand raised above Sarah's body.

"Noooooooooooo!" I shouted, but the orchard was silent. I had not made a sound.

David crashed forward into the trees, and at the same instant I saw Swan grip Elsa's arm, trying to fight the needle from her. She turned on him, and the punch was quick. He fell, lunged, fell again. David reached them just as Jaffer got her in his arms. For an instant they rolled together in the snow, inseparable, almost invisible. I saw Swan raise his fist and hit her, hard, in the throat, and Elsa slumped back upon him where he lay.

David knelt beside his sister and when I got there and fell down in the snow beside her, too, he looked up at me. "Alive," was all he had to say.

Swan had pulled himself up now, braced against a tree trunk, the woman held against him, her long tangled web of curls across his thin chest, his face buried against her cheek. His fierce blow had broken her neck. She was dead.

David picked Sarah up in his arms and made for the greenhouse workshop. Where it had come from, I didn't know—the place had been dark when we arrived—but now there was a light inside and smoke from the stovepipe. Krish picked up the hypodermic needle where it had fallen on the ice-crusted snow.

"She must have known torture," he said softly. "She must have been many years alone."

He threw the needle far off into the darkness and followed David into the workshop to see to Sarah. I was left alone with Swan.

"When did you find out what she'd done?" I asked him. "Before or after you killed Macauley?"

"Nothing to do with her, that," he said quietly. "Bugger killed Elizabeth, I killed him."

"You used the sorrowheart to make him groggy, of course. How did you manage not to breathe it in? I expect you used one of those masks that come with the plant sprayers, didn't you? I saw some on those shelves down in the furnace room. Orchids need almost constant spraying, don't they, so he was probably used to seeing you come in with a mask on. Did he know who you were? Did he recognize the Geoff Glendon he knew in Minnesota?"

"Wouldn't care, would he? Who I was? Only it made it more exciting, filming Hallie, following her around. And Elsa." The breath caught in his thin chest and he made a sound like choking. "He'd got pictures of them, both of them. I went through his desk at home, when I went out to do the plants. I saw the tapes. Christ. I thought—"

"You thought he'd killed your daughter, and you thought Elsa would be next. He wanted her out of the way anyhow, didn't he, to get this place? You'd found a home here, between the two of them, and you thought he was sure to destroy everything. You must've loved them both very much."

"Balls," he said. "Don't lay it onto them. I hated him. Me. For years."

"So you drugged him with the herb you burned in the orchid pot, the herb Elsa taught you about—or was it Axel Engstrom, who thought it was a pesky weed? And once Macauley was half-asleep, you walked him over in front of the desk and laid him down where you wouldn't be seen from the window. Did you think Elsa might see you from down here? Or couldn't you quite do it, looking out

382

and seeing her place down here, seeing everything you cared about?''

He didn't answer. Snow from the tree had fallen on him, snow lay on his shoulders and bits of ice glittered in the dead woman's drift of hair.

"You held him as you're holding her now," I said, pitiless in the cold dark. "As you held Krish that night. And you put the gun in his mouth and held his own finger on the trigger. Maybe he was still just groggy. And you asked him, as you asked Krish: 'Life or death? You choose.' " I paused, but still he gave no answer. "Did he choose? Had he made living such a wretched business that he helped you kill him, in the end?" No answer. "Then you put a bullet in the orchid pot to destroy the rest of the sorrowheart. And you planted the needle and Hallie's necklace and the bottle of diginox on his desk, to make us believe what you thought you knew and couldn't prove, just as you couldn't prove he'd killed Elizabeth Swan." No answer. "Was it you who framed Macauley? Is that how it was?"

"Christ," he said again. "If you say so. Ahhhhhhhnnnnnnnn." With a soft moan he buried his face the woman's ice-jeweled hair again.

"I had no idea it had gone so far." Madam Max stood on the path from the workshop, a kerosene lamp in her hand.

"Oh? Didn't you?" I said. "I don't think there's much you didn't know."

"How dare you judge me!" she cried. "I made a promise to Alois."

"He knew, did he, when he brought her here and married you? Something from the war, was it?"

She sneered. " 'Something'? The Nazi informers, the madman on the radio, the spies on every streetcar. The British bombs, the Russian cannon, then the tanks. All that was left in Berlin were the wounded, old men, children, women. There's hardly a woman who lived through the Russian Occupation and was not raped." She spat the word and took a fistful of the clean snow and put it in her mouth and spat again. "So long as she stayed here, she was well enough. She managed."

"But when Macauley threatened to take the place away from her—"

"Macauley? It was that fool of a husband of hers, the drone!" she cried. "He spent everything, trying not to look like the idiot he is!"

"And he suspected, too, didn't he? He came back here and watched her, and when the police came after Hallie's murder he lied for her. That night she put on his coat and took Swan's book and planted it where she thought he might be hiding, tried to cast suspicion onto him and away from herself. That's why she asked me to find Jaffer and tell him to forgive her."

Swan glanced up at me, then at Madam Max. The old woman swayed in the lamplight, as I went on.

"Those women came to her for herbs," I guessed. "Hallie believed in herbal healing. Isabel Ten Eyck suffered from asthma, and there are herbal medicines for it that you burn and inhale, even asthma cigarettes. Perhaps that's what she did, that day in the park. And even if she moved their bodies, she did it before she used the diginox solution to kill them, and the moving didn't leave its mark on the bodies, done before death as it was. Perhaps she drugged Hallie out here in the workshop that evening, made her sleep deeply enough to last until two, when Swan left her and went on his ramble to Irene's place. That's where she was when you heard the telephone go unanswered at two A.M. She was killing Hallie." I took a step toward the old woman and grasped her arm. "Was it worth it? Alois made you keep his daughter's terror hidden all these years. Look at her! Damn you! Was it worth *that*?"

"I kept my promise!" she cried.

"At what price?"

She stood in the pool of lamplight, her hand shaking, her shoulders pulled painfully back from their habitual slump. "My soul," she said. "I owed him that."

Swan stood up and gathered Elsa in his arms. "I'll take her up, then," he said in his quiet, inward voice. "Late, you know. High time she was in bed. Needs her rest, does our Countess."

He moved off with her, headed for the house, his slight body tilted backward with the weight, his face brushing her hair. Around him the crystal trees glistened in the thin dark, sighing with cold and the weight of their own beauty. In a moment, he had disappeared with her inside the bright house.

I heard a car engine pull into the lane and the whine of tires. Someone was stuck, as we had been, in the deep snow. There was shouting, and I recognized the voice of Lloyd Agate.

"Why?" I said to Maxima. Inside the house, at the upstairs window that was Elsa's bedroom, I saw the figure of Swan, a lamp in his hand. "What could have made her do such things? Other women have suffered rape and healed true again. Other women haven't killed and killed and—"

"Other women were not Elsa!" She laughed, a sound like something tearing free. "I think quite often of those Russian soldiers, of their wives. It is our greatest common heritage, don't you agree? The utter brute stupidity of humankind?"

She walked away from me, back to the workshop. Within a week, Graham would have checked her into Oakview, the old-age gulag by the lake. Within a year he would have married someone else, a woman who spoke no unknown tongues.

I stood alone in the dark orchard, watching the shadow of Jaffer Swan as he moved around the house, putting an end to memory, bidding the place good-bye. Upstairs, the flames licked already at the window shades and in Alois Bergner's study the fire was eating at the leather bindings of the books, brushing fondly over the Dresden plates and the silver pitchers, playing the harpsichord with fingers of flame.

"Holy Christ, Doc!"

Lloyd huffed up beside me, and I saw the thick figure of Graham Worthing on the pathway, staring at the burning house.

"I'll get on the radio," puffed Agate. "They might save something if the fire trucks can get up the bluff in time."

385

I put a hand on his arm. "Let it go," I said.

"But what the—"

"Leave it. It's over. Let it end."

He drew a sharp breath, his eyes trained on the house. The shape of Swan was there, a flicker of shadow on the rising brightness of the fire.

"Jesus," said Agate.

"Yes," I said, and walked away into the snow.

I wanted darkness, and to be alone. Sarah was safe with David, and Agate would in time get the whole story out of Maxima. Now that Elsa was dead, all promises were canceled.

I was very cold, my wet legs numb almost to the knee, as I stood in the orchard away from the others, watching the death of Sorrowheart. I have no idea where he came from, and no idea where he went. It was a night for deaths and entrances. After that Christmas Eve, Piers Ambrose disappeared from Ainsley, his magic ended. I heard his voice before I saw him, leaning on a pear tree trunk.

" 'Put out the light,' " he whispered, " 'and then put out the light.' "

He stood staring at the caving roof, the burning walls, the windows like mad, fiery eyes in the darkness.

"You loved her, didn't you?" I said. "I saw you at the cast party, watching her. You knew it then. What she'd done. Hallie and the others."

"I may have. I couldn't be sure."

"Was it you who gave Hallie that black coral necklace? Did you take it from her body when you were out here in the orchard that day? Was it you who planted those things on Macauley's desk? Swan didn't answer me. Did you plan it together? Piers—"

When I looked round, he was gone.

I made my way back up the path, an ache somewhere at the center of me like a great yawning hole, the end of possibility, of hope for anything. If we could work such ruin on each other, what use was it to keep battling absurdly on against a rising tide of horrors? Let the world eat itself and crumble and be damned.

I stumbled blindly in the snowy dark and fell against a log, my face in the snow, and as I got up I could've sworn I heard the high, clear notes of Jaffer's clarinet out of the night.

> Sorrow got no chains on me
> Redwing blackbird, flying free.

I wanted nothing but silence and the clean, strong, fearless truth that cuts away all need to be deluded by a foolish hope. I wanted the peace that is the heart of sorrow.

I pulled myself back up and saw it standing in the path, outlined by the lights of the police cars and the burning house.

It was Sarah.